FALL OF MACHARIUS

A WARHAMMER 40,000 NOVEL

THE MACHARIAN CRUSADE

FALL OF MACHARIUS

WILLIAM KING

BLACK LIBRARY

To the Agents of Fortune – You know who you are!

A BLACK LIBRARY PUBLICATION

First published in Great Britain in 2014.
Paperback edition published in 2015 by
Black Library,
Games Workshop Ltd.,
Willow Road,
Nottingham, NG7 2WS, UK.

10 9 8 7 6 5 4 3 2 1

Cover illustration by Raymond Swanland.

A CIP record for this book is available from the British Library.

UK ISBN 13: 978 1 84970 850 0
US ISBN 13: 978 1 84970 851 7

See Black Library on the internet at

blacklibrary.com

Find out more about Games Workshop
and the world of Warhammer 40,000 at

games-workshop.com

Printed and bound by CPI Group (UK) Ltd, Croydon, CR0 4YY

It is the 41st millennium. For more than a hundred centuries the Emperor has sat immobile on the Golden Throne of Earth. He is the master of mankind by the will of the gods, and master of a million worlds by the might of his inexhaustible armies. He is a rotting carcass writhing invisibly with power from the Dark Age of Technology. He is the Carrion Lord of the Imperium for whom a thousand souls are sacrificed every day, so that he may never truly die.

Yet even in his deathless state, the Emperor continues his eternal vigilance. Mighty battlefleets cross the daemon-infested miasma of the warp, the only route between distant stars, their way lit by the Astronomican, the psychic manifestation of the Emperor's will. Vast armies give battle in His name on uncounted worlds. Greatest amongst his soldiers are the Adeptus Astartes, the Space Marines, bioengineered super-warriors. Their comrades in arms are legion: the Astra Militarum and countless Planetary Defence Forces, the ever-vigilant Inquisition and the tech-priests of the Adeptus Mechanicus to name only a few. But for all their multitudes, they are barely enough to hold off the ever-present threat from aliens, heretics, mutants — and worse.

To be a man in such times is to be one amongst untold billions. It is to live in the cruellest and most bloody regime imaginable. These are the tales of those times. Forget the power of technology and science, for so much has been forgotten, never to be re-learned. Forget the promise of progress and understanding, for in the grim dark future there is only war. There is no peace amongst the stars, only an eternity of carnage and slaughter, and the laughter of thirsting gods.

CHAPTER ONE

Exhibit 107D-5J. Transcription from a speech imprint found in the rubble of Bunker 207, Hamel's Tower, Kaladon, containing information pertaining to the proposed canonisation of Lord High Commander Solar Macharius and to the investigation of former High Inquisitor Heironymous Drake for heresy and treason against the Imperium.

Walk in the Emperor's Light.

The gigantic face of the skull moon leered down through the clouds. The screams of the dying echoed out of no-man's-land. Strangely coloured mist drifted over the lip of the trench and little lights, like the glow of lost fireflies, swirled inside as it passed overhead. There was something sinister about the movement, as if the tendril of poisonous gas were the limb of a monster furtively seeking out prey.

Shadows danced away from the entrance of the nearest bunker, where some of the troops were toasting lasgun powerpacks in a rubbish fire, hoping to coax a last bit of life into them before the next enemy attack. A partially disassembled flamer lay just inside the doorway. It had an abandoned look to it that did not surprise me. We had not had a sniff of promethium in more than two months and without that fiery element the weapon was worthless. The bunker itself was the shattered remnant of a Leman Russ battle tank, tipped on its side by a direct hit from enemy artillery and partially buried in mud. It had been stripped of any useful parts by the enginseers and its carcass left to decompose. Hundreds of such wrecks were incorporated into the trench lines. It made me nostalgic for the heady initial days of the war when we still believed in the armoured fist of the Imperial Guard, before everything got bogged down in the mud and rain and slurry of this hideous world.

I checked my spare rebreathers for the hundredth time. I had built up quite a collection – every man in Macharius's Imperial Guard army had been issued with a secondary before we arrived on Loki and I had helped myself to a few more from corpses since then. I prayed to the Emperor that they would bring me more luck than they had to their original owners. There had been a lot of filter failures. There had been a lot of failures of every kind.

On Loki, you could never have too many protective masks. You never knew when one might fail, and if that happened you were dead. If the poison gases did not give you a heart attack by showing you your worst fears, the disease spores would clot in your lungs, and if the disease spores didn't choke you to death on your own mucus then the airborne moulds would fill the inside of your lungs with grey fur. There were at least a dozen unpleasant ways to die on Loki that did not involve being shot, bayoneted or otherwise slain by heretics and there were plenty of fanatical bloodthirsty unbelievers to go around, too. The planet seemed to have entered into a conspiracy with the forces of darkness to slay the Emperor's soldiers. I've been on many such since I joined the Guard.

Anton rose up out of the gloom, tall and gangly and weather-beaten. The rebreather covered the lower half of his face but from the way the old scar across his forehead writhed I could tell he was grinning at me. That he was still capable of such idle good humour after all these years of campaigning was testimony to his innate cheerfulness. Or his innate stupidity. It was sometimes hard to say. 'You counting your treasures, are you?'

He was respectful enough when there were others around, but with no troops about we stopped being sergeant and corporal and were just men who had fought and bled for each other over the three decades since we had left Belial.

Anton had not even bothered to maintain his secondary rebreather. He was careless that way, or counting on me to bail him out most likely. He walked a little along the wooden duckboard. A thin layer of mud sucked at his boots. The sound seemed to disturb him, so he stopped walking for a moment and studied the muck thoughtfully.

'Somebody has to make sure there's enough to go round,' I said. 'You never know when another gas attack will come.'

'I don't know why they bother,' Anton said. He looked out into no-man's-land and shook his head at the folly of the generals. 'We all have rebreathers, don't we?'

Like me, Anton had grown up on Belial, an industrial hive. Wearing rebreathers was second nature to us, but it wasn't to everybody. Many of the newcomers had come from agri worlds and feral worlds and the sort of beautiful friendly places where the air was always breathable. Hard to imagine but true.

'We all have them and we sometimes wear them,' I said. 'And they sometimes work. The enemy is playing the odds. And anyway, you are missing the point. The gas is not there to kill us, it's just to add to the general level of misery.'

'I heard a medical adept say that you don't need to breathe in some of the gases,' said Ivan, rubbing at the metal-covered half of his face and then running the artificial fingers of his bionic hand over his prosthetic jaw. 'They just need to touch your skin. That's why we're supposed to stay covered up all the time.'

'Genius,' said Anton. 'Make sure we all get trench foot and lice and shuttle-bugs. I think Leo has it right. They are adding to the misery. I mean, this is the Imperial Guard – misery is what it's all about.'

Somewhere out in the vast field of mud, barbed wire, shell-holes and disease-filled sewage ponds, a man was begging for someone to come and kill him. From the accent I could tell he was one of ours, a Grosslander by the sound of it. I wondered what it was that made him plead so convincingly. Was he suffering the after-effects of some hallucinogenic? Was one of the giant rats that haunted the trench complex chewing on his leg? Or did he have his own personal reason for seeking a quick way out of Loki's killing grounds?

'One moment,' Anton said. He lifted the silenced sniper rifle he had picked up on Dolmen, popped his head above the parapet and scanned the horizon for a moment. There was a soft coughing sound and the begging stopped. Anton dropped back into the trench and said, 'Mission accomplished.'

'You shot him,' I said. 'You shot one of our own men.'

'I gave him what he was asking for. And to tell the truth he was getting on my nerves.'

'You get on my nerves all the time,' said Ivan. Even after all these years and an ever-improving series of prosthetic jaws, he still mangled his words. The plasteel teeth did not improve his pronunciation any. 'Does that mean I can shoot you?'

'The guy had lost half his guts. His entrails were covered in ghost mould. I tell you, if the same thing happens to me I hope you will shoot me. You'll be doing me a favour.'

'I'd be doing the rest of us a favour if I shot you now.'

'Ha-bloody-ha,' Anton said.

'See anything else while you were up there?' I asked. 'You're lucky one of the heretic snipers didn't take your fool head off. They're just waiting for an opportunity.'

'I killed the last one two days ago when he shot Lieutenant Jensen. That will teach him not to do it again.'

'Ever heard of reinforcements?' I asked. 'It's not unknown for new snipers to be sent to the sector to replace the ones who were killed.'

Anton scratched at his head, running his fingernails across the ceramite of his helmet with a slick, scratchy sound – a pantomime of idiocy. 'Reinforcements? Reinforcements? I heard that word once, a long time ago. Aren't they the things the High Command keeps promising to send us, along with more ammo, and more food and new uniforms, and then keeps forgetting about? Or am I confusing them with supplies? It's been almost two standard years in this forsaken place. I'm starting to forget the meaning of words.'

Dumb as he was, he had a point. We *had* been stuck here on Loki for close on two standard Imperial years now. It was the longest campaign of any during the crusade and there was still no end in sight. Things had got so bad that even elements of Macharius's elite personal guard, like us, had been thrown piecemeal onto the front line to reinforce the green troops there. It was how we had gone from occupying a nice suite in a commandeered palace in Niflgard City to squatting in tattered, dirt-encrusted uniforms in these mud-filled trenches, watching assorted moulds grow on our feet and limbs. Most of the commissars had got themselves killed in the endless slogging grind of this war. Those who had not were doing the work of ten, walking the lines, executing the cowardly and those too wounded for medical treatment.

'We'll get reinforced soon. When have you ever known Macharius to fail?' Ivan said. He sounded more like he was praying for it to be true than making a statement in which he believed. None of us had ever known a campaign in which Macharius had taken a personal interest bogged down for so long. Maybe it was true what all the rookies were saying, that his fabled luck had deserted him. Or perhaps it was simpler than that. Perhaps, like the rest of us, in spite of all the juvenat treatments, he was simply getting old.

'He's never fought anyone like Richter before,' Anton said. 'Some say the traitor is as good as the Lord High Commander was in his glory days.' He paused to let that particularly gloomy thought sink in. Anton did not like the fact that the enemy commander here on Loki had been one of our own, a favoured protégé of Macharius and his best pupil, until the day he had decided to start building his own little private empire here on the galaxy's bleak far edge.

'But you don't agree with them, of course,' I said. Saying a thing like that was dangerously close to treason. I had heard it muttered, though, even by soldiers of the Lion Guard, Macharius's personal bodyguard. There was a sense of shock to the whole thing. Some of us had known Richter – we had fought alongside him and his regiment for almost a decade. And then one day, he had just turned, gone native, turned against us here on this hell world. What was most alarming was the thought that if it could happen to him, seemingly Macharius's heir apparent, who else could it happen to?

'Of course I don't,' said Anton. 'What kind of idiot do you take me for?'

A lock of hair poked out from beneath his helmet. It was greying now. The stubble on my own chin was grey too. Juvenat holds back the years but it cannot stop them rolling by. It merely slows down the effects on your body and, some say, it has other side effects. Everything has its price and extended life has the highest price of all. I felt tired sometimes when I should not.

'I don't doubt we'll see reinforcements,' said Anton, suddenly serious. All of his life he had the greatest faith in Macharius and even if he sometimes complained he never liked to leave that faith in doubt for any length of time. 'I just worry about the quality.'

He did not quite bellow it. He was trying in his way to be tactful, but with all of us he shared the veteran's contempt for the newcomers. That too, like old age, is something that sneaks up on you. It did not matter how often I told myself that we had all been as green as these newcomers once, that the only way soldiers got to be veterans was starting as neophytes and living long enough to learn.

I could not suppress a certain irritation any more at the fresh young faces around me in the trenches and bunkers. I was glad none of them had decided to join us for a smoke in the rain. I could barely hide the contempt I felt for the way they did not have sense enough to throw themselves flat at the first hint of incoming shells and at the way they cowered in cover too long afterwards.

They did not move to the same beat as those of us who had been on the front line for so long. You were always having to wait for them to catch up, and then having to tell them at other times not to rush ahead and get themselves killed. I could see some of the Grosslanders looking at us now, heads poking out round the improvised door-holes of their bunkers, unlined faces staring out with scared and trusting eyes.

Or maybe it was just that they were young in a way I was not, all appearances to the contrary notwithstanding. Maybe I was just jealous.

The smaller moon jumped over the horizon and raced across the sky like a drunken charioteer. Its orbit was much lower and faster than its huge brother, more like a comet or a meteor than a satellite. It was visible through the gaps in the clouds as it careened across the sky above us.

A trench rat emerged from its hole and glared at us with its horrible intelligent eyes. It chittered something to its hidden companions and retreated before anyone could draw a bead on it. It had seen no corpses to scavenge, no unguarded food, so why take the risk?

'Sensible beast,' said Ivan.

'I hate those scuttling little frakkers,' Anton said. 'Caught a bunch chewing on Nardile's corpse last night. They'd pulled out his guts and scooped out his eyes. One of them was nibbling on an eyeball like it was a grape.' We all licked our lips at the thought of grapes, even Ivan who only has metal and plastic lips.

'What did you do?' I asked.

'I armed an incendiary grenade and rolled it in among them. One of them tried to eat it too, greedy little swine. Then one of his mates tried to throw it back at me, I swear. He knew what it was for.'

'Did it get you?' I stifled a mock yawn.

'Would I be sitting here telling you about it, if it had?' Anton said.

'I'm not sure I want to be sitting close to a genius who uses incendiaries in his own trenches and can almost be outsmarted by a rat.'

'The key word is *almost*,' said Anton. He sounded almost proud.

Behind him the chanting of the heretics had picked up again. I felt the hair on the back of my neck start to rise. For all I knew it might just be their evening prayers, but I doubted it. It was normally a sign that they were getting ready to attack. Or rather that their priests were whipping them up for an offensive. There was something about that mushy language that set my nerves on edge. It was as if the speakers' mouths were filling with phlegm as they chanted – the mere sound of the words suggested illness and disease.

Anton was on his feet. He cupped his hands over his mouth and bellowed, 'Could you keep the noise down? We're trying to have a cosy little chat over here.'

By pure chance there was a momentary silence from the distant trenches. 'Thank you,' Anton bellowed.

The chanting started again.

'I swear they do that just to annoy me,' Anton said.

'Yes,' Ivan said. 'This war is all about you. Always was. Always will be.'

'I'm tempted to take a few of the new boys, head down the line to the Great Bog and make my displeasure known,' Anton said. About a kilometre away, our trench system blended near imperceptibly into their trench system. If you followed the so-called Grand Trunk Road you'd get there, provided you negotiated the sprawl of barbed wire, trip-mines, booby traps, mud-holes, spore pits and rats' nests that made movement in the abandoned trenches so treacherous. The Great Bog was a hideous swamp of latrines, cesspits and abandoned emplacements constantly fought over. Right now it represented our front line. Tomorrow it might well belong to the heretics.

'You know the rules,' I said. 'We stay here until we are told to do something different. Or until the heretics come and ask us to leave. We don't need to go embarking on any of your wild little adventures.'

'You used to be a lot more fun before you became a sergeant, Leo,' Anton said. 'There was a time when you would have been leading the charge, not sitting there moaning about it.'

'I think you are confusing me with someone else,' I said. 'Someone idiotic. Yourself perhaps.' I could not think of any time when I would have been keen on one of Anton's madcap charges, not even when we were young and had first joined the Guard all those decades ago.

'If I am so stupid, how come I am still alive?' he asked.

It was a good question, but it prompted an easy response. 'Because Ivan and I are here to pull your nads out of the fire before you can toast them.'

'I can think of plenty of times when I have saved the both of you.' It was true, too, but the first rule of arguing with Anton is never to admit that he might have a point. You could go mad if you did that.

'You can also remember seeing little green daemons dancing out in no-man's-land,' I said. During the last attack, there had been a fault in the filter in his rebreather. He was lucky I had dragged him into the bunker before it became something a lot worse than a mild case of seeing things.

'They could have been there,' Anton said. He sounded thoughtful now. 'You hear a lot of strange stories here on Loki.'

'We've been hearing a lot of strange stories since we got to the Halo Worlds,' said Ivan. 'It does not mean they are true. I mean ghosts of old armies from the Emperor's time. The dead coming back to life. Space Marines dedicated to the powers of Chaos. Who could believe any of that?'

The chanting in the distance had become a phlegmy roar. Drums beat amidst it, erratically, like the heart of a fever victim in the throes of a muscular spasm. There was a suggestion of the catechism to it now, of a priest calling a question and a congregation shouting a response. Perhaps it was just my imagination. Now and then I seemed to be able to pick out an occasional word. Sound moved strangely through the trench system. Idly I wondered if any of Richter's former regiment were over there, some of our old comrades. I had killed one a few months back, a sergeant I had once got drunk with back on Morgan's World. He had been dressed in muddy brown robes, pale of face and tattooed with evil runes. I did not like to think about why a veteran of the crusade might have done that.

A light rain started to fall, a cold drizzle that soaked the threadbare fabric of our green tunics, ran down the rebreather goggles, hampering vision. I ran my forearm over the lenses to wipe them and they cleared for a few moments before becoming obscured again. I watched the puddles ripple where the raindrops hit them. The scummy water had a sinister chemical tint to it, the light refracted into rainbows the colours of which were not found anywhere in nature.

'Ah, the rain,' said Anton. 'Just what I needed to make my joy complete.' He pulled the standard-issue overcoat tight around his narrow shoulders, hunched forward with his collar up. He looked over at the bunker door without enthusiasm. It was a choice between returning to that narrow confined space with the rest of the troops or sitting outside in the rain. Neither was particularly appealing.

I picked up the periscope and raised it over the lip of the trench, adjusting the magnification. I could see kilometres and kilometres of earthworks, stretching all the way to the distant mountains. I twisted it and saw the same in every direction. An endless maze of trenches through which two armies slaughtered each other, all caught between gigantic ranges of mountains in which there were more fortified cities. One day, far in the future, the goal was to push all the way into those armoured citadels. Then we would be swapping fighting in trenches for fighting in tunnels. At that moment I would have welcomed it as a relief from the monotony.

The periscope went dark. I looked up. Idiot Anton was standing on the parapet again covering the lens with his gloved hand.

'There's a reason for using this thing,' I said. I might just have sounded a little testy.

'I told you I already killed the heretic snipers,' Anton said.

'Take your hand off the lens,' I said. 'I thought I saw something.'

I hadn't really, but I wanted to annoy him. He shaded his eyes with his hand, looked off into the distance and said, 'Hell, you're right!'

I squinted into the eyepiece and adjusted the focus, trying to work out whether he was having me on or not. It was difficult to tell in the half-light of the moon with the mist and residue gas clouds floating above the shell-churned earth. Then I saw what looked like a tide of shadows, moving across the muddy fields of no-man's-land, gliding from shell-hole to shell-hole, moving smoothly and quickly on a course that would take them to our lines just north-east of where we were. I coughed.

'What is it?' Ivan asked. He grabbed the periscope, wanting to take a look himself.

'Death commando by the look of it. Looks like they're going for another night raid.'

Ivan reached over and squeezed the bulb of the air-horn. It was a primitive thing but we had been reduced to such devices in the mud of Loki. Something about the planet radiation halo interfered with the comm-net, which worked only intermittently. The omnipresent mould and mud were tough on equipment as well. The horn's great bellow echoed through the trench and bunkers and was answered by the sound of other air-horns as the alarm spread. Somebody somewhere let off a flare. It arced into the sky, a green firework leaving a phosphorescent trail behind it, until it exploded into a brilliant flash of actinic light. The shadows took on definition, became humanoid figures wrapped from crown to foot in dark black cloth, carrying black-barrelled weapons. I snatched up my shotgun and got ready to give the attackers a warm welcome.

'No rest for the wicked,' Ivan said.

'You'd think they'd give some of those poor sinners over there the night off,' Anton said.

'Why?' I asked. 'Richter's got millions of them and there's more coming out of the vats all the time.'

'There'll be a few less by the time I'm finished tonight,' said Anton. 'I was just thinking about catching up on some kip. I'm not too happy about being interrupted.'

The chanting started drifting across no-man's-land again. It had an agitated sound to it – the heretics were unsettled by the flares and star shells and the sounds of shooting. The drums took on a more regular, but still feverish, rhythm. A great strangled roar rose like a distant sea pummelling a stony shoreline. It was followed by shouts and the sound of more flares going off.

Warning horns sounded again. Our own troops started to pour out of the low bunker doors, the green uniforms of my Lion Guard crew mingled with the grey of the Grosslanders whose spines we had been sent to stiffen. Some of the likely lads were adjusting the straps of their rebreathers. Others had clearly just snatched up their weapons. One or two had bare feet. I could see the whitish mould on their toes, the places where the skin had cracked and leaked pus. They had probably been washing their feet when the alarm sounded.

They were out of luck now. They'd better hope we didn't run into any contact gas. Then they'd have more than losing their toes to worry about.

CHAPTER TWO

More and more heads popped out of the bunkers and blockhouses. Men picked up guns and stood ready to defend their trenches. I ran along the front and shouted at the Grosslanders to get back in. As senior NCO, command had fallen to me since Lieutenant Jensen had taken a bullet through the brain. There were enemies coming across no-man's-land who would be on us before those coming through the trenches. They needed to be shooting at them first.

I raised the periscope again. The black-clad assault troops had vanished into the cover of shell-holes and behind ridges, but a new wave of heretics was sometimes visible in the distance through the gaps in the mist haze and gas clouds. They were throwing themselves over the lip of their trenches and scuttling forward in a half-crouch that suggested they were somehow less than human. Perhaps it was the case. Rumour had it that some strange things were born in vats in those distant mountain citadels.

Lieutenant Prost of the 66th Grosslanders moved along the line. His gaze passed studiously over us. We were not part of his command. I was a mere NCO but I was also part of Macharius's personal guard and, even with his fortunes at a low ebb, Macharius's name meant something. He was still supreme commander of the crusade, and who knew what influence we might have? It was amazing how much that counted with certain officers in certain line regiments.

The Undertaker had dispatched us here to check on this section of line when communication went down and we had not been able to get back to our own section. Our cold-minded former lieutenant had not become any less strange as he had worked his way up to field command, but his grasp of basic tactics was as sound as ever. We were stuck here in our ambiguous position. We carried papers that told people who we were and they were marked with the seal of the Lord High Commander's office. I had been in such situations before – I knew that if we asked for something we would most likely get it, just so long as we did not provoke the prickly pride of the officer class.

Prost barked orders emphasising what I had already said. I thought about that great human wave advancing across no-man's-land. With proper artillery support it would be smashed even as it set out. Hell, with Old Number Ten, the Baneblade that Ivan and Anton and I had started our careers on so long ago, we could have ended the attack there and then.

Screams sounded now as the bunkers opened up across no-man's-land. Lasguns lit the night. Mortars churned the mud. Here and there explosions flared where someone blundered into a landmine or an unexploded shell.

I looked at the squad of men in tattered green uniforms around me. They were waiting for orders. I was not too troubled by the advance across no-man's-land – the bunkers had been positioned so that their fields of fire raked the open approaches. They would slow or kill huge numbers of the enemy.

My main problem was the suspicion that this was a diversion, intended to focus attention away from the assault squads and attacks coming in along the trench lines themselves. Much as I disliked it, Anton's earlier idea had suddenly started to sound good. We needed to undertake a quick reconnaissance along the front line just to make sure.

I raised my hand and indicated the others should follow me. I kept my head down while I did it. Despite Anton's overconfidence I was not sure that there were no enemy snipers around, and people giving orders always make tempting targets.

We trudged down the line, passing the burned-out remains of another Leman Russ which had been hastily converted into an armoured strong point. A heavy bolter team were poking their heads and their weapon out of the place where its turret had once been. The weapon roared as they took their toll of the incoming heretics.

We passed more bunkers. Over each bunker entrance were bits of wood or scraps of card with joke signs inscribed on them, giving the bunker's name. Some of them had lines scratched through the alien script of the heretics and words in Imperial Gothic written beneath. I know for a fact that during my time on the front some of those signs had been changed around a hundred times. Where once the crusade had leapt from star system to star system, now we were reduced to bickering over a few kilometres of sodden earthworks.

We came to a fork in the trenches. A crossroads sign announced that this was where the Great Trunk Road branched into the Street of a Thousand Taverns and the Night Bazaar. I gestured for Anton and Ivan to take a couple of the lads and move to point down Tavern Street. Heads down, they scuttled by me along the left-hand branch. The joking had gone out of them and they were all efficiency now. Anton held his sniper rifle at the ready. Ivan had a grenade in one hand and his lasgun in the other. I clutched my shotgun tight, made sure no one was in front of me and ran along the duckboards towards the so-called Night Bazaar.

When we'd first arrived all of these trenches were an incomprehensible maze where everything looked alike. Now they seemed as different as two adjoining neighbourhoods in Belial. I made out the midden piled up outside the facetiously named Officers' Quarters bunker, and recognised the scratches on the doors of Hogey's Grand Emporium where shrapnel had sliced the plasteel and peeled away the paint from the shattered remains of a Chimera. They were familiar landmarks now. We headed down Sewer Street, a trench that was basically just one big latrine, moving into the Great Bog, a circular area used as a combination of rubbish dump and public toilet.

The clouds parted and the skull moon glared down. The lesser moon was halfway across the sky. A star shell exploded, sending shadows flickering weirdly through the trenches and illuminating the bodies that sprawled around us. They were in the grey uniforms of the Grosslanders. I was all too aware that death had touched this place. Some of the corpses were already crawling with the fat-bodied bore-flies. They liked nothing more than to feast on the flesh of the fallen, before laying the jelly eggs containing their larvae.

I narrowed my eyes. A man lay with his throat cut from ear to ear, a splatter of red blood down his chest, covered in crawling insects. An officer sprawled face down, a lho-stick near to hand, a wisp of smoke still rising from the tip. A soldier with a faintly familiar face slumped over a packing crate on which lay a deck of cards and an open copy of the Imperial Infantryman's Primer. The air inside my rebreather tasted stale. Something in my brain screamed that I ought to be able to smell the odour of death. I could hear the troops behind me shuffling their feet; all of them knew better than to get in front of me when I had the shotgun in my hands.

My brain continued to gibber. Panicked thoughts raced through it. What was I missing here? Where were the enemy? They must still be close. I checked the ridgeline of the trench. There were faint scuff marks on some of the crenulations. Maybe the assault team had come over there. Or maybe they had come down that branch in the trench. I moved slowly forward, my finger almost twitching on the shotgun trigger, the weapon heavy in my hand.

We moved along the trench beside the open sewer. Someone had been making improvements recently by the look of it. Pipes emerged from beneath the water as if workers had abandoned an attempt at plumbing halfway through the process. My brain registered that, but my eyes wandered on.

I counted corpses. Ten. Twenty. Thirty. I stopped counting. A whole platoon had gone down here and there was no sign of their attackers. With every step I felt like I was sticking my neck further and further into a trap, moving further and further away from safety. Reinforcements were getting more distant. The chanting of the heretics was getting closer.

A bore-fly landed on my goggles. More joined it. They crawled across the glass, partially obscuring my vision. I shook my head but they did not move. They were bigger than bluebottles, with bloated thoraxes and wings that seemed the same colour as the unnatural oils that floated on the surface of the chemically tainted puddles.

Had the enemy used gas? The thought sauntered across my brain. Images of men with cut throats flickered through my mind. Maybe they had taken out the sentries with it, paralysed some of the men, but there was more to it than that. All of the corpses I could see were wearing rebreathers. Not that it mattered much. There had been dozens of consignments of faulty masks sent to the front. Some said it was simply the usual incompetence of the Imperial manufactorums. Other claimed corners were being cut to fatten the profits of the merchant houses. I had heard Macharius rail against such things often enough not to dismiss the possibility.

Rebreathers, I thought. It niggled at my mind. I knew I was missing something but I could not work out what. I moved along the duckboards over the sewage trench. I thought about all of those naïve newcomers who never checked the filters on their masks, who trusted that they would work and who died, their lungs filling with froth, during the first gas attacks. I had tried lecturing them. I had tried setting an example. I had tried many things, but some people always know it's not their problem, that death always comes for somebody else, until that final moment when they realise that they are not immortal after all.

I looked down at the latrine trench and saw the brown mix of excrement, urine and mud. I noticed the faint swirls in it that were not caused by the rain and then I knew…

A bump emerged from the muddy mess. I blinked. It took a heartbeat for my brain to process what I was seeing. Something erupted out of the latrine trench. Instinctively I pulled the trigger on the shotgun and the thing came apart. The impact of the shot revealed the red of blood, the pink of flesh and the white of bone. The torn form of a heretic soldier flipped backwards into the mess.

I heard shouts from behind me as surprised soldiers responded more slowly than I had. The enemy assault squad had been waiting below the surface of the latrine trench, breathing through snorkels, examining us through periscopes. Those had been the strange pipes I had noticed at first.

Along the line horrified Imperial Guard soldiers were engaged in close combat with foes who dripped a trail of slime behind them and gurgled a name that sounded like Nurg-Al from deep within their chests. There was an awful suggestiveness about the name. Hearing it made the hairs rise along the back of my neck, and I felt an ominous sense of foreboding that made me want to stop the chanting any way I could.

The attackers were well trained, had the element of surprise and inspired horror and revulsion, but my men were holding their own. They were members of Macharius's elite guard, after all. They might even have been able to turn the tables on their attackers by the fury of their counter-assault had not more heretics erupted from the bunkers behind us, thrusting with blades, firing autoguns. An attack from two sides was almost enough to erode the courage of any warrior. There is nothing like the sensation that you might be stabbed in the back to get you looking over your shoulder, fighting with less than your customary efficiency and making you think about running for it.

I pumped the shotgun and twisted at the waist. A group of heretics was charging towards me. I took a heartbeat to line up the shot and pulled the trigger. The load of pellets ripped through the enemy, sent them tumbling back involuntarily into the mud and the latrine pit. They would not be emerging this time.

I glanced around and saw that Tomkins was down. His bayonet blade had sliced away mask, cowl and upper tunic from one of the heretics and I had a sudden horrific view of the cultist's exposed features. His skin was near-albino white. His eyes were bloodshot and marred by tiny broken veins. Boils erupted from his skin. Red rashes ran like rivers between them. He looked as unhealthy as it was possible to be and remain mobile, and yet he fought with the feverish strength of a berserker. This was a product of the vats.

I brought the butt of my shotgun down on his head. His skull broke like an eggshell, spilling discoloured brains everywhere. Flies buzzed around him and I had the sudden violent illusion that they had been released when the bones of his head had shattered. I told myself that could not be the case and took a moment to try and understand the situation.

Most of my men were down. All of my squad and the other two squads that had been following me had been overwhelmed by the double-pronged attack from the trench and the bunker wall. A few were still fighting, but it was only going to be a matter of time before they were overpowered by the scores of heretics swarming over them. The shotgun had bought me an extra moment or two but I was going to be hauled down myself unless I did something.

Autogun bullets whizzed around me as I blasted a path to the trench wall with the shotgun, slung the weapon on its strap and hauled myself up over the lip of the parapet out into no-man's-land. There was a small gap, a rise at the trench lip, and at the foot was barbed wire. I could see holes had been stealthily clipped through it and here and there bits of dark cloth clung to the metal spike-knots in the wire. This was where the assault team had made its approach.

I had only a second to register this and while I did I was

unclipping a grenade from my belt. I lobbed it into the trench and sprang forward, half scrambling, half running along the front of the parapet in case anyone got the idea to respond in kind. A few moments later I heard the explosion rip through the trench and a fraction of a second after that I felt its vibration. I threw another grenade in and kept moving, following the line back the way I had come, hoping that all of my own men down there were already dead and that I was not killing them with my grenades.

The muddy earth sucked at my boots. My gloved hands were covered in the reddish soil where I had put them down to maintain my balance. I heard a horrible phlegmy voice gurgle out orders and saw a cowled head poke up over the parapet ahead of me. I swung the shotgun down on its sling and pulled the trigger. The head vanished in a fountain of blood and bone. I kept running, still squatting down, praying desperately to the Emperor.

The muddy earth gave way beneath my boot. I slipped, overbalanced, began to tumble down the slope towards the barbed wire. I threw myself flat, dug my fingers into the front of the parapet, slowed down my slide. Nonetheless my boot slid into the barbed wire and the metal thorns pierced the fabric of my uniform. As I pulled my leg free, the cloth tore along with the flesh beneath it. I was aware of the pain and knew I was badly scratched but in the heat of the action my body was able to ignore it, the way a fighting man can ignore the loss of a limb until he collapses dead at the end of a battle.

I scuttled up the barrier, aware of the sounds of fighting

from below. I tried to calculate how far I had come. I was perhaps at the entrance to the Bazaar now, almost back where I started. I did not want to stick my head over the top and get it blown away so I inspected the cut in my leg for a moment, then glanced out into no-man's-land. Billows of poisonous mist covered it, rolling slowly in my direction. I prayed that when it reached me I did not absorb any of its venom through my open wound.

Where the mists parted I could see piles of corpses, where the heretics had been mown down. It did not seem to have mattered to them. They had come on anyway, rolling forward in a massive wave, as if their lives meant nothing to them. They were expendable: a mere distraction while another more subtle assault had flowed over our position.

I pulled out the periscope and raised it over the parapet, from the wrong side this time. Down in the trench I caught sight of a green-uniformed Lion Guard squad locked in battle with the cultists. I could see Ivan, his mechanical arm covered in blood, brandishing the severed head of a heretic. It looked like he had pulled it clean from the neck. Anton knelt beside him and calmly snapped shots off with his sniper rifle. I could tell from his stance that he was filled with tension and excitement.

I twisted the periscope and saw a horde of heretics rushing towards them along the trench. I pulled out another grenade, lobbed it and crawled back along the brow of the parapet, tossing more grenades as I went. The enemy were so packed in that part of the trench that I could not miss. Gobbets of flesh and fountains of blood spattered me in the wake of the explosions. I kept tossing grenades. I had run out of explosives but I still had the phosphorescents so I lobbed them in as well. Even through the filters of my rebreather I thought I smelt the stench of burning, rotting flesh. I told myself it was my imagination.

A chain of explosions thundered and a line of fire filled the trench. Either I had hit a fuel dump or some of the heretics had been carrying something incendiary and I had set it off. No matter, the results were gratifying. I made my way back along the trench line for the fourth time. Black clouds emerged from it and the sound of shooting had stopped.

'Ivan!' I bellowed. 'Anton! Can you hear me?'

'Is that you, Leo?' Anton replied.

'No! It's my ghost! What do you think?'

'It has to be him,' I heard Anton say. 'It's too sarky to be anybody else.'

'I'm going to stick my head above the parapet now! Try not to blow it off!'

I extended the shotgun above my head with both hands. I figured that if someone was going to shoot me it would be better to lose a hand. I left it over the parapet for thirty seconds.

'What are you waiting for?' Anton asked.

'I'm waiting to see if any one of you is trigger-happy.'

'Well, I think you got your answer.'

I stuck my head up and saw a line of faces looking up at me. I glanced along the trench line and saw more dead heretics, slaughtered by my little ambush and fire from Ivan's squad. Flies buzzed everywhere. Corpses lay all about.

Even through the filters of my rebreather mask I caught the smell. I jumped down into the trenches and Ivan was slapping me on the back.

'I thought we'd seen the last of you there when those heretics came charging down the trench.'

'They got everybody else,' I said. I glanced around at the others, expecting to see blame written on their faces. I had lost three entire squads to the ambush by being too slow on the uptake. No one except myself seemed to be accusing me of anything. I figured I could do a good enough job of that until we got back to headquarters, when doubtless I would have some explaining to do.

'What did you find down your fork?' I asked.

Ivan shook his head. 'Not a thing. Whole place was abandoned. Just like it was supposed to be. What happened to you?'

I told them. Anton's eyes grew ever narrower. 'You mean I need to check for assassins every time I take a dump now? That will take all the fun out of it.'

'Look on the bright side. Think about what it will be like for them,' I said.

The words had no sooner left my mouth when air-horns sounded down the trench line. Three short blasts, then three long blasts, then three short blasts. It was not a good sign. It meant that a huge enemy attack was incoming.

'Best be heading back,' I said. 'We're going to be needed.'

CHAPTER THREE

I could hear the drums sounding along the trenches and more of that phlegmy chanting. Much more.

I was all out of grenades and the rest of the squad had very few. There would be no repeat of my ambush, not tonight; perhaps not any night, unless we could find a better place to make a stand.

As we made our way back along the trenches, I found I was limping. I looked down at my leg, which felt stiff. When I took out a bayonet and sliced at the cloth, I spotted odd black circles around the barbed wire punctures. I swabbed at them, hoping I was not already too late. I'd seen men lose legs from lesser things on Loki.

Ivan was frowning. He knew better than most what these things could lead to. I doubted there would be any bionics available for me out here. We had left access to such things a long way behind the front lines of the crusade. Fewer and fewer supplies were getting through.

'What you think?' Ivan asked.

'We fall back to Brand's Fort,' I said. 'It's got the best chance of holding out against a big assault.'

'It's a death-trap if we're caught in it.'

'This whole salient is, unless we're reinforced soon. At least there we'll be dug-in with food and medical supplies and as much ammunition as we're ever likely to get.'

Brand's Fort was a massive bunker excavated from the inside of a small hill and covered in rockcrete. Over the past couple of years it had been reinforced and reinforced again, with more weapons blisters, more rockcrete and more barbed wire. Effluent sumps poured slimy liquid down the sides. Skeletons lay within clusters of wire. Some joker had built a small wall of human skulls around the base of one of the bunkers and then spelled out the words *Come and die here* in bones on the slope beneath them. Where did these people find the time?

A Banshee scream filled the air and there was the sudden thunder of an explosion. I threw myself flat and all the Lion Guard around me did the same. The distant heretic batteries had opened fire once again.

Anton spidered his way up alongside me – all long legs and elbows – and out of the side of his mouth said, 'I wonder if this is all part of Richter's Great Plan.'

I knew what he meant but I wasn't going to be drawn into a reply. It was possible this was an artillery barrage meant to precede the rebel attack and that there had been some mistake on the enemy side that had resulted in its delayed launch. The Emperor knows I've seen enough such things happen on our side of the trench system. Or maybe this was the harbinger of another assault.

We lay there for long minutes, acutely aware that it would only take one of those shells to drop on our section of trench and we would all be gone. I felt the earth shake beneath me. The pain in my leg was getting worse and I felt a little light-headed. I told myself it was because we'd been on short rations for so long, but part of me knew that it was not hunger.

I raised my head and watched a cluster of explosions stalk up the side of Brand's Fort, carving out new indentations in the rockcrete, destroying the wall of skulls and the message written in bones.

A crouched figure made its way up the trench towards us. He wore the grey uniform of a Grosslander with a yellow armband that marked him as a messenger. His hand was fumbling nervously in his belt for a pistol. I waved at him to let him know that even though we were not part of his regiment we were not enemies.

'What's new?' I shouted in Imperial Gothic.

He moved up to our position and said, 'Big heretic offensive incoming. I'm on my way to the Great Bog to let Lieutenant Snorrison know he should hold his ground.'

'Snorrison is dead, along with his whole command,' I said.

'You sure?'

'I was there not an hour ago. Assault squad hit his position and wiped it out. Not five minutes later a crowd of heretics came through. We bloodied their nose but we didn't have enough to hold them.'

'You should have,' he said accusingly.

'Is my name Snorrison?' I asked. 'Am I wearing a Gross-lander uniform?'

His eyes widened behind the lenses of his rebreather mask and I think for the first time he noticed the lion emblem on my tunic. He probably couldn't tell the colour – with all the grime it would have been hard.

'No, sir,' he said shakily. He looked into the distance, embarrassed. 'You sure the lieutenant is dead?'

'Either that or he's run away,' I said. 'There was nobody left alive in the Great Bog.'

'Lieutenant Snorrison would not do that,' said the youth. I realised now he was very young and very green. I could not quite bring myself to feel sorry for him. I was not sure I agreed with his assessment of the situation either. Lots of men ran away here and it was not because they were cowards. The strain of the trenches under constant bombardment ate away at their nerves and that was not taking into account some of the gases, which induced terror in the unprotected.

He shrugged and made to move past me. 'Where you going?'

'I need to see if I can find the lieutenant.'

This lad was devoted to his duty, that was for sure. I was not even offended that he would not take my word for it. He had been given orders to do a job and plenty of officers and no few commissars would find him to be in dereliction of them if he did not at least try to carry them out. Plus, he was keen. You could tell by the way he snapped a salute and then raced off along the trench. Silently I wished him luck – he was going to need it.

We kept moving towards the fort.

The fort was not quite so easy to enter as the bunkers back in the trenches. I had to shout down an intercom system that was basically just a collection of pipes. I gave my name, number and a password that was several days out of date and stood so that my face was visible in the view periscope.

This being the Imperial Guard, it took half an hour for someone finally to recognise me and let me in. When the airlock door was opened, the gatekeeper looked me up and down sardonically and sniffed. It was Sergeant Matlock. He was recently promoted, a martinet and a disciplinarian who came from Macharius's home world and had been in the service of a family long allied with the Lord High Commander. I did not like him and he returned the favour.

'Sorry to offend your delicate nostrils,' I said. 'I've been fighting.'

His aquiline nose wrinkled further. His nostrils dilated. He was struggling to find a pithy reply. I interrupted his train of thought. 'I need to see the colonel.'

'You were supposed to be back two days ago.'

'The heretics decided that they required my company a bit longer.' I was already limping past him down towards the local command centre. It was not quite a different world in the fort but it was close. The squalor of the trenches was nowhere visible. The floors and walls were scrubbed. Doubtless Matlock had to keep himself busy somehow. There were Guardsmen in sight but they looked like I remembered once looking myself – their uniforms were clean and untattered. They were shaved. Their eyes were not bloodshot. Their hands were not scabbed. Most of them looked at me guiltily, and felt bad about being down here in comparative safety while I was outside.

I can't say it bothered me too much. I knew most of them would rotate out at some point and join the fun in the trenches. All of them except Matlock. Somehow he always managed to avoid the external duty roster. Someday I was going to have to ask him how he managed that – with a bayonet.

I made my way down the corridors into the command bunker. The Undertaker was there looking as cold and calm as the day he had returned to sanity in the wreckage of Old Number Ten. The juvenat treatments seemed to have worked well for him. The only visible differences were some deeper tan-lines around the crinkle of his eyes and the colonel's insignia on his shoulder.

He looked over at me and I saluted. 'Sergeant Lemuel,' he said. His voice was as flat and emotionless as ever but I had served under him long enough to recognise the question in it.

'Lieutenant Jensen is dead, sir. Killed by an enemy sniper. I am acting commander of the recon unit.'

He tilted his head to one side. 'Report,' he said.

I filled him in on the details of the encounter as quickly and calmly as I could. He nodded as if I were confirming something he already suspected, and barked instructions over his shoulder. A clerk moved some tokens on the paper map of the trench complex. This is what we had been reduced to. The holo-pits had all broken down and had not been repaired. The crystals needed had been requisitioned six months ago but had still not arrived.

I saw the clerk put a number of red counters on the map of the Great Bog and remove the small blue token that had represented Lieutenant Snorrison's unit. There were not a lot of blue tokens in our section of the line and an awful lot of red ones. In the face of what looked like a giant heretic offensive our trenches were going to be very difficult to hold.

'What happened to the leg, Lemuel?' the Undertaker asked.

'Barbed wire, sir. I scratched it.'

'Have a medical orderly look at it, get some rest and then report back here in two hours. We're going to need every man who can fight.'

'Yes, sir,' I said. It was clear I had been dismissed. I saluted and limped out of the command pit. Matlock watched me with hate-filled eyes and a sneer on his face.

'You need to be careful with these things,' said the medic, rubbing alcohol onto the cuts and tearing off a strip of gauze. We had run out of synthi-flesh a couple of months back.

'My legs?' I said, just to be annoying.

'Punctures, cuts, abrasions of any sort. The disease spores out there are nasty and all manner of infections can get in. Some of them we can't exorcise.'

'Why is that, sir?'

He looked up at me. He was a middle-aged man in the uniform of the Grosslanders. No juvenat treatments for him. He knew who I was from the uniform so he was prepared to consider my question in a way that he might not have been if it had come from one of his own sergeants.

'Don't know, Lemuel. There's just something about this place. The diseases here seem cursed. They're cross-breeding like dogs.'

I could tell from the reference to cross-breeding that he had come from a particularly agricultural section of Grossland, which was a particularly agricultural world.

'You said the diseases are getting stronger – how can you tell?'

'They kill quicker, spread faster and are getting more virulent. The symptoms are getting more alarming too. It's almost as if someone is using the disease spores as weapons.'

'Is that possible?'

'You hear stories. The ancients did it. Certain tech-magi are supposed to be able to do it.'

'It's a pretty dirty way of fighting a war.'

'Most ways are,' he said, 'when you think about it.'

I thought about the gas shells and the death commandos hiding in latrine pits and I could not disagree with him. I thought of the hundreds of thousands of bodies spread across no-man's-land, of all the men lost in mud pits and eaten by rats and killed by faulty rebreathers. I must have winced.

'What?' he said.

'I was just thinking that the war here has been dirtier than any I have seen before, and some of the places I've been have been pretty unpleasant.'

'You're part of Macharius's bodyguard, aren't you?'

'For more than twenty-five standard years now.'

'You ever met him?'

'The first time I met him he was decorating me for bravery. I was with the Seventh Belial at the time.'

'What's he like?'

I looked at him. He was a middle-aged man, well educated, well balanced and stable, and he still wanted to know about the legend. Even now, in this long season of delay and disappointment, it still glowed around the Lord High Commander like a halo around the head of a saint.

'That's a hard question to answer,' I said.

'Do you think he really has been touched by the Emperor?'

Now we were on dangerous ground no matter how I replied. If I said yes, I was passing a religious judgement that was not mine to make. If I said no, I could be perceived as being disrespectful to Macharius if this man should turn out to be one of the fanatical kind who were becoming more and more attached to Macharius's legend.

'He is the greatest general of the age,' I said.

'You think he will beat Richter then?'

'I think he can beat anybody,' I said, 'given time.'

'We've had plenty of time here,' said the orderly. Had I misjudged him? Was he one of those men who were critical of Macharius, who sought to undermine morale? It might be that he was just expressing his own opinion but that might prove a dangerous thing to do in these times, particularly since he was expressing it to a man he knew to be part of the Lord High Commander's retinue.

'We have however long it takes,' I said, putting an edge into my voice so he would not misunderstand my real meaning.

'I hope so,' he said. 'I can't help but feel that time is running out.' Given the situation he was in – trapped in a fort running low on supplies with an enormous heretic attack coming in – his doubts were completely understandable, but I could not help thinking that in the past he would not have expressed them. In the past no one had doubted Macharius.

For the first time, I wondered if such thoughts were shared by other soldiers of the crusade. For the first time, I asked myself whether I had such doubts. I let the thought flicker across my mind for a few heartbeats and then I ushered it out. Now was not the time to start questioning my beliefs.

I looked at my leg. It had been swabbed. The dark circles around the wire punctures had faded a little, although one of them wept green pus. The orderly wrapped the gauze tightly again and said, 'Keep it clean and try not to get it exposed again until it's healed. Otherwise you might lose the leg, or worse.'

I got up and put some weight on it. It held, but I felt a twinge of pain and I knew I was not one hundred per cent. I doubted anyone on the front line was. I limped towards the door, knowing that I should report to the Undertaker soon.

'If you do see Macharius, tell him the Grosslanders are still behind him,' said the orderly. He sounded determined and clearly meant it as a declaration of loyalty. He did not sound as if he were afraid I would report the conversation. Myself, I wondered at the fact that he felt he needed to make such a declaration at all either on his own behalf or that of his regiment. Once it was simply taken as a given. Things had changed in the ranks of the crusade.

'I will do that,' I said, and laid a hand on his shoulder to reassure him. He was a decent man, trying to do his best under difficult circumstances and I respected that.

I reported to the Undertaker at the appointed time. He studied me for a moment with cold eyes and a manner that seemed as distant as the stars in the sky. There was no trace of humanity in the gaze he turned on me. For the thousandth time I wondered what he had seen in that strange trance in the wreckage of Number Ten amid the ruins of Karsk IV.

'Fit, Lemuel?' he asked.

'Fit, sir.' I was not one hundred per cent but I could fight, and every man was needed.

'Good. We need to hold this line until reinforcements arrive. It's going to be difficult.'

That was a considerable understatement. I looked at the gigantic stacks of red chips representing the heretics. I looked at our own thin blue line. The Undertaker followed my gaze.

'The heretics are breaking through,' the Undertaker said. 'We have neither the manpower nor the munitions to hold them.'

That was a realistic assessment of the situation I thought,

staring down at the complex map of trenches. What he said next surprised me. 'So we are going to let them pass.'

'Sir?'

'We can hold them at choke points at Skeleton Ridge and Plague Hill. We have enough manpower to stop them there if we reinforce those points.'

'But sir…'

Very few officers would have tolerated being interrupted by a sergeant, but the Undertaker's strangeness and our long familiarity made the difference. 'Please, let me finish, Lemuel.'

'Sir.'

He glanced around at the rest of the officers in the bunker. They listened with the air of men who were going over a plan for the tenth time but wanted to make sure they understood completely. He pointed at the huge stacks of red chips. 'The heretics will be funnelled into the Second Sector, by the resistance at Skeleton Ridge and Plague Hill. We will hold the bulk of our troops in reserve at those points. Once a sufficiently large section of heretics is within our trench system, we will close the front with swift counter-attacks from our strong points, leaving a large formation of heretics trapped within our lines. We will then move to eliminate them.'

It was a typical Macharian strategy, I thought, bold and relying on trickery and misdirection. It seemed like the Undertaker had been studying our master's methods. Of course there were huge risks. We might not be able to close the gap once the heretics were flooding in; we might be ceding a huge forward base to them that they could pour men and materiel into. I thought about it for a moment. It was a desperate plan, but we did not really have much of a choice. It was as the Undertaker said – we did not have the forces to hold this whole section of the line.

'The Lion Guard will spearhead the counter-assault, Lemuel. You will be held in reserve until then. Lieutenant Creasey will be commanding. Your men can resupply from the dumps on the hill.'

I thought about the huge horde of heretics waiting out there in the cold and rainy night. 'Very good, sir,' I said.

'You may rejoin your unit,' he said. He snapped off a salute.

CHAPTER FOUR

I looked down from the parapet of Skeleton Ridge at the fighting below. It was all visible through the magnoculars. The flash of the lasguns, the glare of phosphorescent grenades, the bodies impaled on stakes and trapped in barbed wire. The chatter of autogun fire and the roar of explosions drifted uphill. The bulk of the fighting was taking place below us, in the sector in which the heretics had been allowed to pass.

Tens of thousands of corpses were strewn across the hillside. The heretics had not been allowed to pass on Skeleton Ridge. We had chopped them down every time they tried to mount the slope. At one stage it had come to particularly bitter hand-to-hand combat but we had held out, only just.

'I hope the Undertaker knows what he's doing,' Anton murmured close to my ear. I could follow his thoughts. The heretics were pushing forward in their tens of thousands. They were following the line of least resistance, convinced that they had scored a major breakthrough. In a sense, they had. The question now was whether we would be able to use that against them.

'It's a good plan,' I said.

'It's the only plan,' said Ivan. 'Look at those frakkers. How can one lousy planet keep producing so many soldiers? We kill millions of them and millions more keep coming.'

'There's no more down there than a good-sized hive could produce,' I said.

'Yes, but there's a lot more of them than there are of us. And there's something strange about them.'

I knew what he meant. When I searched those corpse faces on the hill below us, they were all pocked with boils and suppurating abscesses. Their eyes were pinkish. Their skin was blotched. There was a sameness about them that was not the similarity that all corpses have, the stricken look of the fallen soldier. I looked from one to the other and saw what appeared to be a family resemblance among the faces. Looking at the nearest corpses, something niggled, and slowly what it was that was disturbing me floated to the surface of my mind.

Some of the faces were more than just similar. They were identical, like twins. I counted the same face a dozen times as if it had been stamped from a mould. It dawned on me that if I kept looking I might find it a thousand times. Once I started looking I saw that there was another face, also replicated, and another and another. It was as if all those warriors down there had come off a production line in a Guild Manufactorum on Belial. It was a facility that produced soldiers and it had maybe a dozen models. The warriors facing us were being grown in vats, or something worse, I felt sure of it. I suspected they fought so hard because they knew they were going to die anyway. They all seemed riddled with disease.

Even as I watched, the stomach of one – bloated hugely with corpse gas – exploded, sending a cloud of blood and entrails and something else into the air. The mortal remains spattered to the ground around it, but the extra stuff seemed to float in the air, like spores adrift on the wind.

'That was quite a fart,' said Anton, trying to make a dumb joke of it as always, but Ivan was ahead of him.

'What new hellishness is this?' he asked. More and more of the corpses were exploding, entrails bursting out, clouds of spores hovering over them. I glanced around and shouted, 'Everybody make sure your rebreathers are tight.'

The men were Lion Guard. They should not have had to be told, but I like to be certain. I walked along the line making sure all of their masks were well adjusted and then I returned to the post where Anton and Ivan were waiting. I raised the magnoculars and checked again, for something had struck me.

I was right. The corpses that were exploding all seemed to have the same face, and it was one I had not seen before in previous attacks. I thought about what the medic had said, about new diseases being cross-bred. Maybe this new type of soldier was a new type of weapon bearing a new type of plague.

Even as the thought was running through my mind, a shot

rang out. I looked at Anton who had raised the sniper rifle to his shoulder and fired. 'One of them was moving,' he said. 'One of the heretics. He must not have been quite dead.'

Lasguns fired along the line now, bolts cutting through the gloom. I wondered whether Anton's shot had triggered a nervous reaction and the men were simply spooked, but a corpse rose from the heap on the hillside and tottered forward a few feet, blood dripping from its eyes like tears. It got caught in the barbed wire and tried to continue, its flesh being raked off by the spikes. Anton's shot exploded its head and it fell.

More and more of the corpses had started to move, pulling themselves up.

'Must have been playing dead,' muttered Anton, but I knew he was wrong. Several of the bodies were trailing their own entrails. One of them had a hole in his chest cavity that showed where his heart had been burned out.

'Steady, lads,' I shouted. The Lion Guard kept firing. The ambulatory corpses were put down again.

Ivan said, 'Tell them to stop shooting.'

I was going to ask why but instead I bellowed the order. I watched and I saw what Ivan had noticed. Each of the corpses staggered forward only a few metres and then collapsed again, and did not rise.

'Must be some new disease,' Ivan said. 'Makes them run around like headless chickens, even after they are dead.'

I kept my eyes on them nonetheless. I was unnerved by this latest development. Corpses moving by some sort of delayed reflex action I could believe, but not hours after they had been shot. Men waking up wounded on a battlefield was a possibility, but not in such numbers and not with such wounds. I felt that some new and evil development in the war was taking place.

I kept watching, but no more corpses exploded. No more dead men stirred. Not yet.

I woke from a bad dream of cadavers gnawing on my flesh. The worst thing about it was the corpses had belonged to Anton and Ivan and now it was Ivan shaking me awake.

'What is it?' I asked.

He gestured to the messenger standing by his shoulder. 'Orders from Lieutenant Creasey, sir. We're to be ready to counter-attack within the hour.'

I nodded and said to Ivan and Anton, 'Make sure everybody is ready to move out. Make sure everybody has their grenades ready too. The fighting is going to be close and personal. We'll be able to smell their bad breath.'

They scuttled away to spread the word. I studied the corpses on the hillside again. None of them had stirred. If we had not all witnessed it I would have suspected I had been hallucinating, that some form of nightmare gas had penetrated the filters of my rebreather.

The messenger was still standing there, looking at me, no doubt wondering why I was studying the enemy corpses so intently. 'Any message to take back, sir?'

'Tell the lieutenant we'll be ready to go,' I said. He saluted and scuttled away, leaving me staring at the cold and enigmatic faces of the corpses on the side of Skeleton Ridge.

* * *

The Lion Guard began to filter down the hillside along the feeder trench. Sandbags lined the way. The stairs were made from planks of wood, bits of metal, old ration tins half-buried in the muddy earth. Anything that would help give a foothold. Obscenities had been inscribed everywhere they could be, along with curses and prayers and the occasional sexually explicit drawing.

At this point the stairwell was only wide enough for one man. I was leading from the front; as I said before, it's unwise to stand in front of a man with a shotgun. As we moved I prayed that another attack was not launched against the ridge. There was merely a small holding force up there now. We had stripped the defences of every man now that we were trying to close the gap and snip off the salient driven into our lines.

I felt tension building in my body. My mouth was dry. My heart was hammering against my ribs. We were outnumbered and we were weary and we were facing an enemy that seemed to have almost infinite resources in men and materials. In the long run we would lose if things continued as they were. We held only small footholds on Loki now and our supply lines back to the Imperium were long and faulty. The enemy had industrial cities full of productive capacity and access to unholy magic that let them create new armies of obscenely fanatical soldiers. In my youth, I would not have believed in such strange technological sorceries, but I had travelled too far and seen too much to doubt them now.

As I marched I wondered about things. How did those bodies decanted from vats learn? Did they come into the world with blank minds? If so, how was knowledge impressed into them? During the Dark Age of Technology the ancients were said to have possessed machines capable of such wicked miracles, but they had been lost a long time ago. Or had they? Was there something surviving on this world that tapped into those grim secrets?

I took a deep breath and tried to empty my mind of such speculations. It was best to concentrate on the job at hand; that would give me the greatest chance of survival. A faint depression nagged away at me.

What would that survival mean? Just another opportunity to go forth and face death again tomorrow, and the day after that and every day until finally death caught up with me, as it did to every mortal man.

I told myself that the world was getting to me, that the long struggle was bringing me down. I felt another twinge of pain in my leg. Maybe I was coming down with something and my mind was simply responding to my body's hints. It had happened before.

I glanced out through a hole in the parapet intended to allow a man to shoot from it. I caught sight of the battlefield below us. Flares of light drifted overhead. A shell exploded somewhere. Through the soles of my boots I felt the vibration of its distant detonation.

Lines of the enemy were still moving across no-man's-land, heading into the deep breach in our lines. The enemy moved slowly but surely. They chanted their gurgling prayers and moved in time to their drummers. They did not seem to have any idea of their own mortality, of the fact that they could die. I thought again of empty minds, and newborn bodies emerging from vats, of unholy innocents being dispatched to fight in a holy war. I felt oddly sorry for them for a moment and then I squashed the feeling as a thing I could not afford.

I was in the trenches proper now. Grosslanders held the position, weapons at the ready, and we Lion Guard filtered past them in the gloom, making for the enemy.

The duckboards of the trenches shifted underfoot as we passed. Bodies lay everywhere. Some of them had the bloated stomachs and twisted faces I remembered from the assault on the ridge. I wondered if they had stirred after death as well.

How many had died here? How many hundreds of thousands had fallen? A bleak vision entered my mind, of all those bodies stirring and beginning to move in the service of some evil power. In those haunted trenches, beneath that evil moon, visible even in daytime, such a thing seemed possible. The Emperor knows I have seen stranger things during my time in his service.

Perhaps there was something about this world that fed on death. Maybe all the killing leached into the soil itself and then fed its dark energy back into those corpses. I told myself to stop thinking about it. There must be other simpler explanations. A disease that temporarily restored motor functions, causing nerves to misfire and muscles to spasm. That's all it was.

I could hear the gurgling chants coming closer now. The earth vibrated under the tread of that oncoming horde. I felt exposed and vulnerable, the front runner of the tiny force that was attempting to stop that irresistible tide. My leg gave another twitch. Black despair swirled like poison in my brain.

The trenches widened out. More bodies sprawled everywhere. Headless, limbless, reduced to bloody pulp by the great ravening beast this war had become. I could hear yelling now. The gurgling voices had a hint of triumph in them, as if every soldier in that onrushing army were utterly certain of victory. They had good reason to feel that way.

I tried to picture the map of the trench complex in my head. I thought I had it all down. My battles along this front line had given me a great deal of familiarity with the layout over the past six months.

Up ahead I caught sight of the first of those brown-clad, mud-covered, sickly looking soldiers. I crouched low, held the shotgun ready, took a deep breath and prepared for combat.

I raced forward and pulled the trigger, blasting a hole deep in the enemy ranks. I pumped it and fired again and then again. The heretics went down like puppets with their strings cut. They had not been expecting this attack. They had thought that the fighting was still a long way ahead of them.

They reacted sluggishly, as they usually did, with the lethargy of men long confined to sick beds, or whose minds were slower than they should be. They were not very good soldiers, those vat-born heretics. There were just a lot of them.

I saw the uniform of an officer and I shot him, knowing that would slow their responses even more. In these sorts of regiments, the enemy officer corps were the only ones among the heretics who seemed remotely normal, who could respond with alacrity to any new threat. Their followers obeyed them implicitly. In a very real sense they were the brains and nerves of the enemy army.

The officer went down along with a bunch of his minions. Ivan swept by me, lobbing a grenade, and then pulling the trigger on his laspistol. Anton moved up to my side and began shooting with his sniper rifle at any enemy that even hinted at turning in my direction. The rest of our men moved forward sending a hail of grenades and small arms fire into the heretics. We smashed into their line like a bayonet tearing through diseased flesh. In my mind's eye I could picture other squads of Lion Guard on the far side of the salient doing the same thing. The jaws of the trap were starting to close. The question was, who was being trapped, the enemy or us?

We charged forward through the trenches, killing as we went, blowing them up with grenades, setting them alight with incendiaries, blasting them with shotguns and lasrifles. They could not stop us; we had them flanked and we were far, far better fighters. Most of the heretics were worse than even the greenest recruits, but there were just so damn many of them. We cut through them, cleaving their line, but such were their numbers that they simply filled the gaps we made like water flooding into a trench.

I smashed the head of one foe with the butt of the shotgun, stuck the barrel into the mouth of another, which broke his teeth. When I pulled the trigger, his skull disintegrated and the heretics behind him fell. Clouds of smoke were everywhere from the small fires started by the incendiaries, chemical blazes that not even the constant rain could douse.

I faced a heretic officer. He was huge and blubbery, with rolls of fat that distorted the shape of his uniform. A tiny red mouth was visible in parchment-pale skin. He was a head taller than me and weighed three times as much. Numerous chins compressed against his neck as he screamed and gurgled his hatred. Like most of their officer class, he did not seem to have any boils or rashes. His eyes were pink, though, and a mesh of tiny red veins was visible beneath the skin of his cheeks and forehead.

His movements were slow and lumbering. I pointed the shotgun at him. A body came falling from my right and deflected my aim as I pulled the trigger. The giant loomed over me, and I found myself locked in a bear-like embrace, my face pressed deep into folds of fat, flabby fingers pressing at my throat. I smelt sweat and something sickly sweet, like curdled milk.

I tried to pull away, but for all his softness the giant was strong. I heard his breath come out in phlegmy wheezes. I heard his stomach gurgle. I had dropped the shotgun. I brought my fist around and buried it in his belly. It was like poking the side of some huge balloon. My hand sank in and then simply recoiled as if I were hitting rubber. I looked up and saw that he was smiling serenely as he choked the life out of me, a look of dreamy satisfaction on his blubbery face.

I reached down with my right hand, hoping to grab his nads and squeeze them, and I found nothing. He was a eunuch. Absurdly I wondered if all the officer caste were. I slumped down, faking a loss of consciousness, my fast-weakening fingers fumbling for the bayonet I had strapped to my boot. I pulled it free from the sheath and I stabbed upwards into that vast belly.

He gave a high-pitched scream and his hands spasmed, and I feared in that moment he was going to crush my windpipe. He toppled backwards, clutching at his stomach, a dark red stain spreading across his uniform tunic. I stabbed again, aiming below the ribs, into the belly once more, blade pulling upwards to cut internal organs. His shrieking continued.

Another heretic closed with me and I slashed his throat. I looked around desperately for my shotgun, a weapon I had carried through more than two decades of campaigning, and which had saved my life on multiple occasions. I had a superstitious dread of losing it. I saw it lying in the mud and I dived for it, almost shaking with relief when my hand curled around it. I returned my bayonet to its sheath and checked the shotgun to make sure it was working.

A brief lull settled on the position. For a moment there was a quiet that sounded almost like silence compared to the roar of battle that had gone before it.

I saw Anton looking at me and glanced around to make sure Ivan was all right. He stood propped up against the side of the trench, his bionic arm covered in blood. The rest of the squad were stretched out behind us. Everyone looked tired, but moved with the nervous brittle energy that adrenaline and the knowledge that you are standing on the knife-edge between life and death brings.

'Tougher than he looked, that last big frakker,' Anton said, 'but I knew you could take him.'

'You could have lent me a hand.'

'You didn't need one and I was busy with some heretics of my own.'

'What now?' Ivan asked.

'We push on,' I said. 'We try and link up with the boys from Plague Hill. I reckon we've only got about another league to go.'

'What about holding the line?'

'Leave it to the lads coming up behind us. We need to break on through and seal off the salient if we're going to have any chance at all.'

Ivan raised an eyebrow and directed a look of the uttermost cynicism towards me. Clearly he felt that our chances were not great. What could I tell him? We needed to follow on through to give ourselves a fighting chance.

Anton's eyes suddenly narrowed and I heard his gasp of fear. I turned to see the corpse of the officer pull itself upright, its fat arms stretching out and its pudgy fingers flexed like claws. An obscene gurgling sound emerged from its mouth – there was an awful suggestion of humour in it. Its glance swivelled to meet mine and I saw hunger and hatred there.

CHAPTER FIVE

'Hell,' Anton said. 'Not again.'

The rifle rose to his shoulder and he pulled the trigger. The body of the fat officer fell over backwards, head removed.

'You can't say I didn't help you that time,' Anton said. 'I put the fat frakker down for good.'

He had too. I wondered at the way the heretic officer had risen. I glanced around and saw some more of the heretics pulling themselves upright. A few of them shambled forward, arms outstretched, and I was reminded of the way their leader had reached for my throat. I blasted one down with the shotgun. It wriggled forward for a bit before it stopped moving.

Of the enemies that had fallen only a few had managed to pull themselves upright and even they had fallen down once more, like wound-up toys losing their motive power.

'You see that?' asked Ivan, pointing at one of the fallen corpses. I did. It was as if all the blood vessels in the corpse's eye had burst and turned all the white to red. A red film had spread over the iris and only the tiny pinprick of the pupil was visible. I checked all of the bodies that had come back from seemingly fatal wounds and they all shared the same red eyes.

'Some new form of disease,' Ivan said. He sounded thoughtful.

'Looks that way,' I said.

'What sort of disease makes a dead body get up and run around like a headless chicken?' Anton asked.

'This one,' I said. 'I thought that much was obvious. Anyway, we don't have time for this. Push on!'

We headed on down the trench, chopping our way through more of the heretics. A few more of the bodies rose – not many, but enough. I came across a few more corpses whose stomachs had exploded like the ones on Skeleton Ridge. There were no wounds on them. It was as if they had fallen down dead where they lay, victims of some terrible disease.

Over a few of the dead something seemed to hover, a sort of foul disease spore. The area around their fallen bodies was discoloured by more than just the remains of their innards. It was as if some vile chemical had been produced by their death and tainted the very earth around them. I began to do some calculations in my head. Whenever we were near a spot where the corpses picked themselves up, we found one of these stomach bursters. They were obviously some terrible new weapon. I was grateful for the fact that they did not seem to work very well.

Up ahead of us now, we heard the sound of bitter fighting, of grenades exploding and lasguns pulsing. I heard officers shouting orders in Imperial Gothic and saw men in the uniforms of the Lion Guard in front of us. We had made it to the rendezvous. We had linked up with the force from Plague Hill and cut the enemy force in half. Of course, that just meant that as soon as the enemy realised what had happened we were going to be attacked on two sides, front and rear. Suddenly the Undertaker's plan did not seem nearly so clever. I glanced out into the darkness from which the heretics had come. For the moment all was quiet. The enemy had fallen back. One of their commanders had clearly realised that something was going wrong and had halted the advance, quite possibly temporarily. It gave us some breathing space.

Behind us the other half of the enemy continued to advance towards our second line. They had not yet realised they were out of touch with their own reserves. A captain emerged from the Plague Hill lines and went to greet our officer commanding. They chatted for a bit and then Lieutenant Creasey came over.

'Sergeant Lemuel, you and your men will hold this section of the line. The rest of us are going to take those heretics in the rear.' He said it with the utter confidence that a certain sort of field officer feels he needs to project.

I snapped off a salute and said, 'Yes, sir.'

* * *

'Mighty quiet around here,' said Anton, staring out into no-man's-land. He was wrong, of course. Behind us we could hear the sounds of combat as our fast-moving assault squads overtook the rear of the heretic breakthrough.

I kept the periscope focused outwards, wondering when, not if, the next wave of heretics would come in. I had a sick certainty that they would attack again in overwhelming numbers, and it was hoping for too much that they would not. In the past few months they had shown no shortage of men and weapons, so it seemed unlikely they were going to start now.

'Too quiet,' Anton said. Ivan made a tut-tutting sound.

'Are you going to just stand there spouting clichés from a prop-nov all night?' I asked.

Anton nodded. 'Yep. It passes the time.'

'You can pass the time checking our position,' I said. 'Make sure everybody has enough ammo and that their rebreathers are tight. The heretics are going to be on top of us soon and I want everybody ready.'

'Your wish is my command, milord,' Anton said. I glanced around to see if there were any officer's in position to over-hear him cheeking me, or worse yet, any of our men.

'You want me to head in the opposite direction and do the same thing?' Ivan asked. I nodded. It seemed like a good idea.

Anton scowled. 'Typical. We do all the work and he just lazes around playing with his periscope.'

'Get going, corporal,' I said. They got. I was left standing in the trench, checking no-man's-land and feeling my leg beginning to ache again. I looked down and noticed there was a sort of green ooze on my trouser leg, level with the wound. It might have come from a heretic, but I did not trust it. I checked the leg – the gauze was leaking the pus right enough. I did not like the look of that at all.

I adjusted my gear again and checked the shotgun, cleaning it with a cloth. I counted the number of cartridges I had left. Only a dozen or so. I suspected there might not be any more forthcoming. Supplies had not arrived on Loki for some time, and shotguns were not the most common weapons among the Guard. Only my exalted position as part of Macharius's bodyguard had kept me in supply for this long, and here on the front line even that was not going to help.

I kept my gaze focused on the war-ravaged land in front of me, at the lakes of mud, the rolls of barbed wire, the piles of bodies, the smashed remains of what had once been tanks. I watched clouds of mist swirl over the battlefield. Where was the enemy? What were they waiting for? Why was there no attack?

I heard a wounded man call out, then the footsteps of a medical orderly rushing to his aid. What was the point? He was most likely going to die anyway. I sneezed and then I coughed. I felt as if a clot of something was stuck within my lung. My breathing had the gurgling quality I associated with the heretics. Damn, it looked like I definitely had caught something. That was not good. The fighting rumbled on behind us; our boys were giving the heretics hell by the sound of it. At least I hoped they were. The thought of any other result was discouraging.

Ivan returned, followed by Anton a minute later. I coughed and wheezed. Ivan's head tilted as he examined me. 'You don't sound so good, Leo,' he said.

'I don't feel so good either.'

'You want a medic?'

'There's others have more need. I can hang on for a bit.'

The words were no sooner out of my mouth when I heard the drumming start up again from the front of our position. It looked like the second wave of the enemy had arrived and was getting ready to attack. I loaded more shells into my shotgun, snatched up a lasgun from a nearby corpse and set it near at hand. I was going to need it when the ammo was all gone.

'These boys just don't believe in giving up, do they?' said Anton.

'Neither do I,' I said.

More and more of our own troops filtered along the trench line. I felt my nerves subside a bit. The door of the trap was being shut. Grosslanders and Lion Guard alike were starting to fill these trenches, most of them currently facing inward, and cutting off the retreat of the heretics behind us. I propped myself up on the trench wall and fought off waves of dizziness. The skull moon beamed down from the darkening sky. It seemed to be smiling, which was not a reassuring sight.

The drums and the chanting had stopped. Despite my fears the next wave of heretics had not rolled in. It looked like we had successfully stopped the latest enemy offensive. Anton was whistling cheerfully. Ivan had produced a flask and was sneaking a sip from it as he oiled the joints of his prosthetic. I crunched on stimm tabs and painkillers and felt a little better. There was a satisfying sense that it was all over, that we had somehow snatched victory yet again. You could tell from the jaunty air of the soldiers. They were chatting in an almost relaxed manner, despite the occasional sounds of combat still coming from within the salient.

It was then that the shells started to howl overhead. I swear they sounded like no other shells I have ever encountered – they made a Banshee-whine as they fell, like the voices of souls in torment. Some of them left a trail of greenish phosphorescence in the air behind them, whizzing across the sky like dim star shells or ghostly meteors. I wondered what they were being aimed at. They were falling in front of us and behind us. It was perfectly possible the heretics were aiming at their own men, but they did not seem to care.

At the first sound of their falling, I threw myself into cover, with Anton and Ivan beside me and other Lion Guard all along the trench line. I heard a weird sound, like a muffled explosion deep underground. It sounded again and again as the barrage rained down and I realised after a while that it was the shells going off. They were not high explosive. That was for certain.

'What are they up to now?' Ivan asked.

'Some new trick no doubt,' I muttered.

Billows of greenish, glowing mist spurted down into the trench. I heard a man cough and retch, and I realised we had yet another case of faulty filters. The man did not fall or start to scream or hallucinate. He just stood there coughing.

'Gas,' Anton said.

'They're covering a new attack,' said Ivan. That was the logical inference certainly. I stuck the periscope up over the lip of the trench and studied no-man's-land. Shells were falling thick and fast out there, huge columns of greenish mist leaping upwards in great plumes and then sinking and spreading. Almost directly ahead of me I could see a shell, big as a man, sticking out of the mud. The detonator had failed to go off, obviously, but small trickles of gas and some greenish viscous liquid were leaking from it. I could see it had oddly curved fins on it, which doubtless were the cause of the wailing sound they made as they fell.

I couldn't see any signs of an enemy advance, though, and I could not hear any chanting or drumming. I turned my head and saw more of the shells still falling behind us. It seemed like the heretics were determined to cover the whole area in gas.

Whatever it was, it did not seem to be working very well. Even men with faulty rebreathers were doing nothing more than cough. I saw Mikals remove his mask and begin to fiddle with the filter pack, his face completely exposed. His eyes were watering and he was grimacing, but he did not seem to have been poisoned. I tossed him one of my spares and told him to put it on right away. He gave me a thumbs up, sat down, still hacking and spitting, and fitted it over his face. Shortly thereafter his coughs subsided.

I turned my attention back to the killing ground in front of us. Nothing seemed to be happening out there yet.

'Looks like we're not the only ones getting faulty gear,'

said Anton. 'They should put whoever made that gas in front of a firing squad. It's not done anything yet.'

I was tired and my leg throbbed, as did my head. 'How do you know that?' I snapped. 'You don't know what it was meant to do.'

'Kill us, I am guessing,' said Anton. 'And it hasn't.'

He sounded like a child in a huff. 'If it was meant to spread disease spores it might still be working. The symptoms might not have emerged yet, that's all.'

'You are a cheery frakker this evening, aren't you? We've won. We beat them fair and square and you're still looking for something to be depressed about. I tell you something, I'm glad they never promoted me to sergeant if this is what it does to you…'

'Calm down,' said Ivan. 'Leo might be right. We don't know what these heretics are up to. They've always got some new badness up their sleeves, or so it seems to me. Let's just wait and see.'

We waited like everybody else. The shelling had stopped and it did not start again. The gas obscured our vision for long minutes but then began to disperse or sink into the earth, adding a new chemical colour to the rainwater pools.

Behind us all the sounds of fighting had faded away completely. A red flare rose over the battlefield, announcing the all clear. It seemed as if we had won. Myself, I did not believe it. The fact that the enemy's gas shells had failed so completely seemed too much like the sort of good luck we had been missing recently. I found it hard to believe that our fortunes might be looking up, and, of course, I was right.

CHAPTER SIX

Not even the stimm could keep me completely awake. I slept standing up, with my eyes open, and I dreamed strange dreams. I saw the faces of people long dead. I remembered girls I had known on half a hundred worlds. I thought about my old man back on Belial, most likely gone to his grave by now.

My head throbbed. My leg ached but when I checked it again, there was no more pus, just a crust that had hardened over the wound. I cleaned it and changed the dressings. I put down my shotgun and picked up a lasgun and sighted along it out into no-man's-land, trying to get a feel for it in case I had to use it again soon.

I sighted along the barrel and checked the charge. I squeezed the trigger. It pulsed light. No real recoil I could detect, which was strange after using the shotgun for so long. The helmet I had been aiming at turned cherry red at the impact point. I could still hit with the thing then, which was good news, considering my trusty shotgun might soon be worthless to me except as an ornament. I let out a long breath. Sweat ran down my brow. My mouth felt dry and my nerves felt stretched, both symptoms of the fact that I had probably been using too much stimm.

'Nice to see you haven't lost your touch,' Anton said. 'You can still hit the side of a barn door at short range.'

'Do you even know what a barn is?' I asked.

'It's an ancient device,' he said. 'From the Dark Age of Technology. That's where the saying comes from. It was most likely a war machine of some sort. Maybe a tank.'

I decided to let him steep in his ignorance. With my sweating and dry palms and racing heart anything else seemed too much like hard work.

'Hello! What's that?' Anton said. Shadowy forms emerged from the murk, moving very slowly. I sighted at one. It was a heretic, but there was something odd about it. It shuffled along like a sick man and it did not seem to have any weapons in its hand. A shot rang out from beside me. Anton had put a bullet between the heretic's eyes. He did not seem to be having any trouble finding ammunition, but then he always made friends with the ratlings wherever we went.

'Got him,' he said with some satisfaction. A mass of lasgun pulses went off down the line. Nervous soldiers were firing in answer to Anton's sniping, or, at least, so I thought. Eventually they petered out, as the soldiers realised that another heretic attack was not inbound.

'Tough shot,' I said, unable to keep a note of bitter irony from my voice. 'Particularly with a sniper rifle. You must be really proud of yourself.'

'Every time a heretic dies, the Emperor smiles,' Anton said.

'You sure about that?'

'I'll find out if I ever get to Terra.'

'Because we must have kept a grin on his face every second since we got to Loki,' I said.

'You always have to quibble about everything, don't you?'

'And if you multiply that across every world the crusade is fighting on…'

'It's only a saying…'

'And if you add in all the heretics the Adeptus Astartes must be slaying yesterday, today and every day…'

'You're not going to let this rest, are you?'

I could see more figures moving out in no-man's-land. They were visible amidst the clouds of mist that floated there, not even making any effort to use them for cover.

'Looks like the heretics have decided to take another swipe at us,' Ivan said. He aimed his laspistol at the nearest figure. It kept coming.

'Must be on combat drugs,' Ivan said.

'You think?' The rest of the figures were shambling forward now. Anton pulled the trigger and another one fell and did not get up.

'That's how you do it,' he said with annoying satisfaction. More and more heretics were visible now, moving towards us with staggering slowness. I aimed and fired and burned one down. It kept moving even when its uniform caught fire from the concentrated las-pulses. It made no sound. Not a single shriek of agony escaped its lips.

Something was very wrong here. The rest of the heretics behaved the same way. I saw one of them cut in two by a burst from a heavy bolter. Its hips and legs kept wriggling like a snake after it has been decapitated. Its upper torso dragged itself along.

'What the...' I heard Anton mutter. 'That's one tough heretic.'

'There's something strange here,' I said.

'Sorcery,' Ivan said. 'Daemon magic.'

'Most likely.'

'Just when things were going so well,' Anton said. There was a childish whining tone in his voice. 'That's not fair.'

I understood what he meant. 'Fair or not,' I said, 'we're going to have to stop them.'

I noticed something else. Many of the heretics were wounded and those wounds were not fresh. They had been inflicted hours ago.

Even as that thought occurred to me, I heard a strange groaning sound from in front of the trench. The bodies out there were starting to stir. I pumped a las-bolt at one of them just as it was rising. Its flesh blackened but it kept moving. I remembered the bodies that had stirred earlier back on Skeleton Ridge; it looked like the same thing was happening again.

The heretics rose. Their eyes were red and they were weeping tears of blood. They did not bother lifting up their weapons. They began to slouch or crawl towards us. One of them was trailing his entrails along behind him; they were grey-furred from one of the local airborne fungal spores, but that did not seem to bother him any.

I took out a grenade and lobbed it among them. They did not dive for cover. They did not pay it the slightest attention. When the grenade exploded, the heretics closest to it were blown to pieces and they stopped moving. The others did not – even if their flesh had been torn open and the bones of their skulls were revealed they kept right on coming. One of them had a huge piece of shrapnel buried in an artery and blood pumped out, but it gave not the slightest sign of noticing.

More grenades rained down on them and tore them to pieces. In the meantime those in the distance kept moving closer. It was as if every heretic we had killed had come back to life to seek vengeance on us. I stopped firing and studied the oncoming horde, looking for some clue to what was happening, to see whether I could find anything that would help us with putting down the red-eyed shambling dead. I raised the magnoculars to my eyes and studied one of the walking corpses.

Its skin was pale and its eyes were red and tears of blood streamed down its cheeks. There was a glow within the eye-sockets like marsh gas seen in the distance, a hint of green under the bloodshot red. Even when a heretic vanished into a cloud of mist you could still sometimes see the dull light of his eyes.

Some of the heretics were chanting. Nuuuughaaal. Nergle. Narghul. Something like that. It was the only sound that escaped their lips. It was as if something had been branded into their brains so deeply they could remember it even after death. Every time I heard the word I felt a pulse of dread inside my skull, as if the mere sound of the name touched some deep-seated source of horror.

Off in the distance now the drums were beating. There were so many of them and they were so in time that I could feel the sound as a vibration in the ground – it seemed that the dead could, too. Their movements started to synchronise, to take on the rhythm of the drum, and they advanced with a raggedness of formation but a precision of step that was eerie.

We kept firing. They kept coming. The only ones who went down and stayed down were the ones Anton shot. What was he doing that everyone else wasn't? Using a sniper rifle, but I could not see why that should make any difference. It was powerful, but not any more so than some of the heavy weapons being used. Then it came to me. Anton always aimed for the head. He was that kind of show-off.

I tried it myself, sending a lasgun shot into one of the dead men's eyesockets. Its head exploded in a bubble of super-heated steam and the corpse fell and did not rise.

'Aim for the head,' I shouted. 'That's where they are vulnerable.'

A few of the men got the message and more of the heretics went down and did not get up again. Slowly word went along the line. The oncoming horde started to slow. I looked at Ivan. There was fear in his eyes and I did not blame him for it. Fighting against enemies who could come back from the dead was a thing to make the bravest men afraid.

'It's the gas,' Ivan said. 'This is what the gas was meant to do.'

He was guessing of course, but I saw the sense it what he was saying. We had seen bodies come back to life before, temporarily, back on Skeleton Ridge. Maybe the gas was some sort of catalyst. Or maybe it had triggered something. I was not a technical adept; I had no real clue. Maybe all of those bodies out there had been specially prepared in some way before the battle began. Maybe we had not been the only ones setting a trap, and as that thought ran through my mind, another raced up to join it.

I turned around and raced to the other side of the trench, facing towards our second line, and saw that my premonition was correct. Over there, in the salient where we had trapped them, the resurrected heretics were moving again. They were coming towards our lines from both sides now. We were being attacked on two fronts, just as we had done to them earlier. The trap had become a trap. The situation was desperate and becoming more so with every moment that passed.

Huge numbers of heretics still shambled in from no-man's-land while their brethren were going to hit us from behind. Even as that thought struck me I noticed that some of the corpses that had not yet been picked up by the burial detachments were also stirring. I dived down from the parapet and smashed the skull of one with the butt of my lasrifle. It fell back into the mud and lay in a puddle of brain and blood and greenish goo.

More of the corpses rose and began to move. If they had

possessed brains enough to use their weapons we would all have died in those few moments, attacked by surprise from within our own trenches. As it was, things were still touch and go. A squad of riflemen obeyed my shouts to come help me and we clubbed and shot and sawed off heads until the heretics moved no more.

Lieutenant Creasey had noticed what was going on and he was dividing the force by squad, sending half to cover the salient and keeping half facing no-man's-land to take out the incomers. I stood up, wheezing and feeling weak again. I was starting to reach the limits of my strength, where neither stimm nor painkillers would help.

'You all right, Lemuel?' he asked.

'Yes, sir,' I responded. I was not looking at him now. I was looking at the dead heretics. He followed my gaze to see what was holding my attention. Something was happening to the corpses we had put down. Their flesh sagged and what was within it, muscle, sinew or vein, was starting to liquefy into a greenish toxic sludge that seeped out and formed puddles around them. It was nasty-looking and something in my mind screamed at me not to touch it.

'At least when we kill them this time we don't have to worry about them coming back,' Creasey said. He was probably right, but something worried me – surely it could not be that simple. I headed over to the inner trench, the part facing out into the salient.

Thousands of walking corpses came towards us, moving slowly, as easy to hit as targets on a shooting range. We kept firing and they kept coming with a relentless, terror-inducing urge to get to grips with us. They seemed mindless and that just made them all the more frightening. Normal men would have fled in the face of the casualties we were inflicting on them. These heretics just kept shambling forward.

Our lads kept shooting, but not everyone can make a headshot every time, particularly not under the circumstances prevailing in those trenches, with mist, bad light, and the sure and certain knowledge that somewhere at your back was another undead monster just waiting to kill you.

I felt it myself, a crawling between the shoulder blades, that had me constantly wanting to turn my head. The assault continued, the dead men kept coming and we kept shooting. More and more bodies fell. As time wore on, the process of dissolution came over the heretics by itself. The bodies did not seem able to keep moving for more than a few minutes before they disintegrated into their component slime, leaving only corroding skin and soiled uniforms.

All the while this went on, the drums kept sounding in the distance like the heartbeat of an angry god.

We stopped them eventually. Or perhaps they stopped themselves, whatever was in them burning them out and reducing them to protoplasmic sludge. The assault lasted for over an hour and by the time it was finished we had taken scores more casualties and used up even more ammunition. My head was swimming.

I slumped down with my back to the parapet. I was starting to burn up and my leg was hurting once more. I thought about the sludge the walking dead had turned into and the pus that had leaked from my wound and my feverish mind found a connection between them.

It seemed to me then that I was just like those walking corpses and that sooner or later I was going to die and be returned to my component parts. I was going to rot on the ground unless I was burned. The sickly stuff oozing from my wound was just a foretaste of that. Even as this cheery notion trudged through my mind, another, even cheerier, followed it.

I started to wonder if I had been infected by the same disease spores as the heretics, if I had somehow picked up the contamination from them. I was sweating. My breathing rasped within my chest, and I was making the same sort of gurgling wheezing noises as they had. It seemed all too likely I was going the same way. Perhaps I had even been infected by the same heretical madness. That might explain why my thoughts had been so disloyal and my feelings so depressed.

Another star shell burst overhead as the drumming reached a crescendo. Heretics were chanting again, the same name over and over again, and it seemed to me that my own wheezing breath was pitched in time to it. Nuuuurghuuuul. Nuuuurghuuuul. Nuuuurghuuuul. Why were they not chanting Richter's name? His men had used to do that back when they fought for the Emperor. And what was it about the name that seemed to echo within my soul and awaken my darkest feeling of dread?

I slumped forward for a bit. Blackness overcame my mind. Strange dreams swirled around me. I saw a mountainous thing, huge and unclean, all green and brown. It clutched its stomach with enormous paws and laughed, and as it laughed thousands of tiny versions of itself poured out of every orifice, like snot, like diarrhoea. Its belly rippled in time to the drumbeat of its heart. All of the little daemons chanted that strange and disturbing name over and over again. I saw them dancing across the battlefield, climbing into the corpses through noses and mouths and ripped flesh and then reanimating the bodies with their evil essence.

Breathing was getting harder and harder and harder. I felt as if I were drowning and at the same time burning. The skull moon beamed down and its face was that of the great laughing daemon. The clouds were the colour of the daemon's skin and when it rained, millions and millions more of the daemon's tiny offspring dropped from the skies, riding within raindrops as they fell.

Lightning split the sky. It flashed like a thousand artillery pieces going off – Basilisks and Medusas and the like. The tiny daemonlings hit the ground and bounced and scurried all over the battlefield with sinister, supernatural energy.

They were all rushing towards me, swirling around me, clambering over me, their tiny talons buried into my flesh, particularly around my leg. They forced themselves into my mouth and nostrils, choking me. They tugged at my hair and clawed at my eyes. I writhed around trying to crush them, but there were too many and they kept on coming...

My eyes snapped open and I came awake to see Anton and Ivan looking down at me with worried faces. 'Wake up, Leo,' said Anton. His hand was drawn back as if he was about to administer a slap. 'It's just a bad dream.'

The mouthpiece of my rebreather was filled with drool and snot. I took a hasty breath, pulled it off and switched it for a new one. I did not feel any better, but at least I did not feel like I was drowning any longer.

'We've got company,' said Anton. I pulled myself upright, weak as a kitten, and looked out into no-man's-land. Another massive force of heretics was moving towards us. They were not shambling dead but fresh soldiers, newly decanted from their vats and ready to do battle.

I groaned, not so much from pain but because I had grasped Richter's strategy now. He could just keep throwing more and more troops at us, alternating waves of living and dead until they ground us down and swept us from the face of the planet.

I looked around for my shotgun, checked that it was loaded and prepared myself for death.

They came on and on, marching in time to their drums and their phlegmy chanting. Their green and brown banners so like and yet so unlike Macharius's own Lion banner fluttered above them. They held their weapons at the ready and fired as they marched, not stopping until they were cut down. Their shooting was not particularly accurate, but it did not have to be – there was a lot of it.

I propped myself against a sandbag and lined up the shotgun where I could reach it. I was not planning on using it until the heretics were very close. I raised my lasgun and fired it, simply snapping off shots. The heretics seemed better trained than the last bunch, who had been mere cannon fodder. These took advantage of cover, threw themselves down in shell-holes and gave covering fire to some of their comrades as they advanced.

They were advancing along a broad front. We no longer had choke points on Skeleton Ridge and Plague Hill and there was no chance of catching this bunch in a trap.

I felt a hand on my shoulder. I looked up and saw Lieutenant Creasey. A frown was chiselled on his craggy brow. 'Word has just come in from headquarters. We're to begin withdrawing.'

'Me and the lads are to be rearguard,' I said. I could see it coming and it suited my mood. I felt as if I was dying anyway and I wanted to take a few more of the heretics with me.

He shook his head. 'You're to lead the first squads out.'

I wondered how this decision had been achieved. I even considered arguing the toss for a second but then I nodded. There was no point asking who would be commanding the rearguard. I could tell from the expression on his face.

'Good luck, sir,' I said.

'Thank you, sergeant,' he replied. I saluted and lurched along the line, tapping the men from my unit on the shoulder. Anton and Ivan tagged along at my heels as if they feared I would fall and wanted to be in a position to catch me. Anton somehow even managed to get his head under my shoulder and was half carrying me along.

'Let go of me,' I said, my words only slurring a little. 'I can walk.'

He shrugged and stepped away. I took a couple of steps and fell on my face. Ivan reached out with his bionic limb to help me up. 'That went well,' I said, but I made no objections when they kept supporting me.

We began to make our way back through the trench system, while the sound of fighting reached a crescendo behind us.

CHAPTER SEVEN

The trenches showed signs of the fighting. There were piles of decomposing flesh and greenish slime scattered through them. There were many fallen men in the uniforms of the Grosslanders and the Lion Guard as well.

I raised my head and looked up. In the distance I could see the fortress line that blocked the way into Niflgard. The city was our drop-point and landing site. That circle of fortifications was the foundation against which our trench system rested, and it stretched out from there. The fortresses themselves seemed almost invincible, great ceramite cliffs bristling with weapons. I say *almost* only because in my long career as an Imperial infantryman I have learned that there is no such thing as an untakeable fortress. Any defensive position can fall if the attacker is clever enough or well enough armed or ruthless enough or has enough bodies to expend. Or preferably some combination of all of those factors.

I wondered if we were going to be driven back all the way to the chain of fortresses in that towering wall, to have to give up all the ground we had taken at such a cost in blood and lacerated flesh.

'No,' said Anton, and it was then I realised I had spoken aloud. 'That's not going to happen.'

'How are you going to stop it?' I asked. He gave me a look that was obviously intended to say *shut up there are people listening*, but I was too feverish to pay much attention to it.

'I won't. Macharius will.'

I nodded. It was touching to see the faith that Anton still had in Macharius. I told him so. He looked at me as if I were an idiot. That made me laugh. He was the idiot – everyone knew that.

He grimaced and said, 'Right you are,' and I realised I had spoken aloud once again. I knew I was babbling now, but I could not seem to stop myself. I began to tell Anton about all the little daemons I had seen, riding in raindrops, animating the corpses. His eyes narrowed. The scar on his forehead squirmed. 'Daemons,' I said. 'Just like that big one on Karsk. The Angel of Fire. Some bloody angel.'

His hand clamped over the filter hole of my rebreather and I realised he was trying to shut me up, by covering my mouth. It was just like the idiot to do something like that. He was going to shut me up all right – by stopping me breathing. I told him so but my words came out as a kind of muffled grunt.

The phlegm was rasping in my lungs again. I felt as if I was choking and I was beginning to cough.

'I think you're suffocating him,' Ivan said. His mechanical fingers removed Anton's from the rebreather's filter and I could breathe again, not quite normally, but I felt as if at least some oxygen was getting into my lungs.

'You think you can stop babbling nonsense now?' Anton asked.

'It's you that babbles nonsense,' was my witty rejoinder, but I was starting to get some sense of the fact that there were things that he did not want me to say, and, even if he was Anton, there might be good reasons for me not saying them. Some of them were even supposed to be secrets, after all, and Inquisitor Drake among others would not like me spreading them.

I felt very tired. The sounds of violence had stopped behind us – no more shooting, no more screaming, no more explosions. It was peaceful, quiet and really rather nice, and I said so.

'Damn,' said Anton.

'There's no need for language like that,' I informed him primly.

'The fighting has stopped, Leo,' he said. 'That means the heretics have overcome our rearguard. You know what that means...'

'They'll be coming after us next. Typical heretics. They can never leave us alone.'

'You two help me with the sergeant,' Anton said. 'We're going to double-time it from here.'

'Yes, corporal,' they said.

They grabbed me by the legs and began to carry me forward through the trenches in the most undignified fashion. Behind us I could hear the heretics chanting again. It sounded as if they were giving thanks to their daemon god.

There were sounds of violence behind us again, much closer.

'They've met some of our lads,' Anton said. Obviously we were not the only people pulling back to the second line. Equally obviously somebody had decided to make a stand. It would not do much good against the overwhelming number of the enemy, but it might give us time to escape.

Anton was looking at Ivan. I could tell what he was thinking. He wanted to go back and get involved in the scrap. I shook my head. 'Useless,' I croaked, my mouth suddenly very dry again. 'You won't help. You'll just get yourself killed alongside them. Macharius is going to need every man who can fight. Get back to the second line and find cover there.'

I was proud of myself for forcing out such a long and coherent sentence and I grinned. No one seemed pleased by my eloquence though. They scowled as if I had just told them to eat a great pile of corpse innards or take a swim in the latrine trench. They wanted to fight. Back there, comrades were fighting and dying and the sounds of that combat played on their nerves and damaged their image of themselves as fighting men.

I wanted to say *they are dying so you can get back to the second line and fight another day* but I resisted the urge. It would not have helped and, anyway, they could see the sense of it themselves, or if they couldn't, nothing I could say would change things.

They picked themselves up and moved on. Behind us the sounds of combat told me that it would not be long before the battle came to us. The heretics were advancing fast.

'It's no use,' Anton said. 'We're surrounded.'

I had blacked out for a moment and I had no idea what he was talking about. My leg felt as if someone had been pumping toxic sludge into it. A small daemon was beating time on my forehead with a sledgehammer.

'What?' I said. It was not the most intelligent thing I could have said, but you try asking smart questions when you're full of the latest plague on Loki. It took me a few moments to realise what he was talking about. The heretics had advanced unopposed on either side of us and it looked like they had made even better time. Of course, they were not slowed down by the walking wounded like we were.

'Heretics ahead of us and on both sides, sergeant,' said Ivan, managing a reasonable facsimile of respect for a superior on the battlefield. 'We're cut off from the second line.'

He sounded quite calm, but it was always difficult to pick out any emotions in his speech. Even before he lost half his face he was a cool one. I looked at Anton. He was sweating and a little pale. The scar was writhing on his forehead, which told me that he was at the very least tense.

'We've been in worse situations,' I said. I managed to sound calm, too, which was quite an achievement under the circumstances.

'Care to remind me of one?' said Anton. 'I'm having some difficulty remembering any at the moment.'

I took a deep breath. The truth was, at that moment, I was not too troubled at the prospect of imminent death. At least it would stop the daemon pounding on my head with its hammer. And I would not have to worry about losing my leg.

'You sure they are ahead of us?' I asked.

'If they're not, our own boys have changed uniforms and decided to shoot at us,' said Anton. I could tell he was in the mood to be sarcastic. He often chose the most unhelpful times for that.

More clouds of the phosphorescent gas were drifting by. There was a slight breeze and it swirled like the mingled ghosts of all the countless dead who had fallen on the trench-scarred valleys and plains of Loki. There were times when I felt certain that it formed daemonic faces who leered down at me. I wondered if any of the others were seeing them or whether it was just me.

I tried to visualise the map of the trench system I carried in my head. With a huge effort I dragged it up from the ill-ness-clogged sumps of my mind. 'Try the left passage, down along Dead Man's Trench,' I said. 'It's narrow and it looks blocked but there's a way through the wire if you are careful.'

'Field engineers have probably fixed that,' said Anton. He seemed only too pleased to be able to contradict me, the frakker.

'Oh, that's all right then,' I said. 'Let's just wait here and die because you're too lazy to go and check.'

'Illness doesn't make you any less mean-tempered,' said Anton.

'Head for Dead Man's Trench,' I said. 'That's an order.'

It was the last thing I managed to say for a while. The daemon faces in the mist were whispering to me and I could not quite make out what they were saying.

Dead Man's Trench had not been repaired. It was long and narrow and for some obscure reason it had been blocked off by barbed wire. The wire was rusty and there were scores of skeletons caught up in it. Some of them wore our uniforms, some of them wore the enemy's rags. None of them looked like they would ever march in a parade line again.

No one had used the trench for quite a while. It had a reputation for being haunted. Even grizzled veterans swore the spirits of the dead gathered there under the skull moon. Soldiers are prone to telling such horror stories, but there was something about the atmosphere of the place that made you believe the tales.

You could pick your way through the wire if you were careful. The dead men did not object; they just looked at you with big, empty eyes that asked why you were still alive and they weren't. Today I noticed that there were lots of little daemons scuttling among them, clutching their fat bellies and laughing at me, at mortality, at the futility of life in general. It was strange that no one else saw them. They were ugly little critters with a curious humour in their mocking eyes.

We moved carefully through the trench, following the

paths that Anton and Ivan knew were there, and we could hear the heretics chanting in the earthworks that ran parallel. We were in the worst sort of death-trap if any of them decided to walk through the gap between the lines. They could shoot down at us from the parapets and we were slowed by the barbed wire.

I could appreciate the danger in the lucid moments that I had when the daemons weren't frolicking around me. It did not make me any happier. Anton and Ivan were taking turns supporting me and I did my best to guide my feet and not get myself snagged on the barbed wire. Just look at what had happened the last time I had done that.

The sound of combat still drifted over us. Sometimes the poisoned mists deadened it so that it sounded leagues away. At other times, it appeared to be coming from the next trench or even right by our ears. Our lads were putting up more resistance than had seemed possible at the start of our retreat.

My limbs felt like lead now and my uniform was soaked in sweat. The crust on my leg wound had broken and greenish stuff was leaking through. I wasn't just worried about the fact that I had been infected with the corpse-walking disease, I became convinced of it. Those little daemons were pointing at me and laughing because they knew it, too.

I looked at Ivan through feverish eyes and said, 'If I die, put a bullet through my head. I don't want to come back like those deaders.'

'I'll do it,' said Anton, a little too cheerfully for my liking.

'On second thoughts, Ivan, you do it. Wait until I kill the idiot boy first,' I said.

'The sergeant is hallucinating,' Anton explained helpfully to the rest of our squad.

'Will do,' muttered Ivan, words garbled by his metal jaw. I did not know whether he was talking about doing it before or after I got Anton. Either would suit me.

We were reaching the end of Dead Man's Trench and there were definite sounds of fighting ahead. I clutched my shotgun tight.

'He's determined I won't have it,' Anton muttered. 'He promised me it, too, ages ago, on Emperor's Glory.'

'Now's not the time for that,' said Ivan, obviously as disgusted by Anton's thoughtlessness as I was.

'I doubt there's any ammunition left for it anyway,' Anton said.

'Enough for me to get you,' I said.

Ivan held up a warning hand. The servo-motors whined as he flexed his mechanical fingers. The thunder of las-pulse and grenades sounded ahead of us along with the gurgling chants of the heretics and the whooping war-cry of the Grosslanders.

I did some swift calculations in my head. We could not have reached the second line yet, not unless I had fallen unconscious without realising. A quick look around told me that we were still at the end of Dead Man's Trench. The skeletons still watched, but the daemons seemed to have gone into hiding. Only occasionally could I see one peeking its head over the parapet and winking at me. It seemed an almost friendly gesture, except that there was an all-consuming hunger in those bloodshot eyes and the teeth revealed by their grins were sharp as those of a needlefish.

'Sounds like some of our boys are still holding out,' I said.

'Sounds like someone is counter-attacking,' said Ivan. As he did so, he snapped off a shot because one of the heretics had noticed us and was announcing our arrival in his guttural language. At least that is what he seemed to be doing when Ivan's shot took him in the mouth and burned out his tongue. He made an odd gobbling sound before he fell.

His companions did not take his death well. They turned on us and launched themselves in our direction, a human wave, bayonets fixed, weapons at the ready. Our lads were deploying out of the trench. Some of them had thrown themselves flat and were shooting, while their companions behind fired over their heads. It was the sort of thing that made the difference between veterans and inexperienced vat-bred troops. It bought us enough time to fight our way out from under the empty gaze of those skulls.

A moment later Ivan was charging forward, bionic arm smashing bones, pistol spitting death. The others were with him, weapons blazing, lasgun butts cracking skulls and splintering bones. Anton stood beside me, sniper rifle tracking, and sent carefully timed shots into the melee. Every time his rifle roared an enemy fell.

I watched, barely able to stand upright, clutching my shotgun in what I hoped was a menacing fashion. Very few people will voluntarily charge a man with a loaded sawn-off if they notice it is there. You can't exactly blame them for that.

For a moment, it looked as if Ivan's mad rush was going to work and our boys were going to break through. It did not matter where at that exact moment. I think we all felt that smashing through the enemy line would represent some sort of victory. I certainly did. It was just one of those mad instants where you lose sight of the longer-term future and experience only the moment and its emotions.

Then I noticed the heretics pushing in from either side of the emplacement and realised that we were surrounded by an enormous number of the enemy. The only way out was back through Dead Man's Trench and that was a death-trap. The wire would slow us down and we would be cut to pieces.

The melee began to turn as sheer weight of numbers started to tell. At least the enemy were not able to use their superior firepower in the enclosed space of the emplacement. They were more likely to hit their own men than ours. Of course, that did not stop some of them. They shot and their comrades paid the price, at least until their officers managed to convince them to stop doing it by the simple expedient of shooting the idiots who were firing.

It was not going to be long now, I could tell. There were thousands of them and only dozens of us. They were climbing over their own dead to get to us, chanting that horrible name in their horrible tongue. Every word seemed to be being forced out through a throatful of phlegm. My personal pet daemons had returned, knee-high to a heretic, waltzing and spinning atop the dead, licking bodies with their metre-long tongues, seeming to feast on the death and decay going on around them. Their stomachs swelled and bloated then deflated as they hiccupped and belched and farted.

A cloud of gas billowed across the emplacement and, for

a moment, I lost sight of what was going on. I could just hear the screams and roars of men fighting and dying all around me. I could still see the ghastly, spectral faces leering out of the fog. I wondered how those men out there could tell who they were fighting and realised that they could not. Right now it was perfectly possible that heretic was wrestling heretic, and Imperial Guard stabbing at Imperial Guard. It happens more often than you would imagine amid the chaos of battle, particularly under conditions such as those that prevailed on the surface of Loki.

I held my shotgun tight, felt the air vibrate as Anton shot something, heard a man scream and prayed it was not Ivan or one of our boys. A moment later the breeze whipped the fog aside as if it were a tattered diaphanous curtain and I saw the bodies piled high and the wall of heretics charging towards Anton and myself.

'Kill the frakkers,' I said.

Anton pulled the trigger and a heretic officer fell. I pointed the shotgun and fired. There was a shell left. It tore a gigantic hole in the heretic line. I pumped and pulled the trigger again and heard nothing but a clicking sound.

'You picked a fine time to run out of ammo,' Anton said accusingly. The wall of shrieking, gasping heretics rushed towards us.

It was another of those moments when I knew I was dead. I have lost count of how many times they have happened but they never get any easier to take.

It's always the same. My mouth goes dry. My heart races. I

feel that sudden sharp surge of fear that is inevitable when your body realises that it is soon going to cease functioning. In this case, the realisation was compounded by the fact that my body was already struggling with wounds and disease. The visions of dancing daemons swirling through my mind didn't really help much either.

I braced myself for the stabbing of a dozen heretic bayonets. I wondered why they were not already charging at us, keen to take revenge for all the comrades we had sent to greet their daemon gods. I could hear the sounds of fighting, of lasguns pulsing, of chainswords splintering bone to white, bloodstained chips. I could hear someone shouting, 'For the Emperor and Macharius!'

The heretics were charging at us, but their eyes were wide with panic. They did not seem intent on stabbing us so much as keen to get past us. A few of them raced by into Dead Man's Trench, while others threw themselves up the parapet. Their officers screamed for them to stand their ground, or at least that is what I assume they were screaming, but none of the fleeing enemy seemed to be paying too much attention to those orders. They were too busy trying to put some distance between themselves and the green-tunicked Lion Guard coming at them from behind.

These troops were new and fresh and deadly looking. Their uniforms were clean and unpatched. Their weapons were being used with brisk efficiency. It was not them I noticed first though – it was the man leading them.

He looked like a great predator, tall and broad-shouldered, golden-haired and golden-skinned. His movements were poised and deadly. He swept through the melee, a human whirlwind of violence, cutting down a heretic with every stroke of the chainsword he wielded right-handed, while blasting away with the bolt pistol he was holding in his left. There was a poise and deadliness about the Lord High Commander Solar Macharius which he never lost even at the bitter end. He was a perfect killing machine, as completely deadly in his own way as a Space Marine of the Adeptus Astartes.

His coordination was uncanny, his movements eye-blurringly swift. Just when you thought you knew where he was going to step and whom he was going to strike, he surprised you.

The bullet aimed at him passed through the space where you thought he was going to be. His stroke turned out to be a feint, never hitting where it was expected, but burying itself in flesh nonetheless. A heretic raised his weapon to block the blade and took a bolt pistol shot through the eyes. Another ducked to avoid the killing shot and found himself impaled on the blade instead.

Macharius fought in close combat the way he led armies: swiftly, decisively, with feints within feints and a defence that consisted of the swiftest attacks. He was a living god of war, perfect in all he did when it came to battle. At least that was the impression he was still capable of giving when he chose to enter the fray in person. Seeing him, fighting beneath the fluttering Lion banner, you could not help but feel your heart rise and know that victory was certain.

He battled his way over to us, and I noticed that Ivan was

by his side, fighting away, a clumsy half-human automaton compared to Macharius, but deadly in his own way. Macharius's gaze swept over me and he nodded encouragingly and then he went by, killing as he went, leading the massive counter-attack he seemed to have organised out of nowhere.

I noticed then that Inquisitor Drake, his permanent shadow, was with him. Pale where Macharius was golden, thin where Macharius was athletic, Drake nonetheless had his own deadliness. His lean form possessed a surprising strength and an incredible resilience. If he was not quite so quick as Macharius, he seemed just as capable of countering all attacks, possibly because he was capable of reading the thoughts of the attackers.

A halo of light played around his head as he unleashed his psychic powers in terrifying bolts of energy. For a moment, his gaze rested on me as well and I shuddered, for his eyes seemed to be boring into my soul, and I felt he could see the contamination there, the doubts I had picked up, the daemons I was guilty of seeing.

Around Drake were the hand-picked storm troopers of his personal guard, their blank, mirrored visors reflecting the grimness of the battlefield on which they fought. Seen in the shimmering armourglass of those helmets, the landscape of Loki looked even more bleak and terrifying.

In a few more heartbeats, they, too, swept by and more and more troops of Macharius's personal guard followed, looking stern and efficient and implacable.

I wondered then if this was another of Macharius's famous feints, whether we had been the bait in yet another trap to draw in his enemies. At that point I was past caring. I slumped down against the earthwork wall of the trench, my back against a couple of stray sandbags, and I contemplated the staring eyes of the carpet of dead bodies Macharius had left in his wake. I wondered whether any of them would spring back into motion, and whether they would come to drag me down into death and I realised, at that moment, that I did not exactly care.

I did not feel at my best when I came to. I found I was looking up at the face of Macharius. He was standing talking with the Undertaker, saying something so quietly that even as close as I was I could not make it out. Over his shoulder the skull moon leered. The lesser moon raced across the sky, a small daemonling perched on it, giggling.

I tried to pull myself upright and I noticed that Anton and Ivan and a number of the other soldiers were there along with a few high-ranking officers. They were inspecting the dead and noting the fact that some of the corpses were dissolving into puddles of greenish slime, while others, in a new twist, seemed only to be lying there, their flesh green and corrupt-looking.

Around everything small pot-bellied daemons gambolled, sticking out their tongues, farting and belching, walking along behind the officers with taloned hands behind their backs, their movements and expressions mockeries of the men they were following.

I wondered where Drake was. Why wasn't the inquisitor sorting these little frakkers out? It was his job, after all.

Part of my mind, the tiny bit that still held a faint crumb of rationality, told me these were hallucinations, that I was feverish, that I was seeing things.

I pulled myself upright, gurgled for water, and noticed that one of the officers with Macharius did not look like the others. His skin had a greenish tinge. His eyes were mocking. There was something about him that reminded me of the daemons. He seemed to be just as inhuman as them and was fumbling in his belt, pulling his pistol free. I shouted a warning and pointed.

Macharius turned and so fast were his reflexes that he was already reacting to my pathetic attempt at a warning and the sight of the attacker he must have just caught from the corner of his eye. Even as the heretic drew a bead on him he was already in motion, pulling his bolt pistol free from its holster and swivelling at the hip to snap off a shot.

It was touch and go. The laspistol shot seared Macharius's shoulder, melting one of the lion's head epaulettes there. Macharius's return took the heretic in the stomach and punched an enormous hole in it, the way bolter shells do when they explode. I pulled myself upright, and snatched up a laspistol from a corpse. I shot the heretic again, but he still kept moving, animated by some spirit of destruction, or so it seemed.

Others opened fire until glittering las-beams made a net around him and through his body and still he kept on coming. A sniper rifle sounded. The officer's head exploded. I heard Anton give a grunt of satisfaction as the would-be assassin toppled and fell. Someone shouted for a medic and men swarmed towards Macharius.

That's another life you owe me, I thought with satisfaction, somehow managing to forget in that moment all of the times Macharius had saved mine.

CHAPTER EIGHT

I was very weak. I was seeing daemons. And I was not the only one. All around me were thousands of beds, each containing a wounded man, or a sick man, or a man who was both. Adepts of the medicae moved from bed to bed, administering potions, stabbing men with huge hypodermics, lopping off infected limbs with massive medical chainsaws.

Every time I heard the whine of the blade, the splinter of bone, I shouted for them to keep away. I did not want to lose my leg. I did not want a mechanical limb, even if there were any to be had, which there had not been for a long time.

The air smelt of purification incense and gangrene, of suppurating flesh and infected blood. The sound of coughs and screams echoed through the halls.

A medicae adept stood at the foot of my bed. He looked at me with something like horror in his eyes. For a moment,

I thought he was going to pronounce sentence on me, to announce that the leg was going to have to come off.

I was almost relieved when he shook his head and turned and looked over his shoulder and said that there was nothing to be done, that they did not have the serums, that even if they did, it was touch and go. He sounded ashamed and embarrassed.

I wanted to tell him not to feel too bad, that we were an army that was running out of ammunition and food and everything else. It was no surprise to me that we did not have the medicine – we had nothing else.

When I tried to speak all I could do was make an odd gurgling noise. It sounded as if someone had injected a gallon of phlegm into my lungs. Breathing was not easy. Speech was impossible. Two faces drifted into view: one belonged to Ivan and the other belonged to Anton. They both looked very sad. I closed my eyes and fell into strange dreams.

I woke to find a daemon sitting on my chest. That was the weight that was making it so difficult for me to breathe. It looked the same as all the others, fat and pot-bellied, with scales the green of snot and the brown of excrement. It had the same maliciously gleeful eyes and when it saw I was awake it began to use my stomach as a trampoline. Its bouncing caused the contents of my innards to explode from both ends of my body.

Anton rose from beside the bed and shouted for an orderly. The daemon by this point had me by the throat and was trying to strangle me. A huge gob of phlegm was stuck in my gullet. The pressure increased. Blackness swept over me.

When I opened my eyes again death was standing over me in the form of a beautiful woman. I knew her name. She was wearing a nurse's uniform very similar to the one she had worn back in the days when we had first met. She was not a nurse, I knew. She was an assassin.

She was holding a vial of some odd blue substance and attaching a needle to it. I smiled at her, pleased in an odd way that I was getting to see her again before I died. I looked around and saw that Anton was slumped in a chair beside the bed. Ivan was nowhere to be seen. She raised a finger to her lips in the universal sign for silence, then she drove the needle into the vein in my arm and pushed the plunger home. A moment later something burning filled my veins and I screamed before a wave of fire burned all consciousness from me. My last thought was to wonder why she was killing me.

'It's a miracle,' the medicae adept said. 'The Emperor himself must have intervened on behalf of this man. I would have sworn there was no way he could survive without a dose of Universal Purge and we have not seen any of that on Loki for a year. There is not even enough for the Lord High Commander if he should come down with the plague.'

It took me a moment to realise he was talking about me. I certainly did not feel like the beneficiary of a miracle; I felt as weak as a starving rat. My arms refused to obey me when I tried to pull myself upright and it was all I could do to keep my eyes open. Even listening tired me out.

I somehow managed to move my head first to the right

and then to the left and I realised that for the first time in days there were no daemons dancing around me. They were not sitting on my chest. They were not poking my eyes and my heart and my liver with their tiny claws. They were not wheezing into my ear and whispering unspeakable promises. They were simply not there. As that thought occurred to me, I thought I caught sight of one scuttling under a nearby bed. Maybe it was just a rodent.

'So you're saying he's going to live then?' said a relieved voice. It sounded as if it belonged to Anton who was going to burst into tears. I started to wonder if I was perhaps hallucinating again.

'It's not one hundred per cent certain,' said the adept. 'Last night I would have said this man was certain to die. This morning, he has at least a fighting chance. The fever will return. His wound may once again become inflamed, but at least he has a chance.'

'I told you,' Anton was saying. I was not sure who he was speaking to. 'I told you he was too mean to die.'

I let myself drift back off to sleep. In the distance I could hear the chainsaws going, and the screams of men in pain and the gurgles of men dying. It seemed I was not going to be joining them just yet.

'What are you trying to do, kill me?' I asked.

Anton looked a little confused. If I had not known better I would have said he was hurt. 'What do you mean?'

'Well, the first thing I see when I wake up is your ugly mug. That's enough to sap any man's will to live.'

'Ha-bloody-ha! And here I was thinking I would wheel you around the ward before I reported for duty today.'

'I thought you would be fighting at the front,' I said. Anton looked around over his shoulder, as if he were wondering who was listening.

'The front is stable for the moment,' he said. It did not sound like he believed it. To be perfectly honest, I did not believe it. 'We're guarding the space port.'

I looked at him. How stupid did he think I was? Actually, maybe he did not think I was stupid. Maybe he was letting me know the true state of affairs without spelling it out in a way that might be construed as a treasonous attempt to undermine morale by any commissar. It was possible that Anton was not entirely stupid.

If the space port was being guarded by the elite troops of Macharius's personal guard it was because there was a possibility that we would need to beat a hasty retreat through it. That was tantamount to admitting that we were beaten, that Richter was about to drive us off the surface of Loki, that for the first time in decades Macharius was drinking from the bitter cup of defeat. That was not something that anyone would want to speak aloud. It had a feeling of being the beginning of the end.

I looked at Anton again. For the first time in what seemed like weeks his face was not concealed by a rebreather mask. I could see that despite the juvenat the subtle signs of ageing were there. Around his eyes was a fine mesh of wrinkles. The flesh beneath his chin hung a little loose like the wattles of a hangman lizard. His hair looked washed out, not the straw blond of his long-gone youth on Belial. He was still springy and power-ful but the long years and countless battles had taken their toll. They sap vitality and the will to live, in other ways.

He looked me right in the eye and said, 'I am glad to see you're still alive.'

'Me too,' I said.

He looked away, obviously uncomfortable. 'I'd best be away. I have guard duty tonight.'

It seemed an odd thing to hear, so mundane after what we had been through, with the endless battles in the trenches, the dead rising, the strange hallucinogenic gases drifting over the battlefields. The phrase *guard duty* conjured up visions of easier nights on easier worlds when things had been going well. At least for me. He tossed me a mocking salute and shambled off into the night.

I tried to pull myself upright, but I was still weak, so I just lay there and thought about the things I had seen. Had the Emperor really intervened to save me? Had I really seen Anna? Or was she just another product of the fever that had fired up so many strange visions out of my diseased brain? I thought about the daemons I had seen and the odd dreams I had experienced. They had been wild hallucinations, surely, and yet at the same time they had been both consistent and convincing, as if somehow I had been peering into another world, one that existed just below the skin of our reality, at least on this cursed planet.

Such thoughts are easy to come by in a hospital bed, sur-rounded by shrieking wounded.

* * *

The hospital was packed with dying men. At first I wondered about the lack of care that had been given to me since, after all, I was one of Macharius's chosen guards, but it came to me after a few days that I was getting the best care that was available. Medicae adepts checked me and shook their heads wonderingly and I realised that I had become something of a celebrity in the wards since my astonishing recovery. It turned out I was the only soldier to have done so from the fever I had suffered.

They checked the wound on my leg, which was no longer inflamed, although it was crusted over. They laid cool hands on my forehead and intoned invocations to the Emperor. They wafted incense over me that brought strange dreams and helped control the fevers that I still suffered.

The road to recovery was a winding, circuitous march through fever country. There were days when I was once again sick, when it felt as if daemons were pressing down on my chest and when Ivan or Anton would spend nights beside my bed. There were times, too, when I would open my eyes and see a sister of the Orders Hospitaller, and sometimes she bore a strange resemblance to Anna.

I dreamed of her often, of how I had first seen her on Karsk when we had escaped from the worshippers of the Angel of Fire together, of how I had seen her again on Emperor's Glory, where Ulrik Grimfang, an Adeptus Astartes of the Space Wolves, had warned me against her. I dreamed of the bodies of the men she had killed and I had found, and I dreamed of how she had saved my life.

I knew then with the odd clarity that such dreams bring

that our lives were linked somehow. It might have been part of some grand design on her part or just the secret unwinding of our interlinked destinies, but our lives had touched in the oddest and most intimate of ways down through the decades. I liked to think there was some bond of affection there but I was never sure, not even of my own feelings. There had been many women in my life, as there always are for soldiers moving from world to world, but hers was the only consistent female presence I could remember.

I was certain of another thing too. That if she was here on Loki someone important was going to die. It was her nature and the nature of her service to the Emperor, and who am I to criticise? How many have I killed in the same cause?

I remembered too many of the campaigns I had fought in the name of the Emperor and Macharius. I experienced them once more in bloody, sweat-inducing dreams that had me waking in terror to stare at the murals on the ceiling depicting angel-winged Space Marines confronting all manner of xenos horrors.

I recalled the jungles of Jurasik and the orks we had fought there. I remembered the great armoured advance on Karsk IV and the burning winged statue of an evil angel perched atop the mountain-sized city of Irongrad. I marched again across the ice wastes of Caledax and watched men's limbs turn black from the frostbite. I climbed over the peaks of Aquitaine and saw monstrous sentient spiders feast on the flesh of the soldiers they had webbed. I saw living weapons, war machines of flesh, remnants of some ancient invasion of xenos that had lurked like termites in the ruins of the human civilisation they had destroyed. I saw the redemption of worlds ruled by ancient evil cults and I saw the armies of the crusade advance, invincible, until we reached the Halo Worlds.

There everything had gone wrong. There the supply lines had grown too long and the armies too war-weary and the distances too great for reliable navigation even by the great starships of the Imperium. There all manner of horrors had emerged. There we had found ourselves bogged down in endless wars of attrition and even Macharius had seemed to lose his total certainty of victory and begun to whisper blackly of plots and betrayals.

I saw another vision now, of Loki as I had first seen it from space, a ball of green and blue and grey with toxic clouds drifting across seas that had died tens of thousands of years ago by being flooded with poisonous industrial waste. A world of manufactorum-cities whose giant chimneys poured choking clouds into the sky as their inhabitants worked day and night. A place whose landscapes had been blasted by pollution and blighted by the deserts of ash the cities had created.

I saw it as it was now, its greatest city ringed by trenches that stretched out to other man-made mountain ranges where heretics lived and bred and performed obscene rites beneath the glow of ever-burning lanterns. I saw networks of trenches that stretched as far as the eye could see, and plains of mud on which lay the corpses of millions of men, unburied, forgotten, degenerating to piles of bones and walls of skulls. I saw the clouds of gas drifting from sinkhole to sinkhole and I saw what lay beneath the ground, all of the ancient and evil and horrifying things that burrowed blindly, waiting for the chance to emerge and devour.

And just as these images flooded my mind, I felt something else, a vast dark presence. I looked up and could no longer see the murals above me. Instead I was looking into the grinning frog-like face of the gigantic daemon I had first seen on the front lines. It was smiling down at me, watching me with eyes full of that ancient malicious humour, looking at me the way I might look at a whining mosquito, a thing it was going to reach out and swat when the mood took it, and that mood might well be taking it now.

It reached down for me with one massive claw, and grabbed me in a vice-like grip and began to shake me. It was like being in the grip of an earthquake. My body was being thrown from side to side, and it seemed to me that if this kept up the life would be shaken from me.

The vast and horrible presence loomed over me and I wanted to shout defiance, but I could not. Instead I felt the vast head lower, the huge jaw distend, as if it were going to swallow me in a single gulp. A long tongue glistening with green mucus extended from its mouth and descended towards me, and I knew that if it touched me I was going to die in the grip of some vile disease.

The head descended, the tongue reached out, the world shook as the thing approached. I tried to scream and I snapped open my eyes.

CHAPTER NINE

I was looking up at an odd frog-like face but it belonged to the man from the next bed. He had been moved there a couple of days ago after the previous occupant's corpse had been dragged away. He seemed friendly enough, but I was still reeling from the sight in my dream and shrank away from him.

He smiled. His teeth were broad and yellow but normal-looking. There was humour but no overt wickedness in his eyes. 'Easy, brother,' he said. 'It was just a nightmare.'

He pointed to himself and said, 'The name's Zachariah.'

I nodded and took in my surroundings. I was in the hospital. The winged Space Marines were still fighting their fanciful battle against a bunch of particularly daemonic-looking orks. Men were still moaning and screaming and dying. I managed to sit upright. It seemed I had at least enough strength to do that now, although I still felt as weak as if my muscles were made out of water.

'It was just a nightmare,' I agreed.

'We all have them,' he said. His voice was light and pleasant with the faint burr that marked him as a Grosslander. The stained white smock he wore gave no clue as to rank or origin.

'Not like I do,' I said. I was feeling sorry for myself and the words just burst out.

'You see ghosts and daemons,' he said. 'You were muttering about them in your sleep.'

'Yes,' I said.

'Do you see them, the disease bringer, and all his children? Little things, they ride in clouds and corpses and spread plague across the world.'

I looked at him sidelong and suspicious. 'Was I talking about them in my sleep?' I wondered what else I might have been talking about. I know some secrets that could get men killed. Me included.

He shook his head. 'I have seen it too. I had trench fever and I saw it in my dreams. I kept my mouth shut because a few others had mentioned it and been shot by the commissar. There's something going on here that normal folks are not meant to know.'

I smiled at that. He was a hick from a hayseed world and he had put his finger right on the nub of the problem. There were things going on here that we were not meant to know about. The whole Imperium is built atop layers of secrets that men have been buried to keep and that no one except the anointed few are allowed to talk about, and then only with each other. I have caught fragments of those conversations in my time, between inquisitors and Lord High Commanders, Assassins and Adeptus Astartes. They are not things I like knowing, but I cannot unlearn them.

'You didn't get shot,' I said and he grinned.

'They didn't think I needed to be, not when the trench fever took me. I was dumped here. This is the place they send men to die.'

'It's a hospital,' I said.

'That's what I said.' He grinned. It was a likeable grin and it made me suspicious. I had never seen him before and here he was talking to me as if I were his long-lost brother.

'Anyway, I am not the only one who had the dreams,' he said. 'Nor are you. I've talked to dozens of men from dozens of battlefronts that have had them. They are omens, that's what they are.'

There was an odd conviction in the way he said the word *omens*. He believed utterly in what he was saying and there was no trace of madness in those cold blue eyes of his. 'They are omens. Something is happening here. Something terrible.'

I could not actually say I disagreed with him so I kept my mouth shut and waited for him to go. If he was going to spout heresy, I would need to report him to Drake or one of his minions. It was even possible he was one of the minions, put here to test the faith of those who were waiting to die. Don't ask me why I thought that. I was sick and I was weary and I have seen and heard stranger things.

'Our dreams are not the only omens,' he said. Once again there was an ominous conviction in that light flat voice. I don't know what it was that was so convincing, but there was something there, a certainty that made you believe, if not in what he said, then in the fact that the man uttering the words took them as the total truth. It spoke of a sort of faith, terrible in its simplicity. It was the sort of faith that many of us had once had in the success of the crusade. In this man, it seemed to have curdled into its opposite.

'What do you mean?' I asked. I was encouraging him because I was honestly curious.

'You hear stories,' he said. He looked over his shoulder to make sure no one was listening, as if, even here surrounded by the dying, perhaps dying himself, he suspected that there were spies. He was quite possibly correct. 'The crusade is crumbling. We came too far, too fast. We came to places where man was not meant to go. We are seeing things that man was not meant to see. We are too far from Holy Terra and the Emperor's Light.'

Again there was that conviction there, the certainty of the fanatic who had no doubts. He might have been a commissar addressing a regiment before an important battle or a martyr preparing to meet his doom in fires stoked by heretics. There was no possibility that he was wrong.

'I had been stationed a few places before we got to Loki – we stopped at all the transhipment points on our way out and I talked to a lot of folks. I like talking and I like listening and I heard some tales that would make your hair stand on end.'

'Like what?'

'Like ghost ships emerging from the warp and destroying our supply craft, enslaving their crews, taking the supplies meant for us and carrying them off to the daemon worlds where the heretics dwell.'

'You always hear such stories,' I said. 'I have been hearing them since I first set foot on a starship over thirty years ago.'

'I know,' said Zachariah. 'But tell me, is this the first time you have believed those stories to be true?'

Again there was no doubt in his voice, only certainty. I *must* believe what he did. The odd thing was that he was right. Oh, in the past, in moments of doubt and fear when travelling between the stars, I had thought of those old stories. Everybody does. But the Halo Worlds were the first place that I really actually thought it was true when I was not aboard ship.

He nodded, as if seeing something written on my face that confirmed what he was thinking. He kept going like a fighter pressing his advantage in a brawl. 'The generals all think of rebellion, if they are not already openly rebelling like Richter. What else could that be but the taint of this evil place finding its way into their minds? Why else would they plot and scheme against the greatest hero mankind has known since the time of the Emperor?'

He was tugging at the first finger of his right hand now, counting off points as he made them.

'Armies, entire Imperial armies, have fallen into heresy. Their generals set themselves up as gods among men, as satraps for old, evil powers. They are crushed and crushed again and still more emerge.' That was another finger. 'You have seen that here on Loki.

'Our armies are falling apart. Our men do not have ammunition. Our vehicles do not have fuel. Among the far stars, the glorified clerks of the Administratum plot against heroes.' He had reached the penultimate digit.

'We face more and more monsters, more and more strangeness, and that strangeness is not to be found just among our enemies but among ourselves.' And he was done.

He sat down on his bed, appearing to have exhausted himself with his tirade. I noticed he was pale and that his eyes were faintly bloodshot. There were spots on his skin that reminded me of something and it came to me that he was very sick.

'These are times of ill-omen,' he said, his voice starting to fade, his certainty still there but his body unable to respond to his fanatic's will. 'All things will end badly.'

He nodded and slumped down, a wind-up toy that had run out of power. He pulled the sheet over himself and lay still. I turned my head a little so that I could see him, closed my eyes for a moment and I was asleep.

The next morning, when I woke, two Sisters Hospitaller were there. Zachariah's body was covered with a white sheet. I felt much better and I sat up in bed. I placed a hand on the woman's shoulder and she turned to face me, flinching as if she had felt the hand of a corpse on her body.

'What happened?' I asked. 'What happened to Zachariah?'

'He's dead,' she said. 'I thought that much would be obvious.'

'I was just speaking to him last night,' I said.

She looked at me. Her face was pale. Her eyes glittered. There were two spots of colour far up on her cheeks. 'That's impossible,' she said. 'He died two days ago. We've only just picked up the notification to remove the body.'

I stared at her, unsure if she was joking. It swiftly became obvious that she was not and I said no more.

I felt strong enough to take a walk around the wards. There was no one present to object. I was still limping and a little weak and I thought sometimes, out of the corners of my eyes, that I could see those small scuttling daemons.

There were many wounded men there, wrapped in bloody smocks. Some of them were legless. Some of them inspected the stumps where hands had once been with listless, uncomprehending eyes. Some were blind, with bandages wrapped around their eyes. Many lay on their beds, their breath wheezing from their chests, phlegm gurgling in their lungs. Their skins were pale. Their eyes were white. I was reminded constantly of the heretic armies as they advanced. If only there had been the sound of gunfire, many of the noises would have been similar.

As I walked I thought about what the sister had said, about the things I kept seeing out of the corner of my eye. It seemed obvious to me that I was not one hundred per cent recovered, that the fever still gripped me, at least some of the time.

I found myself in a great hallway with a soot-smudged stained-glass window. I looked out of it. Below me I could see dark clouds of industrial gas. From the gas lifted immense chimney towers, tall as starscrapers. In the sides of some I could see glowing windows. Roads ran round them, carrying groundcars ever higher. Aircars flew between them, bearing who knew what loads.

Below me the clouds parted and I caught sight of a vertiginous view, of massive pistons rising and falling on the roof of a structure bigger than a starship. Of more effluent billowing forth. Of a huge wheel, stuck in the side of a building, turning around and around for who knew what unguessable purpose. I stood there watching and thinking and trying to sort out my thoughts and feelings.

Had I imagined a whole conversation with Zachariah? Was it merely a fever dream conjured up from scraps of overheard conversation by my own imagination or had I really spoken to a dead man? Whether Zachariah had been dream or reality, he had given voice to many points that had troubled me about the state of the Imperium and the state of the crusade.

I batted this back and forth for the rest of a long afternoon and when I returned to my dormitory bed, Ivan was waiting.

'How goes it, Sergeant Lemuel?' Ivan asked with mocking politeness. I slumped down on my bed. I could not help but notice that his prosthetic arm was dented and that the motors whined even more than usual when he used it. He regarded me steadily through one normal eye and one bionic. It was a trick he used to great effect when playing cards.

'Could be better, could be worse,' I replied. 'Anton could be here.'

'Don't let him hear you say that. And in all seriousness, he spent more time by your side than I did when you were unconscious.'

'How long was I out?' I was curious now.

'Almost a week. For a long time there it was touch and go. The medicae thought you were lost a dozen times. That's what they told me.'

'Anton told me that you're guarding the space port.'

'He told you more than he should have then.'

'You know what he's like. Can't keep a secret.'

'Don't tell anybody else you know. The Lord High Commander is in a bad enough mood anyway.' Macharius was not normally a man to lose his temper. He was brilliant at concealing his emotions no matter how badly things went. Or he had been until recently.

'Any particular reason?'

'Any number of them. Take your pick.'

'What would I be choosing from?' I could see what he was up to now. He was going to make me work for any information I got out of him.

'The crusade is bogged down on half a dozen war-fronts.'

'That's happened before. It will recover momentum eventually.'

'There's some sort of conclave of generals scheming to replace him.'

'There's always some underling seeking glory.'

'These ones have the backing of the Administratum, or so

Macharius thinks.' That was not good news. Macharius had a number of powerful enemies among the bureaucrats who ran the Imperium. It was almost inevitable. For most of the past couple of decades he had been the most powerful man in known space. That caused a lot of friction. 'With everything that has gone wrong they might just be in a position to pull him down. Macharius has a ship on standby to take him to Acheron. That's where the generals are supposed to be meeting with their supporters.'

'I would have thought he would have been gone by now. It's not like him to let any challenge go unopposed.'

Ivan let out a long sigh. 'There's still the challenge here on Loki. He's still obsessed with beating Richter. He won't give up this world.'

'He might not have any choice, from what I've seen.'

'Don't let him hear you say that,' said Ivan. 'He has not been kind to those who preach defeatism. That's what he calls it.'

'He's never had any problem with the truth before.'

'Well, he does now. You can't say you haven't been warned.' Ivan placed a careful emphasis on his words. He wanted me to understand that he was serious. I felt suddenly very tired and I think that weariness showed on my face.

'Things have changed, Leo,' Ivan said. 'He's not the man he once was. You'll see when you recover.'

'I'm not sure I want to recover if things are the way you say.' I sounded petulant and childish and I knew it. I could not help myself though. I was sick and physically weak and I was beginning to be very frightened.

* * *

I had another visitor soon after, although she did not come in the guise of such. I was lying on the bed, listening to the coughing and the screams of pain when a Sister Hospitaller was suddenly standing over me. Her features were very familiar. It was Anna.

'I thought I saw you before,' I said. She smiled at me enigmatically.

'I don't know what you mean,' she said.

'I saw you giving me the serum.'

'No such serum is available on this world,' she said. Her face was utterly bland. I knew she was capable of lying with a completely straight face – she would not blink and her pulse rate would not change. Her entire body had been rebuilt to make her capable of such deceptions and far more.

'I know it was you,' I said. I was certain it had been, too, although I could not say why. My senses had been highly unreliable of late.

'Whether it was or it wasn't,' she said, 'I am glad you are all right.'

And that was as close to an admission as I was ever going to get from her. 'Why are you here?' I asked. I wondered if she had been sent to kill Richter. After all, one assassin can succeed where an entire army might not. And the rogue general must be a prime target.

'You should know better than to ask me that by now,' she said. She was mopping my brow. It made her look more like a Hospitaller, I suppose, but it made me shiver. It was something between us that she never seemed to lie to me directly, or maybe that was just the impression she wanted to give. I have never been sure.

'You're supposed to say you came to see me,' I said.

'I did. Today at least.'

'I'm glad you did.'

'Your friends have visited you often.'

'You could have done so too. They would not be able to recognise you if you did not want them to.'

'I have been busy, Leo.'

'People have been dying unexpectedly, have they?'

'I do more than kill people,' she said. It was almost as if I had criticised her. I have no idea why she should feel offended; she had no more conscience about murder than a cat has about killing mice. 'I gather intelligence. I report it.'

'So you have been gathering intelligence then?' I said.

'You are an exasperating man.'

'Apparently so.'

'Yes. I have been gathering intelligence.'

'And you cannot tell me about it.'

'What would you have me tell you?' She was looking at me directly now and I felt as if, just for a moment, I could ask her anything and I might get an honest reply. There was an unguarded look in her eyes, or so it seemed to me. I looked at her for a long time and the moment passed, and she seemed to be wary of everything and everybody once more.

'Are you comfortable here?' she asked.

I looked around ironically at the wounded and the dying. 'It's better than where I was before,' I said. She tilted her head to one side and studied me very intently. She seemed to hear something more in my words than I had intended to put there.

'You are frightened,' she said. 'That is not like you. Why?'

I told her about the dreams. I told her about Zachariah. I told her about the things I had heard. I told her I was starting to doubt my own sanity. While I told her this she held my hand; when someone walked by she appeared to be taking my pulse.

As I spoke, she nodded, as if I were confirming things that she already knew. It was a way she had. Maybe she did already know. Maybe it was just her method of encouraging me to speak. It certainly worked – I babbled as if I had somehow been injected with truth serum. Only later did I wonder if perhaps I had been.

Once I had finished speaking, she said, 'Speak of these things to no one. Your companion, Zachariah, if companion he was, was correct about that. There are matters here that could get you killed if the wrong person learns of them.'

'Drake,' I said. The inquisitor could read my thoughts if he chose to.

'He has his mind on other things just now.'

'Why do I need to worry about these dreams?' I wanted to know and she seemed to be in a position to tell me, even if it was foolish to ask.

'We have come too far,' she said. 'Into a place where Chaos seeps through. It is very strong here. What Zachariah told you is essentially correct.'

'You are saying we should abandon the crusade, go back?'

'Perhaps it might have been better never to have come

here, but it's too late for that now.' It was easy to be wise after the fact, I thought, and she could see it written on my face.

'We didn't know,' she said. 'We couldn't until we got here and the reports started coming in. Now we do. We need to pull back. If we do not our armies will become corrupt and our way will be lost. It is already starting to happen. The signs are there for those who can see them. Richter had already raised the standard of rebellion and others will follow him down into the darkness.'

'You think the crusade will fail then, and Macharius with it.'

'It does not matter what I think, Leo,' she said. 'What matters is what the High Lords of Terra think. They are the ones who give the orders and will ultimately decide success or failure.'

'History and the Emperor will decide,' I said.

'Faith, Leo? From you? At this late date? I always thought you were a cynical man. It is one of your more attractive qualities in this age, in these worlds.'

I remembered what Ivan had said. 'You think he will be removed?'

It was not necessary to spell out who I meant. 'There are already plots against him,' she said. 'They have failed in the past. Sooner or later one is bound to succeed if there are enough of them.'

I remembered the assassin back on the battlefield and shouting a warning. I told her of him. 'You think he was not a heretic?'

'He might have been in their pay or suborned by them, or he might have been working for someone else,' she said.

'He was very hard to kill,' I said.

She considered this for a moment, appearing to turn it over and over in her mind. If she did know something she decided not to tell me. She rose and said, 'Be wary, Leo. You and your friends are caught in the middle of a great web. The fact that it was not meant to trap you will mean nothing when the spiders come to feed.'

She departed. She had not walked more than a dozen steps when she seemed to vanish amid the people. It was something about her way of walking, her body language. She just blended into the crowd as if she had become invisible.

I lay there feeling the faint lingering warmth of her grip on my hand, wondering if this too was a hallucination.

CHAPTER TEN

A warning klaxon woke me. I sat up too quickly and felt dizzy. I glanced around, wondering what was going on, what the panic was. The constant repetitive blaring sound was a sector callout alarm, the sort that you normally only hear in a hive city when there has been a catastrophic failure of life support systems. If that had happened I was in the worst possible place, garbed only in a medical smock, without weapons or equipment.

Another darker thought occurred to me. The heretics might have broken through; they might have invaded the last bastion of the Imperium on this planet. Our defeat might already have been accomplished.

I looked around to see what I could see. Sisters Hospitaller were moving through the chaos. Their faces showed no emotion but they had been trained to deal with the carnage of the battlefield and not to panic. I noticed a medicae adept moving between the beds. His stride was swift, his manner urgent. I saw fear in his eyes. I pulled myself out of bed and stood in front of him.

'What is going on?' I asked. He made to brush by me.

'I don't have time for this,' he said. I put a restraining hand on his shoulder and he shrugged it off. I applied one of the holds I had been taught in basic training. I have got a lot of use out of it over the years. Even in my weakened state I was capable of holding him in place. I could tell from his expression he was finding the experience painful, even as he struggled to break my grip.

'If you keep this up you will either break your arm or dislocate your shoulder. In fact, I might do that for you.'

He listened to my words for a moment. They seemed to take a few heartbeats to travel from his ear to his brain. He stopped struggling.

'Thank you,' I said. 'Now tell me as quickly and clearly as you can what is going on.'

'The alarm has sounded.'

'I know. I can hear it. Tell me why.'

'I don't know.'

'Guess.'

'There are rumours of a heretic army in the streets of Niflgard. Of a new plague breaking out. I've been hearing them all day.'

No point in asking why no one had told me. No one tells the patients anything in a place like this. I let him go and he scuttled off, looking backwards over his shoulder, angry and afraid. He was not used to being manhandled. He would not have lasted a minute in the streets of the hive where I grew up.

I walked over to the wall, where the emergency rebreathers should have been kept. The cases were open and they were all gone. I guess they had been stripped away and sent to the front a long time ago. Either that or they had been stolen and sold on the black market.

You can fashion an emergency rebreather against certain types of gas from a sheet soaked in your own urine. Don't ask me why it works, but it does. I lifted a sheet from my bed and tore it into strips just in case. If I had possessed an alembic I would have prepared some urine as well, but I did not. I stood there for a moment, wondering what was going on. I needed to find out more. If the heretics really had broken through, Macharius would either be counter-attacking or regrouping at the space port for evacuation.

I needed clothing, gear, weapons and equipment. A hospital was not a place to find any of those. I might be able to scavenge scalpels or a surgical chainsaw but that would be about the limit. Still, it was better than nothing.

I was feeling stronger now. Adrenaline has that effect. One minute you might feel weak as a newborn kitten, but if your life is in danger, you can find the strength to wrestle an ork if you need to. I strode past a bed on which a figure lay covered in a grubby white sheet. Poor frakker, I thought. A cold white hand grabbed my wrist.

My response was reflexive. I chopped down with my free hand, breaking the grip, then stepped back. As I did so the figure under the sheet sat up. If it was a joke, I thought, it was being executed with spectacularly bad timing and poor taste.

It was not a joke.

The sheet fell away to reveal a dead man. His skin was grey, not with ill-health but with the chill of death. It was the colour of processed meat ground from bone and gristle in a distant food manufactorum. His eyes were an odd bloody red with that hint of corpse-light green burning in their depths. A slight trickle of greenish pus ran from his nostrils and the corners of his mouth when the body moved.

The corpse wheezed and gurgled not because it was breathing, but because its lungs were being compressed within it by its movements, and then it seemed the phlegm was being forced out.

What I noticed most was the smell. It was as if with every false breath it were emitting the stench of all the putrefaction within its body, all of the pus and phlegm and rotting innards. It was a stench to turn the stomach and sour the heart and I had no rebreather. Just the stink of it paralysed me for the moment it took to get from its bed and grab at me. They say that fingernails still grow after death and this corpse had long ones that bit into my flesh. I grunted with pain and responded as I had been trained to too long ago on Belial.

I lashed out with my foot, catching it between the legs. Its movements were slow and clumsy and it made no attempt to dodge. My kick had no effect. The corpse felt no pain. I had turned its testicles to jelly and got no reaction whatsoever. It was dragging me closer to its foul-smelling mouth. Its teeth were bared as if it intended to bite me. Its face had a look of total, all-consuming hunger.

I brought my arms up inside its grip, my forearms against the internal arc of its elbows. It was strong, but my motion broke its grip and jerked its arms apart at the cost of leaving some of my own skin beneath its fingernails. I pulled at the sheet it had left on the bed, tossed it over the dead man's head and ran. It did not make any sense to stand and trade blows with something that felt no pain, particularly not when other corpses were rising from beneath their sheets and making a grab for the living.

There were at least a score of them, but they induced a panic disproportionate to their number amid all those beds crammed with the sick, the dying and those trapped in fever dreams. To many it must have just seemed like another aspect of their nightmare, until they died with the teeth of a walking corpse buried in their jugular.

I needed to find a weapon, any weapon. I saw a medicae adept lying on his back with a dead man on his chest that gnawed at his throat and pulled out his entrails with bloody fingers. On a trolley near at hand were medical implements, including a surgical chainsaw.

Grabbing it meant getting closer to the feasting corpse. I told myself it seemed busy and lunged forward. My action distracted the dead thing from its meal. It looked at me with its reddish eyes. I saw a network of small broken veins within them. Tears of blood spilled down its cheeks and a line of mucus like the trail of some daemon slug dripped from its nose and down over its chin. It wheezed its stinking breath. There were flies all around it. They seemed to have come from nowhere; perhaps they had hatched within its flesh.

I grabbed for the chainsaw. There was no way to find the activating rune quickly so I lashed out, burying the serrated teeth in the dead man's forehead. They bit deep and small fragments of brain and juice flowed out, but he kept coming, reaching for me.

I found the runic activator on the grip and invoked a basic technical chant I had learned when I served on Baneblades all those years ago. By chance or the Emperor's Blessing the blades whirred to life, sending gobbets of flesh and splinters of bone spraying away.

I pushed forward and the blade bit into the skull and passed through, slicing the head in two all the way down to the spine. I twisted at the top of the spinal cord and pulled the weapon free. The dead man dropped like a puppet with its strings cut.

I let out a faint sigh of relief. I had found a weapon that worked and a way of putting the things down. That was the best I could hope for under the circumstances. I turned to look at the medicae but he was most definitely dead, his skin already turning a strange greyish green. He looked not unlike the walking corpse.

A thought struck me. These were not infected heretics who were rising this time, these were our own men. Had the disease mutated again, found a way to jump to the uninfected living and lie dormant until they passed on? If that was the case the plague was definitely growing stronger and more deadly.

Why now? Why were they all rising at once? Had some

dark ritual been performed that caused them all to rise and hunger? I resigned myself to the fact that I would probably never know, that I didn't even really want to know, and looked around to see what I could see.

A group of walking corpses was pressing a Sister Hospitaller back towards the door. The woman was trying to keep them at bay, swinging surgical implements at them, slicing flesh, but the walking dead men paid them no attention. I came up on the group from behind and sliced off heads and limbs with all the élan of a woodcutter chopping down trees. It was a crude technique but it was effective.

The ones with the severed heads fell at once, and the others kept coming until I decapitated them. When I finished I turned to the woman. She stared at me. I could not have been a pretty sight, a tall man in a besmirched medical smock wielding a chainsaw and covered in gore. She reacted pretty well, all things considered.

'Thank you,' the sister said. She was tall and dark-haired, and had a calm beauty that would have aroused my interest under somewhat different circumstances.

More and more dead bodies were rising and not all of them were coming out from under white sheets. The medicae adept whose chainsaw I was wielding came lumbering towards me, as if determined to reclaim the tool of his trade. He was hampered somewhat by the ropes of intestine wrapping themselves round his leg and forming slimy pools at his feet. Behind him came more and more dead people, arms outstretched, tears of blood running down their faces, uncanny hunger burning in their eyes.

The disease had certainly mutated. The dead were rising much more quickly and the plague seemed to be being passed on from the dead to the living, perhaps at the moment of death.

I turned to the woman and said, 'It's time to go.'

She did not need telling twice. We raced towards the elevator. It was already in use. I could see the glowing numbers light in sequence as it approached our floor. More walking dead, I thought. I did not see what else it could be. In this hospital at this moment it was the most likely explanation.

I wondered whether to wait and try to clear the elevator with my chainsaw or to make a break for the stairs. As I wrestled with the thought, the elevator reached our floor and the doors opened. I brought up the chainsaw and found myself looking down the barrel of a sniper rifle.

'Typical,' said Anton. 'We come all this way to collect him and he greets us by trying to chop our heads off.'

'It would raise the level of intelligence considerably in your case,' I said.

'And then he makes a smart remark. Not even a hello, pleased to see you, thanks for risking your life to save me.'

'Pleased to see you,' I said and I was.

'You might want to save the sentimental reunion for later,' said Ivan. 'We have other problems.'

The sniper rifle barked. A walking dead man fell, his head reduced to so many blobs of flesh and brain. This in no way discouraged the others.

I hustled the sister into the elevator while Anton and Ivan fired over my shoulder.

'I don't suppose you thought to bring my shotgun,' I said. The door closed, taking off the hand of a dead man as it did so. It crawled around on its fingers like a great spider until Anton stamped on it with his heavy boot. Then he shrugged his left shoulder. The duffle bag hanging from it dropped to the floor with a metallic crunch, just as the elevator began its descent.

'Is that what I think it is?'

'I thought you might be missing your favourite toy. I brought you some cartridges too.'

'Thanks,' I said. There was not just a shotgun in the duffle bag. There was a uniform and some combat boots as well.

'You came well prepared,' I said.

'We thought we had better when the reports started coming in,' said Ivan.

'Reports?' I asked.

'Uprising. The whole city was rebelling, or so it seemed. Only it wasn't that simple.'

'When is it ever?' I said. I pulled off the smock and started fitting on my uniform.

'It wasn't the citizens who were rebelling, it was the corpses. A whole bunch of them seemed to up and leave the morgues and go on a killing spree, and the ones they killed decided to join them and soon the whole bloody party was out of hand.'

I thought of what I had seen back in the ward. It seemed like the hospital was one of the last places to be touched. It made a certain sort of sense I suppose. It was warded against disease.

Anton decided to join in the explanation, possibly because Ivan was getting too much attention from the sister. 'And then, wouldn't you just know it, the heretics decided to attack. A huge offensive, millions of troops, living and dead, pushed all the way to the city wall, and someone opened the gates for them.'

I pulled on the boots. 'Sounds like it was all part of someone's plan,' I said. 'General Richter's, maybe?'

'They've got to get up pretty early in the morning to put anything past you, haven't they, Leo?' said Anton.

'He's right though,' said Ivan. 'It's all too closely timed for it to be any other way.'

'I would have thought you would have your work cut out for you defending the space port.'

Ivan looked away. Anton looked at the ceiling and whistled. The elevator kept going down. I adjusted my helmet and then my rebreather. 'We were off duty when the word came in to pull back, that we'd be taking to the ships in an hour or so.'

'How long ago was that?' I asked, while I loaded the shotgun. It felt good to be putting ammo in it again.

'About half an hour ago.'

'So what you're really saying is that you deserted your post to come here and get me out.'

'It doesn't sound like such a good idea when you put it like that,' said Anton. 'Maybe we shouldn't have come.'

'We'd just have been waiting to board a shuttle anyway,' said Ivan. 'This is way more exciting.'

Neither of them seemed particularly bothered that they

might not be able to get back to the space port in time to escape the impending catastrophic collapse of Niflgard into plague-ridden madness. I was very grateful to them both and I struggled for the perfect words to express my feelings. 'You're idiots,' I said eventually.

'You're welcome,' said Ivan.

The doors opened again. Corpses crawled across the lobby. Some of them were eating others. Some of them were fighting. All of them looked up with glowing reddish eyes when they smelt fresh meat.

I stepped forward, pumped the shotgun and pulled the trigger.

CHAPTER ELEVEN

In my experience there's nothing that clears a hospital lobby quite like a blast from a sawn-off shotgun. The hail of shot tore through the walking dead, severing a few spines and causing them to fall and not rise again. Many more were blasted off their feet. When they rose, there were holes in their flesh. A few limbs dangled from strips of flesh.

Anton opened fire with his sniper rifle. He was more subtle than me and more effective. Every shot took one of the dead men in the head. Ivan had meanwhile decided that he wanted to try out my chainsaw and I saw no point in objecting. The sister kept behind us as we fought our way out of the building.

The street was like the inside of the hospital only on a larger scale. There were bodies everywhere, many of them moving, some of them armed, and all of them looking hostile and hungry. Their nostrils twitched and their heads turned as we pushed our way through the doors with the former patients, staff and guards in hot pursuit.

Anton had left an open-cockpit groundcar outside the enormous building. Around it were a bunch of dead bodies. I mean really dead, with smashed heads and ripped torsos. I could pretty much reconstruct the route he and Ivan had taken into the hospital from the layout of the corpses. There was a lot of greenish slime strewn around as well.

A roar of engines announced the presence of gunships overhead. They were racing somewhere in the distance. Shortly thereafter we heard the distant thunder of explosions. I have no idea who was performing airstrikes or what against, but it fed the general atmosphere of chaos and confusion and provided a momentary distraction that let us move a few paces closer to the groundcar.

More and more of the walking dead men were coming towards us. I ran over to the vehicle and jumped in, the others piling in all around me. I heard a scream and saw the sister had tripped and a horde of the dead had set on her in a frenzy. The way her screams suddenly stopped told me she would not be joining us.

I activated the vehicle and the engine roared to life. I pushed it forward aiming directly for the crowd. There was going to be no other way to get through. The balloon tyres screeched. There was a shuddering bump as the first of the corpses impacted on the radiator grille. Another went cartwheeling away from the force of impact. The car wobbled slightly on its suspension as we went over some more corpses.

The walking dead did not care how fast we were moving. They threw themselves at us. Most of them were knocked clear but one of them managed to get itself onto the bonnet of the vehicle and started to climb its way up. Ivan stood on the bucket seat and swept his chainsaw down. It was not the cleverest thing to do under the circumstances. Gore splattered the windscreen. Some of it arced over the armourglass and sprayed us. I flicked the wipers on and leaned to one side so I could see round the murky windshield. It almost cost me my life.

A dead man stood there. I ducked back in just in time to avoid hitting him. The force of the impact would most likely have broken my neck. I could see through the gaps where the wipers had removed the blood now. In the mirrored reflection I caught sight of something climbing over the back. It was the upper half of the corpse that had been thrown beneath the vehicle. Its hips and legs had been torn away, but its arms still functioned well enough.

'Anton, behind you,' I shouted. He twisted and stood in the back seat, aimed and fired. The corpse was thrown backwards. We hit a speed bump, probably another corpse, and he teetered forward, almost losing his grip on his gun.

'Try to be a bit more careful, would you, Leo? You're not driving a Baneblade now,' he shouted. Something plunged from an overpass bridge above us and landed right in the cockpit. It gave a gurgling growl and reached for me. It snagged my arms and sent the steering wheel to spinning left. The groundcar lurched in that direction, racing along a pavement, heading directly towards the wall.

In the confined space of the groundcar cockpit Ivan could not bring the chainsaw to bear without hitting one of us. There was not even a place where he could set it down. He cast it away and it scythed through the air behind us, decapitated the walking corpse of a woman and buried itself in the chest of a huge man who was lumbering along after us.

Ivan grabbed the corpse and pulled it off me. The bionic systems of his arms whined as he struggled with the dead man. It tried to bite him and broke its teeth on the plasteel of his bionic limb. Ivan tugged its arm from its shoulder. It came free with a strange sucking, popping sound and started to wriggle around like a snake, grabbing at the steering wheel.

Ivan somehow managed to pull the rest of the monster clear and toss it over the side. It fell into another crowd of walking dead. The arm, meanwhile, had locked its fingers around the steering wheel and would not let go. I twisted the wheel to the right just in time for us to avoid hitting the wall and found I had aimed the vehicle directly at a lumen column. I kept twisting and the car went into a spin, the great balloon tyres screeching as the whole vehicle started to rotate.

Somehow we missed the lumen column although it scraped the paintwork along the side of the groundcar. We spun almost to a stop. It was a bad place for that. We were now facing back in the direction we had just come, our bonnet pointed right at an onrushing horde of corpses.

'Well done, Leo,' Anton said. 'You sure you don't want me to drive?'

'Shut up and keep shooting,' I said, and executed a

three-point turn that almost reversed us into a wall and crushed several more dead bodies.

'How long 'til final boarding now?' I shouted.

'About twenty minutes, so you might want to put your foot down.'

He wasn't kidding. It was going to be touch and go. I got us aimed along the road again and accelerated as fast as I could, praying to the Emperor that no more dead men decided to perform feats of acrobatics.

I managed to get us onto the access ramp for the main highway. Overhead a massive airship crashed into the side of a starscraper. I wondered whether the plague had taken the pilot or whether one of the dead was at the controls.

As I gunned the engine I got a clear view of the streets below the great roadway. The dead were everywhere, fighting with the living. Some soldiers were still holding out, garbed in the uniforms of the local militias. Things were not going to go well for them when the heretics entered the city. They would not go well for us either if we were found here.

The air was cool as it swept by us, though, and my rebreather kept out the worst of the pollution. Anton studied the horizon with his sniper-scope. Ivan sat beside me and stared off into the distance, bionic arm hanging out over the side of the car as if we were out on some pleasure trip.

Ahead I could see the massive forms of the orbital shuttles on the space field. They looked as big as starscrapers themselves. I knew we would need to find a place on one of those. 'Which shuttle were you assigned to?' I asked.

'What does it matter?' Anton asked.

'I'm going to drive right up to it and we're going to dive out and hope someone recognises us.'

'We're wearing our uniforms,' Anton said. 'What's the problem?'

I shut up. Maybe he was right. Maybe I was worrying about nothing. But when you're caught up in a massive retreat through a city being overrun by heretics and hungry dead men you tend to worry about these things.

The road sped by. I weaved through a number of cars that just seemed to have been abandoned or crashed and left to burn. The plague had most likely got to their drivers. Up ahead I saw a roadblock. I looked at the dashboard timer. I reckoned we had fifteen minutes.

The men wore the uniforms of the local militia and they had weapons pointed directly at us. I toyed with gunning the engine and trying to crash through, but it was a risk. They might shoot us and the force of the impact might wreck the groundcar.

I hit the brakes.

'Where are you going?'

'The space port,' I said. 'Urgent communication for Lord High Commander Macharius.'

They stared at us and our blood-spattered vehicle. I could see they were wondering exactly what was going on. They recognised the uniform, though, and the voice of authority, so after a few moments of dithering they let us through.

'Just as well,' said Anton. 'I was going to shoot them if they didn't.'

For once nobody bothered to contradict him. I suspect

we had all been thinking the same thing. Up ahead white contrails scarred the sky like the talon marks of some great beast. Even as I watched, the massive squat shape of a shuttle lifted itself into the sky. It was like watching a starscraper take flight.

'Frakkers are leaving without us,' Anton said. He meant it to sound like a joke but there was a faint panicked squeak in his voice. 'Might want to put your foot down, Leo. Shake a leg.'

I was already accelerating, pushing the groundcar up towards the limits of its speed. The roadway here was fairly clear, with less evidence of the plague and the walking dead. My hands felt clammy on the wheel. I was starting to think we might not make it, that we would be stranded in this mad city with an enemy army incoming and no way to escape. I doubted the heretics would be very friendly towards any outworlder they found. I was sure they would find some unclean use for us in their dubious rituals.

There was an odd feel in the air, an ominous expectancy that hovered over the doomed city. The wind carried it through the polluted clouds. It throbbed in the vibration of the great cogwheels whirring on the sides of the starscrapers. The smokestack towers breathed it out along with their freight of effluent. It took me a long moment to realise what it was.

It was the feeling of defeat, that we had been beaten and that we were not going to recover from this. For the first time since we had begun to follow Macharius on his long fiery road across the stars it felt as if we had no hope of victory, that all that was left for us to do was to flee like whipped dogs, tails hanging, and try to get away as far and as fast as we could, leaving the traitorous General Richter in possession of this planet and its vital production facilities.

I watched the road fly by and I tried to absorb it. In all my years I had never really felt it, even when we were surrounded by the hordes of the Angel of Fire back on Karsk. There the Imperial forces had been stabbed in the back and overwhelmed by treachery, but I never doubted that once the Imperium's full might was brought to bear victory would be ours even if I did not live to see it. I did not feel that way now. We had come too far, lost too much, perhaps even our sense of mission.

I tried telling myself that I was just recovering from being sick, that I was still weak, that it was just the lows my body was feeling manifesting themselves in my mind, but I knew it was more than that. I felt that the war was lost, and that even just escaping the surface of this blighted world was most likely beyond our grasp.

Naturally I did not share my thoughts with Anton and Ivan. I did not really need to. I could tell from their hang-dog expressions that they were feeling exactly the same way.

We reached the gates of the space port. In the distance I could see that there were still scores of shuttles on the ground. Men were still clambering aboard and vehicles were still rolling up the ramps. I could see Guardsmen guiding a few battered Leman Russ tanks with hand signals. A few more of them watched the perimeter guns pointing outwards. I wondered if they had enough ammunition to make good on the implied threat.

I pulled up at the gate. Nervous-looking men in the uniform of the Grosslanders turned their weapons on us. They were white-faced. They knew the hour of evacuation as well as we did – they had not been given the order to withdraw. They were wondering whether they would get off-planet just as much as I was. They had that narrow-eyed, sweaty look that soldiers sometimes get when they know that their line of retreat is fast being closed and certain death is approaching. To their credit, they still stood there.

I gave my name and rank and regiment. Anton shouted the password of the day. Their officer stared at us suspiciously. I knew exactly what he was thinking. It was extremely unlikely that three ragged and blood-spattered heretics would roll up at this late hour, with a story as unbelievable as ours.

In the minute he took to debate this, three of the big ships took off, leaving misty contrails behind them as they shucked off the chains of gravity and left defeat below them. Eventually, after what felt like hours but which could only have been minutes, he waved us through.

I weaved through the traffic as deftly as I could towards the towering shuttle that bore the Lion symbol of Macharius. It was still there, of course. It would not be done for the vessel of the Lord High Commander to be seen to leave while any of his men remained on the surface. Not yet anyway. Not unless things got really desperate.

I heard the sounds of gunfire from the edge of the field and then a massive explosion. I glanced right and saw smoke rising in great towers and then a horde of heretic infantry carriers flood onto the space field through the gap. It appeared the war had reached us even here.

Men were already moving to intercept the heretics before they could reach the great spacecraft. It was an act of desperation. Those soldiers knew that if the enemy reached the spacecraft then none of us would be departing.

I looked at Ivan. He looked away shame-faced. Anton pretended not to notice me either. Neither of them volunteered to go and join in the fighting, so I aimed us towards the *Lion's Pride* and gunned the engine.

The great vessel loomed over us, a tower of ceramite and plasteel, resting on great finned haunches. Most of the blast doors were already closed. Men in green tunics guarded the ramps. I brought the groundcar to a screeching halt and vaulted out, striding confidently towards the shuttle. Men brought lasguns to bear on me. I snapped a salute at the nearest officer.

'Sergeant Lemuel,' I said. 'Reporting fit for duty.'

Anton and Ivan strode up behind me and repeated my performance. The officer shook his head and motioned for us to get up the ramps as quickly as we could.

'We seal and blast in three minutes,' he said. He glanced towards the conflict where the walls had been breached. 'Possibly even sooner.'

The ramp flexed under my weight as I raced up it. At the top I turned and looked out. A massive heretic breakthrough had smashed the space port perimeter. At the edges, ships were already taking fire. Space-toughened ceramite was being blasted by Basilisk shells. Lightning danced down the flanks of one vessel where ancient power conduits leaked. Men lay charred and blackened on the concrete. Clouds of smoke and gas drifted across my field of vision. I stepped into the vessel. A starsailor shouted and pointed, guiding me towards the emergency acceleration couches. I strapped myself down knowing this was going to be a rough liftoff.

CHAPTER TWELVE

I strapped myself into the launch-bed, thinking of all the previous times I had done this. Normally it was a simple precaution, but with all the shelling going on there was a very real threat of an emergency take-off. Even as that thought struck me, the whole ship shuddered. A bell-like tone filled the air, as if the ship had been struck with a great hammer.

'That's not good,' said Anton. All around us crewmen were on their knees, murmuring technical invocations and launch prayers. A red light flashed. A warning bell sounded. There was another impact, this time followed by the sound of an explosion. It did not sound at all like the normal launch routine.

'I think we got on just in time,' said Ivan. His mechanical voice held no emotion. He at least always sounded calm.

'I think we're getting away just in time,' said Anton and gulped. He glanced around furtively as if realising that what he had just said smacked of cowardice.

Normally I would have taken the opening and used it to attack. This time I kept my mouth shut. His words echoed my own thoughts too closely. The ship shuddered and for a moment I thought the end had come, but it was only the lifters cutting in. I could tell from the vibration that the shuttle was now airborne, climbing up and away from the planet's surface. I lay there rigid, listening for the small sounds that would tell me that something had gone badly wrong.

'If that last shell has breached the hull then all the air in the ship might be evacuated,' Anton said. He sounded nervous.

'Bulkheads will close and prevent that,' said Ivan.

'Only in the sections not breached. If there's a hole in the hull we'll all be sucked out into space even if the rest of the ship remains sealed.'

'We can't be sucked out,' I said. 'We're strapped to these couches.'

'Then we'll suffocate and flash-freeze. Remember what happened back on the *Tramontane* when that wall blew out?'

How could I forget? We had found bodies frozen so cold that they were like ice blocks themselves. If you accidentally bumped into them bits broke off.

'As far as I can tell it has not happened yet,' said Ivan, 'so why don't you shut up and worry about it when it happens.'

'Because I won't be able to worry,' said Anton. 'I will be dead.'

'Then where's the problem?'

'What was that noise?' Anton asked, turning his head nervously. It was just the all clear, telling us the shuttle had left the planetary atmosphere. I unhooked the harness and stood up, made my way out of the emergency launch chamber and stared out of a small porthole. Beneath me I could see the vast shield of the planet obscuring the lower half of the sky. Green and red clouds drifted over rust deserts and sludge seas of ominous grey. Perhaps it was my imagination, but I could have sworn that I saw small flickers of light below me, as if vast explosions were going off, large enough to be seen from space.

Despite the silence, the shuttle was still accelerating. The great hemisphere shrank to become a ball beneath me. The outline of continents became visible. I felt unutterably weary. I looked at the chrono on the wall, still set to local time. An hour ago I had been among the sick and wounded in the great hospital. Now I was watching the planet recede beneath me. It all had the aspect of a dream.

I felt Anton and Ivan move up to flank me.

'Well, we lost,' said Ivan. His voice was utterly flat.

Anton sighed. He would have liked to deny it but he could not.

'We'll be back,' I said. I did not sound very convincing, even to myself.

Macharius looked weary. It would not have been visible to many but it was to me. I had known him for a very long time, stood guard over him on a hundred worlds. It was evident to my eye as soon as I resumed my bodyguard duties.

There was something about him that suggested the old man he in fact was. It was not his body. The juvenat treatments still kept him slim, tall and athletic, muscular as a warrior god. His hair was still golden. His eyes were still clear. When he strode across the room there was still the same look of electric purpose to him that he had possessed when I had first seen him three decades ago on Karsk.

It was something about the set of the shoulders perhaps. They were not so firmly straight. There was the suggestion of a stoop as well, of a head often held downcast.

The grip he clapped on my shoulder was just as firm as it had ever been, and the way he guided me across the chamber was just as forceful as it ever was. There were more lines around his eyes, perhaps, and on the flesh of his hands. There were a few more scars, barely visible. Macharius always healed well. In this, he was fortunate.

'You are recovered, Lemuel,' he said. The tone of his voice was compelling but it seemed to have lost something, the certainty it had always had. It did not quite command belief the way it once did. Or perhaps it was just my own imagination and my own feelings of depression.

'Yes, sir,' I said.

'It pleases me that you are fit for duty,' he said. To his credit, he did sound pleased. It was not just something he was saying because it was expected. He was a man who had conquered sectors of the galaxy for the Imperium. He could say what he wanted to whomever he wanted.

I looked around the chamber. It was oddly familiar, filled with furnishings that I could remember seeing many times before, mementoes of scores of campaigns, the battle banners of a hundred defeated foes. There was a rune-embossed chainsword he had picked up on Silvermount and the helmet of the Amir of Peshtar, crowned with the Star of Pesh, birthright of a world's rulers for a hundred generations. There was a desk carved from the tip of a Leviathan tusk on which sat a regicide set made from the resonant woods of Kal, whose colour responded to the mood of the player when he touched them.

Macharius looked at me again and said, 'I wanted to thank you for saving my life back on Loki. I would decorate you again but you've enough braiding already.'

One more would always be nice, I thought, but I did not say anything. It was clear Macharius was not in the mood to be giving medals, even for saving his life. There was a grimness about him I had not seen before. He gestured that I should take a seat. I knew then what was coming.

Throughout his career Macharius had made a habit of talking with his common soldiers about the campaign. It was not really the trait of an Imperial general. It was the style of the planetary nobility amongst whom he had come of age, of men used to talking with trusted retainers.

'Tell me about Loki,' he said. His strange golden eyes focused on me. He assumed a posture of intent listening and I will say one thing for him, he did listen. He made you feel as if he had no other interest in the world at that moment but what you were saying.

Under the circumstances, in the face of such flattery, it would take a better man than I not to talk loosely. As I spoke he nodded and tilted his head to one side. It was clear that he was not judging, that I was expected to tell him what I felt honestly, man to man, two old comrades speaking the truth. Except, of course, that I was doing all the talking and he was doing all the listening.

I told him all about the trenches and the walking corpses and the strange things I had seen. He occasionally asked a question, requested more details, a clarification of some point I had made. It was always germane though, always showed that he had been following what I said very closely. I somehow found myself talking about my strange dreams, and the daemons I had seen, and for the first time I noticed a faint widening of his eyes. His fingers flexed and drummed against his thigh for a moment and then stopped as if he too had become aware of what he was doing and what he was revealing.

I told him about waking up in the hospital, about Anna and Zachariah. I repeated the things that were said as closely as I could remember them, even the things unflattering of him and critical. He just nodded and listened and I kept going until I had finished the full tale of our escape.

Only once it was done and he had risen from his chair did I realise the full appalling extent of all I had said. I had criticised the great man to his face, or I had repeated others' criticisms of him, which to some officers would be the same thing. I had spoken aloud things that many would have construed as heretical to a man who was sworn to uphold and extend the Emperor's law wherever he stood.

I held my breath, surprised, as I always was after such

conversations, at exactly how big my mouth was and exactly how much trouble I was capable of getting myself into. And I had the cheek to call Anton stupid.

I watched Macharius, closely aware that even now he might be contemplating orders that would lead to my swift execution. He simply looked at me and said, 'I appreciate your frankness, Lemuel, but you must say nothing of these things to anyone other than Inquisitor Drake and myself.'

He walked over to the regicide board and I could see that he had set up a position there, or perhaps he was playing against himself. Certainly there was no one else in the army who could have played against him and provided any sort of challenge, not even Inquisitor Drake. His hand hovered over a piece and just for a moment he looked something I had never seen him to be before. He looked indecisive and then he looked angry.

'At every turn, I am thwarted, it seems,' he said. I did not say anything. I did not know whether he was talking to himself or to me. I kept very still, and made my mind blank, pretending to be nothing more than a piece of furniture. 'And it seems once again the Dark Powers are raised against me.'

He looked over at me. I don't know whether he was trying to gauge my response or whether he expected me to say something. I kept very quiet. 'There is something on Loki,' he said. 'Something old and dark and evil. Something that stands behind Richter's shoulder and whispers to him.'

He put a world of loathing into the name Richter. I could understand that. He was talking about the man who had betrayed him after all, a former friend and pupil who had also beaten him in battle, and one thing Macharius was not used to was defeat. He strode over to the porthole and looked down. The world was still below us. In the distance I could see Imperial ships exchanging fire with the planetary defences. The flare as they unleashed their ordnance was visible against the blackness of space.

He looked down at the world below as he had looked down at the game board, with a savage intensity, as if he were confronting a foe with whom he was about to engage in bitter personal combat, against whom he was about to fight a duel to the death. I followed his gaze as it turned towards the moons, as if refusing to invest with any significance the world where he had been beaten.

'I have his measure now,' Macharius said. 'I have its measure. I will return and I will be victorious.'

His voice had all of the power that had once held armies enthralled in its spell, but there was something missing, I thought, some inner note of conviction that would have given it the old magic and convinced me of his invincibility. To me, at that moment, it sounded as if Macharius was trying to convince himself.

'Are you sure?' Macharius asked Inquisitor Drake, when he brought his news. I kept my gaze fixed over his shoulder. I could see my face reflected a dozen times in the mirrored visors of the inquisitor's storm trooper bodyguards. I saw Macharius too and I was sure that he was aware of me as I stood by his shoulder. It was a position of privilege, awarded only to the most trusted of house troopers.

The inquisitor looked long and hard at the general. He was not a man who was used to being questioned in such a way even by the most powerful man in the Imperium. His normally impeccable self-control was being tested. Knowing Macharius, this was possibly quite deliberate, but I was not so sure – circumstances were unusual. Eventually Drake nodded.

'I am sure. It has been confirmed by multiple sources. Three of your highest-ranking commanders are already on Acheron. It is only a matter of time and the vagaries of interstellar travel before the others arrive there.'

For the first time ever I saw a look of utter fury on the face of Macharius's distorted reflection. His fist clenched, crushing the metal goblet he held. Wine slopped over his fingers. A servant moved discreetly into place to mop it up. Macharius motioned him away with a flick of his hand, the sort of motion you would use to brush away a fly. He rose from his throne and moved down the dais until he stood directly in front of Drake. The two men were of the same height but somehow Macharius managed to make the other man look small.

'Why would they do this? They must know they cannot get away with it.'

'Must they?' Drake's voice was flat, calm and emotionless. He was not afraid of Macharius even though at that moment he appeared the focus of the Lord High Commander's rage.

'They are plotting behind my back. They have convened to replace me. They…' He paused for a moment, as if he could not quite force the words out.

'If you rush there you will find that it is a meeting convened by Cardinal Septimus. Word was sent informing you but somehow the messenger never reached you–'

'Do they really think I am so stupid?'

'There will be documentation, incontrovertible proof, that the message was sent, that through no fault of the cardinal you were unaware of the meeting. What are you going to do? Call him a liar? Execute a representative of the High Lords of Terra?'

'I might.'

'Now you are being foolish. That would merely give your enemies what they want. It would prove that you saw yourself as greater than the Emperor's representatives, that you plan to set up your own realm here on the far marches of the Imperium, that all the things that have been whispered about you are true.'

'I am not sure I like your tone, inquisitor.'

'Like it or not I am merely doing what I have always done, telling you the truth, although it may not be pleasant to hear.'

Macharius paused at that and suddenly he smiled and looked more like the old Macharius. He knew that Drake was not his real enemy, that the men he was angry with were out of his reach and likely to remain so.

'So it has finally come,' Macharius said. 'They have finally found the courage to move against me.'

Drake shrugged. 'We both knew it was bound to happen. You've made too many enemies, ruffled too many feathers. Too many people want to share in the glory.'

'Richter must be defeated. An example must be made to all future rebels.'

'Is it more important that you defeat one insignificant foe on a flyspeck world or that you remain in charge of the crusade?'

Macharius stared at him. He looked as if he were about to say something. His fist clenched and he closed his eyes for a second as if breathing a prayer to the Emperor. Whether he was asking for patience or inspiration, I could not tell.

'What do you intend to do about this challenge?' Drake asked. His eyes met the Lord High Commander's and did not blink.

Macharius remained silent for a moment. 'What I have always done. Fight!'

And so we were ordered to Acheron and another fight that seemed impossible to win. This time with the representatives of the Imperium and those who had once been Macharius's most loyal followers.

CHAPTER THIRTEEN

Ships filled the sky over Acheron Prime. It was hard to believe there were so many in existence, and it made me realise the full extent and power of the crusade. Here there was no sign of the long, grinding defeat we had known on Loki. Here, the full majesty of the Imperium was evident.

Acheron Prime itself was a vast half-empty city, built amid the ruins of some xenos civilisation on the far edge of the galaxy. Old dark towers loomed over shiny new human buildings. The mix gave the city the look of a regicide board, zones of dark and zones of light intermingled in its architecture.

If the leaders of those conspiring against Macharius were discommoded by his sudden appearance, they gave no sign of it. We were greeted on the edge of the space field by assembled regiments from two score worlds. They raised a thunderous cheer as the doors of the shuttle opened. Macharius raised his hands and waved at the assembled crowd. He turned to Drake.

'There are at least twenty regiments of Guard down there who should be elsewhere.' His tone was low and urgent. I think in his head he was making calculations. He had brought with him only his own personal guard and the remnants of the Grosslanders who had been evacuated from Loki.

At first I thought he was considering using these troops to return there and defeat Richter, but as we walked down the ramp in the chill air of the haunted world, it struck me that he might be considering something else. If it came to a battle we would be greatly outnumbered. I pushed those thoughts aside as I came down the steps. I felt the tug of a new world's gravity, slightly stronger than the Imperial standard of the ship. It made my limbs feel heavier, and it increased my sensations of weariness.

I studied the men who were assembled to greet us, knowing that before me lay an index of those who had conspired to replace Macharius. If they felt the slightest embarrassment it did not show on their faces.

General Tarka looked resplendent in his Hussar's uniform. Piercing icy-blue eyes looked out of his lean, severe face from beneath bushy eyebrows, and his thin narrow mouth was drawn in a tight smile beneath his clipped moustache. He wiped away a speck of imaginary dust from his dress uniform's sash. He could not have held himself any taller and straighter than he did but he gave the impression of suddenly being on parade.

Beside him General Arrian gazed up at Macharius's approach with his bright, mad and fanatical eyes. He was a man who believed in the crusade still beyond any shadow of a doubt. The question was whether he still believed in its leader and the answer, given his presence here, was most likely no.

Looming over the pair like a starscraper over a domestic hab-block was General Cyrus, so tall he looked almost like a mutant, although you would not have said that from a distance. His body was perfectly proportioned. His face looked like it was carved from a block of granite and his eyes were like chips of grey stone.

In his shadow, as if he sought to remain out of sight, there was General Crassus, a man of medium height, almost as broad as he was tall. In the intervening years since I had last seen him, he had put on some weight around the belly and acquired a number of new chins. His face was pock-marked and a scar ran from his brow to the corner of his mouth. There was something about the man that drew the eye despite his attempt to blend in with his companions, an aura of power, of ruthless intelligence, that told you that he was dangerous.

Off to one side, surrounded by a guard of honour, stood another group of robed dignitaries representing the great Administratum of the Imperium. The two groups stood conspicuously apart as if they were having nothing to do with each other. Smiling affably, Macharius advanced to meet them. All of the officers saluted crisply, a gesture Macharius returned with perfect punctilio.

The head of the cabal from the Administratum strode towards Macharius and bowed. It was a complex, ambiguous gesture and it served to remind everyone that he was not part of Macharius's command. He was another tall man, with glossy dark hair going grey at the temples and a small spade beard. His eyes were of such a dark brown they seemed almost black. Three floating skulls orbited his body at shoulder height, a mark of his status, a badge of his power. And those skulls were something more. They were repositories of knowledge and advisors of great cunning.

'Lord High Commander,' said the cardinal, in a rich, rolling bass voice. 'I am pleased to make your acquaintance at long last.'

Macharius's glance was cold and measuring. 'And you are...'

'I am Cardinal Septimus,' said the newcomer. 'As I explained in my message–'

'I received no message from you.' Macharius paused to look pointedly at his generals. 'Or anyone else.'

'But I assumed you were here because you received my invitation.' Cardinal Septimus gave a very good imitation of a man being flustered by unexpected events. If he had not been who he was I might even have believed it.

'I came because I had received reports of my commanders gathering here on Acheron and I wondered what could be so important as to detain them from their duties to the Emperor and the crusade.'

'Alas,' said the cardinal, 'I fear I am to blame for that. I sent the Imperial summons to all of your generals and yourself.' He paused and added with just a hint of irony. 'Clearly some of my messengers have been delayed as the one to you was.'

'So you have summoned me here,' Macharius said. His tone was mild. Only a fool would have assumed that he was anything but dangerous and I doubted the cardinal, despite his manner, was a fool.

'I believe you are still subject to the commands of the Emperor and his chosen representatives,' said Septimus. There was steel in his voice. 'You are a great hero of the Imperium, Lord High Commander.'

He glanced at the skulls floating around him. For a moment, as if subject to some unheard command, their circling ceased and their eyesockets all turned to regard Macharius. My hand went to the shotgun, just in case. 'Once these too belonged to heroes of the Imperium.'

He let the words hang in the air for a moment then said, 'Are you still subject to the commands of the Emperor and his representatives?'

Utter silence descended. Everyone stood absolutely still, straining to hear Macharius's response. There could only be one answer to that question which would not result in civil war, a thing Macharius had spent his whole life ending.

Macharius smiled at the cardinal and said, 'You bear tokens proving you are who you claim to be.'

'My messenger carried documents marked with the appropriate seals.'

'We have already ascertained that your messenger never reached me.'

'Then I can present you with my credentials when we have returned to my palace.'

'Your palace?'

'I have requisitioned a fitting domicile for myself and my staff,' said the cardinal.

'Perhaps you would be good enough to present them to me in person,' said Macharius. The two men stared at each other, locked in a battle of wills. 'At your earliest convenience.'

'Of course,' said Cardinal Septimus, after the lapse of ten very long heartbeats. 'It would be my pleasure.'

Macharius nodded as if he had expected nothing less and swept ahead, through the massed ranks of troops, leaving the generals and the Imperial dignitaries to follow in his wake.

The airship carried us over the ancient city towards the palace that had been prepared for Macharius. I watched the city slide by through the portholes while I eavesdropped on the conversation of my betters. Starscrapers that resembled great ebony tombstones drifted by. Alien runes appeared on their sides and vanished with no apparent reason. Black flames danced through the sky overhead. In the shadows of these monstrous xenos artefacts the human buildings seemed smaller, shabbier and more impermanent.

Many of them had an abandoned half-complete look that showed how recently they had been put up. It had been the intention to make Acheron the capital of the newly created sector. Its strategic position across the interstellar routes made it suitable as such. Now I doubted the city would ever be complete.

Beneath us I could see vast makeshift camps containing the forces of the generals. Around the edges were parked Bane-blades, Shadowswords and other Imperial armour. There was no sign here of the shortages we had known on Loki. I recalled Macharius's suspicions of a conspiracy against him and the gathering of generals here had proved that correct. I wondered if he was correct, too, about supplies being with-held and the supply chain being sabotaged. He was a man who made few mistakes about such things.

'We can't assume that just because they are not here they are loyal,' Drake was saying. His voice was low, urgent, pitched for the ears of Macharius. 'They may, as Septimus says, simply have not gotten the message.'

'Or they may be lying low, afraid to commit themselves, until they see what happens.'

'Equally you cannot assume that just because they are here the officers present are against you. It is difficult to ignore a direct summons from the Imperium.'

'Particularly if one is ambitious,' said Macharius. There was a note of irony in his voice. 'Tell me what you know about Septimus.'

'What does anyone really know about a man like him?'

'I am sure you can tell me more than common scuttlebutt. I am sure your network of agents has been busy here for some time.'

'He is a powerful, clever, ambitious man,' Drake said.

'The fact that he holds the position he does tells me as

much,' said Macharius. 'The Imperium would not have sent a fool here.'

'He will not thank you for making him present his credentials to you.'

'What was I supposed to do? Take him at his word?'

'You could have been more diplomatic.'

Macharius shrugged. 'How do you think this will be played?'

'You will be sent home, summoned to Terra, loaded with honours.'

'My work is not done.' Macharius sounded completely convinced of that.

'Clearly there are those in the Administratum who feel differently.'

'If I am replaced no one will be able to rein in Tarka and his ilk. The crusade will disintegrate as they try to achieve their ambitions unfettered. Give them a decade and they will tear the army apart – it will be the Schism all over again.'

'You cannot be sure of that.'

'I picked those men. I have commanded them for decades. Believe me, I know them and have done so since I humbled every last one of them on the battlefield.'

'There are some would say that was a flaw in your plan,' said Drake. He was not a man afraid to put forward opinions that might have got someone else shot. 'A bid to make yourself irreplaceable. Some would say it was a sign of a lack of humility, of disloyalty to the Imperium even.'

'Some would say, inquisitor? What would you say?'

'I am just setting out the arguments that will be used

against you. Septimus will be able to present himself as just someone seeking to sort out a succession crisis.'

'In order for there to be a succession, I would have to die.'

'You are planning on becoming immortal, are you?'

'I am not planning on dying any time soon.'

'Has it occurred to you that there may well be others who are planning on your death?'

'People have been doing that since I was eleven years old. I am still here.'

'You won't be forever. No man can be.'

'Has it occurred to you, inquisitor, that there are those who would profit by the return of the old Chaos, of a new Schism?'

'Yes. That is why I think some of your command decisions have been unwise.'

Macharius laughed. 'I found those men leading armies that had conquered scores of worlds. They swore loyalty to me. They are the best generals in the Imperium for the kind of war we are fighting. It was not simply vanity and megalomania that made me choose them. They chose themselves. Of all the men in all the worlds, they are the ones who had survived and been victorious. They have conquered more worlds for the Imperium than any men since the time of the Emperor.'

Drake nodded. Macharius clearly had a point. 'You could have replaced them.' He was not about to give up.

'With men just as violent, just as ambitious and perhaps less competent? You don't get to be an Imperial general by being a herbivore, inquisitor. You didn't survive on the killing grounds of the Schism by being the toughest sheep in the herd. You survived by being a wolf.'

'And now your pack is turning on you.'

'You have made your point.'

'I hope so.'

'You think we are approaching a point where I may be of more use to the Imperium as a dead hero than a live general?' There was a trace of mocking humour in Macharius's voice.

'I am sure there are some who might.'

'They will change their minds when I have dealt with Richter.' Once again it was there in Macharius's voice, that note of querulous obsession. He seemed to have convinced himself that overcoming his nemesis would put everything right, would regain any lost prestige, would make things as they once were. Could he really not see how broken things were?

'I have had my people sweep your palace. It is clean, as far as they can tell.' That meant that it was as secure as was mortally possible.

'That is always good to hear,' said Macharius. I knew he had his own people checking as well, just in case. I would see reports about it soon enough.

The airship docked with Macharius's palace.

We accompanied the general to his penthouse chambers and were dismissed.

Knowing there would only be a short respite before the tidal wave of generals and bureaucrats descended on us, we headed down towards the apartments that had been assigned to us. All around an army of servants went about their business, padding through the marble-walled corridors, clad in green tunics, carrying themselves with the bearing of ancient aristocrats. Here at least were those who were still in no doubt of Macharius's status. His glory reflected on them and they looked the part.

'I wonder what they all do when we're not around,' Anton said as we strode past another arrogant-looking houseboy.

'The palace does not look after itself,' Ivan said. 'They still have duties to perform.'

'Aye, and food to eat and wine to drink, while we've been out in the trenches killing heretics.' Anton sounded bitter in a way I had never heard him before.

'What's got into you?' I asked. Behind his head, through a great arched window, I could see a mirrored black star-scraper. On its side pictoglyphs formed and faded, spelling out some unguessable message in a tongue long lost to mankind.

'Nothing,' said Anton. His lips were compressed tightly. His scar looked livid on his forehead. His eyes were narrowed at their corners.

'You sound angry,' I said, just to goad him.

'I am not angry.'

'Petulant, then.'

'I am not petulant.' Of course, denying it made him sound exactly that.

'He's just annoyed there was no victory parade,' said Ivan. 'There's always been a victory parade before.'

'I am not worried about any sodding parade,' said Anton.

'It's the lack of cheering crowds then. You miss them.'

'I don't give a toss about crowds, cheering, booing or otherwise.'

'Then why are you so annoyed?'

'It's them...' Anton said. We paused in front of a mural depicting yet another of Macharius's triumphs. In this one, as in so many others, he was accompanied by his most important generals, each head of one battlegroup of the crusade. They were all there: Sejanus, Tarka, Crassus, Arrian, Fabius, Lysander and Cyrus. All of them looked only marginally less a supreme commander than their great leader.

'Them?'

'The generals, the nobles, the politicians, the high muckety-mucks.'

'What about them?'

'Yeah, what about them?' Ivan asked. 'They've always been frakkers. Why have you picked today to notice it?'

'They're talking about replacing Macharius. You heard what Drake said... It's treason.'

'It would only be treason if they were plotting against the Imperium,' I said.

'They're plotting against Macharius.'

It hung in the air. I looked over my shoulder to see if anyone was listening. No one looked like it, but that meant nothing. In a palace like this half the servants were probably in the employ of someone or other, reporting back every word they heard.

'Macharius is not the Imperium,' I said. Was it my imagination or did one servant girl's eyes widen slightly? I doubted that she could understand the dialect of Belial but you never know – if someone wanted to place an agent badly enough they might find someone who could.

'What have all those other frakkers ever done for the Imperium?' Anton asked.

'Led its armies to victory.'

'I am talking about the bureaucrats who stayed at home and counted their money while we fought and bled over half the galaxy.'

I said nothing. I looked at him disapprovingly, more for discussing this where we could be overheard than because I disagreed with what he was saying. The servant strolled off down the corridor. I told myself it must have been my imagination.

CHAPTER FOURTEEN

The Drunken Ratling was a new tavern pretending to be old. It was in a basement bunker deep beneath one of those old black, mirrored starscrapers. Its walls were covered in murals of Imperial Guardsmen winning great victories in the face of orks, eldar, and a bunch of equally strange-looking xenos the likes of which I had never seen before and which most likely came direct from the imagination of some artist.

The place was full of men in uniform, drinking grog and pivo and brown beer. Hundreds of uniformed soldiers sat at long tables and clutched steins and jabbered at each other in the tongues of their home world. Anton and Ivan and I were no different. We spoke in Belial Hive dialect even though we had less and less use for it down the years. Most of Macharius's guard came from his home world or had been co-opted in from other regiments when they had distinguished themselves in the service of the crusade. Still, it was nice sometimes to speak the old tongue and tell the old jokes and reminisce about a world that none of us had seen for thirty years or were ever going to see again. Sometimes it was good to be reminded of our youth, when life had seemed so simple.

We grabbed a corner table and a serving girl brought us the local beer, a very dark brew that fizzed slightly on the tongue as if there were some strange chemical in it or the water it was brewed from. I raised my glass and spoke a toast to the cog manufactorums of Belial and all those who laboured in them, and Anton and Ivan echoed it. We slopped a small libation onto the table in memory of all those who had fallen beside us on Loki. I don't know where we had picked that habit up, but it seemed to take on more and more meaning as the years passed. We had seen a lot of faces pass and a lot of comrades fall and it seemed appropriate somehow to mark their passing even in such a small way.

I stared through the clouds of lho-stick fug and soma fumes. All around me were soldiers who seemed more subdued than normal, and I noticed that many of them were slipping furtive glances in our direction. One or two of them were even pointing at us and sniggering. I did not think too much of it at the time. In any large drunken gathering there're always going to be a few who behave like idiots.

'You remember when we found Corporal Hesse asleep under Old Number Ten?' Ivan was saying. 'Now there was a man who could snooze under any circumstances.'

'A valuable skill in a soldier,' I said, taking another sip from my beer. It fizzed on my tongue. I saw one lad glance at me, nudge his mate with his elbow and then laugh. He was wearing a uniform with a lot of gold braiding on it. The buttons of his elaborate coat looked as if they might be made of gold. Most likely they were just plated, although some soldiers like to carry their wealth on them in easily transportable, easily visible fashions. Me, I think it just sets you up as a target for thieves.

'Not as valuable as drinking,' said Anton. 'Being able to hold your booze is a talent to be admired.'

'You're talking to the man who tried to outdrink a Space Wolf,' said Ivan. That was something the pair of them were quite clearly never going to let me forget.

'I played my part heroically,' I said.

'I still remember you throwing up in an old helmet the next day.'

'That's a clear misrepresentation of the facts,' I said.

'True,' said Ivan. 'It wasn't a helmet. It was a bucket.'

'Obviously you are both jealous because you lack my prowess,' I said, taking a deeper swig from the beer, 'which commands the respect even of Space Marines.'

It was a slight exaggeration, but neither of them had been present at the banquet in which I had made the mistake of accepting a drink from Ulrik Grimfang of the Space Wolves. I could tell them anything I wanted, but it seemed best to keep things within the bounds of probability.

'You think we are ever likely to see Space Marines again?' Anton asked. He sounded suddenly like a young lad again, keen to get off-planet and meet the legendary heroes of the Imperium.

'We've already met them more times than most Guardsmen will ever encounter them in a lifetime.'

'Ten lifetimes,' Ivan corrected.

'A thousand,' said Anton, not wanting to be left behind in the exaggeration. He banged his glass on the table to emphasise the point. Some of it spilled out, slopped along the table and dripped down onto the highly polished boots of a soldier who was standing there.

Perhaps 'looming there' would have been a better description. He was a huge man, almost as big as an ogryn, with a massive walrus moustache and a bald head. He had lamb-chop whiskers and a ruddy face and tiny eyes of porcelain-blue that looked out at the world with a slightly insane glaze. Beside him were the young man and his mate who had been giggling at us earlier. Behind them was a group of soldiers all in the same elaborate gold-braided uniforms.

'Watch what you're doing,' said the moustached giant in accented Imperial Gothic.

Anton looked at him. 'What did you say?'

'I said, "Watch what you are doing".'

Anton looked at me then looked back at the giant. I could not help but notice that he had arms as large around as my thighs and fists the size of small ham hocks. 'Could you repeat that?' Anton said, putting a hand to his ear. 'I can't understand a word of your turdkicker accent.'

He didn't use the exact word turdkicker, but the Belial equivalent. The sergeant clearly did not understand the word but he understood the tone.

'I don't like you, greencoat. I don't like your attitude.' His voice boomed out and his words cut through the general babble. Heads turned to look at us. A few men smiled. A few cracked their knuckles. I noticed that there were a lot more men from the giant's regiment than there were from ours.

'There's no need for any trouble,' said Ivan. His voice was as flat and emotionless as it always was. The sight of his sharp mechanical teeth was enough to give anyone pause.

'Scared we'll kick your ass?' said the laughing youth. 'Just like the heretics on Loki did.'

I considered his appearance and I realised that there was something about his face that really made me want to punch it.

'It's good you've brought twenty friends to back you up,' said Anton. 'Always makes rats braver.'

The laughter stopped and a look of pure vicious spite passed across his face. I knew that he was one of the sort that was always stirring up trouble. 'I'm not scared of you,' he said.

'Of course you're not,' said Anton. 'That's why you brought your big buddy here to hide behind while you shoot your mouth off.'

That was a reasonable shot and things might have calmed down but he could not resist adding, 'And he looks stupid enough to let you do it.'

'He's not the only stupid one around here,' I said. Unfortunately the giant heard me.

'What did you say?' he asked. His tone told me that he did not suspect me of passing any compliments. Behind him I recognised a group of men in green tunics approaching.

They all had the tall golden look of warriors from Macharius's home world. There were not as many of them as there were of our new friends but the odds had changed a little.

I took a deep breath and I thought about what I was seeing. No one, but no one, had tried to pick a fight with us in a bar since we put on the green tunics. We'd picked a few ourselves, but it just was not done to show disrespect to the Lord High Commander's personal guard. Only now apparently it was. More than anything else this told me how much Macharius's star had fallen.

At that moment, the giant took a swing at me. It was sudden and it was fast. It might have taken my head off as well, if Ivan had not reached across and caught his wrist. The servo-motors in his arm screeched as he halted the blow and the two of them stood there straining across the table. The smirking youth took it upon himself to break a glass at this point and try to slash me with the splinters. I rolled back off the bench and when I picked myself up I could see a full-scale brawl was in progress, spreading across the room, involving the gold-braids, the green tunics and everybody else. By the time the chaos had reached the edge of the room no one had any idea of who was fighting or why. They were just joining in for the fun of it or to make sure no one got the drop on them.

Ivan stood straining with the giant, his mechanical limbs matched against enormous strength. Smirking youth took a slash at him. The splinters of glass ripped his uniform and revealed the plasteel and ceramite beneath the tunic. I decided I had had enough of this. I raised my glass and threw it at Smirker's head. It tumbled through the air, spilling beer as it went, and caught him right between the eyes, sending him toppling back onto the floor.

'Waste of good beer, that,' said Anton. He jumped onto the table and head-butted the giant, dropping him.

'Thought you were taking too much time with that one,' he said and dived into the brawl. There was nothing else to do but follow him.

The cells were small and dark and dim and full of men who all looked the worse for wear. A single glow-globe flickered overhead. Duty guards looked at us through the visors of their riot helms. I had learned a respect for them and their nightsticks a couple of hours back when they had broken up the brawl and thrown us all into the cells to cool off.

'Just think,' said Anton. 'We'd still be drinking beer if Leo here could hold his temper. He had to go starting brawls.'

'I seem to remember I was not the one who insulted the big bald fellow,' I said.

'Classic – trying to weasel out of responsibility for his actions. How you ever made sergeant is beyond me,' he said.

'Now that I can believe,' I said. 'You certainly don't have the intelligence to understand how I did it.'

'See what I mean – can't resist the sarky remarks. Always causing trouble.'

'It was a good fight though,' said Ivan.

'You're only saying that because you broke that big guy's arm when he grabbed you,' Anton said.

'And I would have broken his jaw if you hadn't nutted him,' Ivan said.

'He deserved it and so did his buddies,' said Anton with a sudden change of tone. 'He was disrespectful to our fallen comrades on Loki. And we did not get our asses kicked.'

I let out a long sigh. I did not see any other way of explaining our precipitate withdrawal from Loki but I was not going to say that out loud. I was starting to sober up a little and thinking you never knew who might overhear you and how they might choose to interpret it.

'Not tonight anyway,' I could not resist saying. 'We taught them a lesson.'

I glanced around. Most of the men in the cells with us wore green tunics. The duty guards knew better than to put men from different regiments together. Too much chance of a killing if the brawl restarted. I did not know any of them, but I was glad they had been there and taken our side in the fight. Of course, under the circumstances, there was very little else they could have done.

The door opened and an officer strode in. I recognised his tall, upright figure and his blank-seeming expression. It was the Undertaker. He walked right down to the door of our cell as if he knew exactly where to find us. Beside him were a couple of guards.

'Sergeant Lemuel,' he said, 'you are in trouble.'

I saluted him as he indicated the doors should be opened and we should be released.

I did not expect to be taken straight to Inquisitor Drake. I was shown into his office and the Undertaker departed.

'Brawling, Sergeant Lemuel? I expected better of you.'

Drake's voice was dry. There was a faint hint of disapproval in it but something else as well, a note of curiosity that made me even more cautious.

'As you have every right to, sir,' I said, doing my best to sound contrite.

'Tell me what happened,' he said. I did so, all the while wondering why this powerful man was taking an interest in a tavern brawl. I am not sure whether he read my mind or simply deduced what I was thinking from my expression.

'Because you are a member of the Lord High Commander's personal guard,' Drake said, 'you should not be engaged in such fights. It reflects badly on General Macharius.'

'You are correct, sir.'

'Of course I am correct. The question is, why did you get involved in this brawl at all?'

'I believe I am correct in saying we did not start it, sir.'

'The eternal excuse. Who did then?'

'A group of soldiers from General Crassus's regiment.'

'Did they provoke you?' Even through my hangover I was starting to wonder where this was going.

'A little. They came over to our table. They seemed to be spoiling for a fight.'

'I can see this is going to be a problem.'

'Sir?'

'Dissension in the ranks, Sergeant Lemuel. I suspect it reflects dissension in the upper echelons.'

'You think General Crassus is at odds with the Lord High Commander, sir?'

'I think there are people who are making it their business

at least to make it look that way.' I was starting to wonder why he was telling me this. Again he seemed able to pick the thought right out of my mind.

'Macharius trusts you, Lemuel. And I trust you. You are reliable. It would be a loss to us if you were to be killed in some bar-room brawl.'

'I don't think that was very likely, sir.'

'Men never do until it happens to them, and it happens all the time.' My eyes widened a fraction. The secret world of stealthy killing was more his business than mine.

'Why would anyone bother to remove me?'

'These are strange times, Lemuel. You have spent a long time close to the centre of power in the crusade. Killing you might unsettle the Lord High Commander a fraction and this is a game where those fractions can affect the fate of billions. Also, killing you might open up a space to put someone else close to Macharius.'

I felt suddenly out of my depth. Even after all these years of following Macharius, it was odd to be talked about in this way, even though I could see the sense of some of what he was saying.

'It might all just have been a random brawl, sir. Such things happen all the time.'

'It might, Lemuel, but it is my job to look for unwelcome surprises concealed within the seemingly random.'

'I don't envy you that, sir.'

'We all have our tasks to perform in the service of the Emperor,' he said. 'You have yours and I have mine. Try to keep yourself alive, Lemuel.'

I looked at him then and I wondered at the warning in his words. He actually seemed a little concerned. I dismissed it at the time, thinking I must be imagining things, but I am not so certain now. All of us in that small charmed circle surrounding Macharius had known each other a long time. We were part of each other's lives in all the small intimate ways that long acquaintance implies. Drake was one of the higher ranked ones of the Imperium but he was used to me, as he was probably used to his favourite pieces of furniture. He might indeed be saddened for a few fractions of a second by my loss.

'Is that all, sir?' I asked.

'Yes, Lemuel. You are dismissed.' I wondered about that too. There was no punishment given. We were not restricted to the palace. We were not given any scutwork duties. Maybe in all the great events sweeping along behind us we had simply fallen through the cracks, but I doubted it. Drake was not a man to let anything do that. Neither was Macharius. I wondered if the lack of punishment was making a statement of some kind, not to us, but to General Crassus.

CHAPTER FIFTEEN

'Leo! Leo Lemuel! How are you doing?' The words were spoken in Belial Hive dialect, a language I had not expected to hear on this street on this world. Not spoken by anyone other than Anton, Ivan or myself.

I turned and saw a familiar face, or familiar enough. It belonged to Sergei Krimov, a man I had known once a long time ago, back when I had served with the Seventh Belial. Of course, he was not the same. Ordinary soldiers in the Imperial Guard get no access to juvenat. He looked more like Sergei Krimov's father than the Sergei I remembered. His hair was thinner and greyer. His face was leaner. His skin was more lined and tanned. He had sergeant's stripes on his shoulder.

'Sergei Krimov, is that you?' I asked in the tongue of Belial.

'None other!' He walked up to me and slapped me on

the back. 'I haven't seen you since Karsk and the campaign against the Angel of Fire. You haven't aged a day. Buy you a drink?'

'Why not?' I said. I was genuinely pleased to catch up with an old comrade, and to hear the old tongue spoken. It was a reminder of earlier, simpler days. Sergei grasped me by the arm and led me towards a basement bar. It was a civilian place and it was not crowded at this time of day. He ordered some drinks, slammed them down on the table in front of us, and bellowed a toast before downing his glass in one.

'You still hanging around with those other two from your old neighbourhood?' he asked. 'Ivan and whatsisname, the idiot?'

'Anton.'

'Yeah, Anton. They still alive?'

I nodded and grinned. 'Yes, they are.'

'They've beaten the odds then. Who would have thought it thirty years ago in basic training? Who would have thought we would come this far, conquer so many worlds? Who would have thought any of us would live to see it?'

He was right. The odds against an ordinary Imperial Guardsman lasting so long in the service were great. Of course, neither of us was exactly in the position of an ordinary Guardsman. I was a bodyguard to Macharius. He was in a mechanised unit.

'You still in Baneblades?'

'Yes. Although I don't know how we keep them moving. It's getting harder and harder to get fuel and ammo and they are great hungry beasts. We seem to be short of everything these days.'

'We're a long way from the core and the industrial hives.' I didn't say anything about our failure to recapture Loki. I didn't need to.

'We're certainly a long way from Belial.' He raised his glass again, swigged it down and ordered another. I did the same. 'Man, it's been a long, hard road to get here.'

'Tell me about it,' I said.

'You've done all right for yourself, bodyguard to the Lord High Commander himself. The whole regiment was pleased when you three were selected. It reflected well on all of us, we thought.' There was something in his tone that suggested that he might have thought it at the time, but not now. I let it hang in the air. I wanted some news of the old regiment.

'We fought against the orks on Kassari,' he said. 'And heretics on half a dozen words – Grommel, Mercator, Selenius, Vindicor, Mayama. Crushed them all. We brought a score of worlds into the Imperium. General Crassus led us to victory in every battle.'

'You part of his command, Battlegroup Crassus?'

'Have been since Kassari. He's a great man. I know Macharius gets all the credit but Crassus leads us on the ground, and he's never been beaten.' He paused for a moment, looked long and hard at me. I knew he was seeing the green uniform, not a man from his old world. I took my cap and placed it on the table, unbuttoned my jacket and put it over the back of the chair and ordered more drinks.

'I've always heard he was a great general,' I said. 'All of the field commanders are. They wouldn't be where they are otherwise.'

'That may be true, but Crassus is the best, and the most generous to his troops with plunder, promotions and bonuses.'

'You've done well then,' I said. He tapped the stripes on his shoulders and said, 'I've got something squirrelled away for a rainy day. How about you?'

'I live in a palace,' I said. 'I never saw that coming back on Belial.'

'And you have access to juvenat treatments, unless I am much mistaken,' he said. 'Either that or you are uncommonly well preserved.'

'A little of both, I think.' I was starting to wonder at his tone. There was a bit of an edge to it now. Maybe he was one of those men who get aggressive when they are drunk. Maybe there was some bitterness in him I had not spotted. I did not feel terribly threatened.

'Things are going to have to change,' he said suddenly. 'Too much corruption at the top. Too many people doing too well out of things. Not enough supplies for the fighters at the front.'

'A lot of people seem to think that.'

'Don't you?'

I shrugged. 'Maybe.'

As quickly as it had come on his mood changed. 'What the hell? Why talk about the politics? Let's talk about Belial and the old neighbourhoods.'

I ordered more drinks. They kept coming. It was good to meet someone from the old hive.

I staggered back into our chambers at the palace. Anton and Ivan had returned from their stint on guard duty. I slumped in my chair, nursing a drink. 'You'll never guess who I ran into?' I said.

'A brewer's truck,' said Anton, 'judging from the look of you. Otherwise, I guess you ran into the nearest bar and then ran back out again when you had spent all your money.'

'Sergei Krimov,' I said.

'Slick Sergei?' Ivan said.

'None other.'

'You're telling me the Seventh are here?' said Anton.

'Just got in, apparently.'

Anton folded himself into an armchair and poured himself a drink. 'That's news,' he said. 'I haven't run into anybody from the old regiment since we signed up with the Lion Guard.'

'They are part of Battlegroup Crassus now. Were assigned to it right after Kassari.'

'See any other faces from the old days?' Ivan asked.

'Just Sergei. He was out wandering on his own, checking out the sights of Acheron.'

'Checking out the bars and looking for a criminal connection, if I know him,' said Anton.

'He paid his way,' I said.

'Did you check your wallet afterwards?' Anton asked.

'What have you got against the guy?'

'He was always a fly man,' Anton said.

'People change,' I said.

'And even if they don't, why is it our problem?' Ivan asked. 'Leo was drinking with him, not going into business.'

'Suit yourself, but listen to me. The guy would sell the fillings from your teeth and then come back for your gnashers.'

'Part of Battlegroup Crassus, eh?' said Ivan. 'That's the fourth regiment that follows him arrived then. He has more regiments here now than anybody else.'

'They should be in the field, fighting heretics,' said Anton.

'I'll be sure to mention that to Crassus the next time I run into him,' I said, but I was doing the sums in my head. Four regiments, at least one of them heavy armour, made Crassus the most powerful man on the planet now. And given the proximity of Macharius and the crusade's other leaders, that probably made him the most powerful man in the Imperium. I wondered how he was enjoying the feeling.

'He's got Baneblades and Shadowswords backing him then,' said Ivan. I could tell he was making the same sort of calculations as I was. It was sad how quickly our thoughts had degenerated into forebodings of treachery. It says something for the atmosphere of the time and place as well, I suppose. I think all of us had suspicions about the outcome of this conclave.

'Maybe we should hold a sweepstake on it,' Anton said.

'On what?' I asked.

'On who is going to stab Macharius in the back first.'

'It won't come to that,' I said.

'Won't it?' Anton asked. 'How do you know?'

I had no answer for that. There was nothing I could really say. I did not even believe in my own words myself.

'You really think we're going to end up fighting against the Seventh?' Ivan said.

'If we agree with Anton, it's possible.'

'It won't come to that,' Ivan said. His flat mechanical voice gave his words a certainty I was sure he was very far from feeling. It was hard to believe we were even talking about this, the possibility of having to defend ourselves against the men we had once fought alongside. Was this what the high ideals of the crusade had finally come to?

Maybe Macharius had made a mistake coming here with only his personal guard and the tattered remnants of the Grosslanders. Given the mauling they had taken on Loki it was possible that even they might not stand with us.

Cardinal Septimus strode into Macharius's throne room, his servo-skulls orbiting around him. I stepped forward to bar his way. He looked at me the way a man might look down on a particularly venomous insect. His guards stared at me, but there was not a lot they could do. I had a shotgun and they did not. They had all been thoroughly scanned before entry and their weapons had been removed. I had been instructed to perform another set of checks before they got close. Just to make a point.

Once I had completed the search the cardinal was allowed to approach Macharius's throne bearing the great sealed documents, which he presented to the Lord High Commander. The parchment looked impressive enough and Macharius gave every sign of scrutinising them closely.

'Are you satisfied with my credentials?' the cardinal inquired. He studied the luxurious furnishings of the chamber with a connoisseur's eye. I felt sure he was putting a value on every mobile statue, on every dragon-fur rug.

'It never hurts to be careful,' Macharius said.

'Now that we have established my *bona fides*, perhaps we could discuss the business that brought me here.'

'By all means,' Macharius said. The cardinal turned and looked at me and the others. It was clear he was not expecting to have to speak in front of underlings.

'You can say what you wish in front of Sergeant Lemuel and his men,' Macharius said. 'I trust them with my life.'

'You are entrusting them with more than that if you allow them to overhear the secrets of the Imperium.'

'These men swore the same oaths of loyalty to the Emperor that I did. They can be trusted to the same extent.'

The cardinal looked as if he wanted to argue, but it was clear that Macharius was not going to be moved on this point, and perhaps that *was* the point. 'As you wish,' he said.

'Speak your piece,' Macharius said.

'You have done extraordinary things,' said the cardinal. His voice had changed a little. He was now an orator speaking to a crowd, even if that crowd was just the Lord High Commander and the guards present. Macharius made a small ironic gesture with his right hand. 'You have done a greater service to the Imperium than any man in a score of generations, ten score generations. The time has come for the Imperium to show its appreciation.'

Macharius was smiling now. The smile did not reach his eyes. 'And what form does this appreciation take?'

'You are to be presented with honours suitable to the scale of your triumphs.'

'You have brought these with you, I presume.'

'How could I possibly do so? You are to be granted a

triumph on Holy Terra itself. You and select regiments are to present yourself there and be acclaimed by the elite of the Imperium.'

'I see,' said Macharius. Of course he did. Even I could see it. He was being removed from command of the crusade. Once separated from his armies it was doubtful he would be allowed to return. 'Of course, the commanders who are present on this world will come with me. I could hardly neglect them, or fail to share the glory with them, since they are as responsible for victory as much as I.'

Cardinal Septimus paused for a moment as if this were not quite what he expected to hear. 'They will be honoured in their time. You are the one to whom all the glory has accrued. You are the one whose sole triumph must be celebrated.'

Macharius tilted his head to one side. I would not have liked to have been the man he studied in such a way. It reminded me too much of a great predator studying a herbivore. 'I understand.'

'Good. I shall have the ship prepared for departure. We must set out immediately.'

'Of course,' said Macharius. Septimus looked surprised, like a warrior who had come expecting a desperate struggle and achieved an easy victory.

'There are just a few details that must be taken care of before I depart to ensure a smooth transfer of command,' Macharius added.

'Naturally,' Septimus agreed. Having won the basic point, he was not going to quibble over details, but I could see his eyes narrowing for a moment, as if he suspected Macharius of planning something devious. Pleasantries were exchanged and a few minutes later the cardinal withdrew with every appearance of civility.

'So you have agreed to return to Terra,' Drake said. They were in Macharius's chambers now, surrounded by his honours, seated at his table, staring at each other across the regicide board.

'What else was I supposed to do?' Macharius replied. 'I cannot turn down a direct command from the Imperium.'

'Can't you?'

Macharius stared at the inquisitor. 'I trust you are not implying anything.'

It was clear that even Drake could overstep the mark. 'It has been my life's work to end the Great Schism,' said Macharius. 'I would not wish to undo it all at this late stage.'

Drake nodded. 'I would expect no less.'

'Of course, it is always possible that the cardinal's ship might be delayed by some unforeseen problems.'

Drake smiled a cold smile. 'He could always requisition others.'

'That will take time and those too might have problems.'

'They might.'

'And my departure may be delayed by other unforeseen circumstances.'

'That also is possible.'

'Do not misunderstand me, my friend,' said Macharius. 'I will visit Holy Terra. I will submit myself to the will of the

Ecclesiarchy, but I will do so in my own good time, when my work here is done.'

Drake nodded. 'As you say,' he said.

'Now, I want all of the information you have gathered about Loki and Richter.'

A frown passed across the inquisitor's face. He clearly did not appreciate this development, nor Macharius's mania on the subject, but he produced a folder containing a number of documents. 'These have arrived from the agents we left in place.'

I tried to imagine what it would be like to be left behind among heretics on a world like Loki, amid the walking dead. I tried to imagine how messages could be smuggled in and out of the system. I couldn't, but clearly Drake not only could but had.

The news was not good.

It was not long before another blow to Macharius's prestige descended. I stood guard in his throne room, idly surveying the great murals of Macharius's triumph on Malachite and noting that I was shown standing guard at his shoulder, when the doors were suddenly thrown open and a giant strode in, a barbaric figure encased in ceramite armour.

'Greetings, General Macharius,' he said, in a great booming voice. Macharius rose and bowed in the most formal manner then strode across the chequered mosaic of the floor to slap the giant on the back. The sound echoed across the chamber like a gunshot.

'Greetings, Logan Grimnar. It has been too long.' It had

been a number of years since we had fought alongside the Space Wolf on Demetrius. I frowned at the memories that the sight of him brought back. I had unpleasant recollections of that particular world and the things we had found there.

'Indeed,' said Grimnar. 'But it does my heart good to see you.'

'You did not come here just to exchange pleasantries, though,' said Macharius.

'No. The Great Wolf would have words with you.' There was something about the way Grimnar spoke, an odd undertone, that made me look at him twice. If I had not known better I would have said it was resentment. Of course, the Emperor's Chosen are above such things.

Macharius heard it too. Just for a moment a frown passed across his face. 'And he sent you as his personal messenger.'

'He does us both honour,' said Grimnar.

'A feast will be prepared,' said Macharius. He clearly remembered his last such encounter with the Wolves of Space. 'We shall meet as soon as he wishes.'

'This evening then,' said Grimnar. 'I will bear your words to him.'

And with that he turned on his heel and left. In anyone else it would have been a sign of profound disrespect, but Grimnar and his ilk were above the petty protocols of politeness that bound the rest of us. They were laws unto themselves and had been since before the foundation of the Imperium.

Macharius's gaze followed him gloomily. Clearly he

suspected that whatever had caused the Great Wolf to demand an audience could not be good.

CHAPTER SIXTEEN

It takes a lot of work to prepare a feast for a company of Space Wolves. The tables groaned under the weight of sides of beef, of whole sheep roasted on spits, of Lacedomean calix basted in their own blood and stuffed with steaks. Whole chickens sat on plates. Broached barrels of ale and tankards full of strong, fiery spirits sat beside every plate.

I looked out at the crowd of awed humans and mortal gods and I pledged I would not make the same mistake as last time. At the high table Ulrik Grimfang and his retinue sat with Macharius and all his generals. Cardinal Septimus was present too, smiling his too-satisfied smile, the servo-skulls still orbiting and seeming to take in everything with their dead, empty eyes. Across the chamber I saw Grimfang looking at me. His nostrils flared and he smiled, revealing massive fangs. He beckoned to me with one gauntleted hand and I could do little else but approach.

'You do not seem to be drinking so fiercely this time as you once did,' he said. It could have been taken as an insult by a man more suicidal than myself, but he was smiling in a way that was clearly meant to be friendly. It was hard to take the words in the spirit they were intended. Being smiled at by a Space Wolf is like being smiled at by a sabre-tooth.

'I am older now and perhaps wiser,' I said. He laughed. There was wild mirth in the sound that echoed through the room. It was a contagious sound, although from anyone else it would have sounded crazed. 'I find my stomach cannot take strong drink as well as it once did.'

'You did not dishonour yourself the last time,' he said.

'I thank you,' I said. There seemed little else to say.

'Logan Grimnar speaks well of you,' the Great Wolf said. 'You would do me honour by serving as my cupbearer.'

I looked over at Macharius. Much as I disliked the idea of refusing the Great Wolf anything, Macharius was my commander and it was him that I obeyed. He nodded almost imperceptibly.

I stood beside the Great Wolf and poured his drinks. It was a sign of favour, not a form of being demeaned, and I recognised it for what it was. Thus I came to be standing by the high table during the last exchange between Macharius and the Great Wolf.

'We have come to bid you farewell, General Macharius,' said Grimfang.

'Farewell?' Macharius frowned slightly. He was clearly calculating all the possible consequences of this declaration.

'We depart for the Gothic Sector. There is an orkish invasion there and we must fight.'

'There is fighting to be done here yet and glory to be gained,' said Macharius. He raised a glass and toasted the Great Wolf. Grimfang responded in kind, then said, 'It is as you say, but we have a duty to the Imperium and its defenceless people. Succour has been requested and we must grant it.'

I tried to imagine all that must be going through Macharius's mind at that point. He had just been told that his crusade was of less importance than this new invasion. The fact that this might well have been the truth in no way diminished the scale of the blow. The support of many Chapters of Space Marines, most importantly the personal support of the Space Wolves, had lent him great prestige, had made it seem to many that his campaign had enjoyed support at the highest spiritual and martial level. Its abandonment could not help but undermine that impression. It made a statement that more important things were happening elsewhere, that the crusade was not the focal event in the galaxy.

If these thoughts ran through Macharius's mind, and I am sure that they must have, he gave no sign of it and he knew better than to protest to Grimfang or attempt to change his mind. Not even Macharius's powers of persuasion or his great charisma were up to that.

The drinking continued, songs were sung, tales of the great

battles were retold, but a cloud had descended on the feast and did not lift for the entire evening.

The last song was sung, the last ale was drunk. With many protestations of friendship the Great Wolf and his retinue rose to make their departure, seemingly none the worse for wear from the vast amounts of ale and beef they had consumed.

The same could not be said for the mere mortals present. All of them, even Macharius, were showing signs of having consumed too much, to the extent that many of them seemed to have their thoughts written on their faces. Sober as I was, I took the opportunity to study them, knowing it would be a rare occasion indeed.

Macharius was all controlled charm. His words were not even slightly slurred and his movements had all their usual grace, but there was a narrowness around his eyes, and a grim twist at the corners of his lips that spoke of his anger to those who knew him well.

Drake's face was a mask. His eyes were pits into which you could stare and lose yourself. He seemed unusually thoughtful, as if he were measuring and weighing the events of the evening in his mind, turning things over from every angle, looking for some fault or advantage.

Cardinal Septimus's face was masked by a bland smile. Since his conversation with Macharius, he had been amiability itself, and he was quite as capable of interpreting the Space Wolves withdrawal of support as I was – more so. It all played towards his purposes. Indeed, at that moment,

I asked myself whether the departure of the Space Wolves, the request for their aid, might not have had something to do with him. It certainly removed one of the great props of Macharius's power and prestige. Who would have dared oppose him openly when it was quite clear he enjoyed the support of the Emperor's Angels?

Things had just become a lot murkier.

I thought I detected a look of satisfaction on General Crassus's toad face. Anything that weakened Macharius's position must strengthen his. Just at that moment his mask slipped a little and I knew who the chief conspirator against Macharius must be. As luck would have it, he glanced around and caught me looking at him. Our eyes met for a moment and he seemed to be weighing me up, considering me, then he let his glance slide away. I was not fooled – he knew who I was and he would remember me.

Logan Grimnar rose from where he had been sitting, the last of the Space Wolves to depart. His small retinue remained watching him as he loped over to Macharius and extended his hand.

'We have shed blood together, and fought beside each other. I owe you a debt of honour and it will be repaid.' I thought then that he was merely being diplomatic, throwing a sop to the Lord High Commander to soften the departure of his Chapter, but events were to prove differently.

Suddenly Cardinal Septimus looked a little less smug and General Crassus considerably more wary. Macharius smiled and said, 'I thank you, my friend. I will not forget this.'

He looked directly at Crassus and at the cardinal and said, 'I will not forget any of this.'

After the feast we escorted Macharius to his chambers. Once he was through the doors he seemed to shrink in on himself, to become a smaller man. He looked tired and angry and somehow diminished. I could see how much of a strain the banquet had been on him. He walked over to a cabinet, opened it and poured himself a drink, then slumped down in his chair.

He looked up at me and said, 'The Great Wolf did you more honour than he did me, Lemuel.'

I met his gaze and wondered how angry he was. There was a skull-like quality to his appearance, a gauntness I had not really noticed before, a tightness to the skin of his face. It came to me then that Macharius was very old, and he was finally showing his age, perhaps even dying. Even juvenat has its limits, after all.

'I am sorry about that, sir,' I said eventually. There did not seem to be much else that I could say. Macharius looked down at his regicide board, lifted a piece and toyed with it. 'They think it's over,' he said, so softly that no one but me could have heard it.

'Sir?' I was not sure whether he wanted to be overheard, whether he was even talking to me.

'I said they think it's over, that I am finished, that they can simply replace me and that things will go on.'

'I don't think they can, sir,' I said. They could, but it did not seem my place to say it.

'The Space Marines are going because they think there is no longer glory to be won here. The vultures will see this as a sign to attack.'

I kept quiet. He was speaking to himself, as old people sometimes do, as I could recall them doing back in the hive cities of Belial in my youth. More than ever I found myself wondering about Macharius's health, mental and otherwise.

'I will not be replaced until I am ready,' said Macharius. 'My work is not yet done.'

Looking at him then I wondered if he would think his work was ever done. He had lived on the absolute peak of power for so long I do not think he could imagine living anywhere else. And yet perhaps he was close to realising that in the whole Imperium there was only one man who was irreplaceable and he was encased in the Golden Throne. He rose from the chair, prowled over to a cabinet, produced a map and smoothed it out on the surface of a table. I recognised it at once. It was a map of Loki. He studied it with the intensity of a man contemplating his soul's salvation. I noticed that parts of it had been marked in blood-red ink. I suspected the map was part of the parcel of documents Drake had brought earlier.

After a moment, he seemed to realise that I was still there. 'That will be all, Lemuel,' he said.

I saluted and left him to himself.

Inquisitor Drake awaited me in my rooms. There was no need to ask how he had got there. There were no security systems he could not bypass and he was capable of ensuring that Ivan and Anton would not notice him. I was sure the pair were snoring away in their own chambers.

'You have come from the Lord High Commander's chamber,' Drake said. It was not a question. He knew everything that went on within the palace.

'Yes,' I said. I stared at him, and considered demanding that either he told me what he wanted or he got out. The feast, the departure of the Space Wolves and my last glimpse of Macharius had left me depressed. In the end, though, it turned out I was not quite so depressed as to be tired of living, so I remained silent.

'What did you think?'

'He is not best pleased by the Space Wolves departure,' I said. 'He sees it as a blow to his prestige.'

'Obviously, Lemuel. Obviously. I meant what did you think of him. How did he seem to you?'

'Tired.'

'Tired? Is that all?'

'Is that not enough? For a man like Macharius to be tired is unthinkable. I have never seen him like this before. It's…'

The word had left my mouth before I could recall it. Drake stood taller and more attentively. It was too much to hope that he had not noticed.

'It's what?' he said. 'You were going to say something.'

'Nothing,' I said.

'Do not lie to me, Sergeant Lemuel. We have known each other too long for that to work.'

I supposed it was true, but I found myself resenting this

calm, authoritative man with his aura of absolute certainty, of knowing me better than I knew myself.

'Speak!' he said and I am sure there was some powerful compulsion laced into his words, backed by his strange psyker powers.

'He seems old, as if the juvenat has ceased to work, as if he is wearing out.'

The words hung in the air for a long time. Neither of us said anything. Drake took a seat in one of the chairs. He poured himself a drink from a hip flask and then much to my astonishment, he offered me one. I took it, wondering if perhaps it was poisoned. I dismissed the idea. If Drake wanted me dead, I would be dead.

'The juvenat *has* ceased working,' he said, at last.

'No,' I said. I simply did not want to believe it.

'It stops working for everybody, eventually,' Drake said. 'Otherwise we would all live to be as old as the Emperor.'

He took a sip of his drink then raised it to the light and turned it with his long slender fingers. He looked at it from all angles and I began to wonder whether despite appearances the inquisitor might not be somewhat drunk. His powers enabled him to process as much alcohol as a Space Marine with as little effect if he wished it, but perhaps he did not wish it, this night of all nights.

'I have seen the medical reports,' Drake said. 'His body is suffering from advanced metabolic deterioration. It does not really show yet, but the process is accelerating. It will affect him mentally eventually, if it has not already.' There was a certainty in his manner that made it impossible to doubt him.

'You are saying that he is dying, that all those halted years are going to catch up with him?'

Drake nodded. 'In a way that will likely be most unpleasant.'

'Why are you telling me?'

'Because you are as close to him as anyone. You will notice it sooner or later, if you have not already.'

Once it had been pointed out, it was impossible not to remember the tiny slips, the small failures.

'Do you really think he would have lost on Loki if he had been the same man as he was on Karsk?' Drake asked.

'Is this why the Imperium wants him replaced?'

Drake shook his head. 'The Imperium does not want him replaced. People want him replaced, people with a great deal of power within the Imperium. And the people who want him replaced want him replaced so that they can have his power, prestige and position. Some of them want to be the next Macharius. Most of them simply want power. Macharius is just an obstacle in the way of their ambitions.'

'He cannot be replaced,' I said. 'He is a great man. None greater.'

'You know that. I know that. There are people who choose to believe otherwise. Worse, there are people who would disgrace him if they could, for they do not like to live in a world containing those greater than themselves. They would pull him down to their level if they could. He has outwitted them for a long time but he is slipping. Everyone does eventually.'

'Even you, inquisitor?'

'That remains to be seen,' he said, 'but yes, one day perhaps, even me.'

'Once again I ask you why you are telling me this.'

'Perhaps because I have to tell somebody, and you at least are trustworthy. Also, you are close to Macharius. If you notice anything, you will tell me.'

'You are very certain of that.'

'It is in Macharius's best interests and it is in your best interests. These are dangerous times, for all of us.'

I wondered then at the pressure Drake must have felt himself to be under. He was a friend and long-time comrade of Macharius, one of the architects of the crusade, and yet he too was a servant of the Imperium and somewhere he too must have hidden masters with their own agenda.

'You won't let them replace him, will you?' I don't know to this day why I asked. Perhaps I simply sought reassurance.

'Replace him, no. You were correct earlier. He is irreplaceable.'

He departed, leaving me with much to think about.

CHAPTER SEVENTEEN

The next morning, Macharius looked like his old self. It was as if the previous evening had been a bad dream and I had imagined what I had seen and my conversation with Drake. I would have been a lot happier if that had been the case.

Drake was in Macharius's council chamber. He gave no sign that we had talked the night before. Tarka was there and Crassus and the other generals. Macharius greeted them all affably, and it was obvious, looking at them, that they were surprised by how good his mood was. I wondered if this was just his way of keeping his rivals off-balance. It was always something Macharius had excelled at.

'Good morning, gentlemen,' Macharius said. 'I have good news for you. Before I depart for Holy Terra, I intend to settle matters once and for all with Richter and his heretics, and leave the crusade in a much stronger position.'

Cardinal Septimus shot Macharius a surprised look. Clearly he had not been expecting anything like this. 'How do you propose to do that, Lord High Commander?' he asked.

Macharius tapped the side of his nose. 'At the moment that must remain a secret, but I have discovered a huge flaw in the enemy's defences.'

'It is a pity that you could not have discovered it earlier,' said General Crassus. All eyes swivelled to look at him. It was a direct criticism of the supreme commander and not one anybody would have dared voice in the past. It was a measure of how much respect for Macharius had slipped, and yet there was something about the Lord High Commander's manner that had indeed unsettled his potential successors. No one rushed to support Crassus. Everyone waited to hear what Macharius had to say.

He smiled with all his old charm. 'All of us make mistakes, old comrade,' he said. 'Even you have.'

The words hung in the air, leaving everyone to wonder whether Macharius meant during some past campaign or whether he was referring to the current campaign to have him replaced. It was an ambiguity no one, least of all General Crassus, seemed to want to have cleared up.

'How long will this take?' Cardinal Septimus asked.

'No more than a month,' said Macharius. 'Certainly no longer than it will take for your ship to be prepared for the long voyage to Terra.'

'It would perhaps be as well for you to inform us of the weaknesses you have discovered in the defences of Loki,' said General Tarka. 'In case anything should happen to you.'

He sounded serious – he clearly hadn't lost all of his respect for Macharius's military prowess. He believed that if Macharius said he had found a flaw then a flaw there must be. It was only natural. With a record like Macharius's, most people would have believed that.

'What could possibly happen to me here on Acheron?' said Macharius. 'I am surrounded by the finest troops of the Imperium. No enemy threatens. I am in perfect health.'

Tarka opened his mouth as if he were about to say something, but then snapped it closed again. I wondered if Drake was the only one who had access to the Lord High Commander's medical records. Such a thing was supposed to be a very closely guarded secret, but bribes could buy almost anything provided they were big enough.

Cardinal Septimus glanced at Tarka and something wordless seemed to pass between them. The general said nothing more. I wondered if Macharius really had found a chink in the heretics' defences and part of me agreed with what Crassus had said. It was indeed a pity that Macharius had not spotted it before all the slaughter we had endured there. I kept my face expressionless. The important thing was that Macharius had found us a route to victory.

I could not let myself doubt that.

The Drunken Ratling was crowded. Sergei Krimov made space for me in the corner booth. He ordered drinks and introduced me to a couple of friends. They were not from his regiment, though they wore the uniform. They did not sound like Belial Hivers. They did not sound like anybody from Belial at all.

They did not look at all daunted by the suspicious looks I shot at them. 'These are friends of mine,' Sergei said. 'They wanted to meet you and I could not see the harm.'

His face was carefully bland but I guessed that this was anything but a chance meeting. Perhaps the whole thing was a setup from our very first encounter. I took a drink and tried not to let the thoughts show on my face.

'This is Konstantin and this is Mikhail,' said Sergei. If those were their real names, I was a Space Wolf. I toyed with saying so, but it hardly seemed diplomatic. Konstantin was a big man with cropped hair and a nose that had been flattened by a blow of great force. Mikhail was smaller and lighter. He had a writhing way of turning that made me think of a weasel.

'Pleased to make your acquaintance,' said Konstantin. Mikhail said nothing.

'Likewise,' I said. 'Which part of the Masterforge do you hail from?'

Konstantin ignored my question, probably because he did not have an answer for it. Instead, he said, 'You are one of the heroes who guard the Lord High Commander.'

'I am part of the Lion Guard,' I said. 'The uniform gives it away, I suppose.'

'It is a post of quite awesome responsibility,' Konstantin said, 'and no few risks.'

'The life of a Guardsman is full of those,' I said, 'as you must know yourself.'

The more I talked with Konstantin and looked at Mikhail, the less I was sure this was true. There was something about their manner that suggested they had never been common soldiers, had perhaps never been soldiers at all.

'True, true,' he said, 'but defending Macharius must be especially dangerous. There are assassins everywhere...'

'Surely not here on Acheron,' I said. 'No one could be so disloyal.'

'Alas, perhaps even here,' said Konstantin. He had quite a light voice for so large a man, and a confiding tone of voice.

'If you know of any conspiracy against the Lord High Commander you should inform the proper authorities,' I said.

'Perhaps that is what I am doing,' he said. Mikhail studied his drink, studied his fingernails, glanced at me and returned to studying his drink. I wondered exactly who he was and what he was doing here.

'Perhaps?' Sergei rose from the table and said, 'I shall get some more drinks.' It seemed he did not want to be present for this part of the conversation.

'You do not seem so surprised about talk of a conspiracy,' said Konstantin. 'Perhaps you have heard talk of such things, of such disloyalty.'

'I have heard that there are those who are not happy with the Lord High Commander's recent generalship.'

'There are always disaffected souls,' said Konstantin. I was starting to wonder who he really was. Could he perhaps be one of Drake's agents testing my loyalty? Or was he something else? 'There are those who plot a change in the leadership of the crusade.'

I said nothing. There are times when it is best simply to keep your mouth shut. Konstantin looked at Mikhail, as if seeking support, but the smaller one seemed too wrapped up in the contemplation of his glass, so Konstantin went on speaking.

'A man who uncovered such a conspiracy could become wealthy,' he said.

I wondered if he was seeking a reward for information. It seemed unlikely. There were far better people to approach if such were the case. Of course, it was possible that I was the only potential contact he had.

'Perhaps,' I said.

'You could become a wealthy man if you uncovered such a conspiracy.' There was a strange emphasis on the way he said the words, and I suddenly became aware that Mikhail, despite all appearances to the contrary, was paying close attention to what was being said. He seemed in some subtle way to be straining at an invisible leash.

'Perhaps,' I said.

'You would like to become a wealthy man,' Mikhail said. He was making a statement, passing a considered judgement.

'Who would not?'

'As one of Macharius's Guards you must be rich already.'

'You are sadly misinformed if you think that.'

'The Lord High Commander is not generous?'

'The Lord High Commander expects his soldiers to perform the duties they swore to. Service to the Emperor is reward enough.'

'And you believe in doing your duty?'

'I believe in serving the Emperor.'

'Serving Macharius is not the same as serving the Emperor.'

'At the moment it is,' I said.

'Ah, at the moment,' said Mikhail. 'That is an important qualification.'

'And if Macharius were to be replaced, as it seems he is, you would serve his successor just as loyally.'

'Of course,' I said.

'Tell me, what do you think will become of you when Macharius departs?' he asked. 'He will have no more need of a personal guard.'

'I will serve as I am told.'

'You will be returned to your original regiment,' said Mikhail.

'I can think of worse things,' I said.

'I can think of better.'

'Why don't you tell me of them,' I said.

'You could be kept on as part of the retinue of the new commander, promoted, given special assignments, even retire with honour and great wealth.'

'That would be pleasant,' I said. 'But we were talking about conspiracies against Macharius. We seem to have come a long way from there.'

'There is evidence to be gathered, reports to be made,' said Konstantin. 'We will let you know when things are finalised. For now we must depart. It has been pleasant meeting you. I believe we shall meet again.'

'I look forward to it,' I said. They rose and bowed and departed. Sergei returned from the bar. I could not help but notice he had only brought two drinks.

'Interesting conversation?' he asked.

'Very,' I said.

He smiled. 'I thought it might be.'

I was summoned to see the inquisitor as soon as I returned to the palace. It was becoming quite a habit of his. His bodyguard escorted me to his door and checked me for weapons before allowing me to pass inside. That had not happened in a long time.

'Good evening, Lemuel,' he said. He was standing with his back to me, looking out the window. Across from us the coffin-black starscrapers limned the night, black flames dancing over them. I did not doubt he was aware of me. If he could not follow my reflection in the window, his strange psyker powers gave him other senses than those we mortals are stuck with.

'You wished to see me, inquisitor,' I said. He turned to face me. His cowl was down and his lean, pale face was underlit by the glow-globe on his desk. His features gave me no hint of what he was thinking. He moved to the desk, sat down in the floating chair, leaned forward and steepled his fingers. He looked at me over them as if sighting a gun. I could not help but notice that a bolt pistol sat on his desk, unholstered. It was a not very subtle message.

'I understand you were out drinking again this evening,' he said.

'I was.' I considered telling him that I failed to see what concern that was of his, but I already had some idea of where this was going.

'You met some old friends of yours.'

'One old friend,' I said. 'Or rather one former comrade from the Seventh Belial and two of his friends.'

'Who were they?'

I gave the names of Konstantin and Mikhail and their descriptions.

'And what did you think of them?'

'Their conversation was elliptical.'

'How so?'

'They hinted at conspiracies against Macharius. They hinted that they might be seeking rewards. They hinted at a lot of things and in the end said nothing.'

'Why do you think they did that?'

'I don't know.'

'You don't know, Lemuel, but you can guess. You are a clever man.'

'I think they were feeling me out, to see how I would react to such talk. I get the impression they are hoping that I will become their agent.'

'Why would they think that is possible?'

'I don't know, inquisitor. Perhaps you can tell me.' He looked at me for a long time. I felt cold sweat appear on my brow, but I was damned if I was going to say anything more. Eventually he smiled, showing his small white teeth. It was not a pleasant expression. There was no humour in it.

'Your friends, Konstantin and Mikhail...'

'They are not my friends.'

'I would be obliged if you did not interrupt me again, Sergeant Lemuel.' The words were quietly spoken but there was a world of menace behind them. 'Your friends, or perhaps I should say, your soon-to-be friends, Konstantin and Mikhail, work for Major Kelly, who is chief of staff, chief intelligence gatherer and some would say master of assassins for General Crassus.'

He paused, glanced at his data-slate, then looked at me directly. 'You don't seem entirely surprised.'

'General Crassus seems a most ambitious man,' I said.

'He is. He sees himself as the chief candidate to replace the Lord High Commander when he departs for Terra.'

'Is he?'

'That would be Cardinal Septimus's decision, but my guess is that he is. Or at least he would be, if Macharius actually departed.'

'The Lord High Commander has already said he will.'

'What the Lord High Commander says he will do and what he actually does may prove to be two different things, Lemuel. It seems that General Crassus has already begun to think so. He is not alone in this. All of Macharius's commanders know about his talent for feint and deception.'

'As you say, inquisitor.'

'And you are wondering why I am telling you this.'

'I am sure you have your reasons, sir.'

'And I am sure you can guess them.'

'I am a simple man, sir. I like to have my duties and responsibilities spelled out for me.'

He shrugged. 'If either of these two men approach you again, or anyone else does in a similar capacity, you will agree to whatever they ask, and then report the matter to me.'

'Even if they suggest disloyalty to Lord High Commander Macharius, sir?'

'Particularly if they do that.'

'That would be treason, sir.'

'You are worried that you might be branded a traitor if you do this.'

I nodded.

'You will be branded a traitor if you do not.'

I stared at him. 'What do you mean?'

'There is already enough evidence to suggest you are part of a conspiracy, Lemuel.'

'I can assure you I am not.'

'And I believe you, and I trust you, which is why I am asking you to do this. These are interesting times, and many things hang in the balance. Your duty is to see to Macharius's safety and I am asking you to do your duty.'

'You wish me to help smoke out potential traitors, sir.'

'Precisely so.' He paused for a minute. I looked over his shoulder at the black flames dancing over the black starscrapers and considered his words. Drake did not really need any evidence against me. He had the power to make me disappear at his whim. I was not sure whether he really believed in my innocence, but I could see that did not matter to him. I was simply a tool he was going to use in his hunt for traitors against Macharius. I was a pawn in his great game.

'I will do it,' I said, as smartly as I could, as if I were volunteering for dangerous duty, as if I had any real choice in the matter.

'I am glad to hear that,' Drake said, and sounded as if he really meant it. He stood up and I noticed that there was a hypodermic in his hand. He indicated that I should come closer. I wondered what he was going to do.

'There's no need to be so skittish,' Drake said. 'If I wanted to kill you, I would not need to do it this way.'

'What is in that?' I said. The needle was very long and sharp and I did not like the way its point glittered in the glow-globe's light.

'It contains a very powerful anti-venom,' he said. 'It should increase your resistance to all drugs and poisons for the period of about one moon.'

'You think someone is going to try to poison me?'

'I think someone may try to use certain serums on you.' As he spoke, he slid the needle into my arm. It stung and then an odd coolness spread from it. He reached out and touched my forehead with his fingers. I suddenly felt dizzy. Strange images flickered through my head. He spoke words and I knew I would remember them some day but I could not remember them now. They vanished from my consciousness like mist before a strong wind, leaving only the awareness that I had once possessed the knowledge of them.

I tried to move and found that I could not. My muscles seemed paralysed and I felt a completely stark and utter terror the like I had not felt before. This was what it was like to be totally helpless when danger threatened. My head reeled with the knowledge that something had been done to my thoughts. I glared at Drake, in that moment hating and fearing him in equal measure.

'Tell no one about this little chat.'

I nodded even as I wondered whether Drake had his own agenda in this. I was beginning to get the sense that my life might be in real peril here.

'You are dismissed, Lemuel.'

CHAPTER EIGHTEEN

I met Sergei in the tavern. Konstantin and Mikhail were with him. They were dressed as they had been previously. They greeted me warmly as I sat down in their private booth, which I could not help but notice was in a corner, and commanded clear lines of sight to the exits. Drinks were placed on the table by Sergei and nothing was said except toasts until we had downed a few. All three of them looked at me with slightly glazed eyes that were supposed to hint at drunkenness. I suspected they were less so than I.

'Things go well in the palace?' Konstantin asked. He was taking the lead again, but as before I suspected that Mikhail was his superior.

I nodded. 'Things go as well as can be expected.'

'The Lord High Commander makes ready to depart?'

'That is not my place to say,' I said.

'Your discretion is to be admired,' said Mikhail. 'But everyone knows he has agreed to go to Terra with Cardinal Septimus. Or has he not?'

'Macharius does not confide his plans in me.'

'But you are his trusted bodyguard.'

'And I will remain so as long as I keep his secrets,' I said. If these men were really trying to recruit me into some conspiracy I was not going to make it easy for them. Sergei smiled and nodded as if I were being very wise.

'You are also on good terms with Inquisitor Drake,' said Mikhail suddenly.

'I would not go that far.'

'You talked to him after the last time you saw us,' he said. He was smiling unpleasantly and I felt the urge to punch him in his smirking face.

'I was summoned to his presence,' I said.

'What did he want?'

'He wanted to know who I had been seeing.'

'You told him, of course.'

'I told him I had been drinking with Sergei here and he had introduced me to you two, and that you claimed to have information concerning a conspiracy against Macharius.'

'What did he say to that?'

'He told me to keep in touch with you and report to him any conversations we might have.'

I saw Sergei and Konstantin exchange glances. 'Is that all?'

'Drake is a busy man,' I said. 'I am sorry to have to tell you this but I doubt you are all that important to him. I doubt I am either.'

'Yet he takes enough interest to ask about us.'

'These are troubled times. Like I said, I don't think you are that important to him, but if you insist I can bring your names up again.' I let a little malice show in my voice.

'That won't be necessary,' said Mikhail.

'So do you have any more information about this supposed conspiracy?'

'We do, but first we have some questions to put to you.'

'And what would those be?'

My skin felt tingly now, and his outline swayed a little in my field of vision. 'This is strong booze,' I said. Mikhail's smile became ever more mocking. 'I can't say I've noticed,' he said.

'What questions did you have?' His face seemed to be growing larger. It became just about the only thing in the room I could focus on.

'Do you think Macharius really intends to go to Terra?'

'Not if he can help it,' I said. The words just seemed to slip out. Mikhail looked very friendly and very trustworthy. Surely it was safe to tell him.

'And do you think this is wise?'

'I don't think it's wise for anyone to disobey a direct order from the Imperium.'

'You think Macharius can get away with it.'

'If anyone can, he can.'

'And you, a sworn soldier of the Emperor, don't see anything wrong with that.'

'It is wrong to disobey the Emperor's commands,' I said.

'And yet you have just said Macharius might.'

'I did, didn't I?'

'Do you think Macharius is right to do so?'

'No.'

'What do you think of Macharius?'

'He is the greatest general alive, a hero of the Imperium, a legend…'

'But?'

'But he has made mistakes. He is not the man he once was, not the man I once served.'

I was surprised to hear myself saying the words, even more surprised by the fact that I believed them to be the truth.

'He has made mistakes, you say?' Mikhail's voice was friendly but disbelieving. 'Where?'

'On Loki. We died in the hundreds of thousands there and only afterwards did he reveal he has discovered the weaknesses of Richter's position.'

'You resent that.'

'Yes. I saw thousands of good men die. I saw friends of mine die.' Again I was surprised to find the depths of anger in me.

'Some would say that what you are saying is traitorous,' said Mikhail. I stared at them. There was no denying it. My head was swirling. I realised that I was more than drunk – I had been drugged. It seemed that Drake had lied to me about the anti-toxin.

'You drugged me…' I said. They looked at me and laughed as I fell face forward onto the table.

They lifted me to my feet. I tried to call for help but the words just came out as drunken, slurred babbling. I saw heads turn to watch me go, but all they saw was a drunk soldier being carried out by his not-quite-so-drunk comrades. There was nothing unusual about it.

I was bundled into the back of a groundcar, large and luxurious, and driven off into the darkness. I was aware of the heavy door thunking shut behind me and large men getting in.

The car drove off into the night, moving through the corpse-black, mirrored starscrapers. I was only partially aware of my surroundings. I could hear voices as if from a great way off. They seemed to be discussing something of no great importance, so I lay there, trying to avoid being sick. It suddenly seemed of great importance that I avoid vomiting over the clean, luxurious interior of this great vehicle.

The car drew up at a run-down building on the edge of the city and slipped through a raised door which slid down behind it. I knew that I had vanished off the face of the planet as far as anyone looking for me was concerned.

I was taken into a huge room, lit by dimly glowing globes that just seemed to hover in the air. A man in white robes stood there. He indicated a surgical table with one long lean hand. The men carrying me put me down on it. I tried to struggle, but my hands just flailed the air uselessly as I was strapped down. The man in white robes produced a long hypodermic. If he started making promises about anti-toxins I was going to hit him, I thought, if I was capable of it. I noticed that he was wearing small pebble glasses that caught the light. At times they were like mirrors full of flame. At times I could see cold grey eyes studying me.

My sleeve was pulled up. The needle went in. This time it burned like fire. My muscles suddenly felt under control again. My mind felt lucid. I tried to rise but I was strapped down.

The medic studied me the way a man might study a new and particularly interesting form of insect. He said, 'I am going to give you another injection. It will not hurt you as long as you answer me truthfully. If you answer all the questions with the truth no harm will come to you.'

'For some strange reason, I don't believe you,' I said.

'It matters little whether you believe me or not. You will answer, and you will answer truthfully – your life depends on it.'

I did believe that, so I remained silent. Another injection was given and suddenly things did not seem so bad. I felt relaxed and amiable and I wondered why I had been so bothered just a few minutes ago; after all, these people were friendly.

The questions began, about Macharius, about how I felt about him, about my loyalty. I answered honestly. I spoke of my doubts and resentments and as I did so the questions took on a different tone. I was asked whether I really was prepared to oppose Macharius and what reward I would do it for. I spoke openly and honestly and was surprised to find I had a price, a high one, but it was there. The medic nodded as I talked and I realised what seemed like a high price to me seemed like a small price to him and I told him so. The price went up. He smiled and I could see that he was pleased. He wanted to help me. He wanted me to be happy. He wanted me to have a price and I knew that no matter how high it was he would meet it.

In the end, the questioning stopped and my white-robed interrogator looked over at Konstantin and Mikhail. 'He is telling the truth,' he said. 'He will betray Macharius if his price is met.'

The two men looked at each other and then at me. They were measuring me now, testing me, weighing what I had said against other things that they knew, and I could see that my life hung on their decision. If they decided they did not believe their medic friend they had no reason for letting me live. I looked back at them, numb and a little afraid. I could just move my head. There was no chance of me breaking free from the table. Even if I did I was surrounded by enemies.

Konstantin looked at the medic. 'You are sure?'

'Certain. At this dosage, there is no chance he could lie to us. This man is, for our purposes at least, trustworthy.'

Mikhail still looked dubious. I could tell he did not like me, but then again, it looked like I was the sort of man he had been sent to find. He knelt down beside me and spoke very slowly and very carefully. 'I am going to let you up now. Do nothing sudden and nothing stupid and you will become a very wealthy and powerful man. Do you understand me?'

I nodded. He undid the straps. I noticed a small but powerful-looking pistol was pointing right at me. Konstantin held something similar.

I was led out into another room.

* * *

This room was better furnished. A bottle of Belial whisky sat on the table along with a few glasses. Konstantin poured some and offered it to me. I shook my head.

'You'll forgive my reluctance,' I said, 'but after my last drink with you I am not inclined to take another.'

Konstantin smiled at that, no hard feelings. 'I am sorry, but we had to do this. We needed to know that you are the sort of man to do what is needed and not betray us.'

'A traitor, you mean.' I could not keep the bitterness out of my voice. No one likes to discover they have a price.

'You are not a traitor to the Imperium, Macharius is. He refuses to obey orders from his superiors. He refuses to make way for his successors. You said yourself he is slipping. It is time he stood aside and let those who are still capable get on with the job.'

I thought about him and I thought of the vast whirlpool of intrigue that swirled over this planet. I tried to tell myself that this was only to be expected, that the great generals were all products of the Schism, that they were used to thinking in terms of personal ambition and personal glory. Macharius had once overcome them on the field and bound them to his service; now they saw the chance to break away and follow their own personal interests again. All of them looked at what Richter had done and thought *I could do that*, and Septimus had offered them a way to do it and still remain loyal to the Imperium.

Mikhail said, 'We must apologise for what we did. We are playing for high stakes and we needed to know whether you were trustworthy.'

'I think the question is not whether I am trustworthy but whether you are,' I said.

'We have no reason to betray you. We must trust each other.'

'Really,' I said.

'Yes. If you betray us then you fall with us. We have a record of all you have said.'

'I was drugged,' I said.

'So you will claim. But your words were true, were they not?'

'Yes,' I conceded.

'And it does no one any good for word of any of this to become public. The crusade must present a united front even after Macharius is gone,' Mikhail said.

'Especially after Macharius is gone,' said Konstantin.

'He is not gone yet,' I said.

'But he will be soon,' said Konstantin. 'One way or another.'

'We will return to the tavern now,' said Mikhail, 'and we will drink.'

'Yes,' I said. 'That seems like the best thing to do.'

'You did something to my mind,' I said to Drake. He sat behind his desk and studied the gargoyle lantern. His face was shadowy in its under light.

'If I had not you would now be dead,' he said. 'Those men treated you with powerful truth drugs in dosages that were very close to fatal.'

'I said things,' I said and fumbled for the words to explain what I meant.

'You said things that you have thought in your secret heart,' Drake said. 'You spoke aloud doubts that you have carried for a long time.'

'Yes. No. But…'

'Because you have doubts does not mean you are disloyal,' Drake said. 'It means you are human and that you are quite intelligent.'

I looked at him. It was not what I would have expected him to say. He always seemed a fanatic in his own way. He smiled. 'I can assure you that dealing with doubt was one of the earliest parts of my training and the most comprehensive.'

'They seemed very sure Macharius will go,' I said. 'One way or another.'

'Oh yes,' said Drake. 'They ought to be. I have let it be known, through some informers we share, that Macharius has no intention of standing down.'

'What?'

He raised an eyebrow. He was not used to lowly sergeants taking that tone with him.

'We are surrounded by conspirators here. They need to be drawn out.'

'Is that not rather dangerous? We are outnumbered by more than ten to one.'

'Only if all the regiments unite against us. That will not happen.'

'I wish I shared your certainty,' I said.

'You are assuming that all of Macharius's potential replacements are prepared to work together, Lemuel,' he said, sounding like a schoolmaster explaining the facts to a particularly dim pupil. 'Even a most cursory examination of the situation will show you that is not the case. Simply because a man would like to replace Macharius does not mean that he will support another man's claim to do so. Indeed there are many here who would rather see Macharius stay than have one of their rivals take his place. That is one reason the Lord High Commander has remained in command for so long.'

'I thought it was because he was appointed to the task by the Imperium,' I said.

'There is no need to sound so sardonic, Lemuel. It does not suit you. Of course, Macharius was put in charge, but many of those generals had no respect for the writ of the Imperium before he forced them to have. They were the most successful warlords of the Schism and many of them served the Imperium in name only and only when it suited them. If they did not fear Macharius and covet his position they might well go back to doing so.'

'Then you play a very dangerous game by baiting them.'

'Macharius will not live forever,' he said. 'That is a self-evident truth. Before that happens those who serve him must be brought to heel or the Schism will start all over again.'

My realisation of where this was all going must suddenly have become evident on my face. 'If they are found to be betraying Macharius, they will be discredited.'

He smiled, a teacher whose dim pupil has shown a sudden, unexpected flash of understanding. 'It's always good to have a reason to remove someone. It's even better if that reason is a true one.'

I wondered then at the cynicism of this man, and whether he realised that his own reach might exceed his grasp. The truth of it was that Macharius was surrounded by grasping, opportunistic, ambitious men, and Drake was not the least of them. The difference was that I could understand what it was that the generals sought. I could not understand what it was that motivated him.

'I seek what is best for the Imperium, Lemuel,' Drake said. I wondered whether he had read my mind or whether what I was thinking was simply written on my face for him to read.

'You are playing games with all our lives,' I said.

'It is not really your place to judge me, Lemuel,' he said. His tone was mild but there was steel in his voice.

'Someone has to,' I muttered under my breath.

CHAPTER NINETEEN

I was not surprised to find Anna awaiting me in my chambers. 'You look somewhat the worse for wear,' she said.

'It's been a long night,' I said, stripping off my tunic and sliding into the bed alongside her. She leaned forward and licked my shoulder. It was not in the least erotic. Nor was it meant to be.

'Penthalium,' she said. 'And traces of Morathian anti-venom.'

'You can taste that in my sweat?' I asked.

'Along with a lot of alcohol and some mild narcotics,' she said.

'It's been one of those nights,' I said.

'You have just come from seeing Inquisitor Drake,' she said, 'and someone has been administering truth drugs to you. Given the age of the traces, it was not him.'

'You are about to amaze me with your powers of deduction, are you?'

She smiled at me. 'I am not your enemy, Leo. I may be one of the few people around here who is not, right about now.'

'What do you mean by that?'

'Inquisitor Drake is using you as bait in a trap for some very dangerous men.'

'Did he tell you that?'

'He does not need to. I can see the pattern of things as well as you.'

'You're doing better than me if you can see any pattern.'

'You were abducted this evening and someone gave you truth drugs. Presumably so they could find out what you know?'

'Very good,' I said.

'And what everybody is concerned about just now is Macharius and whether he will go to Terra.' She looked at me and I could tell she was reading me as she always could. 'That's only part of it though. It goes deeper than that. Since Drake is interested in all this, you are part of some scheme of his.'

Some movement of mine confirmed this to her, or perhaps she already knew. She was very well informed. 'He is using you as bait, feeding you information he wants others to pick up on.'

'Is that what you think?'

'Leo, don't try to deceive me. You are not capable of it. I know Drake is feeding disinformation to the agents of half the would-be Macharius replacements. It is his way. He will draw them out and then he will move against them. Or so he thinks.'

'What will stop him?'

'Look around you, Leo. Times are changing. Macharius is no longer secure on his throne. Drake is his shadow, whether he likes it or not. His star rose with Macharius. His star will fall with him, unless he makes a transition to standing behind someone else, whispering in their ear.'

'You think he would really do that?'

'You think he wouldn't? Drake is a political animal, Leo. They all are. You are in a tank full of mud sharks.'

'Of which you are one, if an exceedingly beautiful one.'

She looked at me rather sadly I thought, and considered her response for a long, nerve-wracking time. 'Yes,' she said. 'I am. But for my own small personal reasons I am inclined to keep you alive if I can.'

'That does not sound very cheerful.'

'Wake up! What is left of the crusade is sliding out of anyone's control. Macharius is a sick man. Drake is scrambling to try to keep the whole doomed structure from sliding over the edge of anarchy. The generals are pushing and tugging at it from all sides to try to get what they can. This is a disaster just waiting to happen, Leo, and you are standing right in the middle of it. You'll be right there when the earthquake hits and it all comes tumbling down.'

'So will you.'

'The difference is that I already have a way to get out.'

'I was offered one myself tonight,' I said and then I stopped and wondered if her whole speech had not simply been a lever to get me to admit that. She showed me the sort of smile a wolf shows sheep.

'By whom? By the agents of General Crassus? I would not put too much faith in them if I were you, Leo.'

'I am not entirely stupid,' I said. She reached out and ruffled my hair.

'No,' she said. 'You are not.'

'Anna,' I said. 'There is no way out for me. Whatever happens, I stand behind Macharius. I always have and I always will.'

She looked away for a moment and then said, 'Loyalty has always been your strong point, for better or worse. You are loyal to Macharius and you are loyal to me in your way.' There was nothing much I could say to that. 'It will get you killed in the end.'

'I am an Imperial Guardsman, Anna. I have already lived far longer than I expected when I signed up. And far better too. And that's down to Macharius and to you.'

She kissed me then and we talked no more. There were other things to say and other ways of saying them.

The camp of the Seventh Belial lay on the edge of the city, beyond the circle of those great black starscrapers. In theory, I was simply visiting my old regiment. In practice it was a lot more complicated than that. There were still people there who remembered me, after all these years, although not so many as I would have liked, and I was wearing the green tunic of the Lion Guard, which both made my visit conspicuous and gave it a political undertone. All of the soldiers watching me wondered whether I could be spying or whether I was bringing word from Macharius to their officers. It was a tense little march.

I walked along the ranks of tents and pre-fabricated huts, between the lines of battered Baneblades and shell-marked Shadowswords and I felt a growing nostalgia. I stood in the silhouettes of the great armoured beasts and felt their power and buried rage. I sensed their animating spirits and their fury and I wondered if the time was coming when they would be unleashed on their fellow Imperial soldiers. Such potent armoured vehicles were rare on Acheron at this moment, and whichever side they were on would have a huge advantage in any coming conflict.

Even as that thought occurred to me, I felt a growing fear in my belly. I was taking it for granted that not only was battle possible, it was likely. I was imagining a time when all of these men around me, my former comrades, would be my enemies. It brought back strange memories of Loki and the walking dead. Some of them, too, had once been comrades. Perhaps in this, we were all of us walking dead men.

I nodded to soldiers as I walked past and saluted officers who looked at me with cool, curious looks. There was a time when I would have felt daunted and resentful, back when they had been my social superiors from Belial and I was just a hive-boy who had joined the Guard. Now, I did not really care. I had spent more than half my life around aristocrats with far greater power than these men would ever have, whose families were far better connected, and I had not been so impressed by those. Why should I let these people intimidate me? And yet the fact that I still asked myself that question showed that it was important to me.

I headed towards the tent row and number that Sergei Krimov had given me. He was sitting outside, no doubt waiting for my two old friends Konstantin and Mikhail. I threw Sergei an ironic salute and took a seat outside the tent. We must have looked for all the world like off-duty soldiers, smoking and chatting.

'Find out anything interesting?' Sergei asked.

'I just found out you don't like sharing your booze,' I said.

He produced a hip flask and passed it to me. 'I see you've got over your reluctance to drink with me,' he said.

'Tell me, Sergei. How well do you know Konstantin and Mikhail?'

'Well enough. Why?'

'Are they for real?'

'You mean can they do what they say?'

'Yes.'

'They can and you would do well to believe that. They have powerful backers, serious men with a serious agenda.'

'And you would know this how?' I asked.

'You are the one asking me the questions. If you don't like the answers it's not my fault.'

'How do you know them?'

'They were with the Seventh right enough,' he said. 'They were promoted out to General Crassus's staff years ago. Kind of like you were, only they rank higher and they do more than bodyguard work.'

'You are making me feel inadequate,' I said.

'Look. I know you don't like what happened the other night but I was doing you a favour. Play your cards right and you'll end up rich and powerful.'

'Just like you?'

'Be the smart-mouth, but you are in this thing as much as I am, whether you like it or not. You said things you should not have said.'

'You think that means I will do things I should not do...'

'What are you trying to do, Leo? Talk me into thinking you want out of this? You could, you know. You would not live very long afterwards.'

'You think – what if I went to Drake and told him what I know?'

'Then you'd get me killed and maybe Konstantin and Mikhail and certainly yourself. You don't think they can be tied to anybody higher up, do you? You don't think they wouldn't disappear, just the way you would be made to.'

'All right, all right. You've made your point. I have another question for you...'

'Fire away.'

'How much do you expect to make out of this?'

'I've already made enough so I could retire back to Belial and live like a noble.'

'It doesn't look that way.'

'No. Not right now. But when this is over, I can assure you I will be out of here and away. You will be, too, if you play this sensibly. Look, we've seen all the high muckety-mucks get rich from these endless wars. Why shouldn't we do the same?'

'How rich are you going to be?' He named a sum that

made me whistle. He smiled and nodded and said, 'Look, Leo – you and me are just pawns to these people. We always were. If it wasn't us, it would be somebody else. This way we at least get something out of it.'

He sounded sincere, just a man looking out for an old comrade, trying to do his best in this mean, old world. Hell, maybe he was.

'What if I wanted some proof of that up front.'

He nodded affably. This was something he understood. 'I am sure that could be arranged, with a word in the right ear – leave it to me.'

I was sure that whatever he arranged there would be a cut included in it for him. I could not really begrudge him that. I handed him back his flask. 'Let's drink on that,' I said.

The Red Lantern was the sort of place that soldiers came when they could afford it. Scantily clad women lounged around on red divans. I was greeted like an old friend by the lady in charge and shown through into a private room where I was met by Mikhail and Konstantin. They looked more affable than at any previous time I had dealt with them. I guessed that my session with the truth drugs and my asking for money had reassured them somewhat.

They passed me over a small pouch. It contained three tiny brilliant gems. I had seen their like before. On Belial, they could purchase a large part of a small hive if I traded them to the right person. They were tiny, easily concealed and incredibly valuable. It seemed that my new friends had taken my request quite seriously.

'You can expect more if you play your part well,' said Mikhail. He had a somewhat contemptuous manner now, that of a man who has bought and paid for something he expects to get the use of. Or maybe it was just the surroundings that put that thought into my mind.

Konstantin looked more conciliatory. 'We are all on the same side here,' he said. 'We all want what is best for the Imperium.' He looked and sounded as if he really believed that.

'That remains to be seen,' said Mikhail.

'What do you want from me?'

'Macharius has plans to defeat Richter,' Mikhail said.

'He does not tell them to me.'

'If you hear anything you will let us know.'

'I won't hear anything.'

'Don't be so certain.'

'If it happens, you'll know,' I said, 'but don't get your hopes up.'

'If there's anything else that seems relevant let us know.'

'What do you deem relevant?'

'Any plans Macharius might have, where he might go, who he might talk to.'

'He's not doing a lot of any of those things right now. He spends most of his time in his chambers studying maps of Loki.'

'There now,' said Mikhail. 'That was not so difficult. That is information worth knowing and for which you will be rewarded.'

Again there was a hint of a sneer in his manner. Again

Konstantin stepped in, ever the conciliator. 'Anything might be relevant, Leo. We need to know Macharius's intentions and anything you might know about the people around him. What do you know about the Space Wolf presence on Acheron?'

'I did not know there was one.'

They both looked at me as if they did not quite believe that. I shrugged and said, 'The Space Wolves have left. There was a farewell feast. I was a cupbearer at it.'

'So we heard. It's one reason you are of interest to us.' I considered that. Perhaps they did not intend to just kill me once they were finished with me. I could see how they might think that. I had enjoyed the favour of the leader of one of the most powerful and noble forces in the Imperium. They might think me a useful person to have around in case of any future dealings. I told myself not to get my hopes up. The Space Wolves were a long way away and likely to remain so.

'So you don't know anything about a small Fenrisian vessel in orbit over Acheron?'

'It's news to me,' I said. 'Whether it's news to Macharius or Drake I do not know.'

I could see another reason for them to worry. If the Space Wolves were supposed to have left and one of their ships was still in orbit, who knew what that might represent. Any Imperial commander would be wary of offending the Adeptus Astartes. Perhaps they thought Macharius had cut some sort of secret deal with Grimfang. Hell, perhaps he had. My ignorance was very far from being entirely feigned. As a bodyguard you get to hear far more of what is going on in the Imperial headquarters than any normal soldier, but this does not mean you are privy to all of its secrets.

'If you hear or see anything, let us know.'

'How am I supposed to do that?'

'Leave a message at the tavern for Krimov. He will set up a meeting.'

'Very well. Is that all?'

'No,' said Konstantin. 'We may as well enjoy what we ostensibly came here for.'

He pulled a long cord. The drapes swished open. Three women came in.

'It's getting worse,' said Drake. He rose from the table, strode around the command chamber and studied the great map of the city. All of the armed camps and their commanders were marked on it.

Macharius sat hunched on his commander's throne. He looked tense, not at all like the relaxed, effortlessly calm leader he had always been. He hunched forward, crooked his hands and then stood up himself. 'What did you expect?' he said.

'It is a problem,' the inquisitor said. 'A real problem. There has been a six hundred per cent rise in disciplinary offences. Seventeen officers have been killed in duels. One has lost an eye. Three have lost limbs. Seven hundred and fifty-two enlisted men have been injured in brawls, one hundred and seven of them fatally.'

'Those are not bad numbers for an encampment this size,' said Lazlo, one of Macharius's staff officers.

'That was yesterday,' said Drake. 'Normally we would not see such a rate in a month.'

Lazlo looked as if he wanted to protest but did not dare. The inquisitor turned his attention back to Macharius. 'It's all part of the same thing.'

'I know,' Macharius said. He sounded distant, as if his mind were still elsewhere, dreaming up schemes to defeat Richter. It was the first time I could ever recall seeing him like this.

'Surely the officers and commissars can bring this under control,' said Lazlo.

'They are part of the problem. The crusade is losing all cohesion. Our officers fight duels. Our commissars punish petty infractions of discipline and yet allow the rot to spread unopposed. It starts at the very top. The High Command is too busy jockeying for position to concentrate on any other problem. Their juniors are lax from want of supervision and communicate the ambitions and prejudices of their superiors to the troops. Followers of General Tarka and General Crassus turned their weapons on each other in the streets yesterday. They did not stop until their commissars shot sixty men for disobedience of orders. Even then three commissars were killed.'

Macharius looked at Drake. 'We all know there is a problem,' he said sardonically. 'The question is, what are we going to do about it?'

'No,' said Drake. 'The question is, what are *you* going to do about it? You are our leader.'

Macharius appeared to consider this. 'We have come too far,' he said. 'Our most experienced troops are old and tired.

Our new recruits are untested and lack the zeal our veterans once had. Their officers are disillusioned by the venality of their superiors. It's no wonder things are falling apart.'

'Again, what are you going to do about it?'

'I will speak directly to the troops. I will explain our plans. I will rally them back to the cause of the crusade.'

'It will take more than words,' said Drake.

'Then I will give them more than words. I will lead them forward to crush Richter and his lackeys and after that we shall gather even these Halo Worlds into the Imperium's embrace.'

I wondered at that. I wondered at how distant he now seemed from reality. He made it sound so simple. He would do this and the result would inevitably follow. It was the way he had always spoken and I had always believed him. Maybe the change was in me. Maybe I no longer had the faith I once did. Or maybe the magic of Macharius's charisma had become stretched too thin over too long a time. Maybe it had always been a trick and only recently had I been able to see through it.

I pushed my doubts down into the dark cellars of my mind, but they kept trying to rise up again.

CHAPTER TWENTY

'You say he has a plan?' Konstantin asked. We were once again in the Red Lantern, seemingly met by chance, and in a private room. This time hookahs full of dream smoke had been produced to give a cover story for the lack of girls being summoned. Mikhail got them lit and even sucked away at the mouthpiece for a bit. I shook my head when offered one and stuck with the vodka.

'So he says,' I said.

'And what would that plan be?' Mikhail spoke now, ever the gadfly, ever mocking, ever seeking to provoke a response.

'He declined to tell me,' I said. 'I could ask if you like. I'll tell him you are interested and would really like to know.'

'I am sure Leo is doing his best,' Konstantin said. I noted the fact that I was Leo now. We were old friends, Konstantin and I. At least that was the implication. And Konstantin was on my side, or so he would have me believe.

'Does Leo have even the faintest idea what the plan might be?' Mikhail seemed to be mocking Konstantin now. I wondered if there was real needling there or whether it was just a very good act. It might have been a little of both.

'No, but he seems convinced it will work. He plans to address the troops in three days. Perhaps all will be revealed then.'

'That gives us three days,' said Konstantin, dropping out of character.

'And you didn't see fit to mention this first,' Mikhail said. He was glaring at me.

'I was going to, but I thought I would enjoy a few more of your sneers first,' I said. 'They are always entertaining.'

'Where will this address be given?'

'In the Grand Plaza.'

The two of them exchanged looks. 'He might be able to rally the troops to his side.'

I saw it then in the dismay their glances contained, and heard it in the awed quiet in their voices. They still feared Macharius. They still thought he had it in him to rally even the loyal followers of the conspiring generals to his side, if only he could speak to them. Having heard Macharius on numerous occasions I could understand their fears.

'We'd best get word back to the general,' said Konstantin. 'He'll want to do something about this.'

He turned and stared at me, all pretence of us being old friends and comrades gone. 'Hold yourself ready. We'll be in touch. This is where you earn your baubles.'

There was the same obvious undercurrent of contempt in his voice that Mikhail usually showed. I kept my face bland. I was about to find out exactly why they were hiring me.

'They said the general,' Drake said. His face was a mask but I had known him long enough to detect the unmistakable tone of interest in his voice.

I nodded. 'A small slip,' he said, 'but perhaps an important one.'

'They think that if Macharius has a chance to address the troops, he might be able to rally the crusade.'

'They said that or is that what you think?'

'It's what I think, but I was there and you were not.'

Drake tilted his head to one side and studied me, an owl contemplating a particularly tasty-looking mouse. His mask remained in place, though. 'I will trust your judgement on this.'

'They might be right to fear it,' I said.

Drake shrugged. 'Once, perhaps. Now... I do not know.' His shoulders had slumped and just for a moment I thought I caught a glimpse of a tired and desperate man. I wondered then at how old Drake really was. He did not look any older than me, but he too had access to juvenat.

'They told me to stand ready, that they would be in touch. If they are going to ask me to betray Macharius, it will be now.'

'They will not ask you,' said Drake. 'They will order you. They think you are in too deep to back out.'

I felt a faint twinge of unease. 'You think they will ask me to kill him.'

'No. They cannot trust you enough for that or know whether you will do it. You will be involved and implicated,' Drake said.

It came to me then that only he would know I was not. I could be executed as a traitor and no one would ever know differently unless he said something.

'They might try to assassinate him while he speaks to the army.'

'In full view of all the troops. That would make Macharius a martyr and anyone implicated in his death the worst sort of traitor.' He sounded thoughtful as he said it and I wondered what was going on in the cold clockwork of his mind.

Looking back I can see that it was perhaps then that he got the seed of his last and most terrible idea.

'You've brought the security codes and passwords?' Mikhail asked. I looked around the now familiar chamber at the Red Lantern, taking my time just to annoy him, and then I nodded.

'Good.'

'And you will personally ensure that the lock is opened. We do not trust anyone else to do it.' I had a sudden vision of me opening the great service hatch door and being shot down for my pains. I kept it to myself.

'Of course,' I said.

'Once our men are inside, leave them and go your own way. It will soon be over.'

'Very good,' I said.

'If things go well you'll soon be a very wealthy man.'

Or I'll soon be a very dead man, more likely, I thought.

'Midnight tonight and everything changes,' Konstantin said. He sounded elated, like a man on the verge of realising a long-held dream. Or perhaps a man about to wake up from one.

Midnight found me at the great armoured door on the upper level of the palace. I had dismissed the sentries and stood waiting with the shotgun on my back, wondering for the thousandth time what in the name of the Emperor I was doing. I had the same fluttering feeling in my stomach I have had many times before in the lead-up to a battle. My mouth felt dry and my heart thumped against my ribs. I held up my hands and they were steady. I checked the chrono on my wrist and the smallest hand ticked down towards the stroke of midnight. There were still a couple of minutes to go.

I thought about my life, of all the long mesh of moments that had led me to being in this place at this time. I felt the faint spark of excitement as well as fear, that feeling that something was about to happen, that I had better be alert or I might die, that I was taking my life in my hands. It's a feeling that once experienced is never forgotten, which can be as addictive as any drug.

My mind conjured phantoms. There could be an army out there approaching in the night. There could be an unstoppable horde of assassins. I pictured a vast conspiracy out there in the darkness. I saw tanks revving their engines and soldiers grabbing their weapons and a cabal of trusted generals preparing to strike against their former commander. I was caught at the sharp end of all that. I could be executed by either side for my role in this.

For a moment, I felt as if I were in free-fall. I just did not care. There was nothing I could do but keep my eyes open and my wits about me. It was the only way to survive. I had been doing it for a very long time.

The second hand, the minute hand and the hour hand all reached the same spot at the same time. I opened the door and stared out into the night. At first it looked as if nothing was there, but then I saw a black outline of a Valkyrie gunship and shadowy shapes moving in the darkness. I knew I was outlined against the light and an easy target. I beckoned once and stepped back out of the line of sight.

Black figures scurried forward, moving with professional skill, the ease of men long trained for their task. I backed away and they moved into the light, dark-clad, masked, heavily armed. I became aware of a knife glittering in a man's hand. I levelled my shotgun and said, 'Be careful where you point that thing.'

'Are you mad?' a voice asked. I thought it belonged to Mikhail. 'If that thing goes off it will be heard right through the floor.'

'Then you'd better do nothing that will make it go off,' I said.

'You're not a very trusting man.'

'You are the one with a knife in his hands. I would prefer it stayed there and not between my ribs.'

'You've done your job,' Mikhail said. I recognised the shifty look in his eyes now, just as I recognised Konstantin's huge form looming behind him.

'And I intend to live long enough to collect my payment.'

'You'll do that,' said Mikhail. I suspected that if he had his way I would not live a moment longer than I had to.

'We can stand here all night and bicker or we can get on with things,' I said. 'The choice is yours.'

'Lead on,' he said. I prodded him with the barrel of the shotgun.

'You go first,' I said. 'If a knife should somehow find its way into my back, the shotgun will go off and your head and any chance of surprise will go with it.'

He nodded. 'You think you're clever, don't you?'

'Move,' I said.

We moved quickly and quietly through the top floor towards Macharius's apartment.

'It's very quiet here,' said Konstantin from just behind me. 'I don't like it.'

'It's past midnight and the Lord Macharius requires quiet for his rest. If you like I can summon some servants and you can explain to them what we are doing here.'

He said nothing. I knew that behind us armed men were fanning out through the upper floors of the palace, prepared to bring silent death to anyone they encountered. I prayed that Drake knew what he was doing. I began to entertain a strange fantasy that Drake was the traitor, that his entire plan to entrap the assassins was merely a flimsy excuse to get me to open the door and let them in. It sounds strange now, but at the time with a company of killers at my back and the palace turned into a silent death-trap around me, it was an oddly convincing idea.

'How much further?' Mikhail asked. He sounded a little nervous. I would have been too, creeping through a palace with the assassination of an Imperial hero on my mind and a shotgun pointed at the back of my head.

'It's just ahead,' I said. And it was. It felt like a strange dream to be approaching Macharius's chamber with so many armed strangers around me. I took another breath and counted to seven in my head as I let it out. I was all too aware now that each breath might be my last and I was determined to enjoy them.

We approached the doors and Mikhail stopped. 'No guards,' he said. 'There should be sentries here at least.'

He turned to face me and the knife was raised menacingly in his hand. I sensed Konstantin behind me. I stepped away, putting my back to the wall, and looked at the pair of them.

'I've done my part,' I said, wondering where Drake and his men were, wondering where the others were, wondering what I could say that would keep me alive for another few moments.

'You've betrayed us,' said Mikhail. He moved closer. There was a glittering madness in his eyes. I wondered if he had taken any combat drugs before coming here tonight. 'You fool!'

I swivelled the shotgun to point at him. 'You have a knife,' I said. 'I have a shotgun. I would think twice about calling anyone a fool if I were you.'

Konstantin chose that moment to spring. He moved very quickly for such a big man. The butt of my shotgun had less distance to travel though and it connected with his jaw as he moved. There was a snapping sound as the hinge of his jaw broke.

Mikhail threw himself forward, knife blade glinting in the glow-globe light. It flickered out, aimed at my stomach, point up. He was going to rip towards my heart. I brought the shotgun down, parrying, deflecting the blade. It ripped my trouser leg, and drew a line of blood along the top of my thigh. I hoped he had missed a vein.

He pulled the knife back for another stab. I was lucky. The others had not quite understood what was going on, were still trying to keep the silence so they did not give away the intrusion. That would not last.

I brought the shotgun up, knowing I was not going to be quick enough to stop him. It was not my intention. I intended to take his head off even if he got me through the heart. He saw it in my eyes, the certain knowledge of his own death, and he froze for just the second I needed. The shotgun was pointed at his head. From all around came the sound of a muted struggle and silenced shots. It seemed like Macharius's men were there doing the work after all.

A second later Drake emerged through the door, with Macharius behind him. He raised his hand and Mikhail slumped, a victim of the inquisitor's psyker powers.

Anton and Ivan emerged from a side corridor, a prisoner struggling between them. Drake nodded, satisfied. 'I think we've got enough for our purposes. Let's get down to business.'

He sounded satisfied. We had members of the Seventh Belial caught within Macharius's palace, engaged in an obvious assassination attempt. By the time Drake had finished with them they would no doubt be prepared to confess publicly to anything.

'We don't have much time,' Drake said.

Macharius shook his head. 'We have enough. I've already given the orders to begin the assault on Crassus's palace.'

'Is that wise?'

'Are you going to give me some advice on strategy now, inquisitor?' Macharius asked. There was a note of sardonic mockery in his tone. We raced to the roof, where the Valkyries were waiting to whisk us across the city.

We jumped into the troop carriers and swiftly took to the skies. The mirrored black starscrapers blurred around us. I wondered how many vehicles were out there, running without lights. I wondered if below us drunken soldiers were looking at the skies and wondering about the sleek shadows passing overhead. Perhaps they had already looked up this night and seen Crassus's assassins pass. It seemed impossible to believe that those people down there could have missed the secret war that had erupted in the night.

I looked over at Ivan and Anton. They were hunkered down near Macharius and Drake. The Lord High Commander looked utterly relaxed. I thought of all the ways we could be blasted from the sky. All it would take would be one shot from a Hydra Flak Tank – the enemy would not even have to know Macharius was on board. It just needed one man to fire an anti-aircraft weapon and we would go down. I prayed Macharius's legendary luck would hold at least until we were on the ground once more when I could trust to our skills and weapons.

There are few situations more frightening than hurtling across the night sky in a flyer knowing that at any second a stray shot might kill you, that the slightest miscalculation on the part of the pilot might send you plunging to fiery doom ploughing through the side of a building. It's the not having any control over my own fate that unsettles me.

Ahead of us now I could see fires burning on the peak of a black pyramid, and scores of raptor-like shadows swirling around the building as gunships strafed it. Some of those vehicles were descending and we moved to join them.

Dust swirled into the sky and flames danced away as the Valkyries displaced air. I jumped out of the door, shotgun held ready and scanned the rooftop. I could see no sign of resistance so far. In the distance I could hear klaxons howling and searchlights beginning to probe the sky. Down there was an army that was starting to wonder what was going on, who was attacking it and why?

I raced across the flat rooftop as the rest of the group tumbled out and moved to join me. Drake's storm troopers were already crashing through doors. From below us came the sound of combat.

At that moment I felt an odd sadness descend on me. That which I had most dreaded had come to pass. Imperial soldiers were once more fighting against Imperial soldiers as they had done in the Schism. It seemed as if something had broken that could not be repaired, that even if Macharius were victorious he was in a sense defeated. The long balancing act that had kept him at the top of the crusade had finally failed. Forces had been unleashed tonight that would tear apart the unity he had worked so long and so hard to create. It would not be possible after tonight to even pretend that the army was united. If it had been Cardinal Septimus's plan to undermine Macharius he had succeeded. What was worse was that Macharius had done his work for him.

We smashed through the palace. If Macharius's grasp of the big picture had loosened, his ability on the smaller scale was intact. We stormed through the building with overwhelming force and savagery, taking prisoners by the dozen. What we did not find was General Crassus. He was gone.

CHAPTER TWENTY-ONE

Macharius stood in Crassus's apartments and surveyed the scene of his latest conquest. He looked calm but he was quietly furious.

Drake looked at the hidden doorway behind the cabinet full of ancient statuettes and said, 'Escape route.'

'It goes somewhere,' Macharius said.

'My men are already investigating that.'

'He's gone somewhere.'

'I am getting reports from the space field that a shuttle has taken off.'

'Not his personal shuttle?' asked Macharius.

Drake shook his head. 'Order the field closed if you wish.'

'Too late now,' said Macharius, 'and it would not make much difference anyway. A small craft could be launched from elsewhere on the surface of Acheron.'

'We need to think about what we are going to say,' Drake said. 'We don't have a prisoner to parade in front of the troops. We can still declare him a traitor.'

Macharius shook his head. 'If he had been captured, you could have made him confess. As it stands we have nothing to show.'

'We need to say something. The other generals will wonder what is happening.'

'Let them wonder,' Macharius said. 'I will make my speech tomorrow. No one will try anything until after that and then we can settle things.'

The day of the great speech dawned. Macharius dressed in his most impressive uniform. A dirigible dropped him into the central square of Acheron city, onto a platform set between two massive Baneblades of the Seventh Belial, a deliberate echo of earlier speeches he had given when the crusade first began to drive out between the stars. If any of the tank's crews wondered what had happened to the commander of their battlegroup, they gave no sign.

In the square tens of thousands of men had assembled. They were there to provide a backdrop for a speech that would be recorded by technical cherubim and broadcast to the entire crusade.

Macharius looked much as he had ever done, tall and impressive, a living avatar of war. His gaze was keen, his back was straight, his face like that of a hawk. He did not look nervous as an ordinary man might when about to speak to the assembled armies of the crusade. He had done this before. He was confident that he could do it again.

He stepped out onto the platform and raised his arms above his head. Where once this might have been greeted with a thunderous cheer, it was now met with a watchful silence. Rumours had been swirling around the camp, about the attack on Macharius, about Crassus's flight. Men were wondering what was going on. The peace down there was a fragile thing.

If the quiet daunted Macharius he gave no sign. I took up my position on the edge of the platform watching the crowd as he spoke.

All eyes were on Macharius. Whatever else they felt about him, he still commanded the attention of the assembled regiments as no one else could. I studied faces through a magnifying lens, ostensibly looking for would-be assassins and troublemakers, in reality curious.

The regiments out there were the old guard of the crusade, those that had been with the generals longest, the core of the advancing armies of the Imperium. Every man out there was a veteran or serving alongside veterans. Of all men, they were the ones whose support Macharius should have been able to rely on. They belonged to forces that had fought for the crusade since the very beginning.

And perhaps that was the problem. The faces I looked upon belonged to men who were tired and old and far from home. Most of them did not have access to the juvenat that I had; most of them did not have access to the medical care I had received. They were scarred and wounded. Some of them had crude prosthetics. Some had eye-patches. They looked like hard, deadly men but they also looked like what they were, men who had spent long lives of fighting. They were not the fanatical youths who had set out all those decades ago to rebuild the Imperium and end the Great Schism.

In this I think Macharius misjudged them. He had lived with all the privileges of command. He still wanted more worlds to conquer. His thirst for glory was undiminished and his zeal for the reconquest of the worlds of Man still burned bright. Once it had made him perfectly in tune with all his warriors. Now it made him something else.

'Comrades,' he said. 'We have come far together and we will go further yet.'

He spoke in that confident, confidential way he had. He was not the supreme commander issuing an order. He was a fellow soldier explaining what had to be done. It was a trick of speaking he had that had served him well for a very long time. Perhaps it would serve him again now. He waited, but there was no acclaim, no cheers, no sign that his huge audience was going to respond to the inspiration of his presence.

He made a small gesture of dismissal, shook his head slightly. He smiled. He was not going to let this cool reception put him off from saying what needed to be said. 'We have come to the edge of the worlds that men knew in the time when the Emperor walked among us. We have travelled even beyond those. We have added new realms to the Imperium and we can be proud of that.'

I saw one or two heads nod. The men out there were proud. They knew what they had done and were reminded of their shared achievements. They knew that Macharius had led them to those triumphs. I saw one or two men stand up straighter, prepared to give the general a hearing. Even that filled me with a sense of wrongness, though. They should not have needed to do that. Once all of them would have hung on his every word, been stirred to martial pride by his merest gesture. No more. They just looked at him, some of them hollow-eyed.

'We are gathered together for one last great push,' Macharius said and at last he got some response, a faint murmur of approval, but I sensed it came more from his use of the word *last* than anything else. These were men seeking an end to their labours, not new duties. 'We shall leave Acheron, crush our enemies and add more realms, cover ourselves in new glory, march to new and greater triumphs.'

And there he lost them. He kept speaking, building word pictures of great victories and hundreds of new worlds added to the Imperium, billions of souls redeemed from darkness, of triumphs that would be remembered for as long as the Imperium endured. And the more he spoke, the more he conjured up dreams of victory, the more restless the troops became. They had fought and fought and fought. They had watched their comrades die. They had come to a place where the rules as they knew them had stopped working, where the powers of old Darkness stirred. They were not interested in more battles. They wanted to rest.

They did not cheer as Macharius spoke. They did not raise their voices in acclamation. The Lord High Commander's words were like stones dropped into an abyss. They simply vanished. By the end, even he seemed to realise this. The great speech ended and nothing had been gained.

One way or another the Great Crusade was over. I looked at Macharius and felt sorry for him. His dream had died while he was still alive to see it.

I noticed that Crassus was being painted out of the great mural showing the triumphs of the crusade. The artisans had been dismissed as Macharius had summoned his commanders but the message was clear.

One by one, the generals filtered into the room, accompanied by their staff. Crassus was conspicuous by his absence. Cardinal Septimus was conspicuous by his presence. Those servo-skulls whirling around him seemed to wear the triumphant grin he denied himself.

Under the circumstances I was surprised that any of the generals had shown up. If I were in their shoes I would have feared removal or assassination. Perhaps that is just a comment on the way that I think.

Some of those supremely powerful men looked sullen. Some of them looked defiant. Some of them looked ashamed. None of them looked afraid. Macharius sat on his command throne and surveyed them all. He did not look angry. He looked weary. Of all the men there only Cardinal Septimus looked as if he might be happy with the way things had gone. He still wore his secretly self-satisfied air.

Macharius looked at the generals and they in turn stared back at him. It seemed as if no one wanted to be the first to speak. There was a sense of bitterness and betrayal and broken promises in the air. Things that had simmered away in the background, that had been kept down by Macharius's long unbroken track record of victory, were at long last coming to light. I saw something else too. Each of the generals looked with as much hostility on his companions as he did Macharius. They were all rivals and none of them knew where the others stood.

'Has it come to this?' Macharius asked at last.

'The men are on the edge of mutiny,' General Tarka said. 'Even the commissars doubt their ability to motivate them.'

I saw it then. It was not just each other they were afraid of. I think each one of them saw the potential consequences of their actions rise up to thwart their dreams. If these regiments, the proud core of the crusade, could rise in mutiny, then other regiments could. And no one wanted to light that particular fuse.

Macharius did not say anything. 'Where is General Crassus?' Fabius asked. 'I do not see him present.'

'Alas he will not be joining us,' said Macharius. 'It seemed he, too, was on the edge of mutiny and then he stepped off.'

A ripple of shock passed around the room. 'Apparently he lost faith in my leadership,' Macharius said. 'I doubt he was alone in this.'

His gaze passed from one to another of his former lieutenants and not one of them could meet it.

Cardinal Septimus could barely keep from rubbing his hands together but when he spoke his voice was soft and respectful.

'Now is a good time to return to Terra and enjoy your

triumphs, Lord High Commander. Let another take up your burdens.'

It was like throwing raw meat into a pit full of dinogators. All eyes turned towards the representative of the Imperium. In every cold brain, swift calculations were being made. If Macharius stepped down, he must have a successor. There was glory to be had in leading the crusade, even if it was weakened, even if it conquered no more worlds. Indeed, I am sure that many of those present thought that the current state of the crusade was a reflection of Macharius's leadership, that with *them* in command it would go on to new heights. I saw the fires of ambition light in five pairs of eyes. I saw them glance around and measure potential rivals and allies.

'No,' said Macharius. Suddenly those baleful fires were dimmed as the generals turned to look at their commander.

'No?' said Septimus. His voice was soft, but there was both menace and an undercurrent of glee in it. It appeared Macharius was about to disobey a direct order from the Imperium.

'No,' said Macharius. 'Richter remains and he is a threat to the Imperium beyond measure. I must settle matters with him before I depart.'

'How will you do it if the armies are on the verge of mutiny?' Septimus asked. 'It would be madness to risk it.'

'I do not need the armies gathered here. I can do it with the Lion Guard and the troops of my personal battlegroup.'

'With all due respect, General Macharius, you have been trying to do that for two standard years and you have failed.'

'I will not fail this time,' said Macharius, with utter certainty.

'By the time your ship is prepared to return to Terra, the matter will be settled.'

I could tell that no one there believed him. They thought it was a delaying strategy of some sort.

'You really think that is possible?' Septimus asked. He could not keep the disbelief out of his voice.

'I would bet my life on it,' said Macharius. I felt a sudden resurgence of faith in him. If Macharius said he was going to do this thing, he would do it. Or die in the attempt.

Cardinal Septimus stood silent for a moment. The skulls orbited around him as he considered his options. He squared his shoulders and allowed a smile to spread across his face. 'You shall have your last campaign then, General Macharius, and afterwards you will return to Terra with me.'

The generals departed to plot and try to instil some semblance of discipline in their unbelieving armies. Macharius departed to make preparations for his return to Loki. As we left the chamber, I turned and saw Inquisitor Drake deep in conversation with Cardinal Septimus. Just for a moment they looked like conspirators. It was disquieting.

CHAPTER TWENTY-TWO

Beneath us once more I could see the murky globe of Loki. The crusade had returned to settle with Richter and his minions once and for all. Macharius had announced that he would be victorious here if it was the last thing he did. It was time to put his plan to the test.

All around us the command deck hummed, but it was a bleak parody of the way things had once been. There had been a time when reports would have been coming in from hundreds of distant worlds scattered throughout an entire sector of the galaxy. Now they were concerned only with this one world and its occupants. It showed the terrible narrowing of focus as the energies of the crusade dissipated in internal strife.

Now the holo-sphere showed only the great murky orb of Loki and the two satellites that orbited it, the huge skull moon and the tiny, speeding lesser one. Inquisitor Drake studied them intently as if by staring hard enough he could somehow divine the course of the future. The rest of the commanding officers watched warily. Macharius smiled grimly to himself, in possession of a secret that only he knew, but which would decide all of our destinies.

'Niflgard is once more in the hands of our enemies. It seems we will be starting again from scratch,' said Drake. He was fishing for information.

'It will not be so for long,' said Macharius quietly. 'Once Richter and his staff have fallen.'

Drake shot him a puzzled look. 'What do you mean?'

Macharius gestured to a tech-adept and the view zoomed in to show the area over which we had fought so long and hard previously. Massive armoured citadels lay in a fortified ring. Each was a fortress city holding tens of millions of people. Each had the industrial capacity to supply a dozen armies.

'Niflgard was to be an advance base for a conventional campaign. We needed its hive factorums to provide munitions and material, to supply our war machine, to compensate for the long supply lines. We wanted the world's resources. We don't need them any more. What matters most is that we settle matters with Richter and the powers that stand behind him.

'Previously we got bogged down in endless warfare fighting the way our enemies wanted, to our own disadvantage. Not this time. This time we attack Richter directly.'

'But that ring of citadels is impenetrable. It is impervious to the most potent orbital bombardment of the greatest fleet. You yourself said we would need to take it on the ground.'

'I was wrong,' said Macharius. 'There is another way. We will drop from orbit into the centre of the ring and strike the head off the monster.'

Drake looked at him as if he suspected Macharius had gone mad. I could understand why.

'We don't have twenty Chapters of Space Marines,' the inquisitor said. 'We will die like flies on the ground. You said you no longer wanted to waste the lives of our soldiers. Do you intend to throw them all away at once in some grand gesture, to martyr yourself for the Imperium?'

There was an odd tone in the inquisitor's voice, as if he did not entirely disapprove of the ideas to which he was giving voice. I noticed that the Naval officers nearby were listening intently, a kind of calm curiosity written on their faces. They could afford to feel that way. They would not be trying to force a beachhead on the surface of Loki in the teeth of the defences of those fortified mountains.

Macharius laughed. It was a merry sound with no hint of madness in it but it did not reassure me. 'I am not ready for death yet, my friend,' he said. 'Not until I have settled scores with all my enemies.'

Looking back now, it seems to me that he gave Drake an odd look when he said *all my enemies*. At the time what I noticed was that the calm assurance of his words made all the listeners shiver. He was completely certain of what he was doing. It was like listening to the old Macharius who had always been the still centre of the storm of battle around him. The difference was that I had changed. I no longer shared the Lord High Commander's self-belief. I had allowed myself to doubt my complete faith in him, and once that had happened there was no going back to the old ways.

'We are going to destroy those fortresses,' said Macharius. 'And here's how.'

He outlined his plan, crisply and clearly. It sounded like madness, but as I listened I found myself starting to believe again. It might, after all, just work.

The sorcerer-enginseers of the Adeptus Mechanicus had finished their work. Their ships departed from the surface of the lesser moon. I stood beside Macharius and Drake and the others and watched their ships return to join the body of the fleet.

'How long?' Drake asked. His voice was sombre.

'The drives will be activated in the next cycle, then we shall begin.' He turned to speak to his staff officer. 'I want everyone ready to go within the next twelve hours.'

'All troops are on standby. The shuttles are ready. We await only the coordinates for landing, sir.' He stood tautly to attention and was clearly waiting for Macharius to reveal the landing point.

'Very good,' said Macharius dismissing him. 'I want my personal shuttle ready to spearhead the attack on the ground. I want all the men to know I am going with them. I will be on the ground, sharing the risks.'

I listened intently. Anton caught my eye. His face was a blank mask but I could tell what he was thinking. If

Macharius was going to be on the surface, I was going to be there too, and so were Anton and Ivan.

Macharius issued the final orders and then we were left alone with him and Drake. 'You are playing this close to your chest,' Drake said. 'Do you still suspect there is a traitor among us? Another Crassus, or something worse?'

Macharius shrugged. 'I do not know where we will be landing… yet. I will not know until the divinatory altars tell us where we can set down and that won't be for another four hours.'

The hours crawled by. Macharius and Drake and his upper echelon of command sat in his grand stateroom and surveyed the greenish, polluted outline of the world below them. They smoked and drank like condemned men. I think all of them felt that Loki was going to be their graveyard. It had been an unlucky place for Macharius, the crusade and the Lion Guard. We had fought there for so long and to so little effect that no one quite believed that this time it was going to be any different.

And yet, for all that, they sat there tense and drawn, ready to respond to any command. No matter how the rest of the crusade now felt, these men were still ready to follow Macharius to their deaths.

'What if it doesn't work?' Inquisitor Drake asked. He sounded worried. All of the officers gathered in the chamber looked at him as if he were expressing a heresy.

'It will work,' Macharius said. 'I have every faith in the Adeptus Mechanicus. Their scholars have performed every calculation a thousand times. All of the engines are placed correctly. There will be no mistake.'

At that point the moon was on the far side of the planet, hurtling along its final orbit. I looked at the chrono on the wall and realised that very soon now we would find out whether Macharius's plan was going to work or whether his final desperate gamble was going to fail. The man himself showed no sign of being worried. If there were any doubts in his mind there was no clue to that fact upon his face. He glanced around at all of his sub-commanders and smiled.

'There is no need for all the long faces, gentlemen,' he said. 'I want you all to be prepared to descend upon the surface of Loki at a moment's notice and to destroy the heretics there with complete and utter ruthlessness. Now is not the time to have any doubts. Now is not the time to show mercy. Now is the time to seize victory for the Imperium with our own hands and to show the watching worlds that the crusade is still a force to be reckoned with.'

One by one the officers around the table appeared to relax. One by one they became infected with the confidence that their leader showed. It was just like the old days when Macharius had seemed invincible and just for a moment it seemed that he was once again the unbeatable strategist that we had believed him to be.

'I don't like this,' Inquisitor Drake said. 'Too much can go wrong. Too much has been left to chance. What if the engin-seers have failed to take some factor into account? What then? You will not have another chance to do this.'

Again Macharius smiled. 'There is no one more aware of that than me, I assure you, inquisitor. I also assure you that if something goes wrong we will have lost nothing. We will be no worse off than we were before. And if things go according to plan – which they will – then we will have crushed the most vile citadel of apostasy and wickedness in this sector. We will have demonstrated to all of those who doubted us that we are still a power to be reckoned with.'

There was compelling force in his words, but I wondered as I listened whether he was talking about the crusade or himself when he was talking about the doubters.

The hands of the chrono circled just as the moon raced around the planet. The shape of the planet floated within the holo-sphere, as if seen from a distance somewhat greater than that at which our fleet orbited. On the far side through the world's ghostly representation I could see the red dot that represented the lesser moon. It was three-quarters of the way around the planet now and I wondered whether or not it had performed this partial circuit much quicker than its previous ones.

Drake's eyes were focused on it almost obsessively. He might have been watching the last seconds ticking down to his own execution. He seemed completely wound up to a pitch of nervous tension that I had never seen him at before, almost feverish in his excitement.

At the time I wondered whether it was simply nervousness about Macharius's chance of regaining the leadership of the crusade in one mighty stroke. He had spent decades attached to the Lord High Commander's cause to the point where its success was identified with his success and its failure with his own. In many ways he had as much riding on the coming campaign as Macharius himself.

Silence filled the room and the only sound was the occasional cough of a nervous officer. Occasionally someone lit a lho-stick. Someone drummed his fingers on the table top until he noticed and stopped.

'Twenty minutes,' an officer announced. Macharius nodded and looked at the holographic representation for a moment. An expression of satisfaction passed across his face even though he could not have seen anything more than the rest of us. He was still a supreme actor and this might be his last great show.

Minutes stretched out like hours. I was aware of the drumbeat of my own heart. All the officers stole stealthy glances at the globe and its hurtling satellite. This three-dimensional representation began to change now. It zoomed in to show the small moon in greater detail rushing across a quarter-section of the planet. A tech-adept made some adjustments and for a moment I caught sight of the pockmarked surface, so like that of a large asteroid, except that huge machines had been placed at various points on its surface and those machines were now surrounded by the eerie glow of ancient drives slowly drawing more and more power into themselves.

Drake barked an order and the technician hurriedly changed the point of view again. Now we could see that the circling moon had begun to shudder slightly and deviate a little from its orbital path. Perhaps it was an illusion, but it definitely seemed to be picking up speed.

I heard one officer gasp as if he could not quite believe what he was seeing. The moon was definitely changing course now and it had begun to move downwards towards the planet's surface. I found that I was holding my breath awaiting the outcome of this last titanic throw of the dice. I looked at the chrono again and suddenly it seemed as if the hands of the clock had raced forward, gaining speed like the moon, for there was less than one minute left on the timer.

A comet trail of vapour was starting to form around the lesser moon now. Drake drummed his fingers on the table. 'This is where it could go wrong, if they have miscalculated and performed the invocations wrong.'

I suspected he meant that the atmospheric turbulence might cause the moon to deviate from its trajectory. Even a slight change in its course would mean it would land hundreds of leagues off target. Even as he spoke the words the moon was changing colour. Trails of red and yellow plasma joined the greyish vapour. It was heating up like a shuttle decelerating into the atmosphere. I wondered if there was anyone down there looking up at the night sky now. Perhaps they would think they were seeing a large meteor. If there was any gap in the clouds they might witness something strange and unnatural, the satellite that had been orbiting their world for millions of years drifting out of position, hurtling downwards towards them like a hammer wielded by an angry god.

I imagined the dead men wandering across the shell-churned landscape and looking up with their greenly glowing eyes to witness this terrific descent. I stared at the image of the moon. It was surrounded by a red halo now, as it began its final fall. The mountains seemed to rise to meet it as it descended through the clouds, and then came the moment of impact.

I held my breath. For a brief heartbeat, almost impossibly, nothing seemed to happen. The thought skittered across my mind that it was impossible. Millions of tons of rock accelerated to such terrific velocity must have some effect. The point of view of the sphere pulled back and I saw shock waves rippling out from the point of impact, as if a man had smashed into a mud ball with a hammer. Mountain ranges bent and tumbled. The moon burrowed into the cold crust of Loki like a bolter shell seeking a heretic's heart.

The whole area of the planet's surface around it seemed to be being pushed inwards by the enormous impact. Lava lines appeared as the fiery heart of the planet spilled out in a huge wave that would destroy anything in its path. An enormous mushroom cloud of dust rose skywards, obscuring everything from sight.

For long, long minutes everything was silent. I think everybody, even Macharius, was appalled by what we had witnessed. In our mind's eyes we were all imagining what it must have been like to be at the focal point of that vast impact. We waited and we waited and we waited for the dust to clear, for the divinatory sensor images to stabilise so that we could see what had happened.

Terribly slowly it all became clear. The ancient moon had smashed the crust of the world, toppling mountains, destroying fortresses. The land over which we had fought so bitterly for so long had been swept clean of earthworks and emplacements by a tidal wave of shuddering earth, the ripple of the planet's skin, leaving huge new heaps of rock and dust and rubble. Niflgard was gone, a child's sandcastle kicked over by an angry giant. Even the most distant of the heretic fortresses had suffered terrible damage. Their armoured carapaces had been cracked open. They looked like vast termite mounds that someone had riddled with autogun bullets until they had fallen apart.

Clouds swirled everywhere, contrary to any normal weather pattern, their movements driven by the awesome turbulence caused by the staggering impact.

'There,' Drake said. His pointing finger stabbed out to indicate something. By some strange chance, or perhaps by design on the part of Macharius, one gigantic hive citadel was left standing, its surface ruptured but its structural integrity intact. It stood now on the edge of a vast crater from which an immense red-hot cliff-spire emerged. I realised it was a fragment of the shattered moon. It must have broken up on impact and been tossed scores of leagues through the sky. 'That is Richter's citadel.'

The earth around it was a maze of new canyons, where the earth had folded and rippled. In the midst of a new valley was a large flat area. 'Then that is where we must go,' said Macharius. He turned to the officers. 'Be ready for action. We descend when the land has cooled and the air turbulence settled.'

The officers leapt into action. In a moment the chamber was clear of all except Drake and Macharius and their bodyguards. Macharius said, 'Now we shall see what we shall see.'

He strapped on his chainsword and picked up his bolt pistol and made ready for his final battle.

* * *

As we raced through the ship, I thought I caught sight of a familiar face among the officers watching us head to the shuttle. It raised a hand to wave to me and I thought I saw a fleeting expression of sadness; then it was gone, vanishing in the direction of the shuttles.

Anton caught the look on my face. 'What is it?' he asked. 'You look like you've seen a ghost.'

It was not a ghost, it was Anna. She was on the ship again, moving in disguise through the corridors. No doubt she had intended for me to see her, because she could easily have concealed herself in a hundred different ways had she so wished. Was this farewell?

'Nothing,' I said. There was no time left to stop and explain. No time for me, no time for her and no time for any of us.

We joined the rest of the Lion Guard within the shuttle and waited for the warning klaxon to sound, telling us it was time to descend once more to the surface of Loki. A feeling of dread filled my heart at the thought of it.

CHAPTER TWENTY-THREE

The shuttle, massive as it was, shook on the way down. Atmospheric conditions were still not settled after the moon-strike. I stared at the faces of my companions. They were all partially concealed by rebreathers but their eyes looked grim.

It seemed to take forever until the shuttle touched down. It hit the ground with a shudder and then vibrated as the ramps were lowered. A moment later we were heading down onto the soil of the world we had vacated what felt like a short lifetime ago.

The first thing I noticed was how cold it was. Loki had never been exactly tropical, but now it was chillier than it had been in the depths of winter. The dark clouds in the sky that obscured the sun might have had something to do with that. It felt almost like night even though dawn had already risen in the east. No stars were visible. Unconsciously I looked for the hurtling lesser moon but, of course, it was no longer to be seen nor would it ever be again.

There was a strangeness about the advance down onto the planet's surface. This was not an area we had ever reached during our original advance. It was too deep in the enemy heartland, surrounded by a maze of fortified trenches and citadels. Now there was no sign of any work of man. The ground had a crumpled, crumbled look, as if a huge hand had dug its fingers in deep and squeezed. As far as the eye could see were ridges and deep craters and vast blocks of splintered moon-rock. Fires burned all the way to the horizon. Some were distant volcanic eruptions, and others were hive cities venting gas and chemicals in sheets of flame a kilometre high.

Shadows danced everywhere. Our breath came out in clouds. Tiny motes of dust or perhaps disease spores swirled everywhere. The headlights of armoured vehicles caught the dancing particles. Some of them glittered, though I have no idea why.

We hit the ground hard and fast and moved to establish a perimeter. We needed to establish the beachhead as quickly as we could. The heretics had not responded and there was no guarantee that they would, but we could not count on that. Company by company, squad by squad, the spearhead of the crusade dispersed across the shattered landscape, digging in where it could, establishing strong points, guard posts and lines of sight for artillery and armour and heavy weapons.

A converted Baneblade had been made ready as Macharius's mobile headquarters. It had been requisitioned on Acheron from the defeated remnants of Crassus's forces and hastily repainted in Macharius's colours. It was equipped and fuelled and I was to be its driver. It felt good to be back behind the controls of a Baneblade once more, making the invocations, feeling the great beast come to life beneath my hands. It gave me a sense of nostalgia, as if I were back at the beginning of my career and not at its end. Ivan and Anton were my gunners once again. Part of me felt that this would be an appropriate ending, and part of me knew that was not a healthy thought.

I was glad I had my bucket seat. The inside of the Leman Russ was crowded and not just with crew. We were carrying Drake and his bodyguard. It seemed Macharius did not want to be parted from his great advisor at this late stage.

In a way it was a sad sight that greeted us. Where once there would have been thousands of armoured vehicles, now there were barely hundreds and those had a battered, hastily made-ready look to them. Most of the tanks were Leman Russ Exterminators or Vanquishers; the remainder of them were Chimera troop carriers. Once the force was assembled at the bridgehead we roared off across the landscape towards the last standing citadel of heretics on this world.

Macharius wanted his reckoning with Richter and he was going to have it.

It was not a huge distance from our landing site to the citadel, a matter of a score of leagues, a distance that a Leman

Russ battle tank was capable of covering in a matter of hours even over this broken terrain.

The land around us was as bleak as the surface of a moon. The sky remained dark save where the clouds were underlit by the eerie glow of distant firestorms. The ground was rough and we bounced and shuddered along. All the time Macharius responded to incoming reports from his commanders.

I listened as he briefed the column commanders, telling them where to go and what to do. So far none of them had met any resistance, which was hardly surprising in the aftermath of the moon-strike. I wondered how long that would last. I doubted anything could live through the colossal impact but then, in the past, on Loki, we had not only fought against the living.

Ahead of us the new ridgelines rose towards the horizon and on that horizon loomed the jagged hive citadel that was our ultimate destination. There was something strange about it, a warped look that was not simply a product of the impact shock. Looking at it I thought the place had always been twisted. It had been built that way or had become so over the long years since it had been constructed.

Things were starting to grow around us. Slimy luminous moulds covered the boulders, like veils of greenish mucus. Large mushrooms glowed spectrally in the gloom. I wondered if they had always been here or whether the impact had brought buried things from deep underground to the surface.

Here and there were the broken bubble domes of what once might have been hab-bunkers. Gigantic pipes emerged from the soil like broken and empty veins protruding from an amputated limb.

Black snowflakes swirled around us. Perhaps they were not snow, but that is what they looked like and it was certainly cold enough. I intensified the spotlights so I could see to drive by and kept us heading in the direction we had fixed upon, as visibility dropped to almost zero and I prayed to the Emperor we did not encounter a chasm opened by the fall of the moon from the sky.

Suddenly we emerged from the murk. The black flakes swirled away and I could see ahead once more. The landscape was even more broken, the way forward running through huge gullies over which needles of rocks stood guard like sentinels.

We passed huge drops and chasms and I knew we were slowly gaining altitude as we advanced. In the distance the citadel loomed larger, and appeared ever more twisted. More reports came in telling of figures sighted in the distance. Perhaps they were refugees, perhaps they were survivors, or perhaps they were something different. It did not matter now. The important thing was to reach our destination before the enemy became aware of us.

All of this was part of Macharius's plan. He knew that all communication on Loki as well as all of the sensor networks would be disrupted at this moment in time. He also knew that our enemies would be much more concerned with dealing with the disaster than with any possibility of attack. The planet had just taken the single most powerful attack it had ever received, something far more powerful than an orbital bombardment, and it was unlikely that even if anyone spotted us that the enemy would be able to respond. It would be far too busy dealing with the disaster.

At least that is what we hoped and believed.

We came to rest on a ridge overlooking Richter's citadel. The fortress had taken an enormous amount of damage from the moonfall. The great armoured carapace had been cracked and there were gaping holes inside the structure from which greenish fluid poured. Fires blazed in the side of the building and clouds of poisonous-looking smoke rose to mingle with the dust in the air.

The place looked more like a living thing than a building. It had an organic look reminiscent of an insect hive, as if it had been grown rather than built, and it looked diseased. Great bulges emerged from its sides like tumours and long tendrils of living tubing, like veins or intestines, flowed over it. Sphincters as large as city gates pumped out loathsome effluent.

In areas where the external walls had been ripped away by the impact, it was like viewing a body whose skin has been ripped away by a grenade explosion. There was a suggestion of fleshiness to the rockcrete and hints that the internal structure was reinforced with something more like bone than metal. It had the hallucinatory quality of something seen in a drugged nightmare. Looking at it, I could not help but think of the gloating daemon face I had seen leering down in my dreams.

'What is that?' I asked. It was a breach of discipline but no one took me to task.

'I do not know,' said Macharius. His voice was quiet and

calm, but I sensed unease in it, perhaps for the first time in my recollection.

'It looks like the work of the Ruinous Powers,' said Drake, very quietly so that no comm-net would pick up his words. I shivered. In my experience those were not things that any sane man would choose to encounter, although its presence here explained a lot of things.

'Nurgle,' the inquisitor said, and the word made it sound as if he were clearing his throat and spitting. Once again terror swirled somewhere in the depths of my mind when I heard that name. 'Lord of Plague.'

He was talking more to himself than to anyone else now. 'That place will be a disease pit,' he said.

'Our men are as well protected as they can be. They have rebreathers and full body covering. We cannot let fear keep us from covering the last kilometre.' Clearly Macharius was not about to retreat now, whatever Drake said. 'We have broken the walls, destroyed the defences.'

'Have we?' Drake asked.

On the walls some of those great blister turrets were swivelling to bring their weapons to bear. 'It looks like some defenders are still alive within the place.'

The turrets fired. A great explosion tore the cliff top not too far from our location. The Baneblade vibrated at the shock of the impact. I put the vehicle into reverse gear and pulled us away from the edge. The explosions might set it to crumbling away and send the tank tumbling to its doom in the valley below. Macharius was already giving orders for the remainder of our column to do the same.

We were fortunate that the citadel had been so heavily damaged. If more of those great weapons had survived we might have been destroyed along the ridgelines. As it was casualty reports came pouring in; it looked as if we had lost many men and vehicles.

'What now?' Drake asked.

Macharius looked calm, but there was something strange about his voice. 'We regroup and prepare to advance once more. You saw how damaged the citadel was. We can take it. This is the closest we have ever come to doing so. I will not be denied victory at last.'

There was a note of almost maniacal obsession in his voice. He wanted victory and he was prepared to pay any price to get it.

We may have been out of line of sight of the citadel's batteries but we were not out of range. Shells arced down out of the sky to raise new craters all along our line.

The enemy gunners did not know where to aim but sometimes their shots hit home anyway, churning the landscape, raising new dust clouds to add to the fug in the air. Looking back, I suppose they had no real idea of where we were. It was most likely they were simply firing in panic, but at the time it did not feel like that. When a shell smashed another Leman Russ to pieces, it was as if we were being personally and individually targeted by foes who knew exactly where we were.

'They let off a thousand shots for every one that hits,' Macharius said. He was right, of course, but it did not make me feel any better. It was always possible that we would be the ones that sheer random chance selected to be the next victims.

'That will not matter if they have enough shells,' said Drake.

'Then we shall just have to hope they do not,' said Macharius. He began to give orders to the force. As ever he did not really need a holo-sphere to be able to envisage a battlefield. He carried the information in his head.

A vast explosion lit the sky.

'Take us forward and let's have a look,' said Macharius. I obeyed his command and began to edge the Leman Russ back towards the crumbling ridgeline. I peered hard through the gloom, all too aware that the ridge might have disintegrated under the impact of all those explosions.

As we reached the edge I saw that more gaps had appeared in the side of the citadel and a few of the turrets had gone.

'A magazine explosion,' Macharius said. I could picture an eruption in an ammunition dump with the huge explosion tearing through the loading tunnels built to feed those huge turrets with shells. Of course, it might not have been any such thing. It might simply have been a power-core exploding. In any case, the citadel looked dead. The turrets in its sides did not swivel. Many of the visible lights had failed as if the systems had collapsed. Even as that happened the comm-net kicked back in and we could hear the chatter of reports coming in through the static.

'It looks as if we might have got lucky,' said Drake.

'It is a trap,' said Macharius.

'You think they staged a magazine explosion to lure us forward?' There was obvious disbelief in Drake's voice.

'No, I think Richter is taking advantage of the explosion to do that,' said Macharius. 'I know how he thinks.'

'Can you lead us into his trap and out again?' Drake asked.

'Let us see,' said Macharius.

We rumbled down into the huge crater valley left by the aftershocks of the moonfall. A piece of the shattered satellite loomed over us like a fallen mountain. It still steamed despite the cold of its surroundings, or at least it looked that way.

Long lines of armoured fighting vehicles made their way down narrow ridgelines into the chasm. Ahead of us the shadowy bulk of the great hive citadel rose like a hungry ogre. It felt as if a vast hungry daemonic presence was looming over us, waiting for us to fall into its clutches. I wondered at Macharius's confidence. He seemed totally untroubled, even though he knew we were driving right into the teeth of an ambush.

In my mind's eye, I pictured the huge daemon I had seen during my fever dreams. I told myself I must still have a touch of the fever, but that was not it. There was a very real fear in my heart, and a terrible sense of foreboding in my mind. My mouth felt dry, my heart hammered against my ribs. I made myself concentrate on keeping the drive treads pointing in the wrong direction. Having the Baneblade slide off the ridgeline would kill us all just as quickly as any shell-blast or manifesting daemon god.

Macharius gave the order for the tanks to fan out as soon as they completed the descent. He did not want a vehicle being taken out along the ridgeline and blocking our advance, leaving us helpless prey trapped on the approaches. Once we were in the area between the ridges there was space to spread out so that individual vehicles did not make such tempting targets.

Looking ahead I could see the slope rising to the side of the hive. Once there had been roads and mono-rail tracks there, but now the roads were worn away and the rail-lines were just tangles of twisted girders. The land up there was broken by great menhirs of tumbled rockcrete. Rivers of burning chemicals flowed down the sides of the hive and polluted slime trails bubbled out of broken vents. From close up, the hive looked less like one vast monolithic structure and more like a collection of jumbled features on the landscape. Its sides were pitted and fissured. The great gaps loomed ahead of us like enormous chasms.

Some of the tension had drained out of Drake. He looked almost relieved. Perhaps Macharius had been wrong about the trap. 'We need to get inside and begin to cleanse this place of the last of the heretics,' he said.

The words had no sooner left his mouth than lights flickered on once more in the hive citadel and the great turrets on its side began to swivel on their mounts.

'Indeed, we do,' said Macharius.

The batteries opened fire, tearing chunks out of the landscape around us, sending the shattered metal remains of main battle tanks hurtling into the sky. Wreckage rained down all around us along with dust and soil and broken rockcrete. New craters appeared where the munitions struck.

I could feel the vibration of the explosions through the hull of the Baneblade. The darkness around us was shattered as our forces returned fire. Battle-cannon shells sleeted down on the enemy position. They had no effect on the huge armoured structures.

'Forward,' Macharius ordered. I wondered if he had gone mad. His intention was clearly to get us under the arc of fire of the enemy batteries into the dead zone that they could not reach, but I doubted it would work. The turrets were set at measured distances to each other so that they could cover each other's blind spots. We might get below the angle of fire of the forward turrets but the ones further up the hive's sides could still shoot at us.

Huge shells thundered down from on high. They destroyed more of the Leman Russ. Because of the formation's dispersal they could not get them all or quickly.

'To the left,' Macharius said. 'Lemuel.'

It took me a moment to realise he was speaking to me but I did as I was ordered. A shell hurtled by overhead and tore up the rockcrete to our right. I did not ask how he had known. Macharius could read a battlefield like no man ever born. Perhaps knowing where the shell had been about to descend was just part of his talent. I had seen him do similar things before.

'Keep moving to the left,' he said. He spoke a string of commands into the comm-net, telling other vehicles to follow more or less our path. The shells continued to hurtle over us, tearing up the terrain to our left and behind us and it slowly dawned on me as I followed Macharius's instructions what he was doing.

The turrets had been set up to be able to cover all of the approaches with multiple redundancies set in. Under normal circumstances there would be no way through without being hit by an inferno of shell-fire, but these were not normal circumstances. The hive citadel had been badly damaged, with the bulk of the turrets taken out already. There were blind spots in the enemy's arcs of fire and there was a pathway through. With one view of the hive side from the ridgeline Macharius had plotted it. There were still terrible killing zones but they could be avoided and once through we were relatively safe.

At least I thought we were; then I noticed that there were lights moving on the side of the hive and things were coming out through the gates and taking up position on the citadel's sloping sides. I upped the magnification of the driver's periscope and saw that they were Basilisks and something that looked like a Hydra modified for anti-tank service with an open turret mounted on the chassis. The fixed turrets might not be able to hit us but the mobile artillery was moving into position to attack. It seemed Richter had anticipated Macharius's move. We had merely exchanged one form of killing ground for another.

The enemy opened fire. Explosions once more lit up the sky, shattering the darkness. All around Leman Russ burned, reduced to heaps of slagged metal. We returned fire at the enemy hull on the ridges above us.

It was impossible for me to tell exactly what was going on. I had a very limited perspective of the battlefield from my driver's position. I knew only that Macharius calmly continued to give orders and respond to the enemy's attacks. From what he was saying I sensed that some of our drivers had panicked and left his carefully chosen route up the hive side. I thought I could hear screams and explosions over the comm-net.

Even as that thought occurred to me the hail of fire intensified around us. A shell impacted on the side of the Baneblade. I felt that moment of sheer stark terror you always get when you've taken a heavy impact in an armoured vehicle.

This is it, I thought. I am dead. I'd seen too many nasty brew-ups in tanks, far more than enough to get my imagination working overtime. Sparks flew around the cabin and a terrible clanging sound of repeated impact on the side of the vehicle all added to my panic.

'What the...' I heard Anton say.

A smell of burning filled the inside of the cockpit along with gouts of smoke.

'Everybody out!' Macharius ordered. I undid the harness holding me in the driver's seat and scrambled for the evacuation hatches. All around me things sparked and burned. An army of evil possibilities invaded my mind: I saw us stuck within the burning tank by hatches that refused to come unsealed, the magazine might detonate at any minute if the power-core went up, and another hit might come lashing out of the darkness as the enemy concentrated their fire on the crippled tank. I held my breath against the smoke and the possibility that each breath might be my last.

I flipped open the escape hatch and tumbled out into the cold night of Loki.

CHAPTER TWENTY-FOUR

And it was cold. Loki had always been cold, wet and cheerless but this was something else. The effect of the moon-strike had dropped the temperature significantly. The dust cloud covering the sky and blocking out all sunlight had changed something. This was the sort of cold that brought snow and blizzards in other worlds. My breath came out in clouds. At least there was a source of heat behind me. The Baneblade had caught fire.

Macharius had pulled himself up through the top of the turret and had turned to aid Drake. The two of them jumped clear. One of Drake's bodyguards leapt behind him. Anton and Ivan joined me.

'Get clear,' I shouted. 'The thing's going to brew.'

I did not have to tell anybody twice. I turned and fled over broken ground. The strain of running warmed me against the chill. There was a crawling sensation between my shoulder blades. I was free of the burning tank but I had found something else to be afraid of. The tank might explode or it might not. In any case it was a beacon for incoming fire and the enemy had already proven it had weapons powerful enough to take out a Baneblade. To make matters worse I was running towards a firestorm of explosives. I had bailed out on the side facing the fire zone of the big turrets. They were tearing up the earth ahead with huge explosions.

I dived flat behind a boulder and moments later I was joined by Ivan and Anton. Anton still clutched his sniper rifle in his left hand. He had paused in the middle of bailing out to grab it and had somehow managed to get it through the escape hatch. There was dedication. Or idiocy. Most likely the latter.

'You showed a clean pair of heels,' Anton said. 'Looked like you were trying for the regimental running championships. I've never seen anybody flee so fast. I thought there was a dust cloud rising behind you.'

'You seem to have kept up,' I said.

'Never fancied going up in a brewed-up tank,' Anton said.

A huge explosion rocked the dark from off to our left. It was not a shell from one of the turrets. Anton stood up, his lanky form casting a long shadow in the light of its burning.

'Yep, there she goes,' he bellowed.

'Get down, idiot boy,' I said.

Shrapnel clattered off the rock.

'Why?' he asked. 'They are not shooting at me.'

'No,' I said, 'but those guys might start.'

Moving downslope was a mass of heretic infantrymen. They had bayonets attached to their lasguns and they looked anything but friendly.

'Good point,' Anton said. He brought the rifle up to his shoulder, aimed through the sight, snapped off a shot and dropped back into cover all before I could tell him not to. We were isolated on the slopes of Richter's citadel with no help in sight and facing off against a regiment of heretics and, of course, he had to draw their attention to us.

'You had to draw their attention to us, didn't you?' I said.

He showed me his idiot grin. 'Suppressor on the sniper rifle makes it difficult to see, and if they could hear me shooting over this racket they have better hearing than an Anatarean devilhound.'

Something about his confidence made me smile. 'Sometimes I suspect you might not be as stupid as I thought.'

'I am touched,' he said.

'Sometimes I think you are even stupider.' He nodded, stood up and took another shot then another and then another. I stood up and risked a glance. In the flickering darkness, at range and without a sniper-scope, it was difficult to see what he was shooting at. It was not difficult to see the enemy though.

A horde of them was out there, thousands upon thousands, armed with every form of man-portable weapon I could think of. They moved to the beat of great solemn drums, with the mindless collective will of insects swarming to defend their hive. I thought of the walking dead we had fought and the truth is I could not see much difference between them and these living soldiers. The heretics might still be breathing but they seemed just as mindless and just as insanely brave.

Of course, that is not necessarily an advantage on the field of battle. There is a time for bravery as there is a time for turning tail and fleeing. The heretics were moving into position to face a battle-line of Leman Russ battle tanks. The tanks' weapons blazed and cut them down.

'This is madness,' Ivan shouted. I thought about it for a second. He was right. Even if the heretics had just a small hope of taking out a Leman Russ, it did not stop some of them advancing and trying to use grenades. 'They don't have a chance.'

From above us, the enemy field artillery kept shooting and I realised what was going on. 'They're not meant to have a chance. Richter, or whoever is in command here, does not need to keep them alive. They are a distraction. They're there to keep our lads' attention focused on killing them while the enemy artillery does its job.'

'A masterly summation, Lemuel,' said Macharius. He and Drake and a group of Drake's bodyguards dropped into the shell-holes around us. How had the inquisitor summoned them, I wondered? They must have been close by, to have found us in the chaos.

'Surely you can order our tanks to return fire.'

'I have,' said Macharius, 'but if they do that the infantry will swarm over them. In their numbers, with grenades and melta bombs, they will inflict heavy casualties.'

He was right and there was something he was not saying,

which was that no matter how well disciplined a tank crew might be, they were not going to ignore an immediate threat to their own safety in order to concentrate on those distant batteries. Whoever had ordered this suicide attack had known what he was doing. 'What are we going to do then?' Drake asked.

'Whatever we can,' said Macharius. 'But our first order of priority must be to silence those guns.'

All around us artillery spoke in voices of thunder and tanks replied by spitting spears of fire. The earth shook. The cold air swirled. The chanting of the heretics throbbed. Macharius continued to speak into the comm-net. I saw figures begin to converge out of the gloom. They wore the green of the Lion Guard, but their uniforms were torn and bloodied. Many of them had been wounded, but they were prepared to fight alongside their commander. If we were lucky there was perhaps a company of us. The Emperor alone knew how many men waited for us up at those gun emplacements.

That was at the moment though. I felt sure we were going to find out.

Macharius gave it five minutes for the crews of the destroyed tanks to converge on our position along with infantry from the brewed-up Chimeras. They came out of the shadows in twos and threes, moving cautiously along the ground, using every scrap of cover. Their caution was warranted. The enemy had other things to do, but if they had noticed those stragglers they would have taken the few seconds required to wipe them from the face of the planet.

We assembled on the edge of a blast crater, and Macharius spoke. His voice carried over the cacophony of the battlefield, clear, precise and thrilling. 'Our comrades are pinned down and under assault by the foul heretics on the hill,' he said. 'We are going to do something about that and then we are going to enter that hive and put an end to this war once and for all.'

His voice held no doubts, only absolute certainty of victory, and I could tell from the faces of the men around me that they all believed him. No matter what doubts they might have had back on Acheron, they had none here. They could not afford to have them. They were under fire and facing superior numbers. They *needed* to have faith in the man leading them if they were going to come through.

'We are going to wipe out those heretics in the name of the Emperor, and we are going to cleanse this world of all evil.' He made it sound so easy. We were just going to march up there and settle the matter. No matter that we were outnumbered ten thousand to one.

'You are all chosen men – picked by me, selected for your courage and your skill in soldiering. Those deranged madmen up there are no match for true soldiers of the Imperium. And we are going to show them that.'

And we were. All of the men stood taller, breathed more deeply, held their weapons ready to fight. Macharius continued giving out orders and we listened and made ready to obey.

When he gave the command we moved out.

* * *

Macharius had read the battlefield as if it were a map. Our route along the flanks of the rising ridgelines kept us away from the bulk of the enemy horde and out of line of sight of the guns. Even if we had been noticed, we would not have seemed like much of a threat to the heretics. They were concentrating all of their attention on the Leman Russ below us. Most of the tanks had withdrawn to use what cover the ridgelines provided. Their lack of mobility would soon leave them easy targets for the oncoming infantry. At close range, grenades could smash the drive-cogs of the tanks. Filter covers could be wrenched away and explosives dropped down the pipes. At very close range a tank without infantry support becomes extremely vulnerable.

As we clambered up the hillside I paused for a moment to look back. Below us the great green and brown stain of the enemy infantry raced downhill. A number of Leman Russ tanks hull down on the broken ridges of the hive's side blazed away at them. Huge towers of rockcrete dust erupted around the tanks as a human wave of screaming diseased bodies threw themselves forward to die beneath their tracks. Above us, the artillery blazed away from their emplacements.

Macharius led us, crouched low, moving forward and upward with no sign of fatigue. His bolt pistol was in one hand, his chainsword in the other. The ground was broken and churned, the light uncertain, the footing dangerous and yet he picked his way forward with absolute sureness. I advanced as fast as I could to catch up with him and Drake. It was my duty to be there and defend him and to do that I needed to be close.

Anton and Ivan followed in my wake, scuttling along on hands and knees, moving ape-like through the darkness, keeping out of sight. We progressed up the side of the hive, moving from cover to cover, from extruded ventilation tower to impact crater, moving sometimes through fissures and sometimes in the shadow of great leaking sump pipes.

Beneath me the ground shook, and not just from the impact of the shells. It was like being an insect scuttling over the skin of some great beast and feeling the beat of the heart and the rasp of breathing beneath. The hive citadel was still functioning. Systems down there still worked. Sweat stained my tunic. Condensation had begun to form within my rebreather mask – I could feel it running down my cheeks. My lips tasted salty when I licked them.

Guns were firing somewhere off to our left. At first I thought Macharius had misjudged our path as he led us ever higher but then I realised it was not so. He was moving us into a position where we could get to the batteries' defenders and, hopefully, take them by surprise. We were going to need to do that. It was just about the only advantage we would have.

Macharius stopped. He crouched in the shadow of an industrial pipe, looking down upon the gun batteries below us. He studied them carefully, head tilted to one side as he tried to gauge the weaknesses of the enemy position. It took him only a few heartbeats, then he extended a finger.

'Lemuel, take those dozen men and attack that gun when you see the signal flare.' His hand indicated Anton and Ivan and a group of other green uniformed troops. All told there could not have been more than a hundred men with us and we were attacking ten times our number. Macharius never let little things like that stop him, though. His eyes narrowed. 'Destroy as many other guns as you like but leave that one intact.' His fingers stabbed out indicating the one second-nearest to our position.

'Yes, sir,' I said. The others nodded. He gave instructions to the rest of the men and his plan was clear – we would attack the flank of the enemy position closest to us and destroy as much as we could. It would certainly disrupt the battery's fire on the Leman Russ below but it would probably not do much for our health. That was hardly an objection though. We were doomed unless our tanks broke through and overran the position. The enemy would simply destroy them and at some point they were bound to notice we were here.

Once the orders were given, I looked at my men and gave the signal to move out. We scuttled downslope and headed towards the enemy.

It was dark. The only real illumination came from the muzzle flare of the enemy guns and the huge explosions caused by the turrets above us. They kept firing regardless of the fact that there were no real targets for them to hit. Most of our surviving tanks were in their blind spots. Those that weren't had not survived. In any case, they did not seem to be suffering from any shortage of ammunition.

The slope was cold and slippery. Some of the rocks were razor-edged. There were trenches and furrows left from the moonfall impact that were invisible until you were almost on top of them. They were only intermittently visible in the flash and glare of the guns and you needed to remember where they were in the periods of darkness as you advanced.

To make matters worse, our own boys were not exactly inactive. The Leman Russ kept up a hail of punishing fire on the heretics. Some of their shells went astray and arced down near our position.

'It would be just my luck to live through a brew-up and be killed by a shell fired by my own side,' said Anton. His voice cut through a sudden silence on the battlefield.

'Some of those boys down there know you're up here,' said Ivan. 'They're not aiming at the guns at all.'

'Ha-bloody-ha.'

'Quiet, idiots,' I said, making a chopping gesture with my hands.

'Yeah, because they are going to hear us from down there while they are deafened by their own gunfire.'

'No,' I said, 'but they might hear us when we get closer. Anton, find a place where you can cover us. The rest of us are going in. We need to be able to rush the place when we get the signal.'

'I get the boring job again. It's not fair.'

'The Emperor help us all, I am relying on you to give us cover.'

I could tell he was grinning by the way the scar writhed across his forehead.

'So it's come to this,' grumbled Ivan. 'We are dependent on Anton. We're doomed.'

The flare rose over the enemy position, lighting everything up in its brilliant glow.

'Move!' I said.

We raced downslope, keeping to cover. Ahead a few of the heretics were staring up at the flare, wondering what was going on. Most of them were concentrating on shooting. Gunners stared into sights, fiddled with loading mechanisms, muttered technical prayers over their weapons.

None of them had thought to look behind them and I prayed to the Emperor that none of them decided to do so now. I glanced off along the ridgeline. There were a score of guns there along with their crews. There did not seem to be anybody else. All of the heretics who could be spared were below us, charging under the tracks of our armour.

I charged forward, shotgun at the ready, followed by Ivan and the rest of my improvised squad. No one paid any attention. No one expected such an attack and certainly not by such a tiny group of men. We had almost reached the enemy gun when someone looked up. He did not pay any attention to us at first, probably assuming that we were heretics like himself, but then he did a double take. It was the last thing he did before I turned his head into bloody mush and removed it from his shoulders.

I pumped the action of my weapon and readied another shot. Anton opened fire and one of the enemy gunners slumped forward over the side of the weapon. His companion turned and said something to him, then pushed him, shaking him by the shoulder as you would a companion who has fallen suddenly asleep; then he noticed the blood on his hand…

Anton's next shot took him in the head and sent him tumbling backwards. Most of his companions continued to fire but one or two of them had noticed something was wrong. An officer turned to glare at us and reached for his sidearm. I pulled the trigger and he collapsed in a welter of blood and entrails.

The rest of my squad opened up and more of the enemy went down. Then we were among them, carried by the momentum of our rush and our enthusiasm for killing. It might have been my imagination but I thought I heard the sound of more shots being fired in the distance. It was difficult to tell over the roar of the guns and the thunder of battle.

A man jumped at me, screaming, aiming a heavy metal power tool at my head. As he did so, another heretic raced towards me, raising an autogun.

I sprang to one side and aimed the shotgun as I fell. Autogun fire chewed up the ground where I was standing. The jumper, worse luck, landed on the far side of the trace of fire and came towards me.

I aimed the shotgun at the man with the rifle and pulled the trigger. The weapon kicked against my shoulder. The shooter fell, his legs cut off at the knees. He screamed and let go of his gun. I twisted, pumping the shotgun as the man with the huge spanner swung it down, intending to shatter my skull.

I wasn't fast enough. Even as I swivelled the shotgun to bear on him, the power tool had begun its downward arc. I tried to twist myself to one side but slipped in the blood and dust.

My attacker's head exploded, covering me in brains and body fluids. It happened as if by magic and I wondered for a moment whether Drake had used his psyker powers. Then the same thing happened to another member of the gun-crew who was drawing a bead on Ivan with his sidearm and I realised that my saviour had been Anton.

On his own he seemed to be doing as much damage as the rest of us. I realised that in our own way, on a smaller scale, we were doing what those heretic fanatics down in the valley were doing, providing a distraction while a distant lethal attacker wiped out the people fighting against us.

Bodies fell and we surged up to the gun. Even as we did so, a line of blazing fire cut in front of us. An enemy Hydra, deeper in the position, went up in a ball of hellfire. I glanced over at the gun on the extreme left of the battery and it had wheeled on its mount and was firing across the emplacement and into the other heretic guns. Macharius had seized the first gun and turned it on our enemies. I could see him standing on its side, partially covered by its armoured shield, directing fire deeper into the enemy position.

I laughed and ordered my men to get behind the controls of the weapon we had seized. Soon it too had been turned on the enemy position. It was part of Macharius's plan that we would not be discovered too soon. The enemy were concentrating their fire on the Leman Russ below and any of their own weapons that went up would be taken as victims of the tanks' response, at least to begin with.

Our captured gun roared as we joined in, sending bursts of armour-piercing shells tearing through the enemy position. In the rage and confusion of battle, we managed to take out all of the enemy guns in our line of sight before anyone noticed us. There were still guns firing at our troops down below but they were out of sight, hidden from us by the curve and roughness of the ridgeline.

A moment later, Macharius came racing up with the rest of his bodyguard. 'Very good, Lemuel,' he said. 'Now we must repeat this at the other side of the emplacement.'

'Nothing is ever easy,' muttered Ivan from my side. Anton came loping down from the hillside to join us. He had a satisfied air about him, that of a man with a job well done.

'I got twelve of them,' he said as he reached my side.

'Only a few million more and we're done then,' I said. He nodded pleasantly, as if he had no doubt in his ability to kill that many and it was just another day at work. It was all right for him, I thought sourly. He did not have to get into close combat with these heretic frakkers.

'Soonest done, soonest we get some beer,' he said.

'And where the hell are we going to get beer in this forsaken place?' I asked.

'Maybe the heretics will have some,' Anton said, ever hopeful.

CHAPTER TWENTY-FIVE

We moved along the ridgeline, skipping from the tangled remains of one destroyed enemy gun to the next, using them for cover, killing any of the enemy wounded we encountered. As we rounded the bend, we saw more enemy guns emerging from an arch in the hive side as well as more infantrymen. An unending stream of heretics seemed to be coming from that gate.

I took a deep breath. There was no way we could fight our way through so many of them and no way that they could fail to notice us once our attack began. There were thousands of the enemy pouring out from underground. I realised that even if we had killed ninety-five per cent of the population with the moonfall there were still millions of enemy below us. Not all of them would be soldiers but even if it was one in a hundred we were still colossally outnumbered.

I turned to Macharius for guidance. 'Sir?' I said.

'Take the nearest guns,' he said. 'Turn them on the gate. Close it.'

All hope left me. Even if we closed the gate there were still thousands of the foes out there on the ridgeline, more than enough to put paid to our small force. All we could do was lay down our lives so that our comrades would live. Our own were already over.

'Right you are, sir,' I said.

The one good thing about being such a small force was that nobody noticed us at first. I doubted I would have if our positions had been reversed. I mean it was madness for fewer than a hundred men to attack an enemy with fifty times their number.

Of course, we had some advantages. Most of the enemy ordinance was pointed at ninety degrees to us, firing down into the huge battle going on below, and that's where most of the enemy attention was going as well.

I saw officers ordering their men to the front line. They were moving in columns through gaps in the ridgeline, heading down into the battle below, an endless line of human sacrifices offered up to the hungry gods of war, by a High Command who did not care whether they lived or died. I felt a sudden flash of sympathy for them that I quickly quashed. That was no attitude to enter a battle with.

Macharius looked up at the sky as if he expected to see something, glanced at the chrono on his wrist and then gestured for us to begin the attack.

We advanced taking advantage of every patch of shadow, every scrap of cover. We did not want that vast army of enemy faces turning in our direction until the absolute last second.

Anton took up position amid the smashed remains of one gun, lying along its twisted barrel, allowing himself to peek out over the top and set his rifle. Anyone looking at him in the bad light would most likely see only wreckage. They would have to be looking directly at his rifle to see the muzzle flash as well, and if they were looking at it that way they were most likely dead anyway. It was a nice choice for a sniper's nest and it meant that Anton would most likely outlive the rest of us by a couple of minutes. Until he ran out of ammunition. Even if he wasn't spotted he would be a lone Imperial soldier on a battlefield surrounded by heretics, in sub-zero conditions, on a world where plague was all too common.

I dismissed that thought. It was pointless worrying about Anton. I had my own skin to think about and Ivan's and Macharius's.

The Lord High Commander loped forward like a great stalking cat. In the thunder of battle he did not need to creep silently but I knew he was doing so. He moved as if there were every chance of an alerted enemy sentry overhearing him and still managed to outpace the rest of us.

Next to him was Drake. The inquisitor glided forward over the ground, as if his feet did not quite touch the ground, and when I looked I could see no prints in the dust. His cloak fluttered around him; his shadow performed a sinister dance behind him in the flickering, multi-sourced light. His ten remaining bodyguards moved along in his wake, silent as ever. Some ancient techno-magic had darkened the mirrored face-guards of their helmets so they would not give away their positions. They held their weapons ready to use at any moment.

I wondered if they were still the same guards that had followed Drake back on Karsk, back at the start of our adventures with Macharius. I had never really spoken more than a few words to any of them, never seen them off guard, and never got to know them. I thought perhaps the movements of some were familiar, but that might just be the product of similar training. I was most likely going to die without ever knowing them.

Ivan moved along beside me, keeping Macharius in sight. All of his attention was focused on the Lord High Commander. He was ready to throw himself forward and take a bullet for the man if needed. Even with all my doubts, I was prepared to do the same. It takes a lot to alter the habits of a lifetime.

We had almost reached the first enemy gun. A column of troops moved past it on the far side, still heading for the battlefield. Macharius's mouth moved and I could see he was still talking into the comm-net, giving orders, keeping commanders' morale up, doing whatever needed to be done. I prayed to the Emperor that the comm-grid remained functional enough for those on the receiving end of his commands to follow instructions.

Maybe they were. A sudden hail of detonations exploded around the near ridgeline, sending the enemy ducking for cover. Macharius gave the signal for Ivan and me to move forward to the nearest gun. I hooked the shotgun over my shoulder and drew a knife. I was going to try to do this without drawing attention to myself. To my surprise four of Drake's bodyguards moved with us, blackened wires held in their outstretched hands. Garrottes, I realised.

We scooted forward, holding ourselves low, keeping the bulk of the gun between the enemy column and ourselves. The gunners on the back of the chassis loaded as an officer gave them instructions. They were brave men or uncaring. They somehow managed to ignore the hail of fire raining down near their position as if confident that it would not touch them.

They had faith in their own way, I supposed, and it was, in a strange fashion, justified. They were not going to be hit, save by accident, because Macharius had ordered it so. Of course that did not mean a stray shot could not hit them. I had been on enough battlefields to know that nothing ever goes completely according to plan.

Not waiting to take any more chances I raced forward to the side of the vehicle. It was in firing position, with great armoured legs extruded from its sides to hold it in position despite any recoil. I ran into its shadow, alongside the tracks. I pressed my back against them and waited for Ivan and the others to catch up with me.

There was something at once reassuring and unsettling being so close to the great armoured fighting vehicle. Reassuring because of the metallic smell and the strange incense of the engine emissions, because the vibration of the internal power systems reminded me of other vehicles I had ridden in. Unsettling because there was a strangeness to the scent, an odour of rot and corruption, the like of which I had never quite smelt before. It was as if the metal of the gun itself held some sort of disease. I wondered if that was even possible.

I grabbed my bayonet in my teeth, reached up and caught the top of the track, below the armoured mudguards. I pulled myself up, feet resting on the bolts holding the great drive wheels that powered the tracks when the vehicle was in motion, and I swarmed over the side. Just ahead of me was an officer. I stepped forward, threw an arm over his throat, pulled his head back and stabbed with my knife.

A moment later Ivan and the others were over the sides. Ivan dived on the nearest crewman and the storm troopers leapt forward like shadows, looping their garrottes around the necks of their targets. The officer died beneath my hand, kicking out in frantic agony, his bowels voiding, urine and blood soaking the legs of his tunic. I let him fall and I moved over to the open hatch on top of the gun. I dropped in through it, into the dimly lit interior of the modified Hydra.

In a way it was like coming home. Ever since basic training I have felt comfortable within the hull of an armoured fighting vehicle. I like having metal walls around me, shutting me out from all of the dangers of a battlefield, or at least minimising them.

I had never driven anything quite like this modified Hydra. The fact that it had been manufactured by heretics made it even less familiar. Nonetheless most vehicles of human construction share some common design elements – the ancient templates from which they are worked make it so. Almost invariably the drivers' sections are at the front of the vehicle so that they can get a clear view of where they are going.

I moved forward in a fighting crouch, knife at the ready. The body of the tank cut off much of the sound of battle. It seemed almost quiet after the hellish clamour outside. I could hear the voices of the heretics up front as they talked to each other in their wheezy, guttural tongue. I heard one man cough, and it was as if a great mass of phlegm moved around within his chest as he did so.

I had no idea what they were saying and no desire to find out. Even as that thought crossed my mind, one of them started to gabble at the other. Perhaps his companion had insulted him or perhaps he was excited by the carnage all around him. It seemed much more likely to me that he had just found out something was going on around him, as if he had received a message about the attack on the gun above.

I stuck my head around the corner and saw what I expected. Two men sat together in the traditional drivers' bucket seats. Before them was a command altar with the standard controls one would expect on a vehicle like this. The one who I assumed to be the driver looked up as I came in and reached for his sidearm. I stepped back, angled the shotgun around the corner, pulled the trigger and stepped away.

The roar of the gun was deafeningly loud within the close confines of the tank's interior. Even so I could hear the screams. The pellets of the shotgun blast ricocheted within the cockpit like thousands of small angry metal wasps, bouncing off the metal surfaces until they came to rest in something soft and massive enough to stop them or until they lost all momentum.

I had chosen to fire at an angle that reduced the chances of the pellets flying back to hit me. Even so some of them did. It was difficult to imagine the convoluted course they must have followed, but if you fire enough of something, dumb luck dictates you have a chance of hitting anything, including yourself, even when you are standing around a corner. I took a pellet in my hand. It drew blood. Another gashed my cheek. Another tore a strip from my leg. None of the wounds were serious. I waited for a second and risked a glance around the corner again.

I put my head lower this time so that if the driver was aiming for where I had been it would take him a fraction of a second to alter his aim. I need not have bothered. The two heretics were a mess. One of them had lost an eye and his face was covered in blood. So was his neck, as the flesh had been torn and an artery had been hit. Blood pumped between the fingers he was using to try to hold the wound closed. It was not going to do him much good – he would bleed out in a minute at most.

His companion looked worse. He was clutching his stomach. It had been perforated in a hundred places. He too was splattered in blood, his own and his companion's. He had absorbed most of the blast. His sidearm lay on the cockpit floor. His mouth was open and blood ran from it. The shots had smashed his teeth in a score of places. One of them had buried itself in a molar and glittered at me.

I was not going to risk another blast at close range in this tightly enclosed space. The cockpit was too small to risk it. Instead I stepped forward and slammed the butt of the shotgun into the driver's face. Bones snapped, and so did his neck. He had been strapped into his chair and braced and the force of my strike pushed his head back at an unnatural angle.

His companion said something in a terrified, pain-filled voice. I felt something like guilt and that made me hit him all the harder, smashing his skull until it was little more than jelly.

When I was sure they were both dead, I pulled the driver from his chair. There was no time to wipe it clean of blood or other stuff. It squelched as I sat down. The place smelt like the inside of an abattoir but all the time there was that strange, sickly sweet, mould-like smell I had come to associate with the battlefields of Loki.

I wiped the blood off the driver's periscope with the sleeve of my tunic. The seat of my trousers felt wet and I knew it was because of the blood there. My boots squelched when I moved my feet on the control pedals. I made a few invocations experimentally as my hands danced over the controls. The Hydra still followed the patterns of the old rituals and the vehicle roared to life beneath my hands. I glanced into the periscope and studied the battlefield.

The enemy troops flowed past us, heading down into the battlefield. They had not yet realised that the tank was under enemy control. Hopefully they would not for a few seconds yet. A shudder on the ceiling above me told me that the turret had started to traverse. I had no idea what it was aiming for. All I could hope was that Ivan had managed to take over the controls. He had always been a better than competent gunner.

The thought struck me that even if Ivan was not in charge of the guns there was still something I could do, even if it cost me my life. I hit the controls, heard the engines roar to life and got the great vehicle into gear.

I won't say that driving the heretic Hydra was exactly like driving an Imperial vehicle but it was close enough. The basic principles of guiding a tank or anything else with tracks remain the same no matter what it is you are in. If you put forward power on both treads you go forwards. If you put both treads into reverse, you go backwards. If you put one tread into forward gear and the other into reverse you rotate. That's what I did now. When I heard a grinding sound from the sides of the tank I realised I had forgotten to retract the stabilisers.

Gibbering, wheezing noises came from the comm-net. There was an angry, interrogative sound to them. Given their volume and the fact they were coming from the ear bead of the nearest corpse I could only assume that someone was asking me what I was doing. I kept my attention focused on the periscope even as I fumbled for the controls that would retract the stabilisers. I did not want anything to slow us down once we started to move.

Pistons hissed and there was a clanging sound from the sides and rear of the tank as the stabilisers retracted. I had guessed correctly. In the periscope I saw the faces of a few heretic soldiers turn to look at me. Most of them kept marching with the strange, drugged discipline that had been so common in the trenches.

I fed full power into both tracks and the tank raced forward, almost leaping from the pit in which it had been hull down. I prayed to the Emperor that one of the Leman Russ down there did not choose this exact moment to aim an accurate shot at us. My heart was in my mouth until the Hydra was on the other side of the slope heading right down into the marching army emerging from the hive side.

I saw eyes open wide in panic and men turn to scramble away as they realised what was happening. Only a few had and as they turned they barged into their annoyed companions and were tripped and fouled, their flight impeded by all the marching men around them. By then I had the tank in their line. It bumped and juddered. Faint gurgling screams came from outside.

I had seen enough men run over by tanks to be able to picture the results of my driving in my mind's eye. I was leaving bloody smears and jellied bones on the rocky surface of the hive.

An officer held up his hand palm outward in the universal gesture that means stop. Perhaps he thought that the Hydra's driver had just made a mistake, taken a wrong turn, and needed someone to tell him what to do. I ran him over along with the company behind him that was already turning and starting to flee.

The chaos increased as they ran into the men behind them who had not yet realised what was happening. I fed the engines more power, trying to move as far and fast as possible and kill as many of the heretics as I could before order was restored, but they realised what was happening and someone set up an anti-tank weapon.

The tank left a trail of mangled flesh in its wake. The gun above me barked, sending a high-powered shell smashing into the top of the gateway through which the enemy marched. The rockcrete above the entrance cracked. A huge piece of statuary dropped, crushing the men below it, partially blocking the way through, disrupting the smooth flow of enemy soldiers emerging to do battle. It looked like Ivan had taken control of the Hydra's primary armament.

The gun fired again and once more the shot smashed into the arch of the gateway. To any outside observer it looked as if the gun was being fired wildly but I knew better. At least I hoped I did. The third shot convinced me that the gunner knew his business. The arch finally cracked and sent tens of tons of stonework dropping onto the soldiers below, sealing the exit from the hive until heavy equipment could be brought up to clear it. At least the murderous army below us on the slope would be getting no reinforcements. That only left the thousands of them already on the surface to deal with.

I threw the Hydra into reverse and increased the speed as I brought it round in a great arc, feeding slightly more power to the left track than the right. It was a simple evasive manoeuvre, intended to make it more difficult for anyone to draw a bead on us. I realised that less than a minute had passed and that the enemy were still struggling to understand what was going on. That would not last – even if they were still assuming it was incompetence or madness that was responsible for our actions, there was going to be a response soon. In the meantime…

I sent the Hydra forward again, crushing more heretics. The gun above me spoke in a voice of thunder. One of the enemy guns along the ridgeline went up in a pillar of fire and smoke.

'Well done, Lemuel,' Macharius's voice said over the comm-net ear bead. 'You somewhat exceeded your orders, but good thinking.'

'Thank you, sir,' I said.

'Keep them busy for another two minutes and thirty seconds. Help is on its way.'

I wondered what he meant by that. It did not seem possible that the Leman Russ had made so much progress against the enemy below us. I knew the tanks could not cover so much ground in so short a time. Perhaps he was only talking to keep morale up but that was not like Macharius. Perhaps he knew something that we did not.

I heard another gun opening up from behind us and saw another of the enemy weapons go up. It looked like Macharius's other bodyguards had captured a second mobile gun.

Of course, now that meant there were two of us facing off against the enemy. I hoped doubling our firepower was not the full extent of Macharius's plan.

CHAPTER TWENTY-SIX

I crushed more of the heretics. The gun destroyed more enemy vehicles and, at last, they started to respond. Men lobbed grenades at us. The Hydra shook with the impact. Some of the grenades were fragmentation and their shrapnel pattered on the sides like rain. I worried about the gunners exposed in the turrets but there was nothing I could do for them, except try to keep us moving and thus make us a harder target. I offered up a prayer to the Emperor that Ivan was safe and I brought the vehicle round hard. I was trying to keep the forward armour, always the strongest part of a tank, towards the enemy as much as possible.

Something hurtled into us from the side. I caught a flash from the corner of my eye. There was a detonation and the whole vehicle shook. For a moment I wondered if I was dead. Sparks flickered from the Hydra's systems, but the engine kept roaring as the power-core fed it energy. Then I heard a strange slithering, scraping, knocking sound like someone drawing steel against steel with a great deal of power. There was a metallic screaming noise. The vehicle juddered as if it were rolling over very bumpy ground on one side. The weirdest thing was that the other side was stable and the area around us was quite flat. The Hydra began to circle. The left control stick fought against my grip as if the spirit of the machine itself had decided to disobey me.

Then I realised what had happened. We had taken a hit to the left-side track. Tracks are the weak point of any armoured fighting vehicle. Judging by the sound of it, the treads had broken and were in the process of becoming unwrapped from the mechanism.

I cursed. The tank could still move, for the moment, unless the mechanism became completely fouled, but the left-hand drives would gain far less traction. That was what was sending us circling. I cut power to the right tread and we began moving straight again but at a fraction of our normal speed.

Another shot slammed into us. It was as if we had taken a punch from a giant's armoured fist. There was the sound of an explosion, the smell of smoke and burning. I heard something clattering metal on metal deep within the hull. I tasted ozone on my tongue and all the lights on the command altar flickered and died. The right stick stopped responding as well. The pedals were simply sprung-steel mechanisms beneath my feet. Nothing happened when I pushed them.

I wasted no time on invocations to try and resurrect the spirit of the dead war machine. It was gone and it was beyond my power to bring it back. Worse than that, the Hydra had ceased to move. It was a sitting duck for whatever weapon had already reduced it to a powerless hulk. If I remained within it I was most likely going to die there.

It was dark within the cockpit now, save for the brief flickers of sparks from the shorting-out systems and the lightning flash illumination of the battlefield being filtered in through the periscope. There was barely enough light to see by. I unstrapped myself and rose from the chair. My boot plunged into something soft and sticky which sucked and resisted when I tried to lift it. I felt soft snakes entangle my leg along with a sopping wetness and I realised I had put my foot into the remains of the dead driver. I pulled it free, filled with an urgent desire to get out of the doomed vehicle before I joined him in death.

I banged my head as I stood up in the unfamiliar small-ness of the cockpit and I stretched out my hands to touch the sticky bloodstained walls and guide myself through the gloom.

My heartbeat thundered in my ears and my breathing came in short gasps. Every moment I expected another shot to smash into the tank. As I moved down the corridor I could see a hole had been blown in the Hydra's side. It was not big enough to scramble through or I would have done so. I made my way through the gloom towards the hatch. The opening had been deformed by the impact of whatever had damaged the tank and the ladder had been bent out of all shape.

I reached up and pulled myself through. My tunic snagged

on a protruding edge and held me in place. I glanced around and saw that an enemy gun had been brought to bear on us. The loaders were working frantically and it was set at the perfect angle to hit us. It would not take them more than a few seconds to complete their actions and I was doomed to a fiery death when they did so. The shell would flash across the distance that separated us in a heartbeat. I squirmed and tried to get myself free. Nothing happened for a moment and then I heard fabric tear. The enemy gunner reached for a lever. I knew he was about to fire and that my life was over.

At that moment, brilliant trails of light split the sky overhead. I saw the gunner look up for a second, confused by what was happening. I took advantage of the moment to leap clear of the doomed Hydra. I noticed that Ivan and the others had already done the same. I hit the hard ground with a grunt and rolled, looking for cover. As I did so, I saw the comet trails of light sweep down towards the battlefield, each attached to a glowing dot.

In the first second I cursed. Was this some sort of orbital bombardment? Was I doomed to die under the guns of the Imperial fleet? Or was this a of meteor cloud, fallout from the moonfall?

I wondered if it could be an aircraft, but none I could think of moved that fast. In the few seconds since I had noticed them, they had come noticeably closer, flashing down with the speed of falling comets. They seemed to be aimed at the ground.

I found a fold of rock and threw myself behind it. For a

few seconds my thoughts were distracted by the explosion of the gun I had abandoned. Obviously the heretic gunner had remembered to fire. His shot turned the Hydra into a pile of burning wreckage. A smell of burning machine oil and roasting flesh filled the air and it struck me that if I had been but a little slower I would have been charred meat within its metal remains.

My heart pounded within my chest. There was a taste of bile in my mouth and my eyes were dazzled. When they cleared again the comet trails had descended further. I saw glittering lights at their tip and I was struck by their familiarity. They seemed to be slowing now, although their velocity was still fantastic. They must be missiles of some kind, aimed at the ground.

I fumbled for my shotgun and glanced around. I was surrounded by heretic soldiers, all of whom were looking up now. I could have taken a clear shot at the nearest but that would just have drawn their attention to me so I scuttled from rock to rock, crab-wise, seeking my way back to Macharius and the Lion Guard.

The flashing comet trails arced towards the battle and I saw for the first time they were aircraft decelerating at an insane speed that would leave anyone within them crippled by the force of gravity exerted on them. Fires flickered around them and the guns near me began to explode. It took me a second to realise that they were being destroyed by the newcomers. It took me another second to recall where I had seen those blessed vessels before.

They were Thunderhawk gunships and they were coming

in to land. As they did so there was an enormous earth-shaking noise as the sonic boom they had been outracing caught up with them.

The Space Wolves had arrived riding on the thunder.

The heavy bolters on the Thunderhawks blazed, sparking along the armoured sides of the modified Hydras, cutting through the bodies of men as if they were simply not there. One of them hovered in the air giving covering fire while the others landed, or rather hovered just above the ground. Hatches in their side opened, disgorging massive armoured figures. They leapt to the ground, legs flexing on impact, bolters blazing, not in the least discomposed by the deceleration of a landing that would have left an ordinary man crippled.

I rolled into cover, not wanting to be taken for a heretic and killed by accident. I needn't have bothered. One of the warriors noticed me. His head twisted to one side, attracted by the movement. His nostrils flared and he looked away, dismissing me as a threat. I might have been insulted if I had not been so relieved.

The Space Wolves numbered fewer than a hundred but that did not stop them. They bounded across the battlefield, moving into the heavy clumps of surprised heretics, turning them at once into prey and cover. Howling battle cries rose over the chaos of the battlefield. Blood fountained and chainswords flickered. In the distance I saw the captured Basilisk lurch forward, gun blasting, picking off its fellow heretics. Somehow the Space Wolves knew to leave it alone, that it was on their side.

They cut through the heretics like a chainsword through bone, smashing into them, leaving piles of corpses in their wake. They were a whirlwind of violence passing over the field.

I kept crawling, hoping to find a position from which I could contribute something to the battle. I found myself staring at a pair of ceramite-encased legs and looked up to see the face of Logan Grimnar looking down at me.

'We meet again, Sergeant Lemuel,' he said. His voice was a fierce growl but I thought I detected a glint of humour in his eyes. I pulled myself upright, using his massive armoured form as cover. I am not a small man but compared to him I felt like a child. He turned for a moment, snapped off a shot and said, 'It has been a while since we fought alongside each other. It pleases me to do so again.'

'Not as much as it pleases me to see you here,' I said, and I meant it. The Space Wolves might only have doubled our number of troops on the ground but they were turning the battle. They had arrived at precisely the right moment to take advantage of the chaos. I noticed that squads of them had already captured the modified Hydra and were holding them against the oncoming tide of heretics. They were firing the weapons down into the battle in the valley below and I guessed they were not shooting at the Leman Russ.

I could hear the roar of approaching armour now. It mingled with the sounds of shooting, the cacophony of battle and the howl of Thunderhawk engines overhead. Glancing around I saw that Macharius and the others had abandoned their captured gun and were making for higher ground. I understood why at once. They did not want to be mistaken for an enemy when the Leman Russ arrived. The Space Wolves kept fighting and shooting, pulling their captured tanks back from the ridge and out of the line of fire. Clearly they were not going to abandon their prizes until absolutely the last second.

'I must get to Macharius, sir,' I said. 'I am his bodyguard.'

'That is well, for I must speak to him. Let us go together.'

And so once more I found myself racing across the battlefield in the company of a warrior who was already legendary.

A detachment of Space Wolves fell into place around us. I would have said they were Grimnar's bodyguards but clearly he did not need any. He was quite capable of looking after himself. I have felt more threatened crossing the streets of a hive than I did running through that inferno of battle with the Space Wolves.

They wore armour so heavy a mortal man could not lift it and I wore only my normal uniform but still I struggled to keep up with them. They moved with long, easy loping strides that ate the ground beneath them. Nothing that got in their way lived. They laughed and growled as they shot and hacked.

I caught a hint of movement from the corner of my eye. I began to turn, raising my shotgun. By the time I had done so, a Space Wolf had lifted his bolter and removed the threat with a single shot. It happened again and again as we moved. I was never quick enough. There was never a threat

I perceived before they did. They were superhumanly aware of all that went on around them, raking the battlefield with senses that mortals simply did not possess. At least that was the way it seemed to me.

As we raced over a hump in the hive side, Grimnar turned, bringing his bolter to bear. The other Wolves did the same. A moment later we saw a group of heretics moving cautiously into view. The Wolves could not have seen them, could not have heard them over the roar of the battle and yet they knew the enemy were there. I struggled to work out how. Had they smelt them? It did not seem likely, but what other explanation was there?

More to the point, they opened fire at once. They shot with control and precision. There was none of the confusion you would have got in such a situation with a normal group of even veteran *human* soldiers. Every Wolf picked a different target and shot him, and then did it again and again. There was no hesitation, no moment when they did not seem to know exactly what they were doing. And they reacted as one, like the pack of feral hunters that they were. They shared an understanding that went beyond the merely human and made them seem almost like one large organism. I had seen Macharius forge units of men into well-honed machines but the Space Wolves seemed to operate that way on instinct, but I know not how.

We came at last to the position that Macharius and the Lion Guard held. I saw Anton watching us, eyes wide as we approached. He was standing guard on the lip of a crater, covering the battlefield with his sniper rifle, occasionally taking a shot when a clear target presented itself. He made the sign of the aquila over his chest when he saw the Space Wolves arrive. There was something odd about the movement. It was jerky. His tunic seemed much darker as well. He waved at me cheerfully.

A moment later we were bounding down into the position, where Macharius waited with Drake and the remnants of his bodyguard. They stood amid a ring of wounded and dying soldiers. Clearly it had not just been the heretics who had taken casualties. Macharius finished saying something into the comm-net and then looked up and gave a smile of greeting to Grimnar.

'As always you have chosen a good time to make an appearance, Logan Grimnar,' he said.

'I came looking for a battle, but this was only a skirmish,' said the Space Wolf. His voice boomed out. His words should have sounded bombastic but there was a confidence and a humour in them that made me smile.

'You will have your battle yet,' said Macharius. 'We are only knocking at the enemy's door. He has yet to let us in.'

'I am glad to hear that. We have come a long way for things to end so swiftly.' He sounded as though he meant it, as if he would be disappointed that a fight in which he was outnumbered a mere twenty-five to one by heretics was a let-down. I wondered what it must be like to feel so certain of victory. It was certainly inspiring in an odd sort of way to be confronted with such confidence.

'Well, if you have nothing better to do, you could perhaps secure the entrance for us,' Macharius said.

With Grimnar to think was to act. 'That we can do.'

No other words were spoken so he turned with his honour guard and raced away, heading back out onto the battlefield.

'Lemuel,' said Macharius. 'I find it reassuring to see that your luck or the Emperor's favour has not deserted you.'

'The Space Wolves brought me back, sir,' I said. 'It was their doing, not mine.'

'Yes, but they found you, Lemuel,' Macharius said. 'In all the chaos of battle, you ran into Logan Grimnar. And not for the first time.'

He turned to say something into the comm-net and his attention slid away from me. Even as he did so, he nodded his head to me. I was clearly dismissed. I looked around the vast shell-hole in which we were encamped. There was no sign of Ivan.

I walked over to the perimeter and took up a position beside Anton. 'You seen Ivan?' I asked. He leaned forward and studied the battlefield through his sniper-scope.

'Last I saw of him he was with you, on the thing that looked like a Hydra,' Anton said. His voice sounded odd. He squeezed the trigger. Somewhere below us a small figure fell. The barrel of the rifle tracked a little to the right. Anton sought another target.

I looked down and saw that his tunic was soaked in blood. I took a closer look at him and noticed he was pale and his face was twisted. 'What in hell has happened to you?' I said. 'Sit down.'

'No need,' he said. 'I am a goner.' He removed his mask

and I could see there was blood trickling from his nostrils and mouth.

'So you are a medicae now?'

He laughed until it became a horrible choking sound. 'Take a look for yourself, if you don't believe me.'

I pushed him down and opened the tunic. A huge sliver of shrapnel had sunk deep into his belly. It must have been agonising but he did not give much sign of it. 'Standard,' he said. 'I come all this way and I get taken out by my own side. It was those frakkers in the Russ down below. Overshot their target, shell exploded here. Can't feel my legs now.'

'Don't talk,' I said. 'We'll get you down to Drake, maybe he can do something.'

'Don't bother. It's getting dark and I feel a bit dizzy.' He stopped for a moment. 'At least I got to see the Space Wolves fight again,' he said. 'How many hivers from Belial can say that?' He sounded proud and pleased and his eyes were wide open.

'Shut up and I'll get you down to Drake,' I said but I knew it was too late. His skin was cold and his breathing had stopped and I knew that the idiot boy had contradicted me for the last time. I piled some rocks up over him and stuck his sniper rifle in the cairn to mark the spot.

It took me some time and then I made my way back to Macharius and waited for instructions. There did not seem to be much else to do.

CHAPTER TWENTY-SEVEN

With a mighty rumble of engines the first of the Leman Russ roared over the ridge and slammed down into the enemy position. It was at that moment they were most vulnerable, when their underbellies were temporarily exposed by the climb. That's when the enemy should have hit them with every anti-tank weapon they had. But the time for that had passed. The Space Wolves had descended from the assault guns they had captured and were ripping through the enemy lines. Macharius's small force kept up what fire they could in support while the Thunderhawks swooped overhead like great birds of prey, turning their guns on the enemy positions from above, slaughtering ground targets by the score, constantly in motion to stop them from becoming easy targets.

Once our armour arrived the battle was over. The terrified

and distracted enemy infantry had their hands full trying to cope with the constant strike and withdrawal of the Space Wolves. They did not think to defend themselves against this new enemy until it was too late.

By then, the Space Wolves all seemed to have somehow moved out of the killing ground. They were fighting their way towards the entrance that Ivan had partially sealed earlier, moving forward squad by squad, giving each other supporting fire, striking with a precision and assurance no mortal soldier could match.

Macharius moved into position nearby and surveyed the battlefield through his magnoculars, picking out points of weakness, giving directions to the tank commanders, acting as a spotter even as he read the tactical situation. He stood tall and confident and radiated power and assurance. It was as if he fed from being on the battlefield, a god of war drinking mead distilled from blood and terror. In some ways he reminded me of the Space Wolves, with his more than human ferocity and energy.

'It is done,' he said. And at that moment, as if he had commanded it, there was silence. I looked down on the field and saw that he was right. Every heretic was dead or had fled. We were in command of the entrance to the hive. He had achieved his victory.

We walked up to the hive entrance. The Space Wolves had settled into easy possession of it, standing or sitting in small groups amid the rubble and the corpses. They seemed as much at their ease as they ever were.

'Well met,' said Macharius. Grimnar rose from among his companions. He walked over to Macharius and loomed over him. He was one of the few men I had ever seen who could make the Lord High Commander seem small.

'Perhaps not,' Grimnar said.

'What do you mean?' asked Macharius.

'I do not like the way this place smells.' I doubt anyone else would have dared to say something like that to Macharius but Grimnar not only did so, but he also made it sound serious. And, truth be told, we all took him seriously. His instincts had been proven correct too many times in the past.

'What don't you like?' Macharius asked.

'There is the stink of old Darkness here, of ancient enemies, of the foes of the Allfather.' Something told me that by that he did not simply mean heretics. He pointed to the fast-decomposing corpses of our former enemies. I remembered all too clearly the way such bodies had come back to a hideous unlife. Perhaps I should have wondered why it had not happened here yet. 'These ones have been twisted,' the Space Wolf said. 'There is something unclean about them.'

He gestured at the hive with one huge armoured hand. 'There is something unclean about this whole place.'

Macharius turned to Drake. 'We must find Richter,' he said, 'he must face the Emperor's justice.'

I felt sure Macharius was more concerned with the traitor escaping his justice than the Emperor's, but it did not seem my place to say it.

Drake nodded. 'We must go below,' he said.

'It will take some time to clear the way,' Macharius replied. He turned to us and said, 'Get some rest.'

'We have only just arrived,' said Grimnar. He looked up at the turrets higher on the hillside. They had continued to fire down into the killing zones. 'I think, though, I can find something for my men to do while you recuperate from your labours.'

He turned on his heel and marched away, bellowing orders to his fellow warriors. I stood there, feeling numb. For the moment the fighting was over and I had some time to think.

It was cold. Ice had formed in the shadows of the rubble. Snowflakes were crystallising in the air. A vast cloud still hovered overhead and the dim greenish lights of the hive flickered on emergency power. A drumbeat of thought sounded in my mind. I had not seen Ivan since I drove the Hydra through the heretics. No one else seemed to have seen him either. It looked like he was another casualty.

I refused to accept it. The three of us had not gone thirty years in the Imperial Guard together just so I could lose them both in one day – it just did not seem possible. The pair of them had always been indestructible, emerging from every deranged adventure with a collection of scars and stories. I told myself to be realistic, that I had seen enough death to know that it came to everyone and often at random. Stalk around battlefields long enough and your number will come up. You'll find yourself in someone's sights.

I needed to find out what had happened to Ivan. I could not rest till I had done so. I got up and tried to retrace my path away from the brewed-up enemy gun where I had last seen him. It was not going to be easy.

I felt pressure build up on the back of my legs from the strain of moving downslope. Somewhere above us a turret fell silent and the sound of shelling dropped off a fraction.

I came to the burned-out remains of the Hydra chassis. It was just a pile of scrap metal now, twisted and fused and blackened by the passing of war. Bodies lay all around it. Most of them were in the state of advanced decomposition I associated with the heretics. One or two of them were the torn remains of more normal mortals.

I walked over and inspected the nearest. It wore the grey of one of Drake's storm troopers. Its mirrored visor was cracked and broken with droplets of blackened blood congealed on it. Within I saw the face of the storm trooper, for the first time ever. It looked normal and peaceful in death but it did not look like anybody I knew. I thought about burial, of saying the funeral rites, but I was just too weary.

I tried to recreate the path along which I had driven. You'd think it would be easy, what with tanks leaving tracks behind them and all, but there were bodies and signs of blasting everywhere. And that realisation did make it easier for I could trace from the blast circles every impact point at which the tank had been hit.

I studied the corpses of the fallen and noticed something familiar lying downslope and off to the left. I had found Ivan's body.

My heart sank when I saw the shattered remains of the broken bionic that lay close to the fallen figure. Ivan lay face down, his back bloody, coils of wire and metal emerging from his shoulder. Heart in my mouth I walked over to where he lay.

He was pretty badly beaten up. His back was riddled with shrapnel. His legs were wounded. His arm had been removed by the blast. I turned him over, worried by what I would see. Maybe his front was worse than his back. Maybe he was going to spill his guts all over the ground.

He didn't, but his eyes were closed. I checked his heartbeat and was relieved to find there was still a pulse. At that moment his eyes flickered open.

'What the hell happened to you?' I asked.

He looked up at me and said, 'Damned if I know.'

His jaw was twisted out of shape and his words mangled even more than usual.

'I was running away from the anti-tank gun. There was an explosion and I felt a pain through my shoulder.' He looked down at the metallic stump where his bionic arm had been.

'Can you walk?' I said. I tried to lift him to his feet. He stretched himself and rose shakily then walked over to where what was left of his arm lay. It did not look as if it were going to be repaired any time soon and we were a long way from getting any spare parts.

'How did it go? We win?' Ivan asked. 'The last thing I remembered was seeing some lights in the sky. I thought it was the explosion.'

'Space Wolves,' I said. 'Grimnar pulled our nads out of the fire again.'

'That was good of him.'

'I think he feels he owes Macharius for what happened on Demetrius.'

Ivan nodded and then took another experimental step or two. 'It's lucky he felt that way then. I was pretty sure we were all doomed. Where's the idiot?'

I wanted to tell him but I could not. The words just seemed to get stuck in my throat. I tried to force them out again and still nothing came, only a strange gasping noise that I could not even make sound like words.

'Damn,' Ivan said, his words mangled. 'Damn. Damn. Damn.'

We limped up the slope again towards where the rest of the Lion Guard were encamped. 'How did it happen?' Ivan asked eventually.

'Shrapnel in the gut,' I said. I paused for what felt like an hour and added, 'Our own side.'

He looked away and shook his head. 'Typical,' was all he said.

I lay on the side of a vast daemon. It was as big as a hive but its flanks were green and slimy. Warts the size of turrets emerged from its side, burst blisters made huge gates in its skin. When I looked up I saw a great grinning face looking down at me. It was the same daemon I had seen when I lay in the hospital back on Niflgard. It smiled, revealing huge glistening yellow teeth, but there was no humour in its eyes. They were empty abysses cold as the darkness between the stars. There was a vacuum in them that threatened to suck my soul right out of my body.

I knew I had to look away or I was doomed, so I forced myself to look down. For a second I was looking at the daemon's skin but that faded into translucence and I was looking at its internal organs, veins the size of streets, intestines big enough to hold a city. Corpses lay everywhere. They looked as if they had died all at once. Those street-veins were filled with them. They had that strange decomposed look I associated with the walking dead. I wondered what had happened to them.

It took me a moment to realise: life support failure, the nightmare of every hive dweller. The moonfall must have taken out the power and the circulation of air and all the cleansing systems must have failed. With the strange logic of dreams I was no longer looking at a daemon's innards but a dead hive city and I always had been.

It was not entirely dead though, for within it, like maggots wriggling through a corpse, things still moved. Some were monstrous, partially human, but too big and too large, with white skin that somehow reminded me of slugs. There were other monsters born of men who had fed on the diseased corpses and been twisted by it.

They could not be real, I told myself. I must be dreaming. And it came to me that I had experienced such dreams before in other places like this and they had always contained within them seeds of truth. I felt breathing become difficult as one of those walking corpses turned his glowing eyes to look at me and stretched out one gauntleted hand. I knew without being told that if he completed that gesture he would become fully aware of me and I would die. I turned to flee…

I came to wakefulness around the gate of Richter's cita-del. I could see Drake nearby and Macharius and Grimnar. A halo of light played around the inquisitor's head and I guessed he must have been working some strange sorcery of his. Perhaps the backlash of it had touched my dreams and those of the other Guardsmen around me.

Drake's whole posture spoke of weariness, as if he had been overstraining his gifts. He looked like a man who had just run for a day carrying a full pack. 'Richter is down there,' he said, 'and so are other things. If we go down there, death is waiting for us all.'

'It awaits every man around every corner,' said Macharius.

'That is well said,' Grimnar agreed.

'You are resolved then?' said Drake.

'Aye,' said Macharius.

'Very well then,' the inquisitor said. 'We should make ready to depart.'

'I want to get my hands on the traitor and put an end to this once and for all,' Macharius said. I picked myself up and looked around. Ivan lay nearby. He was awake and studying his surroundings. He had the veteran's gift for being able to sleep anywhere and at a moment's notice and wake in an instant. I walked over to him and drew my boot back.

'Cold here,' he said. He was looking in the direction of Anton's burial mound. I had shown him where it was.

'Then we'd best get you into the warm, little man,' said Grimnar.

I heard men discussing the arrival of the Space Wolves and how victory was certain with the Emperor's Angels beside us. There was a confidence in the air now, as if the presence of the Space Marines were a sign of the Emperor looking with renewed favour upon Macharius. Knowing the circumstances in which their aid had been granted I was a bit less confident but I said nothing. On a battlefield, morale is everything, and the presence of Grimnar and his band was good for our morale.

I heard the roar of Leman Russ engines and the grinding of great blocks of rockcrete being dragged away from the entrance of the hive. It seemed as if the gloom of this world had really infected me, for I did not share the soldiers' confidence in our ultimate victory. I had the feeling that none of us were going to come out of this alive.

The Space Wolves had already scouted ahead before we even entered the hive. They moved in advance of us now as we roared into the depths.

I rode along within the Leman Russ Macharius had chosen to be his new command vehicle, and eyed the streets warily. Dead bodies were everywhere and I half expected them to come springing to life around us.

In some ways Richter's citadel was like any other hive, smaller than most perhaps but otherwise the same. It was a complete city with its own life support systems, built level upon level, rising hundreds of metres into the air, sinking thousands of metres into the planet's crust.

The effects of the moon-strike were evident, though. The city was cold and dead inside. Corpses filled the area massively: life support systems had failed and air purifiers had ceased to function. In whole sectors people had choked to death on poisonous fumes. Obviously someone somewhere had been working on bringing the systems back on stream but it had come too late for the people who had died here.

Drake sat with Macharius in the command cockpit. 'There is an odd psychic pulse here,' he said. 'I don't like this at all.'

'You think this is another trap?' Macharius asked.

'I know it is.'

'Good,' Macharius said. 'Then we are in agreement.'

I thought again about the dead bodies and the lack of walking dead and I realised that the most likely reason they had not risen and attacked us yet was because it was not time for them to do so.

'There's something else here,' Drake said. 'The feeling of something tainted and evil. I sense the presence of Nurgle's daemons.'

'Grimnar said something similar,' Macharius said. 'He caught the scent of an ancient enemy, whatever he means by that. He looked happy about it, though.'

'He would. He lives to die in battle,' Drake said. 'I can think of few things the Space Wolves count as ancient enemies that I would like to meet.'

'If it is our fate to do so, it is our fate,' said Macharius. He sounded at once mocking and resigned. There was weariness in his voice and in his manner. 'All I ask is to settle my score with those who have betrayed me.'

I wondered if it was worth the lives of all the men who were going to die for that to be accomplished. I pushed the thought out of my mind. After all I was only there to drive the Leman Russ and put myself in the way of any bullets aimed at Macharius. I wondered at the fact that I had become so cynical. Had I been infected with something more than illness when I came here? Anton's death had hit me hard and made me all too aware of my mortality.

Ivan had been silent since we mounted the Leman Russ. We were not a cheerful crew as we pushed on deeper into the hive of the dead.

There were more and more corpses as we made our way down. They looked as if they had fallen to some disease. We drove for hours and everywhere we found death.

No one engaged us. No one attacked us. The hive lights were dim and flickered as if still on emergency power. The air had a greenish tinge to it that was in no way natural.

I don't know what Macharius had been expecting but I doubt that it had been this. I could sense the tension when Grimnar's signal came in. It seemed some of his Wolves had taken prisoners.

CHAPTER TWENTY-EIGHT

'We found them holed up in a hab-block,' Grimnar said, indicating the huddled group of pale-faced humans cowering in the shadow of the Space Marines. 'They're the only ones we've found alive so far. They must know something.'

Drake nodded. His security people had already scanned them to make sure they had no sub-dermal explosives and were not assassins. Looking at them I would have said they were typical hive workers or what passed for such on this world. They were about medium-sized for humans, pale-skinned, blond, with pinkish-tinted eyes and a look that reminded me of albino rats.

'Very good,' said Drake. 'Let us find out what they know.'

He strode up to the nearest, making no attempt to reassure them. A nimbus of light played around his head. When he reached out, a second halo of light jumped around the local's head. The man's face contorted, the tendons on his neck stood out, sweat appeared on his brow. He looked like a man losing a deadly struggle, which he probably was.

Drake's breathing became shallow. When he spoke his voice held the tension of a man who was trying to concentrate on performing two difficult tasks at once. 'I see,' he said. 'There was a plague. It struck down the local population after the moon-strike. This one thinks the world has come to an end. That these are the end-times.'

'As far as these people are concerned he could be right,' said Grimnar.

'He thinks we are daemons,' Drake said. 'More specifically he thinks you are.'

It was easy to see how a heretic could have got that impression of the Space Wolves.

'Was the plague released deliberately?' Macharius asked.

Drake's expression went blank for a moment. The local ground his teeth. 'He does not know. It's possible. The plague could be a weapon.'

'Even if it is,' Grimnar said, 'it might not have been released deliberately. The hive took terrible damage when the moon-strike hit. If the plague was being stored in an incubator it might have got loose by accident.'

'How did this one survive when so many died?' Macharius asked.

'There are always those who are immune to diseases,' Drake said. 'They have resistance. Even to the most virulent of plagues. This one may have it and there will be others.

It should be possible to create a serum against the disease from his blood.'

Macharius spoke into the comm-net, ordering all precautions against contamination to be redoubled. We had all been exposed to the plague now.

'How long did it take to strike people down?' Macharius asked.

'It all happened within hours of the impact.'

'Right through the hive?' Macharius said. 'That does not sound like an accident.'

'You're right. I also suspect that the whole population might have been particularly susceptible to this plague.'

'You mean it was intended to harm them.'

'Yes. Tailored to their genetic runes, so it spread swiftly and fatally.'

There was silence. There was no need to ask why. It was a recruiting drive on Richter's part, to bring about an army of the dead. I had no doubt that it would only be a matter of time before we met them. I thought of all the corpses on the fields outside. They had been activated by the gas shells fired upon us.

'Gas,' I said. 'They will introduce it into the life support systems once the disease has had time to do its work.'

'They've probably started already,' Drake said. 'That's what that greenish stuff is.'

'We need to find Richter and quickly,' Macharius said, 'otherwise we will be cutting our way through a whole city of the walking dead.'

Drake smiled. 'I know where to find Richter.'

Macharius looked at him. 'How?'

'His palace is below us. Everyone in the city knows where the Chosen One lives. Even these maggots.'

'The Chosen One?' Macharius asked.

'The warlord from the sky. He bears the Sacred Amulet of the Lord of Mortality,' Drake said. His eyes were closed once more and he seemed to be plucking the words directly from the hiver's mind. 'He was the first living man in ten thousand years to enter the Vault of the Great One and live. He came out bearing the symbol of their daemon god's power. That is why they follow him without question. That is why the plague priests believe he will lead them forth from this place to conquer the galaxy.'

Grimnar laughed. 'I have heard such stories before on a hundred worlds. They have all ended the same way.'

The hiver must have understood the Space Wolf's tone. His religious sensibility was outraged. He did something braver than I could. He spat on the ground at the Space Wolf's feet and gabbled something angrily in his local tongue.

'He says the Chosen One will kill you. He is invincible. He cannot be slain.'

Grimnar took no offence. 'I have heard that one before too. I will tear his heart out and make him eat it.'

'We move,' Macharius said. 'Now.'

Not even the Space Wolf disagreed with him.

Richter's palace was located exactly at the centre of the hive, spread over multiple levels, with an enormous dome above it. The area around it looked as if it had once been a park or a garden of a very strange sort. There were fungal trees which looked as if they had once been landscaped. Clouds of spores swarmed the air and webs of slime clung to the great mushroom-like structures. Everything looked diseased and strange. There were bodies strewn everywhere, blotched with black mould. Some of the corpses hung on what looked like ropes of snot. Others had become so overgrown with fungus that they were being held upright by it. The mould appeared to have emerged from within their bodies and turned them into strange pillars. In some places a dozen or so of the overgrown corpses had been piled together and looked like a disturbing many-headed, many-limbed statue.

Here, as in so many other places around the hive, the moon-strike had done its work. The area around the palace was filled with rubble and the central structure had suffered as well. There had been emplacements and turrets in its sides. There still were but most of them were broken, their weapons twisted piles of scrap, the fortifications cracked and splintered. That did not mean they were useless. Right now I could see figures moving up there, for the first time since we had reached the city. It looked like there were living inhabitants.

I considered that for a moment. They were moving, but that did not mean they had to be alive. I turned the periscope of the Leman Russ to bear on them and saw that cowled and cloaked figures garbed in green and brown, their garments stitched with unholy runes, appeared to be performing rituals amid diseased-looking cultists in the garb of soldiers. Glowing nimbuses of light surrounded the priestly figures. The soldiers seemed involved in more mundane tasks, bringing weapons to bear on us.

Even before Macharius spoke orders into the comm-net, our tanks opened fire. Shots flashed between the palace and our army. And already the Space Wolves were in motion, racing through the fungal gardens, heading towards the building in which Richter and his allies lurked.

'A ritual is being performed here,' said Drake. 'This is the centre of all the evil in this world.'

'Then it must be cleansed,' said Macharius. The first wave of tanks raced forward, moving towards the obscene forest. As they did so, spores erupted from the trees and began to clog their treads. As they ploughed into the trees, tendrils of mucus erupted and sprayed over them, coating hatches and exhaust pipes, to no visible or immediate effect.

The tanks pushed forward, slower than before. The guns in the side of the palace opened fire, concentrating on the lead vehicles and turning them into smoking wreckage. A leading Leman Russ exploded and the flames transformed its surroundings into blackened muck, which formed a swift-hardening tar, sucking at the tracks of the vehicles that followed.

It became clear that the plants were not there simply for decoration but formed as much of a defensive barrier as a minefield. A crewman bailed out of a brewed-up Leman Russ and dived for cover. One of the fungus-covered corpses came to life and grabbed him, hugging him close. Even as I watched, the mass of spores covering the animated corpse shifted to the Imperial Guardsman, flowing over his body, covering his eyes, entering his mouth and his lungs, choking him. The luckless man collapsed onto the ground and sprawled there.

Macharius considered this for a moment and then gave orders. A wave of incendiaries descended on the fungal forest, setting it alight. More of the black sludge appeared where the mushroom trees went up. They caught fire, exploding and popping in the extreme heat.

While this was happening the heretics kept a stream of fire pouring down on us, and I noticed now that more and more bodies were starting to appear around us, shambling into place, moving to attack us. The walking dead had risen to do battle once more.

Reports came in from the back of our column. The soldiers there were under attack from an army of the walking dead. At the moment they did not seem to be any great threat to the tanks, but they were costing ammunition and distracting our forces.

A heartbeat later I heard the faint sound of distant explosions and screams and static buzz on the comm-net. It seemed like something had, after all, managed to destroy at least one of our tanks. A shiver passed through me. How could walking dead men manage to destroy an armoured vehicle? They were strong and their mindlessness made them fearless, but that was just not physically possible.

Macharius asked for reports from the vehicles nearby. His head tilted to one side. Clearly someone had seen something.

He ordered the tanks of the rear-guard to keep firing, gave clear, clipped, concise instructions and then fell silent.

'What is it?' Drake asked.

Macharius looked at him. 'Some of the corpses had bombs attached to them. And there were heretics concealed in the masses of walking dead, using them as cover to get close enough to use grenades and anti-tank weapons.'

As I listened a vision of what had happened became clear. Our boys had been overconfident, simply running the undead over, splattering them under the tracks of their vehicles. The enemy had used that to their advantage and closed. Now our troops were being forced to expend ammunition on them. Macharius did not need to explain the implications of that to anyone. We did not have unlimited ammo. The enemy had an almost unlimited supply of walking corpses.

I imagined what I would do if I were them. Now we were firing at the oncoming horde, the heretics could pull back and let our troops exhaust their ammunition on the fearless walking dead. If our soldiers looked like slacking, they could renew their attacks with anti-tank weapons and grenades until they forced us to start shooting again.

It was a tactic that favoured them. Sooner or later our troops would tire or run out of ammunition. The heretics had a whole hive city of walking dead to draw on. We would run out of bullets and shells before they ran out of bodies to throw at us.

Macharius swiftly gave orders dividing our force into six columns and sent a column to cover each entrance into the plaza. The powerful Leman Russ war machines formed a barricade across the main entrances that would be all but impossible for the walking dead to pass through while the tanks had ammunition. A dozen tanks could block the widest of the entrances and the remainder formed a ring around them, turrets facing outwards, to cover any lesser approaches and to keep firing at the palace.

It was not a perfect plan but it would keep us safe for as long as we could keep shooting. It left two columns to work with. One was to form a flying reserve to interdict any enemy force that broke through or appeared unexpectedly. The last column, led by Macharius himself, was to take the palace.

Watching the Lord High Commander at work I was reassured. He had risen to the challenge swiftly and well. We might not make it out of the citadel alive but it would not be for want of trying.

More reports came in over the comm-net, this time from the Space Wolves. They had blazed a path through the fungal forest, had secured one entrance and were spreading out through the palace, killing any enemy they encountered.

Drake was listening in and said, 'They are hideously outnumbered in there. Even if one Space Wolf is worth a hundred heretics.'

'In those circumstances more like a thousand, but you are correct,' Macharius said. 'They will need our aid, although they would not thank me for saying so.'

I had seen Grimnar in action before and it was easy to imagine him stalking silently through the palace ahead, picking off enemies and retreating into the shadows to strike again. Even so, given the number of enemies in there, all they could really do in the long run was buy us time by distracting them.

Also, it has to be said that Macharius was not a man to let anyone else, even the mighty Adeptus Astartes, do his fighting for him. I looked at him out of the corner of my eye and saw there was something feverish about him. Here was a man who might be entering the last great battle of his life, facing his last test, seeing his last chance to grasp at glory. He had won every major battle except his last one here on Loki. He did not want to leave this life with an account unsettled. He did not want his last campaign to leave a mark on his unbroken string of victories. He had one last enemy to take down, Richter, and he wanted to be there at the kill. He knew he was dying and he wanted to go out in a blaze of glory. That was what I thought, at least.

He gave the order for the final column to advance towards the palace. At his command we laid down a curtain of fire, not at the palace, not at its defenders, but at the obstacles in our way. The hail of fire smashed through the blazing fungus. The sticky tar beneath the treads slowed the tanks but did not stop them.

Then the enemy opened fire with incendiaries and I saw the purpose of that dark residue. It caught fire, blazing up with incredible heat. It was something that would have fried an infantryman on the spot, but a tank is massive and it takes some time to heat.

'Push on!' Macharius ordered. We drove forward into a curtain of flame.

* * *

I held my breath. I could see nothing except flames and oily smoke ahead of me. I was simply driving forward in the direction of the palace entrance as I remembered it and praying to the Emperor that we did not deviate too far from the line.

There was nothing out there that I could think of that would deflect us by sheer mass, but even a slight inclination caused by an obstruction could shift us a fraction of a degree out of line and the cumulative effect of those might cause a lot of drift. I was tempted to make adjustments to the controls, but that way, too, might lead to disaster. My own imagination could take us out of the correct line.

Something smashed down into the Russ from above. The guns on the palace walls were still firing at us. The Leman Russ shook under the impact but its armour held.

'Keep moving, Lemuel,' Macharius said. His voice was calm and confident. 'We will soon be under the angle the guns can fire at.'

In his head, he was keeping the speed and range of our tank to the palace as well as all the other factors in the battle. He started giving out orders in response to reports coming in from the gates behind us. It sounded like the walking dead were attacking in force.

Ahead a burning man emerged from the flames. His flesh had been seared black but still he struggled to move. The dead were rising even in the former fungal forest but the flames incinerated them as that happened. It was a small mercy but I was grateful for it.

Suddenly we were clear of the fire. Ahead of us I could see

a massive ornate staircase, flanked by two huge statues of diseased angels. Both were cowled. Both had great bat-wings rising from their backs. One of them had a skeletal face, the lower half of which was covered in a rebreather mask. The other apparently depicted a man in the throes of a plague. He was smiling malevolently, his mouth a death's head rictus, his eyes narrowed in glee. The statues were so realistic they appeared to be alive.

I aimed the Leman Russ at the stairwell and drove up it, splintering the marble beneath the treads of the tank. The vehicle roared up and I glanced out ahead of us. Space Wolves held the hallway beyond us, crouched in cover behind pillars and obscene statuary. A hail of incoming fire splashed over us, until our own guns spoke in response.

A grinding sound behind us told me that other vehicles had arrived. I nudged the Leman Russ forward as gently as I could into the hallway, and pulled up, hull down alongside a stagnant ornamental pool. We could take the tank no further.

The guns kept firing. Macharius reached up and flipped the seal above him, opening the hatchway and pulled himself out. I followed swiftly, determined to guard him with my life.

CHAPTER TWENTY-NINE

I went up through the hatch, unslinging my shotgun, feeling the warmed metal of the hull vibrate beneath my feet. I risked a glance around and saw more and more Leman Russ emerge at the top of the stairs. There were so many of them now that the entranceway was all but blocked. Behind the tanks, towers of flame leapt and danced, and clouds of oily smoke spiralled upwards towards the roof of the hive.

I looked around and saw that the ornamental pool held scummy, stagnant, diseased-looking water. It was greenish and clogged with algae. Obscenely fat, whitish, slug-like bodies floated in it. Most of them bore the exploded-from-the-inside look that I associated with bolter shells.

There were corpses everywhere. Every single one of them either had its head torn off or its skull destroyed by bolter fire. The Space Wolves were taking no chances of having their foes return from death to trouble them again. I suspected it was less because the thought bothered them than because they did not want to waste the time.

The palace might have been beautiful once. There was a lot of marble and a lot of statuary but the place was *contaminated*. That was the only word I could think of to describe it. Things were blotched by mould and covered in curtains of mucus. A statue raised both hands to the sky, a bolter held between them. Yellowish slime dripped from under its arms. Paintings on the walls were covered in a fur of whitish mould. Small things scuttled everywhere. They might have been rats, they might have been beetles or they might have been some unholy hybrid of both.

Who could dwell amid all of this, I wondered? No one sane.

Macharius jumped from the side of the tank and landed on the edge of the pool. He kept his balance like a great cat. I dropped after him, and my boots slipped on the slimy lip at the water's edge and I almost tumbled in. I flailed my arms to keep my balance, somehow pulled myself upright and let myself drop to the ground. The thought of touching the polluted liquid made me shudder. Ivan dropped down from the side of the tank directly to the ground, which struck me as entirely more sensible.

Drake and the two members of his guard joined us. More troops moved up all around, taking cover where they could find it. Macharius moved over to one of the pillars to join Grimnar and his honour guard. The Space Wolf grinned at us, revealing his sharp fangs. He was not wearing a helmet or a rebreather here and seemed to feel no need for one.

'Glad you could finally join us,' he said. 'These unbelievers are most unwelcoming towards the Allfather's Chosen.'

'This is where the traitor Richter is,' Macharius said. 'We shall find him.'

'Of course, Lord High Commander,' said the Space Wolf. 'It will take more than a few thousand of these heretics to stop us.'

'What have you found out so far?'

The Space Wolf indicated the mould on the wall with one armoured finger. With no squeamishness whatsoever he drew a swift map of the entrance hall and the surrounding area using his finger. Once he tilted his head to one side as if listening to something and then drew a swift correction. He was obviously picking up reports from his scouts still.

I studied the diagram. It was large and covered a score of rooms radiating out from our position. One large corridor ran ahead and it had chambers running off it. An x marked rooms that had been cleared; a large number of them marked the map.

Grimnar started another map, indicating the levels above us. He sketched in the balconies on which the heavy weapons were mounted and swiftly marked those destroyed as well. It looked like he had cleared the area overlooking the route we had taken into the palace even as we advanced. It was an astonishing feat considering how few warriors he had compared to the defenders.

'The majority of the heretics were hardly fit to be counted as foes, more like target practice,' he said and laughed. It was an eerie sound. I could not detect anything like human mirth in it although his face showed something of the expression of a man making a joke. 'There are some present who appear much tougher than others. They have been changed.'

'Changed?' Drake asked.

'They look diseased but in their cases their illness makes them stronger and faster and feel pain less. They show signs of mutation.'

'Suffer not a mutant to live,' said Drake.

'Indeed. Though the stigmata these ones bear may be signs of their disease.'

'You mean the plague within them causes mutation.'

'It may be. I have encountered such things before among the worshippers of the Ruinous Powers. They shout the name of Nurgle as they fight and claim they are blessed even as we slay them.'

I saw Drake give a small shudder when the name Nurgle was mentioned. I knew why. The sound had the same effect on me. 'The Father of Pestilence has this world in its grip.'

Grimnar tilted his head to one side, gestured extravagantly and showed the inquisitor a sardonic grin. 'What gave it away?'

Drake stood up primly. He was not used to being mocked, but for all his power he was not fool enough to challenge one of the Emperor's Chosen.

'This is invaluable information,' said Macharius. 'What else can you tell us?'

'Monsters roam the corridors deeper in the building. More mutant creatures like great plague-riddled slugs. Our most advanced scouts report encountering alchemical laboratories with tank-grown abominations. They have cleansed those with fire and chainsword.'

I did not like the picture Grimnar was painting with his words but there was nothing I could do about it. We were going to have to fight our way deeper into the building – that seemed certain – and we were going to find horrors there. I consoled myself with the thought that it would not be the first time, but it came to me then that I had always had men there with me at the time, Anton and others, who had seemed in some ways immortal. Now even Macharius had lost his aura of invincibility. The shadow of mortality hung over him.

'Also, we have found some interesting altars,' Grimnar said.

'What do you mean?'

'It would be best if I showed you.'

We moved forward from the main entrance hall. The firing had slackened off as the heretic counter-attack faltered. We kept to the walls, picking our way through more headless corpses until we found the entrance to another chamber. This one was heaped with bodies and it was clear that the heretics had fought hard to keep it from the Space Wolves.

In the centre of the room was a massive altar. Great pipes ran from it to the walls. They had an organic look, as if they were alive. On the altar itself were numerous skulls, gilded with metal. They reminded me of the servo-skulls of Cardinal Septimus. Light flickered within their eyes. As we entered they spoke, emitting what sounded like curses in a language I did not understand. I wondered why the Space Wolves had not destroyed this accursed object. It did not seem like them to spare any obscenity created by the enemies of man.

We advanced into the room and I noticed there were Adeptus Astartes keeping guard at all of the entrances. They had quite obviously been stationed here and told to hold their position. Given how outnumbered Grimnar's men were they must have thought this thing important. Drake rubbed his hands together like a man well pleased.

He said something in what sounded like the language the skulls were speaking and they responded as if to a catechism. 'What is it?' Ivan asked. Drake shot him a look, warning him to be silent, and kept speaking. This went on for long minutes. The inquisitor's hands danced over the altar moving dials and pushing sliders. All the while an aura of psychic fire played around his head.

Macharius and Grimnar watched him. Their expressions gave nothing away, but I sensed a tension in the Lord High Commander. The Space Wolf looked interested, as if watching a show put on for his amusement.

The skulls' chanting took on an aspect of horrific plainsong. Some of their voices seemed to gurgle, some were so high as to sound like screams. Eventually Drake said, 'I have the key to the thing now. Richter is indeed here and so is the traitor.'

He returned to chanting and the air over the altar swirled as a holo-sphere came into being. It displayed a complex array of lines that I realised were a map of the palace. A blue area represented our position. A red area much deeper in the three-dimensional structure represented what I presumed was our target. Even as I watched it started to flicker and disintegrate, coming apart in lightning-like flickers and the smell of ozone. The singing skulls' voices changed until they were static screeches, howls of the damned.

'It seems someone objected to my intrusion,' said Drake. 'Did you get it?'

He looked at one of his bodyguards who nodded. 'Yes,' said Macharius.

Grimnar growled. 'I could find my way there.'

I doubted I could have from the brief glimpse of the map and the route, but it seemed I did not need to. All that was required was that I follow those who did.

'As can I,' said Macharius. 'Let us go and settle our scores and then leave this accursed place.'

Macharius formed us up in companies. Ivan and Drake and Grimnar went with him, surrounding him. I was also part of that select crew. The Space Wolves moved along in advance of us, scouting the ways. They moved along parallel corridors too, making sure we were not flanked.

We passed an elevator going down. Macharius did not even look at it. In combat it would be madness to take such a thing. They could be turned into death traps with very little effort. Instead we pressed on towards the first stairway. From up ahead we could hear the sounds of fighting.

The enemy must have known from the images Drake had conjured out of their data grid where we were headed. Heretics held the head of the stairs, lying down where they met the landing, providing as small a target as was possible.

Grimnar snapped off a command as well as a shot, and the heretic heads exploded. Guns skittered from their suddenly loosened grips. A grenade came arcing up the corridor towards us. Grimnar stepped forward, snapped it from the air and returned it to where it came with one throw. The resulting explosion sent gobbets of flesh flying.

A greenish cloud rose above the site of the explosion. I wondered whether it was a by-product of the grenade or from the bodies it had hit. The plague-infected corpses of previous battlefields were still on my mind.

'There are other routes,' Macharius said. 'We can easily be bottle-necked if we take only one approach.' He gave orders to the company commanders and sent them moving in the direction of different stairwells.

We moved down the stairwell, passing through the hovering green cloud. Bloated flies with chemically coloured thoraxes buzzed against the visor of my rebreather. There was a horrible glow in their eyes and pus dripped from their tails as if they contained poisoned stingers.

I slapped at one as it landed on my arm. The thing squelched, leaving a greenish stain on the cloth of my tunic. I heard a man gasp and turned to see one of the Lion Guard clutching at his arm. He looked as if he had been stung.

Drake raised his arms. An aura of fearsome power crackled around his head. He gestured and a wave of force erupted from his fists. Suddenly small orbs of greenish-yellow light blazed in the air. The flies burst and splattered with a strange frying sound.

'Who was stung?' Drake asked. Half a dozen Guardsmen

replied in the affirmative. Drake's eyes narrowed and he stepped over to the nearest. He gestured to one of his guards, who produced a blade and sliced at the man's tunic. The man's pale skin was blotched and where the insect had stung him was already starting to swell. Drake indicated again and his bodyguard sliced at the swelling. A small amount of yellowish pus bled out. 'Dress it,' he told the affected soldier and moved along the line. 'Anyone else who was affected should do the same thing.'

There was something about his voice that brooked no argument. I saw men begin to slice at their own flesh through their tunics.

'What is it?' Macharius asked. He kept his voice low but I was close enough to hear.

'Those flies were contaminated and their venom was too. Draining it may help.'

I did not like the way he said it. His tone made it sound as if he thought the victims were already dead. His bodyguards studied the wounded as if considering killing them. I am sure if Drake had given the command they would have.

We followed the stairs down. Grimnar went in the lead. I followed him and then Ivan. Macharius, Drake and his bodyguards remained close behind. My skin crawled as we went down. One grenade might take out all of us. Perhaps Grimnar with his superhuman reflexes and his ceramite armour might survive. I was pretty certain the rest of us would not.

My heart thumped against my ribs as we reached the foot

of the stairs. We looked out into a hall, at least a kilometre on either side and with a ceiling perhaps twenty metres high. Glass tanks lined the walls and in each, attached to the walls by an umbilical, floated bodies. They were not corpses. Each was the size of a full-grown adult man. Some had no skins, and flesh and muscle were visible for all to see. Some were still growing stomachs or hearts or internal organs.

It looked as if this was the place where Richter was growing his soldiers.

The floor of the hall was covered in more huge tanks, all filled with greenish fluids. The aisles between them were as wide as roads. In the tanks more bodies floated. These ones looked nearer completion. They had skin and features and as we walked by them their heads turned and their pinkish eyes followed us. I was reminded of the soldiers we had fought on the battlefields near Skeleton Ridge, but these warriors were larger and their faces were more wicked. There was a malign intelligence in their eyes, as if something ancient and evil looked out through them. I told myself I was imagining things but it was hard not to feel a shiver of suppressed nervousness when I passed them.

Hands reached out as I did so. White palms pressed flat against armourglass and I knew that, if they could, those floating figures would gladly have grabbed me and strangled me. As it was their hands and feet made constant slow bumping sounds as we passed them.

I felt the urge to turn the shotgun on the tank and shoot but I resisted. The pellets might not be able to break the armourglass and we would all be caught in the ricochet.

And something whispered in my mind that being touched by that greenish fluid would be very unwise should the glass break.

The company spread out, moving along the aisles between the tanks. I kept close to the Lord High Commander. I made sure the shotgun was always pointing more or less directly along the aisles, not wanting to risk the consequences of me being right about the tanks.

Over each tank were metal pipes that obviously fed chemical supplies into the fluid. Walkways ran along the side of the pipes and every so often ladders led up to them. I kept looking upwards, fearing that they would make a good site for an ambush.

We passed a junction between aisles still following the route Macharius had mapped out for us in his head. Grimnar sniffed the air and looked up. I followed his glance and saw a heretic lift himself up from the top of the overhead pipes and raise something in his hand. He got no further before Grimnar shot him.

Warned by some instinct I turned my head to the walkway on the other side. More figures were rising there. Most of them held bolt pistols or autoguns but one of them had raised his arm as if about to throw a grenade. I lifted the shotgun and pulled the trigger, sending him tumbling backwards. Screaming and kicking he splashed down into one of the tanks. There was a muffled explosion and green liquid gouted upwards into the air. The pressure of the blast cracked and splintered the glass. Snot-coloured fluid spilled forth onto the floor.

I raced to the nearest ladder, slung the shotgun and pulled myself up towards the pipes.

A hail of fire descended from above and was met by a response from the Lion Guard. It all sounded incredibly loud in my ears. I clambered upwards, rung by rung, hoping that everyone else was too focused on the firefight to notice me.

The people on the pipes I was climbing towards could not see me in my current position, but all it would take would be for one of them to lean outwards. The heretics on the opposite side had a clear shot at my back. I felt a constant crawling sense of anticipation between my shoulders. At any moment I expected to feel a surge of pain in my back and then experience a swift fall into oblivion.

I resisted the temptation to take a look over my shoulder. It would do me no good and I needed to put all my effort into the climb. I counted rungs. Nine, ten, eleven. The itch between my shoulders became almost unbearable.

Twelve, thirteen. I was almost at the top. A shot clattered off the pipe near me. I felt something sting the skin of my arm but I did not let it distract me. I pulled myself up once more, looked over the edge of the pipe and found myself exchanging glances with a green-faced corpse. Its skin was marked with boils and blotches. Pus leaked from its eyeballs, oddly discoloured blood from a sucking wound in its chest. I glanced along the walkway and saw nothing but corpses there. They had tumbled from the pipe above.

I pulled myself onto the walkway and my boot squelched on the dead body that had first met my gaze.

I kept my head down and tried to keep out of the line of fire of my comrades on the ground. I unslung the shotgun, took a deep breath, tried to calm my racing heart and sprung upright, half expecting to get my head blown off. I saw more cultists along the top of the pipe. Some had fallen. Some of them were crouching. Some were snapping off shots.

They were ugly men with strange reddish eyes. They wore no rebreathers or protective masks and their skin was covered in abscesses, warts and boils. They bore the marks of a dozen different diseases and yet appeared to feel no ill effects from most of them.

One or two of them moved oddly, like men whose coordination was impaired. Some of them bled from large wounds, but that did not seem to slow them down.

One of them had lost the fingers of one hand, not to our gunfire but to what looked like para-leprosy. His nose was gone too, leaving an empty crater in the middle of his face. From the way he shouted orders, he seemed to be the leader. That made him an instant and obvious target.

I lifted the shotgun and pulled the trigger. Half-hand threw himself off the pipe and into space. My shot missed him and cut through the heretics standing behind. I pumped the shotgun, pulled the trigger again and cut down a few more.

Half-hand landed below me. His legs gave way as if broken and still he gave no sign of feeling any pain. It was as if every nerve in his body were dead. He pulled himself up and swung his pistol to bear on Macharius. The general was faster and blew his head to smithereens with a single shot.

The rungs of the ladder creaked below me. Something

massive catapulted overhead. Grimnar had joined me on the walkway. He ran along, shooting and cleaving with his chainsword. Nothing could stop him. Shots puffed up around his feet and pinged off his armour, threatening to overbalance him, and still he moved on.

I glanced around and saw enemies firing at him from the top of the facing pipe. I blasted them while their attention was distracted and I was glad it was. I did not have the Space Wolf's armour or his eye-blurring speed to protect me, and the guard-rails of the walkway would provide me with no cover.

I was lucky. I managed to take out half a dozen of the enemy fighters while my comrades climbed up the ladder on the opposite side. I could see there were no more than twenty of the enemy there. Judging by the screams there were few of the heretics left on my side of things. Grimnar was seeing to that.

I looked down and saw a web of cracks had appeared in the armourglass of the great tank. Macharius was already clear, along with Drake and his guards, when the glass gave way. The greenish fluid and shards of crystal sprayed over our nearby troops.

Men screamed, flesh gouged by translucent shrapnel. Some of them shrieked oddly. Some of them tore off their masks. Viscous slime stained their faces and dripped from their rebreathers. It looked like the fluid had found its way in through badly adjusted mouthpieces or impaired filters and the side effects looked anything but pleasant.

I looked around for Ivan, hoping that he was not numbered

among the fallen. I caught no sight of him until I looked up at the opposite ramp and saw him there. His bolt pistol was in his hand and he was snapping off shots. He looked as strange and ungainly as the cultists without his bionic arm but its absence did not slow him.

I heard more screams below and looking down saw that some of the white bodies that had been in the tank were flopping towards our troops. They moved with a malevolent mindfulness that suggested that they had been aware of what was going on the whole time. They clutched at men's ankles, and slowed them down. When men fell, they went for the throat with their blotched teeth.

Grimnar had cleared my section of the piping now. I could not fire into the melee below with the shotgun, so I advanced along the walkway behind the Space Wolf, took aim at the enemy across the gap and pulled the trigger. The shotgun kicked and cultists died. I took another step and fired again. In short order the ambush site was cleared.

Below us were more casualties, from enemy fire, from the splintered tanks, from the newborn monsters. It did not stop us though. We continued our advance through the hall.

The place seemed endless, lit with a daemonic emerald glow, filled with the bubbling sound from the life-vats and the gurgling of chemicals through the pipes. There were more ambushes and more killing but we were ready for them now, and fell into the rhythm of clearing them.

As we neared the exit from the hall, I heard screaming again behind me.

CHAPTER THIRTY

It came from one of the soldiers who had been stung by the diseased insects on the stairwell. He was clutching at his arm, and howling curses and imprecations. There was agony in his voice and madness in his eyes and I started to understand why as I moved closer to see if I could help him.

Small boils had erupted on his skin. They had spread out from the place where he had been stung. At first I thought it was a trick of the light, some weird distortion caused by the lenses of my rebreather mask, but as I squinted I could see I was wrong. The lumps in the man's skin were shifting. One of them crawled beneath the flesh on the back of his hand. Another had reached his throat and was moving up towards his jaw. There were further ripples beneath the sleeves of his tunic.

The lump on his jaw moved across his cheek, heading

towards his eye. There was something eerie about it, like watching some evil spell doing its work. I wondered if it was some new disease or the result of daemonic influence. Even as that thought ran through my mind, a blue, chitinous fly erupted from the soldier's eye in a spurt of jelly and a clicking of mandibles. Dragonfly-like wings stretched wetly and the creature prepared to take to the air.

The infected man brought his fist crunching down on it even as more and more of the creatures erupted from his flesh. They had a wet, glistening, newborn look to them. I brought my boot down on one, even as the dying man rolled over to crush others. From down the line came more screams and I guessed that more of the infected soldiers were discovering what they carried.

The insects were slow and dazed, at least at first, and easy enough to kill, but some of them slipped away and I had an uneasy feeling that they might infiltrate my clothing or suddenly appear when I least expected it.

Men were swiftly assigned to stand guard over the wounded and the company moved on. I returned to Macharius's side. Drake was speaking.

'Confusion and demoralisation. That is their purpose. We must leave men to look after the wounded or we reduce morale yet further.'

Macharius gave a weary smile. 'Those men knew what their lives became worth when they joined the Imperial Guard. They know what is going to happen to them. We cannot take them with us for they are time bombs waiting to go off.

Any who have been infected must be left behind. We cannot risk another outbreak at a crucial time.'

Drake nodded. The sound of bullets began to be heard from behind and a commissar emerged from the line. 'I have made sure we will suffer no liability from those men, Lord High Commander.'

Macharius nodded and with a curt gesture indicated that we should proceed.

From ahead came the roar of bolter fire. The howl of Space Wolves echoed through the great hall of the vats. In response came the eerie chanting of diseased fanatic voices and the thunder of autoguns.

Macharius indicated that we should advance. I took charge of a section and raced forward up a flight of stairs. I entered what looked like a demented combination of a temple and a sorcerous laboratory. Vast carved idols, resembling the huge daemon I had seen in my fever dreams, flanked a gigantic altar that crackled with magical energy. From an area behind the altar a strange glow emerged along with the sound of bestial chanting.

I glanced around, taking in an evil parody of an Imperial cathedral. There were nooks in which statues of what might have been plagued saints stood, and smaller altars were arranged along the walls. Galleries lined the higher walls. Perhaps once a congregation of Chaos worshippers had howled prayers to their evil gods there. Now they were packed with armed men, firing down at us.

Half a dozen Space Wolves did battle against an army of

disease-infected, plague-worshipping mutants. Richter's palace guards were almost as large as the Adeptus Astartes. They were armed with bolters and marked by the stigmata of a dozen diseases. Their eyes were pinkish, their flesh blotched. Running sores wept greenish pus but seemed to leave their owner's fighting ability unimpaired.

A score of them opened fire on a running Space Wolf. A trail of shells chewed up the carved pews through which the Space Marine ran in search of cover. One of the shells took him in the shoulder, exploded and twisted him around. Another took him through the throat. Another impacted on his chest-plate, breaking it open and revealing flesh and bone beneath.

Still the Space Wolf kept moving. He raised his bolter and snapped off a shot at one of the heretics, removing his head, then he fired again and again, killing two more Nurgle worshippers. Sensing blood their comrades kept pouring on the firepower. More shots hit the exposed innards where the ceramite carapace had been torn away, ripping through flesh and doing terrible damage to the Space Wolf.

I noticed that his bones were not like normal human bones. They were larger and in places had fused together to form what appeared to be another layer of armour around vulnerable internal organs, but not even that was enough to save the luckless Space Marine.

He must have sensed that his death was upon him for he changed direction in an eye-blink and ran into the hail of fire. I did not think anything living could move through the storm of death around him but somehow he closed the distance with the cultists and was among them, bolter still spitting death. He reached out with one armoured hand and crushed the skull of the nearest heretic, broke the neck of another and then stumbled and fell backwards as the heretics hit him with a dozen shots. Even then he managed one last discharge of his own bolter before falling to the ground dead.

For a moment there was silence. The entire chamber was aware that some enormity had occurred. All around echoed the howling war cries of the Space Wolves as if they had, at that moment, sensed the death of their battle-brother and gave vent to their mourning.

I froze for a second, scanning the chamber from the top of the stairs, then I ordered my men down and directed them to shoot at the cultists in the gallery above.

Seconds later I heard the roars of the Space Wolves coming closer, as they converged upon the spot where their comrade had fallen. Although the sound was redolent of wild fury, and the faces of the Space Marines were transformed by feral rage, nothing impaired their fighting ability.

Several of them gave Grimnar and their brothers covering fire as they advanced, putting out such a storm of bolter fire that they pinned down the enemies most likely to shoot. Once in position Grimnar and his companions then gave their comrades covering fire as they advanced. Thus they moved forward, mutually supportive.

The heretics had made the mistake of standing gloating over the corpse. I looked up and saw one of them had painted his face with Space Marine blood. Another was chewing on the flesh as if somehow he could absorb the fallen warrior's power by this cannibalistic act. Perhaps he could. I have seen stranger things in my campaigns among the stars.

Grimnar closed with the bloody-faced one and tore his head from his shoulders. He used it as club, smashing it into the face of the cannibal, knocking him from his feet. Then in an unleashed whirlwind of violence, he tore through the Nurgle worshippers, shredding flesh and severing limbs with his chainsword, moving with such speed and ferocity the enemy never drew a bead on him.

All eyes were on the havoc being wreaked by the Space Marines. I ordered my men to follow me. I had spotted the stairwell leading to the gallery above. Now seemed to be a good time to take it. I raced across the nave of the dark temple, running along bullet-chewed pews, heavy boots clattering on the wooden seats. They had been carved with strange symbols: evil eight-pointed stars containing strange runes, skull faces leering from the centre of eight outward-pointing arrows, icons carved in a language that hurt the eye.

I could hear chanting now from deeper within the temple, a gurgling, ghastly roar that sounded as if it had been torn from the throats of a thousand diseased and dying men. The air started to thrum as if echoing to the sound of the wings of some huge insect buzzing overhead. I raced up the nar-row winding stairs, praying to the Emperor that no one was waiting at the top to roll a grenade down them.

I reached the head of the stairs and looked out onto the great gallery. It had clearly been intended for the use of the local nobility. Individual carved seats were strewn across the place. On each one decaying cushions showed signs of the neglect that characterised this place. The mixture of richness and rot spoke of the insanity that ruled here. Behind the low balcony wall heretics crouched, firing down on our forces below. Their faces were a ghoulish green, scarred with the stigmata of the diseases they proudly wore. I stepped out into the gallery, making room for my men to emerge alongside me.

As I did so, one of the heretics glanced at me. Clearly he had expected reinforcements because he nodded and then did a double take. I levelled my shotgun and pulled the trigger, sending him flying backwards over the barrier to drop down into the nave below. His companions looked around, bringing their weapons to bear, and I threw myself flat behind one of the carved thrones. I heard them begin to shoot as the remainder of my squad emerged from the stairwell.

I crawled forward on my hands and knees, readied a grenade and lobbed it. It exploded amid the heretics with a deafening blast. I popped head and shoulders over the back of the seat and opened fire from almost point-blank range, sending shots ploughing through those who had survived my grenade.

The explosion had torn through part of the balcony, sending more of the heretics tumbling to their doom. One of them had survived by one of those freaks of chance that always occur somewhere on the battlefield. He must have been standing right beside where the grenade went off, and he was painted with gore, but still he stood apparently unscathed.

He launched himself towards me. Las-blasts filled the air all around as my men opened up. I pumped the shotgun but he was as quick as any Space Marine. His enormous wart-covered hand grabbed the still-hot barrel of the shotgun, almost wrenching it from my grasp. Diseased flies buzzed around his body. He smashed a massive fist into my face. The lenses of my rebreather mask shattered into a web of fine lines. The sudden stench of his body told me the filters were broken. The sickly sweet foulness of rotting flesh made me want to vomit.

I tried to hold my breath, even as stars danced before my eyes. My vision swam. Enormous hands gripped me. I thought dizziness was overwhelming me but then I realised that he had swung me up into the air and was turning to throw me over the balcony.

I had an excellent view of the conflict far below. I could see Macharius and Drake in the midst of fighting across the nave. It was flooded now with our troops, moving forward using the pews and alcoves for cover. Beyond Macharius and the Space Wolves were ranks of chanting heretics. The air around them shimmered and swirled with a green light. Something foul seemed to be clotting out of the very air, coagulating around a human-like figure that seemed somehow familiar.

It's strange the details the mind picks out in what it thinks might be its final moments. A Space Wolf crouched over the corpse of his fallen brother, perhaps mourning, perhaps removing something from the body. I thought I saw something wet and red like an internal organ slopping within his hand. One of Drake's bodyguards looked up, and tilted his head to look straight at me. I had a good view over the long drop and struggled frantically to tear myself free from the heretic's grip, knowing that I was too late.

Las-bolts flickered through the air, searing the heretic's flesh, turning it into blackened charred meat. He grunted and raised me higher, despite his pain. I knew then that whatever happened I was going to die. Even in his death spasm he could send me catapulting into the void.

Drake's bodyguard raised his bolt pistol and did not even stop to aim. The weapon blasted and I felt the impact in the body below me. A fraction of a second later, there was an explosion and the heretic was blown backwards away from the edge, sending me tumbling back into the seats behind. A flash of pain seared my arm and I knew I had taken a glancing hit from my own side. Thoughts of Anton's accidental death filled my mind.

'Cease fire,' I bellowed. 'It's clear up here.'

The firing continued. When men are driven to the brink of madness by the presence of danger, they do not necessarily pay close attention to the orders of their superiors.

'Cease fire!' I ordered and then repeated myself again. Third time was the charm. They stopped shooting at me and the dead heretics. I waited for a few heartbeats to make sure they had definitely given up the attempt and then raised my head to order them to the balcony edge and give covering fire to our lads below.

My heart pounded against my chest. I felt giddy with relief. With one lucky shot, that bodyguard had saved my life. I made up my mind to thank him in the unlikely event that we made it out of this place alive.

As my men opened fire I found something new to worry about – my rebreather. I removed it from my face, and knocked out the lenses. I had feared that at any moment they might break, sending sharpened armourglass into my eyes. With the filter broken the mask was useless anyway. I found I was holding my breath and then realised it was pointless. I had already breathed the stinking, corrupt air anyway. I was most likely already infected with whatever disease spores were about.

I thought this way for all of thirty heartbeats before noticing that one of my own men was down. A bolter shell had taken him in the stomach. Being dead he had no use for his rebreather mask, so I removed it and put it on. It was a small thing and probably useless anyway given what I had been breathing, but it brought me a measure of comfort, and that's not something to be discounted.

The Space Wolves smashed through the heretics, backed up by the mass of the Lion Guard. They had reached all the way to the back of the place near the altar. The chanting had reached a crescendo now. The air shimmered around the glowing figure. I had a sense of dizziness and distortion. I recalled experiencing something similar before, long ago on a different world. Terrible psychic currents swirled in the air and I knew that we were reaching the climax of an unholy ritual.

Green and yellow light flickered around the heads of the cultists and illuminated their cowled forms. Macharius and Drake raced towards those performing the ritual and I realised that I was in the wrong place to protect the Lord High Commander if things went wrong. I ran along the balcony, heading towards the stairwell on the far side. I ordered my men to follow me. I knew that events were now rushing towards a climax and realised that soon it would all be over, one way or another.

I was weary and battered and dizzy. I could not tell if it was the after-effects of the heretic's blow or whether I had been infected with something. All I knew was that Macharius was down there along with Ivan and Drake and it was my duty to be with them and that I had better get down there quick.

I heard mocking laughter ringing out from the figures around the altar. Bolter shells sprayed at them but were halted by some strange force. A shimmering aura swirled in the air above the altar and such was its potency that it could stop even the blast of a Space Marine's weapon.

I saw a man garbed in an ornate uniform, like a general. He was tall and gaunt, almost skeletal. His skin was grey and his eyes burned with a fierce internal light. So warped and changed was he that it took me a moment to recognise him. It was Richter. Something hideous and greenish glowed on his chest, an amulet of some sort, blazing with mystical energy. From its centre a monstrous eye looked out with a malignant mockery that reminded me of the great daemon of my fever dreams.

When Richter spoke, his voice was out of all proportion to his wasted form. It was rich and mellow and full of malevolent humour and it easily filled the room despite all the random background noise. Perhaps it had something to do with the acoustics of this part of the temple but I doubted it.

'Lord High Commander Macharius, we meet again,' Richter said.

Macharius replied, 'For the last time, traitor.'

'I regret that will prove to be so,' said Richter. 'You have been a most worthy foe. Bringing down the moon was a masterstroke. I salute you. I see you finally decided you could spare the world's industrial capacity. You should have done that two years ago.'

'We did not come here to bandy words with heretics,' said Grimnar. 'End this.'

Richter turned his mocking gaze on the Space Wolf. 'Ah, I see the Wolves of Fenris have not developed bigger brains or better manners over the last ten millennia.'

There was a familiarity and a contempt in Richter's voice that I had never heard the like of before and it came to me then that we were not hearing merely Richter the man, but some mighty entity speaking through him, some daemon in the service of the powers of Chaos who had a history with the Space Wolves. It was no wonder then that the general had managed to stymie even Macharius in battle, for he had access to the understanding and intelligence a daemon could provide its host.

'By the Allfather you will regret those words,' said Grimnar.

'I already regret hearing yours,' said Richter with a dismissive gesture. He gave his attention back to Macharius. 'I am glad you are here, general. We have much to talk about.'

Grimnar leapt forward, pushing through the shimmering defensive field, his movements slowed by it, along with those of his honour guard. Richter gestured and the field coagulated around them, slowing them more and more until they could not take a step further. By a superhuman effort of will, Grimnar raised his bolter and aimed it at Richter's head. There could not have been more than a couple of strides between them and it seemed that there was no way he could miss. His eyes blazed. His fangs were bared in a terrifying rictus.

Richter gestured, a man shooing away a fly, and Grimnar was suddenly catapulted across the room to end up sprawling against one of the cathedral pillars. The rest of his companions were forced down almost to their knees by the field of power surrounding them.

CHAPTER THIRTY-ONE

'As I was saying, we have much to talk about,' Richter said.

'I do not see how that can be the case,' said Macharius. 'I require only your death.'

Richter smiled. 'You are dying, Lord High Commander. Mortality has finally caught up with you. The servants of the Father of Plagues are already working away within your body, within your brain. You have lived too long. You are not what you were. Your enemies can see this, too – and some of those you think of as friends.'

Macharius tilted his head to one side. He appeared to be listening.

'How much longer do you have? A week? A month? Not more. And what happens to all you have achieved when you are gone? It disintegrates, torn apart by the ambition of fools. Your life is ending in defeat. All you have worked for is turning to dust. With a few more years you might have left a monument that would have endured as long as men remember. Now you will fall and your memory will fade.'

'It is the fate of all men,' said Macharius.

'Not so. It has not been the fate of the False Emperor. It has not been the fate of those who have accepted the gifts of my liege lord.'

'As you have divined, I have already had more than enough of his gifts for my liking,' said Macharius. Drake's gaze flickered between Macharius and Richter. He clearly did not like the way things were going here.

'It does not have to be that way,' said Richter. 'My patron can reverse his gifts. The seeds of death within you can be turned into the seeds of immortality. You do not have to die, Lord High Commander. You do not have to watch your empire turn to dust and see your legacy destroyed by lesser men. You could join with us and gain life eternal and power immeasurable.'

'You mean I could serve a daemon.'

'No. I mean you could *become* one. In the long run, you are worthy. You could become the mightiest champion of Chaos in this millennium. You could overthrow the False Emperor and take his place as the ruler of mankind.'

I should have thought Richter was lying. I should have *known* it, but instead I knew he was telling the truth. He believed what he was saying implicitly and because he did, it made him convincing. I believed him and I was not the focus of his power and attention the way Macharius was.

I thought of what it meant to be Macharius. Any man would have wavered in the face of such temptation, but Macharius had been tempted before, back on Karsk, by the Angel of Fire and I knew what he was made of.

'And all I would have to lose would be my soul,' Macharius said. His face was grim. He raised his bolt pistol and aimed it squarely at Richter.

'Go ahead and pull the trigger,' the traitor said. 'I am invulnerable to your puny weapons now. My god makes me so.'

Macharius pulled the trigger. The bolter shell ricocheted off the field of force surrounding Richter. All eyes went to it. Distracted.

Drake gestured. A bolt of psychic energy smashed into the screen and just for a moment, parted it. Macharius dived forward, his chainsword arcing down and smashing into the traitor's forehead, splitting it open as far as the nose. Bits of brain and skull spurted off the teeth of the chainsword.

Richter did not fall. He stepped away from Macharius, his eyes now several centimetres further apart than they had been but still focused on his former commander. When he spoke his words seemed to come from the surrounding air, the voice of an angry god who had been defied.

'I told you I am immortal,' he said. 'It appears you do not understand what that means.'

His flesh and bone started to knit together again, leaving his features deformed but intact. I noticed that the amulet at his throat had changed colour, losing some of its lustre as it did so. More bolter shells impacted on his body, ripping flesh to the bone.

Instead of blood a strange green pus emerged. With a hideous sucking sound, the flesh began to flow together again, leaving the heretic's form intact but a little more deformed. I glanced around to see where the bolter shells had come from. Grimnar had risen, his carapace armour cracked and bloody. His bolter was steady in his hand. Drake's bodyguard too had taken careful aim and opened fire.

'Do not let up,' Drake shouted. 'Do not give him a chance to concentrate or we are doomed. That amulet holds awesome power.'

He unleashed another psychic bolt at Richter. The heretic screamed and shuddered and Macharius brought his chainsword down once more. Richter stepped aside and grabbed Macharius by the wrist. His strength was daemonic. Bones splintered as his fingers closed. The chainsword dropped from Macharius's grip.

The two generals went to the ground still grappling. Macharius fought like a wounded lion but Richter was stronger and appeared to feel no pain. The baleful amulet glowed on his chest as he exerted his greater strength. Macharius rolled over and over, his motions taking the two of them towards the chainsword. No one save Grimnar and Drake's bodyguards continued to pump bolter shells into the heretic's body. I held my fire for fear of hitting the Lord High Commander.

With the force field down, a melee erupted. The heretics raced forward, as did the Lion Guard. Like their leader they seemed superhumanly strong, and like him they had no doubts as to ultimate victory. I pulled the trigger on my shotgun and sent them tumbling backwards, flesh torn, but they rose again, apparently as unkillable as Richter. Their wounds knitted more slowly but the same process seemed to be in effect.

I fired again, moving towards Macharius. I heard wolf howls as more of the Space Marines recovered and hurled themselves into the battle. One of the cultists launched himself directly at me. I sidestepped and smacked him on the side of the head with the butt of the shotgun. Bone broke but the cultist still moved. His fellows opened up. A hail of bullets erupted around me. Something heavy hammered into me and I hit the ground, convinced for a moment that I had taken a bolter shell.

A heavy weight lay on top of me and I felt metal touching my flesh. I looked around and saw it was Ivan, his body riddled with bullets. He had thrown himself forward to push me out of the way and taken the blast of fire meant for me.

'What th... Where's Anton when you need him, the useless frakker? He's the one who's supposed to stop bullets.' He looked around, the light dying in his eyes. 'Protect Macharius!'

They were the last words he said. I pulled myself out from beneath him and looked around. Macharius and Richter had rolled right over to where the chainsword lay, still sparking as its teeth bit into the rocky floor. Macharius tried to reach it but Richter was on top of him, casually battering him with his mighty hands. In the surge and press of the melee, no one else could get a clear shot. I pushed forward until I could get the barrel of the shotgun against the heretic's chest and pulled the trigger.

The shotgun kicked. The force of the blast lifted Richter off Macharius. The Lord High Commander rolled to one side and grasped the chainsword with his off-hand. He raised it up and slammed it down against the heretic's neck, pushing it forward, cutting through muscle, vein, gristle and vertebrae. The expression froze on Richter's face as his head rolled clear. Macharius grasped the chain of the amulet and tugged it from the body, pulling it away until it separated from the flesh.

A wailing noise emerged from Richter's mouth. His body suddenly collapsed in on itself like a balloon deflating. Black corruption boiled up from the middle of it. Rot spread across the flesh and drove along a tide of white mould – within a few seconds his armour was all but empty, leaving only blackened bones and a scum that might once have been his flesh. His henchmen lost all cohesion, seeing their champion defeated. Their wounds ceased to mend, as if the killing of Richter had caused his unholy sorcery to stop working.

We tore through the heretics like a chainsword through diseased flesh and then the battle for Richter's citadel was over, leaving us to count the cost.

Grimnar surveyed the carnage around the cathedral nave with something like satisfaction. He wrinkled his nose when he looked upon the outline of Richter's fallen form. He strode over to Macharius and extended a hand to aid him to his feet. Macharius was not too proud to take the Space Wolf's grip. He stood triumphant in the midst of his final battlefield.

'I thank you for your aid, Logan Grimnar,' he said. 'Whatever debt of honour you feel you owed me is more than repaid. I am in your debt now.'

Grimnar shook his head. 'Such a battle as this is its own reward. By the Allfather, there will be those among my battle-brothers sorry to have missed this fray.'

'It is done here,' Macharius said. 'Richter is defeated.'

He looked down at the amulet he held in his hand, 'And this thing – it must be destroyed.'

He looked at the Space Wolf expectantly.

'I will see to it,' Grimnar said. 'It is a bauble not meant for mortal men.' He picked up an ammunition drum, dropped the amulet into it and then sealed it. 'This will do until it can be properly dealt with.'

He tipped his head to one side, obviously listening to something on the comm-net and then said, 'There is still a battle to be fought out there and I must go and aid my brothers. Till we meet again, Lord High Commander,' he said, tipping his arm in salute and with that he was gone.

Drake watched him go with something like an expression of relief on his face.

'It seems we have survived after all,' he said. He sounded like a man who did not quite believe it. His bodyguard returned; it seemed he had been exploring the chambers at the back of the cathedral.

'Inquisitor, Lord High Commander, there is something you should see,' he said. Drake nodded and looked inquiringly at Macharius.

'Lead on,' Macharius said, clutching his crippled hand. The pair of them moved towards the chamber. I moved to follow. The bodyguard raised a hand. 'This is for the eyes of my master and the Lord High Commander alone.'

There was something familiar about the voice. 'I don't take your orders,' I said. 'I take them from General Macharius.'

'As you wish,' said the storm trooper.

The room was a small antechamber. The corpse of a cultist sprawled on the floor, a heavy autopistol clutched in his hand. On an altar table were spread a number of grimoires and sheets covered in strange and evil runes. Macharius stood over them and shook his head uncomprehendingly. I heard the door click closed behind me.

Drake stood alongside him, shaking his head. 'These are an unholy ritual. With the amulet and these words, a man could draw on the Ruinous Powers. How long were these in Richter's possession, I wonder?'

'Why don't you tell me?' Macharius said.

'What do you mean?' the inquisitor asked.

'You have been in contact with him all along. That is where your information about the location of his headquarters came from.'

'I had agents in place,' said Drake.

'No. It was not as simple as that. I saw his followers. None of them were sane enough to be your agents. They had lost all semblance of intelligence long ago. Someone informed Richter of my plans. It was the only way he could have kept anticipating my moves. You saw that ranting madman. He was not capable of it.'

'Crassus,' said Drake. I saw the storm trooper bend down over the cultist's corpse, examining it as if he had found something curious.

'Crassus could not have known all the details. He was too far away, and interstellar communication is too unreliable.'

Drake sat down at the table wearily. 'He had an agent in place, just like I did.' He offered it up as if he did not expect to be believed. He was just going through the motions.

'Why?' Macharius said.

'Why what?'

'Why betray me, betray the crusade and then come here with me to die? Do you feel so guilty?'

My gaze jumped between the two of them. I felt trapped in a nightmare. Had Macharius finally fallen victim to madness? Had the idea that everyone was plotting against him cracked his mind? Or was there something to his theory? It seemed impossible. Drake had been with us so long, had supported Macharius so fervently.

'A martyr was needed,' Drake said at last. 'You were dying. What better way for you to leave the Emperor's service than in one last battle against overwhelming odds, leaving an example of service unto death.'

'And I spoiled it by winning,' said Macharius. He smiled as if he saw some humour in the situation.

The storm trooper moved so swiftly I could not even follow his actions. There was no chance to even raise my shotgun. He lifted the cultist's pistol, aimed it squarely at Macharius's head and pulled the trigger. The greatest general of the age died victorious, with his smile still on his face.

Drake looked at his bodyguard and then at me. 'What are you waiting for? We don't need any witnesses. We have our martyr, gunned down by a hidden cultist in his moment of triumph.'

The pistol was turned on me. I found myself staring down its maw. I started to raise the shotgun but I had seen how fast the storm trooper was. I knew I had no chance. The pistol spoke again. I expected a blast of pain to tear through me and closed my eyes involuntarily. When I opened them again, Drake was dead, killed just as messily as Macharius. I looked at the storm trooper.

'What?' I said.

The storm trooper raised his visor. I saw Anna's face. She winked at me, took my shotgun and pulled the trigger, blasting the cultist's corpse with it. A moment later, she was gone from the chamber, announcing that a hidden assassin had killed Macharius and Drake and that I had killed them in turn.

And so all the great men died. And my friends. And I wonder to this day about what happened. There are times when I think that Anna killed Drake because, like Macharius, he had outlived his time and become a liability. There are times I think she was employed not by the inquisitor at all but by his rivals, or by the High Lords of Terra, and she was simply making sure that all the loose ends were tied up.

Which of course does not explain why she spared me. There are times when I think it was because she wanted to leave a witness who could both corroborate her story or be called upon to tell a different version if it was required. There are times when I wonder if it was because she actually cared for me. I do not know.

I do know that we fought our way out of Richter's citadel and brought the corpses of Macharius and Drake with us. They both burned on funeral pyres. I stuck with the story Anna had given about the cultist, in part because she had spared my life, in part because it was her wish and in part because it was a better story for the Imperium. Of course Macharius died a hero in his hour of triumph. Of course Drake fell valiantly trying to protect him. Of course I cut down the heretic responsible.

And in the end it was all for nothing. Most of the men who fought on Loki died of the plagues they caught there. Macharius's generals fell to fighting over the spoils of the empire he had built. The Schism returned in a new form and the threat of a Secessionist empire disappeared like morning mist, if it had ever really existed.

I was decorated for killing the monster that killed two of the Imperium's heroes. Anna vanished into the night between the stars. I never saw her again and for that at least I am glad.

ABOUT THE AUTHOR

William King is the author of the Tyrion and Teclis saga, the Macharian Crusade trilogy as well as the much-loved Gotrek & Felix series and the Space Wolf novels. His short stories have appeared in many magazines and compilations, including *White Dwarf* and *Inferno!*. Bill was born in Stranraer, Scotland, in 1959 and currently lives in Prague.